"With profound truths on one page [...] on the next, *Like Never Before* q[...] novels I didn't want to end. Meliss[...] ful story that took hold of my heart and didn't let go. Superbly well done!"

—**Katie Ganshert,** bestselling, award-winning author

"In *Like Never Before*, readers are invited to revisit the much-loved Walker clan in a story that delivers on the promise that even if lost once, love can be found again. In true Melissa Tagg style, the dialogue is smart and the romance is real and raw in all the right places. This series is witty storytelling at its best."

—**Kristy Cambron,** author of the HIDDEN MASTERPIECE series and *The Ringmaster's Wife*

"*Like Never Before* is a gem of a story. I never knew Iowa could be so charming until I met the Walker family from Maple Valley. Logan and Amelia's story is pure delight—funny, sweet, romantic, poignant—and it even has a touch of historical mystery! The perfect weekend read—Melissa Tagg just keeps getting better and better!"

—**Susan May Warren,** RITA® and Christy Award-winning, bestselling author of the CHRISTIANSEN FAMILY series

"In *Like Never Before*, Melissa Tagg once again delivers a wonderful romance—and a fun little mystery!—with her signature swoon-worthy characters and laugh out loud moments that will make every reader fall in love with both the story and the author. As always, a wonderful read by a very talented writer!"

—**Sarah Price**

"*Like Never Before* is like a warm embrace from the Walkers with the added sweetness of a heroine who feels like your best friend. Amelia just wants a home. Logan just wants to keep moving. Both are burdened by deep pain from the past. In *Like Never Before*, you will be reminded that love is worth the risk no matter what has hurt you in the past. And by opening your heart, you may just find a home. This is another keeper from an author who somehow makes each novel better than the last."

—**Cara Putman**, award-winning author of *Shadowed by Grace* and *Where Treetops Glisten*

"In *Like Never Before*, author Melissa Tagg once again welcomes readers to the fictitious town of Maple Valley, even as she crafts characters you come to care about like real-life friends. The story, woven through with Tagg's trademark humor, highlights an abiding love of family and the importance of anchoring yourself to God when life is hard. One of my favorite books by this author!"

—**Beth K. Vogt**, 2015 RITA® Finalist, author of *Crazy Little Thing Called Love*

"Warm, witty, and insightful, no one crafts a romance like Melissa Tagg. After just a few pages, I found myself sighing with happiness—prepare to be charmed!"

—**Hillary Manton Lodge**, author of *Reservations for Two*

"Reading a Melissa Tagg novel is like sharing coffee with a close friend in cozy diner where the conversation and laughter flow freely. *Like Never Before* offers readers a charming setting with passionate characters, snappy dialogue, heartfelt moments, and threads of faith woven throughout the story to pull everything together. Another book on my keeper shelf."

—**Lisa Jordan**, author of *Lakeside Redemption*

Like Never Before

Books by Melissa Tagg

Made to Last
Here to Stay

THE WALKER FAMILY BOOKS

Three Little Words: A Walker Family Novella
From the Start
Like Never Before

Like Never Before

Melissa Tagg

BETHANYHOUSE
a division of Baker Publishing Group
Minneapolis, Minnesota

Published by Bethany House Publishers
11400 Hampshire Avenue South
Bloomington, Minnesota 55438
www.bethanyhouse.com

Bethany House Publishers is a division of
Baker Publishing Group, Grand Rapids, Michigan

Printed in the United States of America

Library of Congress Cataloging-in-Publication Data
Names: Tagg, Melissa, author.
Title: Like never before / Melissa Tagg.
Description: Minneapolis, Minnesota : Bethany House, a division of Baker
    Publishing Group, [2016]
Identifiers: LCCN 2015039202 | ISBN 9780764213083 (softcover)
Subjects: LCSH: Man-woman relationships—Fiction. | GSAFD: Christian fiction. |
    Love stories.
Classification: LCC PS3620.A343 L55 2016 | DDC 813/.6—dc23 LC record available
    at http://lccn.loc.gov/2015039202

Scripture quotations are from the *Holy Bible*, New Living Translation, copyright © 1996, 2004, 2007 by Tyndale House Foundation. Used by permission of Tyndale House Publishers, Inc., Carol Stream, Illinois 60188. All rights reserved.

Cover design by Faceout Studios/Kara Davison

Melissa Tagg is represented by MacGregor Literary, Inc.

16 17 18 19 20 21 22   7 6 5 4 3 2 1

To my nephew Ollie

Someday you'll be old enough
to read this and understand
how much your strength
and personality inspire me.
For now, I'll settle for spoiling you
every chance I get.

I love you, buddy!

For I am about to do something new.
See, I have already begun! Do you not see it?
I will make a pathway through the wilderness.
I will create rivers in the dry wasteland.

—Isaiah 43:19

1

To: Logan Walker
From: Amelia Bentley
Subject: Hello?

Hi, Logan,

Yep, it's me again. Amelia Bentley. I know, you'd think after three unanswered emails I'd give up. But reporters—even small-town Iowa ones—have spunk. Except, hmm, maybe you're some Lou Grant–type and you hate spunk.

In that case, I've got persistence, determination, and, fine, a fair bit of stubbornness.

Which is why I'm writing you this third email to see if you have any interest in coming back to work for the *News*. Since Freddie passed away, we're short a reporter. I know you live in LA now, so this is probably crazy talk. But you told me yourself you miss the newspaper world. So I can't help asking . . .

Amelia Bentley

Editor, *Maple Valley News*

p.s. It just occurred to me that maybe the reason you haven't replied is you don't remember me. I was the reporter at your sister's boyfriend's nonprofit's grand opening last month.

(World record for most possessive nouns used in one sentence?)
We talked for a few minutes. You complimented my Nikon.

———

To: Amelia Bentley
From: Logan Walker
Subject: RE: Hello?

Amelia—

I do remember you. And your Nikon. Sorry that I haven't responded until now. My inbox is like something out of a horror movie.

And I remember telling you I miss reporting. I have to be honest: That might have been mostly small talk. Yeah, I miss it now and then. But I don't have a ton of desire to go back to writing about school board meetings and really tall asparagus. :)

—L

———

To: Logan Walker
From: Amelia Bentley

If that's a crack at how often small-town newspapers run photos of oversized produce . . . well, then, okay. (This is Iowa, after all.)

So would you consider coming back if I promised to cover ALL the school board meetings?

Just kidding. I knew it was a long shot. But aren't the best reporters the ones who chase long shots?

—Amelia

p.s. Is signing off with just an initial an LA thing?

———

To: Amelia Bentley
From: Logan Walker

There are long shots and then there are looooong shots.

But hey, it's almost graduation time. Check with the area colleges. I bet you can find a journalism major in need of a job.

—Logan James Walker (There. More than an initial this time. Happy?)

To: Logan Walker
From: Amelia Bentley

I don't want a journalism major. I want you.

And yes, I realize how that sounds. Don't get smug or anything! I'm just saying, your award plaques still line the office walls. When you worked here, subscriptions topped 5,000. Freddie talked about you constantly. If you change your mind . . .

—Amelia Anne Bentley

To: Amelia Bentley
From: Logan Walker

The only thing I'm smug about is the fact that I finally figured out the Lou Grant reference in your earlier. email. *Mary Tyler Moore Show*, right?

By the way, I should've said earlier: Sorry about Freddie. He was a good guy, great editor. I wish I could've made it home for his funeral. When I heard he died, I kept kicking myself for not keeping in better touch since moving out here.

—Logan

To: Logan Walker
From: Amelia Bentley

He knew you were busy. And he always talked about how proud of you he was.

Truthfully, Freddie was ready to be done with the newspaper biz long ago, too. The flood last year did a number on him (not to mention our equipment). He was in the process of selling the paper and retiring before he passed. He only passed on the editor mantle to me a month ago. It's all up in the air now—we don't even know who our current owner is.

That's not meant to be a guilt trip, by the way. Just letting you know why I'm grasping at straws and trying to talk an Iowa boy home.

—Amelia

To: Amelia Bentley
From: Logan Walker

I get it. And I do appreciate you asking me to come back. Believe it or not, I did actually consider it for a few nostalgic seconds. Most of my five years at the *News* were good ones. But my life and work are here now.

Besides, I'm not a reporter anymore.

To: Logan Walker
From: Amelia Bentley

Aw, come on. Newspapering gets in a person's blood. You don't just stop being a reporter.

—Amelia

To: Amelia Bentley
From: Logan Walker

Whatever you say, Hildy.

To: Logan Walker
From: Amelia Bentley

Hildy?

To: Amelia Bentley
From: Logan Walker

You're a reporter. Figure it out. :)

On days like this—when sunlit snowflakes fell like tiny, glistening jewels and a crisp quiet brushed through the cold— Amelia Bentley could almost believe she'd never led another life.

Never stood in front of an altar one morning to begin what a hastily scrawled signature, smudged by tears, would eventually end. Never carved open a chamber of her heart, only to later lock it tight, hiding away the goodbye she'd never asked to say.

Amelia pulled open the front door of the *Maple Valley News* office, bells chiming overhead as she stepped into a cocoon of warmth and familiarity.

Today there were no brick-heavy yesterdays. Only the inky scent of newsprint and the embrace of this wintry town—*her* town. Well, and the yipping voice at the back of her mind reminding her she was—

"You're late." The *News's* receptionist peered over thin bifocals, silver-tinted hair coifed with enough bobby pins to pick every lock in the county.

Amelia loosened the turquoise scarf at her neck, camera bag slinking down her arm. "I know. Just need fresh batteries for my flash. But Mae . . ." The rubber soles of her fur-lined boots squealed against the laminate floor as she slid to the reception desk. Her voice lowered to an awed whisper. "It's snowing."

"You think I don't know that? You're tracking it all over my space."

Amelia glanced down at the puddle forming around her feet. "Sorry. It's pretty, though, don't you think?"

"If it were December, sure. But it's the middle of March. No way you'll hear me calling snow pretty in March."

"You just said *snow* the way most people say *oral surgery*. Or *taxes*. Or *beets*."

Mae only harrumphed and turned back to her computer. Amelia nudged the camera bag back up over her shoulder, stomped the last of the snow from her boots, and hurried through the room that contained the ad department—if two women and a part-time intern counted as a *department*. She waved at Kat, Mikaela, and Abby as she passed. Pin-ups of ads for this week's issue dangled from the cloth-covered cubicle wall separating their desks, and sunshine spilled in through generous windows.

She pushed through the newsroom door.

Just inside, Owen swiveled in his chair. "You're—"

"Save it. Already got the third degree from Eeyore at the front desk." Amelia dropped her bag onto the sprawling island counter that gulped up most of the newsroom's space. Back issues of the *News* and other area papers covered the high tabletop.

"The fire chief's already called twice."

"I'm not even five minutes late. You told him to keep his pants on, right?" She bypassed her own cluttered desk and bee-lined for the row of pale blue cupboards lining the back wall. She hoped that at some point she'd remembered to pick up a pack of spare batteries.

Owen stood, straightening the gray vest that matched his slacks, lavender shirt underneath. He was the only sports reporter she'd ever met who dressed like he belonged at *InStyle* magazine rather than a small-town weekly with a circ of barely 3,500. He perched on the corner of his desk, arms folded. "No, I did not tell him to keep his pants on. I didn't think that the best choice of words, considering your little incident last year."

Amelia opened a cupboard, hiding her almost-smile. "How

was I supposed to know they'd just gotten back from a drill? How was I supposed to know that door in the station led into the room where they change?"

Nineteen volunteer firefighters in various states of undress. Some things you couldn't un-see.

Nor could she, apparently, live down.

"Twelve months I've endured the taunting of the entire Maple Valley Fire Department." But ooh, score, a foursome of double-As loose in the cupboard. "What are the chances they'll drop it one of these days?"

"Not gonna happen. They love teasing you. Same with the police. The EMTs. Every farmer at the co-op." Owen moved away from his desk, unzipped her camera bag, and pulled out the flash.

Behind him, the mockups of this week's paper still hung from two long, metal strips on the opposite wall, held in place by magnets. Twenty-four pages, final edits visible in red ink. Four spreads less than the issues they'd put out even just two months back.

But short a reporter and with both circulation and advertising down, Amelia was doing good to churn out a paper at all.

Her gaze slid to the dark closet of an office in the corner. How many mornings did she waltz in to work, still half expecting to see Freddie settled in his raggedy chair, slurping on a vanilla shake for breakfast? The window in his office looked out on the riverfront, where late afternoon brushed shades of tangerine and pink through the sky's wispy clouds, and the Blaine River, ice-frosted and calm, cut through the center of town.

"Admit it," Owen's voice cut in. "You may not be a native, but you're the whole town's kid sister."

"If thirty counts as *kid*." But Owen had a point. She'd wandered into town a wounded heart three years ago. The people of Maple Valley had begun sweeping up her broken pieces before she'd even decided to stay. She'd spent the time since doing all she could to repay that gift. Made sense that she'd earned some friends along the way.

"You're forgetting Mae, though." She took the flash from Owen. "She's never warmed to me."

"Mae's never warmed to anyone. Except maybe her cat. By the way, Cranford called while you were out."

A groan worked its way up her throat, and she chucked the flash's dead batteries at an already-overflowing trash can. Missed. They hit the wall and clunked to the floor. "Way to bury the lede."

"You can't keep ignoring this."

"Why? It's been working okay for a few weeks now." She reloaded the flash.

"Amelia—"

"Besides, lawyers are still hashing out if the sale was even final before Freddie died. Until I know for sure Cranford Communications is the new owner of the *Maple Valley News,* I don't feel any obligation to take C.J. Cranford's calls. Especially since I know exactly what he'll say." She plopped the flash back in its bag. "He'll do to us what he's done to dozens of small papers—dissolve us and roll us into a larger regional pub. He owns the *Central Iowa Communicator,* you know." A four-color beauty of a paper with a tri-county reach. She could admit to ogling the *Communicator's* zingy headlines and pretty photos each week.

Didn't mean she wanted to see it swallow up the *News.*

Owen only shrugged and picked up the batteries rolling across the floor.

Maybe she shouldn't expect him to share her worry. He was a twenty-four-year-old transplant from Omaha with his eyes on grad school. She'd seen the applications he worked on during his lunch hour, the ones he minimized on his computer screen whenever she walked past.

He couldn't understand Amelia's ties to this town, the paper. Didn't know—*couldn't* know—how they'd filled up the hollowed-out spaces inside her. "Did Cranford leave a message?"

"Mae's the one who took the call, but according to her Post-It—" He walked to Amelia's desk and peeled the note from her monitor. "He's coming to town and wants to meet with you."

"When?"

"Doesn't say. But there's a number."

"He's going to have to wait until after the fire department photo." Which could end up being one of her last tasks as editor. Because if Cranford *did* own the *News* now, what were the chances she'd still have a job after he swooped in? Even if he did keep the paper open, he'd probably take one look at her empty résumé and her nonexistent college degree and wonder why Freddie ever hired her.

Owen stood close to her now, fingers still wrapped around the strap of her camera bag. "Look, it's going to be okay."

"I'm not so sure, but I appreciate the optimism." She started to turn, but Owen's hold on her camera bag halted her.

"Just return the call, okay? Meet with the man." His expression took on an abrupt intensity. "You'll impress him like you do everyone."

She blinked at his shift in demeanor but reached up to pat his cheek. "You're a good guy, Owen Berry. But I gotta run."

He released her bag, and she angled around the counter but stopped halfway to the door. "Hey, does the name Hildy mean anything to you?"

He shook his head. "No, why?"

"Just a reference that has me stumped." Two weeks and she still couldn't figure it out.

She retreated the way she'd come. Mae was helping a customer as she approached the receptionist's desk—a tall woman with the kind of burnished chestnut hair Amelia could only dream about and lipstick a jarring shade of magenta. Mae glanced at her as she passed. "Amelia—"

"I know, I'm late." She swung to face Mae, arms out. "If Chief Daniels calls, tell him to hold his horses." She fingered on one glove. "And if C.J. Cranford calls again, tell him he's got the wrong number."

"Amelia—"

"Better yet, pretend *you* called *him* and try to order a large pepperoni pizza. If he laughs and goes along with it, we'll know maybe, just maybe, he's not the corporate buzzkill I'm imagining him to be."

"Amelia!" Mae barked.

Amelia fumbled pulling her second glove from her pocket. "What?" And why was the woman at the counter looking at her like it was a hand that'd just fallen to the floor, not merely her glove?

Mae gestured to the woman. "There's someone here to see you." Her words were slow, measured. "*This* is C.J. Cranford."

Amelia's breathing hitched. Her glance darted from the woman to Mae and back to the woman. Oh no. No, no, no . . .

The woman stepped forward, held out one palm. "You must be Amelia Bentley. I'm C.J., but you can call me Corporate Buzzkill, if you like. Now, that was a large pepperoni?"

⁓

A few neatly arranged words, clever and concise, shouldn't be enough to make or break a reputation.

Then again, if they weren't, Logan Walker wouldn't have a career.

"I can't believe we're driving forty-five minutes in stupid LA traffic just to find a napkin from dinner three nights ago." Impatience rattled in Theodore Tompkins's voice and the drumming of his fingers on the armrest of the passenger's door.

"Four nights." A blast of cool from the car's rasping air-conditioner chafed over Logan's skin. He may have lived in California for a good seven years now, but the Midwesterner in him still hadn't adjusted to eighty-degree weather in March. "Trust me, it's a piece of rhetorical brilliance written on that napkin. You *and* the senator will be glad we fought the freeway to get it from my apartment."

He glanced over at his friend, sandy blond hair still leftover from the man's past as a competitive surfer. These days, Tompkins was all pressed suits and glossy-hued ties.

Not that Logan was any different. Sure, he'd loosened his tie into a droop, unfastened the top button of his shirt, and abandoned his suit jacket in the backseat before they'd left the firm. But just like Tompkins had deserted his surfboard and tan, Logan had traded in the life of casual jeans and tees, with a reporter's notebook in his back pocket, plenty long ago.

Logan veered his Ford four-door around an SUV and then onto an off-ramp. Only ten minutes from his apartment building now. Maybe he should've waited until tonight to ditch the office and go in search of the napkin he'd used as a notepad earlier this week, but frankly, he welcomed a midday stop at home. A chance to see Charlie for more than his usual too-few minutes at the bookends of each day.

Besides, his house was on the way to tonight's legislative fundraiser.

Theo pulled out his phone. "If what you wrote on that napkin was so brilliant, why can't you remember it?"

"Because I'm a thirty-four-year-old single dad whose brain is at capacity. This morning I called the nanny Kristy instead of Krista." The phrase *If looks could kill* had taken on a whole new meaning. "She pretty much eviscerated me with her scowl."

"Eviscerated. Nice word. That's why you're the speechwriter and I'm just the measly political strategist." Theo tapped his phone's screen. "But maybe start writing those fancy words on something other than napkins. Just a thought."

"When the muse hits, I scribble on whatever's handy, my friend."

A siren screeched somewhere in the distance. Not an uncommon sound in this claustrophobic city, even in the relatively nice neighborhood where Logan and Emma had settled down.

Nice or not, they'd sworn the apartment was only temporary, a short-term campout until they picked a house to call home. Then, in a blink and a phone call, everything had changed.

And Logan hadn't been able to make himself leave.

He reached for the sweating water bottle in the cup holder between the seats.

"What the—!"

Logan dropped his bottle at Theo's outburst. It plunked to the floor and rolled to where his foot had just slipped on the accelerator. "Man, trying to drive here."

"Sorry, but this can't be for real. Seriously. It can't."

Logan steered onto Shoreline Road, stretching cement apartment buildings lined up like a welcome crew. Lanky palm trees bowed overhead, the only brush of color on an otherwise beige and gray canvas. Even the sky seemed tinged with an ashen hue.

With his left foot, Logan kicked the swaying water bottle out of the way. "Fantasy surfing team lose again?"

Theo slapped his phone to his thigh. "You will use any excuse to bring that up."

Logan pushed a flopping piece of dark hair from his forehead. *Emma would've made me cut it by now.* She would've called the barber, scheduled an appointment, driven him there herself if she had to, and—

He swallowed the swell of memories before he had a chance to taste them. In the distance, the siren's peal grew louder. "I'm just saying . . ." The words took extra effort. "Fantasy surfing? What're you going to pseudo compete in next? Fantasy tetherball?"

"You going to keep mocking the only hobby I still have time for or you going to let me tell you about the email I just read? You're copied on it."

"Fine. Talk." Parking on both sides of the road narrowed his lane, the street seeming to shrink as he reached the final turn toward his unit. Eight more congested blocks.

"It's an email from Roberta S. Hadley. She wants to meet with us."

"Roberta S. Hadley." Two-term senator. Party darling. Shoe-in contender in next year's presidential primaries.

"Roberta. S. Hadley." Theo drew out each syllable, awe hovering in his voice. "You know that can only mean one thing."

"Roberta S. Hadley's putting together an exploratory committee. She's gonna run."

"And she's actually considering *us*."

Of its own accord, Logan's foot nudged the brake, and his car slackened to a crawl. He glanced at Theo. "Is it weird that we can't say her name without saying the full thing?"

"What's weird is we work this campaign, and two years from now, if she actually wins—maybe even if she doesn't—we could have jobs on Capitol Hill."

Washington, D.C. A political speechwriter's Mecca. Every homily he'd ever begun on a napkin—or Post-It or magazine margin or even his hand—had been a resting place for his own hopes and dreams.

'Course, the thought of uprooting Charlotte held about as much appeal as stepping in hot tar. Not even four years old yet and she'd been through so much already. People told him one day he'd consider it a blessing—Charlie's young age at the time of the accident. Meant she wouldn't remember it, they said.

Yeah, well, what kind of blessing was it, knowing she'd grow up with so few—maybe no—memories of her adoptive mother? That she had to make do with a father whose career, though promising, was too often all-consuming?

"We'll schedule it as soon as possible, of course." Not even a hint of a question in Theo's voice.

"A presidential campaign, though. Think of the time commitment. We'd basically be putting the rest of our lives on hold."

Theo snickered. "What lives? It's not like either of us is swimming in free time right now."

True. Running an independent political consulting firm didn't exactly equal a life of leisure. "But don't you ever miss the old days?" Pillars of smoke rose in the distance. "You know, back when we were working on local campaigns?"

"Are you crazy? Low-profile races that drew as much attention as ants on the sidewalk?"

A fire truck's lights appeared in his rearview mirror, and he pulled over to let it wail past. "Yeah, but to this day, I've never had more fun than that first campaign back in Iowa. There's something about local politics. Makes a person feel like they really have a voice, you know?

"Maybe, but it also pays a lot less. If I never see another package of ramen, it'll be soon enough. You're just having a homesick day. That reporter or editor or whoever got to you more than you're letting on."

He started forward again, grin stretching past his hesitation. No, Amelia Bentley's emails a couple weeks ago hadn't gotten to him, not really. They'd made him laugh more than anything. Leave a career on the brink of actual success to go back to small-town reporting? No thanks.

But he could appreciate her persistence.

"Theo, all I'm saying is—" He broke off as the scene ahead came into view and dread burrowed through him. Fire trucks, police cars, people milling about on the sidewalk, all looking toward . . .

His apartment building.

Instant fear lodged in his throat. "Oh no."

Theo had gone silent, eyes wide.

Logan swerved his car to the curb, yanked it into Park, and bolted from his seat.

"Logan!" Theo's call and the sound of his door closing faded as terrified instinct sent Logan flailing down the sidewalk and toward his building. Smoke tunneled from windows halfway up its rise.

Charlie!

He pushed through the barrier of people crowding the lawn behind the emergency responders' activity, his first prayers in forever beating through him in spurts and fits.

Let her be okay. Let me find her.

His phone—he'd left it back in the car in a cup holder, still silenced following a morning meeting. What if the nanny had been trying to call and—

Strong arms pushed against him. A firefighter, blocking his path. "Sir, this isn't a drill. You can't go in—"

"My daughter's in there. Charlie . . . Charlotte." He hurled forward once more, but the fireman's arm jutted out to stop him.

"Please, stay here."

The man's firm grip held him in place, his face hidden behind his helmet. He heard jogging steps coming up behind him, Theo's panting breath.

The firefighter looked over his shoulders. "Your friend?" Theo's rasped "yes" drew a nod. "Make sure he stays here, okay? I'm sure his daughter is fine. We've already evacuated almost the whole building."

In a daze, Logan watched the man hurry away, terror twisting every nerve inside him and a voice from the past feeding his dread as he stared at the building.

"I'm so sorry, Logan. If you'd gotten here ten or even five minutes ago . . ."

The shake of a doctor's head.

An ER nurse unable to stop her tears.

"You almost made it."

The snap of his heart, like a broken guitar string, sharp and callousing.

Almost wasn't good enough.

Theo's hand found his shoulder. "Come on. Let's start asking around. She's probably out here with the nanny somewhere."

Logan nodded, blinked, tried to reach through the fog of alarm for something solid—common sense or courage or . . . something.

Nothing.

"Mr. Walker!"

He pivoted at the frantic call. Krista? The nanny.

Without Charlie.

She reached him, tears streaming down her face, head shaking before he could even ask the question. "I couldn't find her. I called and called and I couldn't find her. The alarm . . . and then this firefighter made me leave the apartment and . . ."

Beside him, Theo sprang into action, running after the fireman they'd just talked to. Krista kept talking, waving her hands.

But Logan couldn't hear over the roaring waves of his own panic.

2

*L*ogan couldn't make himself let go of Charlie.

A chugging breeze, carrying the bitter odor of smoke, sent his daughter's reddish curls tickling against his jaw and cheek, her head buried in his neck. Her limbs hung loose around him, her breathing heavy. Amazing that she'd been able to fall asleep amid the clamor of angst-ridden residents and firefighters swarming the lawn.

It'd been forty-five minutes since the fireman had come jogging from the apartment building, Charlie in his arms, and Logan's pulse still hadn't steadied.

"I heard someone say it was a microwave fire."

Theo was still here? Had he been standing next to Logan this whole time? The muscles in Logan's arms pinched. "Bad?"

"Not from the sound of it. I bet they'll let residents back in soon. I already called the committee for the fundraiser, let them know you won't be there."

"Thanks." His voice was flat even if his heart rate wasn't. Didn't matter if the fire hadn't amounted to any real damage. Didn't matter if he ever found that napkin scribbled with whatever important wording about whatever important political issue.

Only thing that mattered was his little girl.

And those minutes of terror, when he'd instantly morphed into the same Logan Walker who'd stood by Charlie's crib the night of Emma's funeral, three days after the drunk driver had stolen his wife from him, suddenly so horribly abandoned, despite the relatives who still lingered in the living room.

Convinced he couldn't do this by himself.

Alone.

"She's okay, Walker."

Theo. Theo with his wife waiting for him at home at night. Theo who couldn't possibly understand, despite his best intentions.

"Tell me you're going to fire that nanny, though."

Logan shifted Charlie to his other shoulder. She barely stirred at the movement.

"He doesn't have to fire me. I quit."

Both Logan and Theo pivoted at the voice. Krista stood with her hands on her waist, ponytail askew and frown glued in place. Gone were the tear streaks from earlier. In their place, a biting resentment hardened her eyes.

"You quit?" Logan's arms tightened.

"That's what I said."

Theo visibly bristled. "You've got some nerve, kid—"

Logan cut Theo off with a glance, then pinned Krista with the kind of glare he used to give when his younger brother hustled him at basketball. "You left my daughter in a building on fire, and *you're* the angry one?"

She cocked her head. "Yeah, I'm angry. She wouldn't answer. Charlotte never answers." She flung her hand toward Charlie. "I'm yelling for her, panicking, looking everywhere I can think of. Do you have any idea how freaked out I was?"

"*You* were freaked out? I'm her dad."

"Then act like it." The words burst from Krista, pummeling Logan with their force. "Get her some help. She's three. She should be talking by now. She should at least be able to answer when someone calls her name."

Every defensive nerve in his body surged, anger throbbing through him. "You have no idea what you're talking about." Their argument had begun to attract attention. He could feel the curious stares of neighbors he'd never had time to get to know.

"Keep telling yourself that if you want, but it doesn't take a child psychologist to know something's not right." Krista swung her backpack over her shoulder. "And I can't handle just standing by and watching while you neglect—"

"That's enough." Theo's firm voice severed Krista's tirade. "You obviously don't know the person you're working for. Neglect isn't even in Walker's vocabulary. You want to quit, quit. But no one needs to hear your lectures."

Krista's frown deepened, and she looked from Theo back to Logan, then to Charlie's still-sleeping form draped over Logan's shoulder. For a fraction of a second, her expression softened. She met Logan's eyes. "If you need two weeks—"

"I don't."

She nodded stiffly and turned as if to leave. But then she looked over her shoulder once more. "Did they say where she was hiding?"

"My walk-in." The fireman hadn't needed to be any more specific. Logan had known. Emma's side of the closet, behind her dresses, wrapped in the tulle of her wedding gown.

A shudder ripped through him now, the ache pleading for release. And Krista saw it, didn't she? Saw the panic-induced pain threatening to undo him right here on the lawn, in front of everyone.

But she only turned, walked away.

Logan made himself blink. Swallow. One deep breath and then another. And the second he'd lured the grief back into its hiding place, a bevy of questions rocketed to the surface. What would he do without a nanny? Who would watch Charlie during tomorrow's press conference? Was their apartment still livable?

Charlie stirred in his arms, a tiny whimper feathering against his skin. He pressed a kiss to her head. He'd figure it out. He'd figure it all out. Because that's what he did. What he'd been doing for two years now.

"Listen, I should probably get back."

He blinked for what felt like the hundredth time and turned to Theo. "Of course. Need to take my car?"

"Already called a cab." Theo patted Charlie's back. "Glad she's okay."

But . . . she wasn't okay, was she? Krista was right. Charlie would celebrate her fourth birthday this August, and she had yet to start really talking beyond a word or two here and there—no full sentences.

A pediatrician had momentarily quelled Logan's concerns last summer. Explained that without an older sibling to mimic, it might simply take her longer. *"Bring her back in six months if she still isn't talking. But I bet she'll be jabbering your ear off in no time."*

The beating sun heated him now. Six months. It'd been eight. And he hadn't even called to schedule an appointment.

"Oh, before I go . . . we should probably get back to Hadley ASAP." Theo had his phone out as he moved toward the taxi that'd somehow wound its way through the crowded street. "You okay with me taking the lead?"

Had it only been a couple of hours ago that he and Theo had gushed about the senator? Dreamt about futures that looked like something off *The West Wing?* "Sure, go for it." His voice came out dull, croaky, as if he'd been the one to enter the smoke-filled building.

But he hadn't. *Someone else* had been watching his daughter before the fire. *Someone else* had rescued her during it.

He was just the guy who clung helplessly to her in the aftermath.

Just like so many evenings, when he arrived home hours after dark, only minutes before Charlie drifted off to sleep for the night. He'd rock her long after she nodded off, trying to convince himself this was working, this single parent thing.

But it was getting harder and harder to believe his own assurances.

A male voice speaking through a megaphone blasted in. "Attention, please."

Theo paused, leaning over the open taxi door. "Don't do it to yourself, Walker."

Logan glanced at his friend. Was he that see-through?

"Don't beat yourself up for not being there earlier or think you're a horrible dad. Anybody would admire the way you've raised Charlie since Emma . . ."

The fireman's voice droned in the background, letting the crowd know there'd been only structural damage to a couple apartments. Most residents could reenter the building in a few minutes. A couple units on the sixth floor, though—Logan's floor—had suffered heavy smoke damage.

"I'll tell you what Roberta S. Hadley says after I talk to her, okay?"

Logan grasped for the interest he knew he should be able to muster. *Roberta S. Hadley. Presidential campaign. She wants us.*

Minutes later, he watched the taxi cut a path through the maze of vehicles and fire engines blocking the street. He felt the softness of Charlie's palm on his cheek and looked down at her. She'd awakened, emerald eyes grinning at him, whatever fear had driven her into his bedroom closet now gone. Did she even remember being carried from the building?

"How's my Charlie?" He touched his forehead to hers, and she giggled. "Daddy's home early. Sounds like we might need to camp out in a hotel for the night. Maybe one with a pool."

Her lips rounded into a surprised and happy O, and for an elastic moment that stretched with hope, he thought she might actually verbally reply. *Come on, honey, let me hear your voice.* But instead, she only clapped her hands, kissed his cheek.

He'd take it. For now, he'd take it.

Charlie wriggled then and tapped his back. She may not talk all that much, but she didn't have any trouble communicating. He bent over to slide her around his body, piggyback style, and started for the apartment building.

"Logan Walker?"

He paused and turned, squinting against the evening sun, and saw the silhouette moving toward him. A mailman?

"Yes?" Charlie's feet bumped against his sides.

"Got a piece of certified mail for you. You'll need to sign."

Hard to do with Charlie on his back, but he managed. "Surprised you could find me in this mess of people."

"Someone pointed you out. Most of the rest of the building will have to wait for their mail 'til tomorrow. Fire truck's blocking the mailboxes."

Logan glanced at the manila envelope. Maple Valley address. A law firm?

"Glad I could at least deliver this, though. *Certified* usually means important." The mailman winked at Charlie and moved away.

Afternoon warmth tinged with coastal humidity curled around Logan as he tore open the envelope and pulled out the packet of papers. Skimmed what looked like a cover letter crowded with legalese until his attention hooked on Freddie Fitzsimmons's name—the old owner of his hometown paper, his one-time mentor.

And the words *last will and testament.*

⟳

"Want to tell me why we're sitting out here in the cold? Is there a reason we couldn't talk at your office?"

Amelia winced at the impatience huddled in C.J. Cranford's voice. The woman rubbed her hands together, breath forming clouds of white and heels tapping against the shoveled sidewalk underneath the park bench.

"Just wait." Amelia dipped her chin into her scarf. "You'll see."

"Will I? Or will my eyeballs get frostbite first?"

So maybe this hadn't been the best plan ever—the short trek around the block toward downtown. Wasn't it enough Amelia had already blown any chance at a good first impression with the woman who might be her new boss?

But if C.J.'s presence in Maple Valley meant what it had to—that Freddie had indeed signed all the documents before he'd died, gone and sold the *News*—then there was only one thing to do: Convince Cranford the paper was worth salvaging.

Forget the flood-damaged equipment. Forget the paltry advertising numbers. Forget all the reasons print publications in small towns were folding around the country. The *News* could be the exception.

Because it wasn't just any old newspaper. And Maple Valley wasn't any old town. In about five minutes, C.J. would see for herself.

The downtown fanned in front of them like a quiet audience— quaint storefronts brushed with the peachy-pink hues of an ambling dusk. The shadows of bony trees and globe-topped lampposts patterned the blanket of white covering the town square.

C.J. glanced over. "You do know eventually we're going to have to talk business?"

"I thought that's what we did back at the office." After begging Owen to cover her scheduled photo, Amelia had given C.J. a quick tour of the *News's* domain. She'd recited recent headlines and rattled off newspaper history—like the fact that this summer the *News* would celebrate its 100th year. An effort at damage control that may or may not have done any good. Because all C.J. had done after Amelia ran out of words was tilt her head and say, "Coffee?"

"That wasn't talking business," C.J. said now. "That was a tour. A very . . . perky, tinsely one."

Because she'd overdone it, hadn't she? Pumped too much cheer into her voice and brown-nosed it. "Sorry—"

"You like your job. Nothing wrong with that." C.J. crossed one leg over the other. The zigzag stripes of her tights were the one standout feature of her attire—black blazer over black pencil skirt. Black heels. Black purse.

"I do like my job."

"Which is why you've been avoiding my calls."

Couldn't argue that. Across the square, Mr. Baker locked the front door of his antique shop under a flapping awning. He turned, caught Amelia's gaze, waved, and then hunched his way toward his station wagon. "I did mean to get back to you." Eventually.

The first light in the park flickered as Mr. Baker's engine sputtered down Main. "Oh, here we go. It's about to happen."

"What's about to happen?"

"You'll see."

Just a breath later, as if tapped by a magic wand, everything blinked to life at once, a glow of yellowy-white against the deepening sky—the globe lights atop the lampposts, the lanterns hanging from the band shell, strings of twinkle lights draped over wrinkled branches.

"Wow." C.J. released the word in an awed sigh.

"Pretty, isn't it?" Wind-dusted snow sparkled against the light.

"Magical." C.J. uncrossed her legs and leaned forward, elbows on her knees. "Possibly worth the cold."

Satisfaction, warm and sweet, glided through Amelia.

Until C.J. tilted her head. "I wonder how much it costs the city to keep it lit up like this."

The question landed with a thud. "The lights don't stay on all night."

C.J. stood. "So where's the coffee you promised?"

Amelia swiped at her disappointment as they retreated the same way they'd come, their footprints from before already smudged out of sight. Silly, probably, thinking a few minutes and some pretty lights might change a businesswoman's mind.

But then, that was the problem with Amelia. Always hoping in the wrong things. Almost three years post-divorce and apparently the lesson still hadn't sunk in: *Some minds don't change. Some fights you don't win.*

Yeah, well, C.J. wasn't Jeremy.

And Amelia wasn't the same Amelia she'd been back in Des Moines: broken, emptied, drained of any fight.

The riverfront came into view as they rounded the block. Sheets of ice bobbed in the tumbling waterway that split the town in half. The river had flooded early last fall—damaging not only the *News* office, but the bridal store next door and the coffee shop they were about to enter. Amelia had been out here, sandbagging with the rest of the town in the hours before the flood had its way. That same summer they'd been pounded by a tornado.

But there'd been happy times in the last year, too. Seth Walker had turned an old, abandoned bank building into the coolest restaurant around. An ex–NFL quarterback had moved to town and opened up a nonprofit. The community had pulled together to keep its historic railroad running.

And in the midst of all the big things, everyday life moved in a rhythm not all that different than the river's—fast and whooshing some days, slow and serene others. But always, it moved.

"You're upset." C.J.'s heels clipped against the sidewalk as they neared the coffee shop.

"Not upset, just . . . frustrated. It's not only paper and ink we're talking about. It's people's jobs. We're a family in that office. Kat's a single mom trying to put two sons through college. Owen's saving up for grad school."

"Amelia—"

"If you close the office, their jobs will go away." Along with her dream of running the paper herself, finally cementing her place here in Maple Valley. If she'd had the money, she'd have bought the *News* herself the second Freddie mentioned selling. "I'm just asking you to consider—"

"What in the world?" C.J. halted in front of the coffee shop, focus hooked on its stretching windows, a clamor of rising voices, along with the brisk aroma of Coffee Coffee's brew, eking outside.

Amelia glanced at the crowd inside. "Not unusual for Coffee Coffee to have mobs reminiscent of Depression-era bank runs. We've sorta got a town-wide caffeine dependency." She cupped her hands to the window and peered through. "But this looks way more organized than usual." Yes, there was Mayor Milton Briggs up near the order counter, waving his hands from his perch atop a chair.

Great. Just when she needed this town to make a good impression . . .

"Whatever's happening, the only important question is, can we still get coffee?"

"Oh, we'll get you your coffee." This one thing she could get right. She pushed through the entrance, the jingle of bells above the doorway mingling with the commotion inside.

"Now, I know it's confusing." Mayor Milt, with his salt-and-pepper beard and usual cardigan, stood on a chair up front, exaggerated exasperation in his voice. "But since the mother insists she doesn't like the traditional pink and blue, you'll see the ribbons are green and yellow. Green for a boy, yellow for a girl."

All around the eclectic coffee shop, townspeople sat at tables of varying heights and lounged in leather furniture. Behind the mayor, an espresso-hued counter fronted the back wall, with its chalkboard menu and mosaic backsplash.

"What is this?" C.J. leaned toward her. "A community-wide baby shower?"

"I don't think so." She would've heard about that kind of thing. This smacked of exactly the kind of impromptu town meeting Mayor Milt loved to throw.

"So pick whatever gender you think the baby will be. Wear the ribbon any time you come in to Coffee Coffee until next week to show your support for Megan."

Megan. Of course.

The pang started in Amelia's heart and landed in her stomach.

"Double shot espresso."

Amelia blinked. Right, coffee. "Got it. I'll be back."

She arced around the throng and made for the counter, scooted behind it and—not seeing any employees in sight—went for the espresso machine. She had the cup half filled, the machine's whir nearly drowned out by the crowd, before the voice cut in behind her.

"What're you doing back here, Bentley?"

Amelia finished filling the cup before turning toward the droll voice. Megan, the coffee shop's young owner—jet-black hair and charcoal-like eyeliner, as surly as she was resilient. Meg had been forced to close for nearly a month after the flood last year.

But that hadn't been the biggest of the young owner's challenges.

Amelia glanced at Meg's protruding stomach under her purple apron and felt the knobby ache grappling through her—familiar, dense with memories.

What should have been one of the happiest days of her life taking a sudden and harsh turn.

Dani's decision to back out of the adoption.

Mary's wails in the hospital nursery.

And the chafing realization that Amelia wouldn't be the one to soothe her. Not now. Not ever.

Should it still sting so much this many years later?

"Well?" Meg's fists were on her waist. And oh, she reminded Amelia of Dani in that moment.

Amelia swallowed. "I'm making sure you get at least one paying customer out of this chaos, that's what."

The girl, who couldn't be older than twenty-one or twenty-two, lifted one pierced eyebrow. "Can you believe this town? I tell one person I'm finding out the gender next week, and before I know it, they've turned it into a full-blown event. Maple Valley will use literally anything as an excuse to celebrate." She pushed a strand of hair out of her eyes. "Even a single girl's unplanned pregnancy."

Amelia had to work not to flinch. "I thought you didn't work on Thursdays."

"Keeping tabs on my schedule?"

"Uh, no, not keeping tabs." But maybe, truthfully, avoiding. Was it so wrong to know her weak spots? To do her best to keep the whispers of her past entombed where they belonged?

Focus. C.J. Cranford. The News. *The jobs you need to save.* Things she might be able to change.

Versus things she couldn't. No matter how hard she tried.

Megan kneaded the small of her back just below her apron's knot. "Hired a new girl last week and turns out, she's about as dependable as an untrained puppy."

"Too bad. I gotta run, but here's hoping you survive the next week." She handed Megan a five. "Keep the change."

She didn't run from the counter, but she might as well have for all the polish of her escape. Meg probably wondered what her deal was. They used to be friends—or friend-ish, at least. Amelia had even worked a few shifts at the coffee shop just to pad her income. Meg had asked her back when she'd reopened after the flood.

But by then Amelia had heard the news about Megan's surprise pregnancy.

And she just couldn't.

She found C.J. where she'd left her—now wearing a green-and-yellow ribbon.

"Twins," C.J. said as she accepted the cup from Amelia. "That's my vote."

"Don't say that too loud or Megan might chuck a sugar shaker at you."

"Will I get in trouble for voting even though I'm not an official Maple Valley citizen?"

"Are you kidding? The mayor—everyone, really—would love the thought of sucking in an outsider."

Amelia followed C.J. to a counter crammed with coffee supplies. C.J. set down her cup and reached for the sugar. "Listen, I need to get back, and we haven't even touched on why I'm here yet. You clearly think I want to talk about the closing of the *News*." She popped the lid off her cup. "You're wrong."

"I am?"

"Freddie never finalized the sale. I don't know who your new owner is, but it's not Cranford Communications." She mixed her coffee with a stir stick.

"I shouldn't be smiling right now, should I?"

"Don't get too excited. Our board is already prepping a package for the new owner, whoever he or she is. We'll likely acquire the *News* by the end of the summer. The new owner would be crazy not to sell. It's not a financially solvent business, you have to know that."

"Finances can change. We can work on upping our subscriptions, maybe put together some new ad packages—"

"Like I said, I'm not here to talk about that."

The ruckus of the disorganized town meeting still rose around them.

"It's gonna be a girl. I can tell by her stomach."

"A boy. No doubt."

"It's a crapshoot, and you all know it."

Amelia swallowed, too many distant moments trying to swarm in. Jeremy. The hospital nursery. The social worker's gauzy voice. *"I'm sorry, this happens more often than we'd like."*

"Amelia?"

She blinked.

"I'm not here to talk about the future of the *News*. I'm here to talk about *your* future." C.J. lifted her cup. "I'd like to offer you a job."

❧

"You're not seriously doing this."

Logan momentarily ignored Theo as he accepted a stack of files from the intern. Alena would put an executive assistant at a Fortune 500 company to shame.

"The senator's office still needs wording for that energy policy press release." She added another folder to the pile in his arms. "And the Cohen Foundation wants a bullet-point overview for the governor's fundraiser speech next week."

"Not happening." Logan pulled the pencil from between his teeth, eyes on the top file. He perched on the corner of the mahogany desk that claimed one corner of the small office.

So much to get done today. Especially if he meant to pack up and travel back to Iowa this week. Which he did. Theo might throw a fit, but what could he do? That certified letter from the law firm in Maple Valley hadn't left him much choice.

Oh, Freddie, you were great in so many ways. But why me?

Couldn't he have left his newspaper to someone who . . . well . . . wanted it? And how horribly ungrateful was that thought?

"Are you even listening to me, Walker?" Stress curved Theo's brow from where he stood behind Alena.

"They're concerned the governor will go over his allotted twenty-five minutes," Alena said as she moved around him to straighten the contents of the plastic shelf on his desk marked *Inbox*. The one he rarely remembered to riffle through.

Logan dropped the files onto his chair, attention darting to Charlie playing in the corner. Books, dolls—he'd brought all her quietest toys to the office today. "Gov goes over one time and suddenly we're incapable of pacing his speech. Tell them the speech will be perfectly timed down to his every pause—twenty-three and a half minutes, with ninety seconds for applause before and after."

Alena used the edge of her shirt to dust off his laptop. "Whatever you say, boss. Though I think it'd be funny if you pared the whole thing down to, oh, fifteen minutes. Just for shock value. Let the event organizers scramble to fill the extra ten minutes." She stopped cleaning his desk and stood in front of him, playful smirk in place.

He nudged up the glasses he wore today instead of bothering with contacts. "Better yet, we give them their bullet points—*ninety* minutes worth. Then take bets on how long it'll take for the foundation director to call."

Laughter bubbled from Alena—and then Charlie, who obviously had no idea what she was laughing about. But she giggled all the same, leaving the play mat he'd set up for her and walking to him. She stretched her arms, and he stooped to pick her up. Two nights in a hotel while the apartment aerated obviously hadn't bothered her. "What do you think, kid? Make the foundation squirm just for the fun of it?"

Alena reached forward to straighten the barrette Logan had attempted to fasten in Charlie's hair this morning. "You should bring her to the office more often."

"I'd never get another page written."

Alena kissed Charlie's cheek, then picked up a stack of papers from his printer. "I'll proof these for you by this afternoon."

She retreated from the office, leaving Logan to face the disapproval written all over Theo's face. "What?"

"She likes you."

"Of course she does. I keep her stocked in punch cards for the coffee cart. It's the least I can do since she's not getting paid."

"You know that's not what I meant." Theo walked to the mini fridge against one wall. He plucked a water bottle from inside. "She's got a crush on you."

"You should start a stand-up act. You're funny."

"Wasn't joking."

"I bet she's, what? Ten years younger than me? Probably has a boyfriend."

"She's so into you she might as well embroider *I Love Walker* onto a shirt and wear it to work." He took a swig from his water bottle. "Tattoo your name on her arm."

"You're seeing things."

"Whatever." Theo capped his bottle. "Not here to talk about your love life anyway."

Logan let Charlie down and returned to his desk, picking up the files Alena had delivered. "Then what are you here for?"

As if he didn't know. He'd figured the second he pressed *Send* on that office-wide memo, he'd have Theo in his office.

"You're taking a personal leave of absence? So nice of you to tell me first. You didn't even say how long you're going to be gone."

"Two weeks, tops." *I hope.* His gaze fastened on the slit of a window carved into the wall, which let in just enough sunlight to keep alive the one plant on the corner of the desk. His focus flitted to the plant, now wilted and brown. Well, *almost* alive.

"Is this because of your apartment? I told you Jill and I would be happy to put you up in our guestroom."

"It's not that." Although the apartment did smell like a forest post-wildfire. And the unit next door was going to be under construction for weeks.

But it wasn't their living space that'd kept him awake the past two nights. It was the fact that Freddie had gone and left him a business—and with it, employees, obligations. It should be good news, a sign of the man's fondness and respect. But it felt . . . weighty. Another responsibility when Logan could barely keep up with the ones he already had.

But maybe this is a good thing.

The same whisper wandered in now that had last night, when he'd finally made the decision to go back to Iowa. *Maybe this is exactly what you and Charlie need.*

A break. A chance to spend real time together. Vacation. The word tasted foreign.

Theo took another swig of his water. "You couldn't have worse timing."

"I could, actually. We could be mid-campaign. We could be dealing with a PR crisis. It's political off-season right now."

"There's no such thing as off-season and you know it. We're drowning in work. Your home and nanny situation are up in the air." Theo pointed to the plant. "You can't even keep a plant alive. No way do you have time for this."

Logan dropped his files onto the desk with a thud, his last grip on restraint slackening. "You want to talk about time? I have poured myself into this business, Theo. I haven't taken more than a handful of days off in two years. I forgot what a weekend feels like forever ago." He could hear his voice notching, forced it down. "I barely see my daughter."

"Log—"

"And if there's anything I really don't have time for, it's an argument about how I don't have time. You heard Alena. I have a dozen things to finish before tomorrow."

"Tomorrow. You're leaving tomorrow." Statement, not a question. Theo abandoned his water bottle on the windowsill and stepped closer to Logan, blocking his view of Charlie. Voice low, deliberate. "We have a flippin' presidential candidate vetting us for her campaign team. And you're just going to leave?"

"A man *I* hugely respected died." He'd already told Theo about Freddie yesterday. Not just about inheriting the paper, but about Freddie himself. How he'd offered Logan an internship at the paper when Logan was still in high school. Taken him under his wing when Mom first got sick and Dad had been so consumed with caring for her.

Why couldn't Theo muster some understanding?

"I'm sorry about that editor. I am. But this is everything we've worked for."

"Yeah, well, I won't be any good to Hadley if I'm burnt out. You're the one who just said I can't even take care of a plant. That speech Alena had mentioned? I've been trying for days to get it right. Usually I'd whip it out in a few hours. This is what I need. What Charlie needs." His voice was a strained whisper now. "That stuff her nanny said—"

Theo shook his head. "She was frightened and blowing off steam."

"She was *right*. I've been pretending things are fine for way too long."

He brushed past Theo. Charlie held a book toward him, green eyes so much like Emma's most people never would've guessed she was adopted. The resemblance to Emma made sense—Charlotte's birth mother was Emma's little sister, after all.

"So this is for sure."

He looked back. Resignation marred Theo's expression. "Yes."

The Logan from a few years ago would've thought longer. Would've prayed about it.

But he didn't have the luxury of time or the comfort of faith this time around. No, what remnants of belief loitered in his spirit these days were immobile, passive.

He had to figure things out on his own.

"And Hadley?"

"I'll do whatever I need to. I'll fly back here—or over to D.C. if that's where she wants to meet. This is just temporary." He walked to Charlie, sat down beside her, and accepted the book. "Two weeks, tops."

Dear Mary,

If you were my daughter, I'd tell you about how I ended up in Maple Valley, Iowa—a little town west of Ames, tucked into a rolling landscape of quilted fields and patches of trees and prairie grass. We like to call ourselves a tourist spot with our heritage railroad and more antique stores than any one town needs.

I came here on a whim, looking for a man I'd never met—his name was Kendall Wilkins. I was two years too late.

I didn't find Kendall. But what I found instead was home.

3

"*Y*ou have a potentially career-altering decision to make by tomorrow, but instead of hashing it out or making a pro/con list or even just flipping a coin, you're making cookies for a woman who doesn't like you."

Amelia couldn't help but smirk at the exaggerated disbelief in Raegan Walker's tone. As if her friend was one to talk—she and the revolving door that was her employment status.

Amelia opened the stainless-steel door of the oven in the Walkers' kitchen, heat billowing over her cheeks as the impatient rhythm of Raegan's nails tapped behind her. She could've made the cookies in her own kitchen. But there was something enchanting about the Walker family home—nestled into a clearing between a cornfield and a twisting, tree-packed ravine. The spacious kitchen, with its cherry cupboards and coppery-beige tiled floor, the collage of photos stuck to the fridge, the window above the sink overlooking a frosty backyard dappled with pale moonlight and evening shadows—all of it tingled with peace and calm and family.

And on nights like tonight—when indecision buzzed like a plague of mosquitos, it was just what she needed. Yes, she owed C.J. Cranford an answer tomorrow. Accept the job at the *Communicator* and move? Or stay in Maple Valley, holding out hope that the *News* somehow survived its change in ownership?

She was no closer to a decision tonight than she'd been nearly a week ago, when she'd stood in Coffee Coffee, listened to C.J.'s out-of-the-blue offer, and for the first time in three years, considered leaving the town that'd become home. But the Walker house and Raegan's company made up for a world of confusion.

Amelia used one oven-mitted hand to pull out the metal sheet, chocolate chip cookies goldened to perfection. "Mae may not like me, but she loves my cookies."

"She doesn't even know they're from you." Raegan twirled in a half-circle atop a barstool edged up to the counter in the middle of the room, her feet bumping against its base.

True. Amelia had taken to dropping off baskets of cookies at the *News* receptionist's house late at night or early in the morning. Sometimes she left a plateful in Mae's little Honda. *Thank you, small-town Iowa people, for not locking your car doors.* As far as she knew, Mae didn't suspect a thing.

"She doesn't need to know they're from me. I'm convinced she's simply lonely. That's why she's so grouchy all the time. The cookies let her know someone cares."

Raegan stilled on her stool. "You're kind, Amelia Bentley, you know that? A little weird, way too into grunge rock—"

"Long live the nineties."

"—and obsessive about winter—but kind." Raegan slipped a shock of blue-streaked blond hair behind her ear. She was one of the first people Amelia had met when she'd moved to town—and easily the most buoyant. Amelia might have a few years on her, but they'd become fast friends.

Amelia used a spatula to pry a cookie off the tray. "Speaking of things I'm obsessive about . . ."

Raegan's laugh rang through the kitchen, and she shifted

to pull a wad of rolled-up papers from the back pocket of her faded jeans, then held the papers in the air. "I'll trade you for a cookie." She snatched one and took a bite. "Make that two cookies."

Hands still encased in oven mitts, Amelia nabbed the papers from Raegan, focus immediately landing on the words in the upper right corner:

Logan Walker, speechwriter
Tompkins & Walker Consulting

"One of these days I'm going to start charging you money for transcripts of my brother's speeches." Raegan stood. "I need milk. And don't get me wrong. Your cookies are de-lish, but the way you gobble up Logan's writing, I have a feeling I could make some serious moola."

"Just as long as you never tell him I'm the one who reads them." Amelia scanned the first few lines, the same awe as always settling in her stomach. Raegan's brother could *write*. Oh, he could write. And every time she read one of his speeches, it was a reminder of why she'd taken up writing herself.

Words could impact. They could shape opinions and per-spectives. They could move a person to action.

Maybe, given enough time, they could even heal.

Raegan poured milk into two glasses, offered one to Amelia. "Don't worry, I won't tell him. Logan still thinks his little sister is all fascinated with his career. Probably hopes it'll influence me to find one of my own."

Amelia glanced at her friend as she accepted the glass of milk. Rae often seemed younger than her twenty-six years—the hair that always changed colors, the graphic tees, the fact that she still slept in the daybed in her childhood bedroom. Was it hard to be the youngest in a line of such successful siblings? Beckett, the lawyer in Boston. Kate, the movie scriptwriter and novelist who'd just moved home from Chicago.

And Logan. The guy who could weave emotion with words.

There'd been a time when Jeremy had been the one to woo Amelia with his speeches, back before his fame and her failure curdled her dreams for the future.

She sluiced the thought with a shake of her head. "Does it bother you, Rae?"

"You mean the fact that I have a hodge-podge of part-time jobs instead of a *career*-career?" Raegan shrugged, took another bite. "Not usually. Just every once in a while, I'll get this feeling that everyone's waiting for me to figure out what I'm going to do with my life. And I just want to say, what's wrong with being content right where I am?"

That was exactly what Amelia had wanted to say to C.J. Cranford last week. The woman had offered her the job of Features Editor for the *Communicator*. Reminded her the paper was one of the state's leading weeklies.

"We own publications in three states. You know that, right? I've read your stuff, Bentley. You should be writing for something with an actual readership. It's a guaranteed step up."

Amelia hadn't been able to find a reply behind her surprise. C.J. had kept talking while she'd stared across the crowded coffee shop, watching Megan rub her belly.

Problem was, she'd stopped believing in guarantees long ago.

The sound of the front door banging open drifted through the house, pulling Amelia to the present. Probably Case Walker, Raegan's dad. Or Seth, the cousin who lived in the basement. Whoever it was bypassed the kitchen, footsteps sounding on the stairs that led to the row of bedrooms on the second floor.

She settled on a stool beside Raegan, bit into a perfectly chewy cookie. How many evenings had Amelia spent in this house, pretending she was part of this close-knit and supportive family? They were one of Maple Valley's staple families—

the kind everyone loved and not-so-secretly wanted to be a part of.

The kind of family she used to think she and Jeremy might have before . . .

"So, are we ever going to talk about this?" Raegan's voice cut in.

"My job offer? The possibility of the *News* going under?"

"No, the fact that you're in love with my brother."

"*What?*" Amelia choked on a cookie, crumbs spewing to the counter.

"At least admit you've got a crush on him."

She downed half a glass of milk in one swallow. "You're delusional."

"I'm right."

"I love his writing, Raegan. There's a big difference between admiring someone's talent and whatever you're thinking." She shuffled the speech papers into a pile and dropped an oven mitt on top. "I've only met him one time."

He'd been in town for Colton Greene's press conference announcing his new nonprofit. A former NFL player, Colton was an old friend of Logan's. He'd come to Maple Valley last fall for a temporary stop that'd turned permanent once he'd fallen for Kate Walker.

"I know, I was there. I saw you turn about a dozen shades brighter than these." Raegan wriggled her fingers in the air, hot pink polish coloring her nails.

"I did not."

Except that she had. She could still feel the way the warmth had practically scrambled over her cheeks. It was that mellow, baritone voice that did it, the dancing laugh. Logan had seemed observant, a little quiet. Which made her think there probably wasn't much he and those inky-dark eyes missed.

And then there'd been the disheveled hair and crooked tie.

And, fine, maybe for a few ridiculous minutes there, Logan Walker had made her think it really was possible to finally forget Jeremy.

But that was only in-the-moment silliness. The man had unknowingly become her writing hero—three years of reading his past articles, listening to her old editor talk about him, and following his speechwriting career could do that to a person. She'd simply had a fan girl moment, that's all.

"Look at you, you're blushing right now." Raegan's smirk dared her to argue.

"Am not."

"I could roast a marshmallow from the heat on your face. Don't feel bad. Most girls who meet my brother who aren't related to him fall for him. And some who are related to him. I have this third cousin who, I swear—"

Amelia fumbled off her bar stool, sweeping up her empty milk glass and plate. "I'm regretting coming over here."

"I could set you guys up."

"Rae—"

"Besides, you haven't gone on a single date since I met you. So—"

"Shouldn't you be at one of your forty jobs?" Her voice came out harsher than she'd intended, punctuated by the clatter of her dishes in the sink.

And Raegan's silence.

She whipped around. "Rae, I didn't . . . didn't mean . . ."

But Rae was standing, wiping crumbs from her fingertips, refusing to meet Amelia's eyes.

Why had she said that? Obviously Raegan's lack of career direction bothered her more than she let on—and Amelia had gone and trampled on what was already a sore spot.

"Your next batch is burning." Raegan thumbed toward the stove, then left the room.

With a sigh that was as much frustration as regret, Amelia flicked off the oven and pulled out the tray of overly brown cookies. She transferred them to a cooling rack, plated up the leftovers from her previous batch, and covered them with Saran wrap, then went looking for Raegan. Up the stairway leading to the second floor. Down the dim hallway.

She stopped at the soft lilt of a voice. A low whisper, singing a gentle melody she didn't recognize, coming from one of the bedrooms she'd never been inside.

And she couldn't help it. She slipped closer to the open door, allowed herself to peek inside. Her heart turned to liquid at the sight. Someone leaning over a bed, pulling the covers over a curled bundle, hushed song melting to an end.

Logan?

She peered in. *Can't be him. He's in LA.*

Whoever it was, she shouldn't be intruding on this moment.

So why was she standing in the doorway? Watching the man arrange the covers? Holding her breath . . .

He leaned over to kiss the child in the bed, then stood. "Goodnight, Ladybug."

And then Logan—yes, definitely Logan—turned. He started only for a moment when he saw her there. And before she realized what was happening, he'd crossed the room and wrapped his arms around her, pulling her to a solid chest. Her face landed in the crook between his shoulder and a stubble-covered chin that brushed over her forehead. And oh, he smelled good—woodsy, masculine.

Did he think she was Raegan or Kate?

She could feel the muscles in his arms as they tightened around her.

Men don't hug their sisters like this.

What was she thinking, leaning into the hug as if she belonged there? Words not fully formed climbed up her throat, but a stubborn, indulgent piece of her swallowed them down until—

"Emma."

He rasped the name.

And icy realization darted through her.

Emma, his dead wife.

The second he heard his own voice, Logan jerked. As did the woman in his arms. The woman who couldn't possibly be Emma.

She stumbled from his grasp, strands of hair toppling from her ponytail, shock written all over her face. Completely justifiable shock, given what had just happened.

You went off the deep end.

He closed his eyes, exhaustion from the two-day drive clawing at him. That had to be it. The fatigue. The dark room. The fact that as he'd sung Charlie back to sleep after carrying her into the house, memories of being here in this room with Emma had risen like fog and obviously confused him.

And for one longing-filled moment, he'd actually thought . . .

"I'm . . . you're not . . ." He willed his words to work, whispering lest he wake Charlie. "I'm sorry."

"It's okay, Logan. I shouldn't have barged in here."

She knew him? "Who . . . ?"

But then she stepped back, moonlight filtered through filmy curtains highlighting her profile—button nose, freckles. Even in the wan light, her eyes were familiar.

"Amelia," she supplied. "Amelia Bentley. From the *News*."

The editor who'd tried to coax him home in a one-day email exchange. The one with the camera at Colt's press conference.

But why was she here?

And could she see the warmth crawling over him? It was more

than embarrassment. *Try mortification.* Partially because of the hug, but mostly because of the stinging whiplash his mind and heart had just gone through.

And the stark reminder. *Emma. Gone. Two years.*

"Sorry for walking in. I just heard you singing and, well . . ."

"You heard that?"

"It was sweet." She nodded to the bed. "Your daughter? Rae's told me about her."

She was friends with Raegan, then. That explained what she was doing here. Too, the laughter he'd heard from the kitchen when he'd first walked into the house. He'd purposely skirted past the main living area, intent on getting Charlie to bed before his family could get ahold of her. They'd rile her up and he'd never get her back to sleep.

He followed Amelia's gaze toward Charlie now. She sighed in her sleep, turning to her side, a stray curling drooping over her forehead.

"About that hug—"

"It's really okay."

He met Amelia's eyes—hazel, flecked with amber. He remembered meeting her back in February. She'd rambled on about how she'd read all his old articles while he'd stood there thinking he'd never seen irises so shifty in color. Like sunlight through autumn leaves.

And the way she looked at him now . . . it was like she knew all about Emma.

"Logan?" Raegan's squeal bounded into the room. "What in the world?"

She barreled toward him. And it wasn't a minute until half his family barreled in. Seth, his cousin. Kate and Colton. And of course Charlie woke up. Laughter, rounds of hugs. Then Dad, too, wandered in.

Ten minutes and a drawn-out explanation later, they found

their way to the kitchen. The smell of cookies hovered in the air, voices all talking over one another. Charlie was already playing catch with Colton, a pair of rolled-up socks for a ball. Kate was pouring glasses of milk and handing out cookies.

"I'm making decaf." Raegan held up a coffee pot.

He felt a palm on his shoulder. Dad.

"You sure know how to turn a house into an uproar, Logan."

"Sorry to get here so late. I know the plan was tomorrow, but once we hit Nebraska, I got eager. You sure you're okay with us staying for a couple weeks?"

Dad grinned, eyes on Charlie. Colton had once said Dad reminded him of John Wayne—same height and broad build. Same etched face. But to Logan, Dad was just Dad. The man he most admired in the world. "Are you kidding me? You know I love having a full house."

Which was exactly what he was about to have. Although surely Kate and Colton would end up married before long, and Kate would move out once more.

For the first time in a long time, Logan's heart hitched on the thought of, well, love, he guessed. The kind of romance that looked to be a lifelong thing.

Then again, he knew more than anyone that *lifelong* wasn't a guarantee.

No, not more than anyone.

He looked back to Dad, now sliding onto a seat at the island counter. The crinkles in the corners of his eyes when he smiled, the rumble of his laughter belying the heartache his father had been through—the slow-churning tragedy of losing Mom to cancer.

But Dad had healed, hadn't he? Settled into running Maple Valley's historic railroad and depot museum, carved out a new life for himself.

Unlike Logan, who mistook a random woman for his dead wife.

"Amelia." Her name slipped out.

Raegan paused at the coffee pot. "Oh yeah, where'd she go?"

He had no idea. She'd come down to the kitchen with them and gathered up some papers on the counter while everyone else was a tornado of activity.

The coffee pot moaned, and Raegan pushed it under the counter. "I hope she didn't think she needed to leave because this suddenly turned into a family night. I'll go see—"

"Let me," Logan interrupted and pivoted from the room before anyone could question him. He toed on his shoes in the entryway. Sharp cold pricked his cheeks as soon as he stepped outside. The light over the garage hummed against the still of the night.

He scanned the driveway before his attention hooked on footprints leading to the side yard. And there she was . . . building a snowman?

The porch swing—the one where Mom and Dad used to sit at night, their muted voices drifting up to his screened bedroom window—creaked in the breeze. He followed the footsteps. "Amelia?"

She turned at the sound of his voice, his snow-packed steps. "Oh . . . hi."

He stopped in front of her, breath visible in front of his face. "What are you doing?"

A gust of wind sent a cloud of snow curling off the roof and into her hair. "I coerced Raegan into building a snowman with me earlier this evening. When I came out to leave, I noticed his head had fallen off." She shrugged. "Decided to help Frosty out."

"Do you often play in the snow at ten o'clock at night?"

"I love snow. I'd play in it any time of day. I think I'm the only person in all of Iowa who mourns the end of winter."

How could he have possibly—even for a hazy, yearning second—mistaken her for Emma? The hair should've been a giveaway. Or the frame. Emma was slighter. Even with a coat, he could see Amelia had . . .

He cleared his throat. "You didn't have to leave."

Although now he kind of wished he'd let her. He was cold—should've grabbed a jacket on his way out—and he was embarrassed all over again, uncomfortably cognizant of her probing study.

"I figured you Walkers could use some family time. So, what are you doing home? Did your family know you were coming?" Her grin turned playful. "Decided to take up my job offer?" Moonlight brushed streaks of gold in her hair and eyes.

"You ask a lot of questions."

She shrugged. "I'm a reporter."

Yes, at the paper he now owned. The paper he planned to sell. Because it made sense. Because his life was back in LA. Because he had a presidential candidate waiting on him, and because he'd promised Theo.

And because for all the good times he'd had working with Freddie at the *News*, one lousy story had been enough to sour him. Local politician. Big secret. Scandal and a wrecked career.

And Logan's name in the byline.

This many years later, he shouldn't still feel guilty. But it made the desire to sell even stronger.

Amelia dotted two eyes into the snowman's face with her finger. He should tell her.

Instead, he found himself reaching down for a handful of snow, patting it into the side of the snowman. "You know, if you'd made the base bigger, the head might not have fallen off."

"Way to critique my snowman-building skills instead of answering any of my questions."

He laughed. An honest-to-goodness, unadulterated laugh. Possibly his first since leaving California. "How's the newspaper biz?"

"Fine. Could be better, I guess. There's a strong chance we're going to get sold off. And I was offered a job at the paper that's likely going to buy us out. I have to make a decision by tomorrow. A logical person would take it, but I happen to love the *News*, this town. First place that's felt like home since forever, and I keep thinking if I can just come up with the right plan, maybe I can save the *News* and—" She broke off. "I don't know why I'm telling you this."

Cold burrowed through his thin coat. "And I don't know why I hugged you earlier, thinking you were . . ." He coughed, breath forming clouds of white. "Anyway, again, sorry about that."

"Again, it's really okay." Her voice was soft. She drew a smile onto the snowman with a stick. "I guess I'd better get going. I still have cookies to deliver, after all."

"You made the cookies?" He trailed her from the yard to the driveway.

"My one and only specialty." She stopped at the tiny two-door that must be hers. "Raegan told me you're a health nut."

"Not a health nut. Just a believer in the food pyramid."

"Well, try one of my chocolate chip cookies and you might be tempted to give them a spot on the pyramid. I burned the last batch, but if you snag one of the early ones, you'll see."

"You're modest."

"Or just honest." He reached for her car door, but before he could grab it, she stopped with a questioning look. "Hey, Logan, how would you do it? Save a dying newspaper, I mean."

Tell her. "Amelia—"

"Just hypothetically. If a newspaper you loved was about to go under, how would you turn the tide? Impress a new owner?"

He sighed. "Hypothetically? I'd work my tail off enticing advertisers. Shave off a couple spreads to lower print costs and make sure the space I have is filled with good material." He shrugged. "And I'd go hunt for a riveting front-page story.

Something I'm passionate about. Because passion shows, and a good story can't hurt."

He could practically hear her latching on to hope at his advice. He could kick himself. "Amelia," he began, fully intent on finally being honest as he opened her car door. But the second the door opened, a sheaf of papers came fluttering out. They slapped against each other, and he rushed to catch them before the wind stole them away.

Amelia managed to catch one of the rustling pages. He snagged the other two and started to hand them to her but stopped when his gaze landed on familiar words. Wait a sec.

"My education speech?" His gaze whipped to Amelia. "What are you doing with this?"

"I . . . Rae . . ."

Either her winter coat and scarf weren't nearly warm enough or that was a blush, plain as day, painting her cheeks. "Amelia?"

"I read your speeches sometimes, okay? I think they're great. Raegan gets you to send them, and she passes them on to me, and I just like reading them, all right?" Her words released in bullets. "I bribed her with cookies for this one. Go ahead and laugh."

"I'm not laughing." Though he couldn't have stopped the tease from infusing his voice if he'd tried. "I am, however, entirely flattered."

She snatched away the papers he held. "Don't get smug. It'll ruin my image of you."

"You have an image of me? And tell me, how do my speeches match up to your cookies? Am I as at the top of my game with my skillset as you are at yours? Allegedly, anyway."

She thrust the papers inside the car and turned back to not-entirely-convincingly glower at him. "There's no *allegedly* about it. Go inside and eat a cookie, Logan Walker." She dropped into her car.

One hand on her door handle, he leaned over. "Happy speech-reading." He closed her door, and her engine sputtered. He turned back to the house to see Dad waiting on the porch.

But before Logan made it up the stairs, he heard a car door closing again and pivoted to see Amelia outside once more.

"*His Girl Friday.*"

Even from across the driveway, in the dark, he could see her eyes light, realization dancing through them.

"Hildy. From the classic movie *His Girl Friday*. Cary Grant. Rosalind Russell. Cary's the editor who keeps trying to get Rosalind's character, Hildy, to come back to the paper."

Oh right, from that email exchange. He'd called her Hildy and told her to figure it out. "Well done," he called back at her.

Behind him, Dad whistled. "Flora would be proud."

Mom had loved old movies. So much so that he'd wound up with an impressive storehouse of trivia.

Except Amelia looked more impish than impressed. She shrugged as she leaned against her car. "I got the movie right even if you got the characters wrong."

"Say again?"

"In our scenario, I'm Cary Grant's Walter Burns, trying to lure you back to the paper. *You're* Hildy." She straightened, one eyebrow lifted. "If you're going to whip out a classic, Walker, don't botch the reference."

And then she dropped back into her car and backed out of the driveway.

Dad's chuckles, then his footsteps, sounded in the snow beside Logan. Gawking stars blinked overhead.

"She doesn't have any idea you're her new boss, does she?" Dad said.

Logan folded his arms, the heaviness he'd felt ever since receiving that certified letter finally whisked away, at least for now, by a yawning wind. He grinned. "Nope."

4

July 24, 2008

Dear Logan,

If you're reading this, it means I've passed away and you've just discovered you now own a newspaper. Surprise! I'm sure you're wondering why I'd leave a paper to you that you've only just recently walked away from. I'm happy to explain.

But first of all, you need to know, you're the closest thing I've ever had to a son.

*H*e couldn't read this now.

Logan folded Freddie's letter along its creases, slow and deliberate, giving himself time to swallow the emotion pooling inside him. Why hadn't he realized how important he was to Freddie?

How important Freddie was to him.

"You read that quickly." Hugh Banner, the lawyer who'd sent

the certified letter that had pulled Logan home, folded his fingers atop the expansive mahogany desk in his office. The man's wiry frame was dwarfed by his high-back leather chair. Thin, white hair and eyes that might've been labeled beady if they didn't contain such compassion. He probably knew perfectly well Logan hadn't finished the letter.

Maybe, depending on how much Freddie had told him, he even knew why.

"I wouldn't have a career today if it weren't for Freddie."

Hugh leaned back in his chair. "Oh, I doubt that. You're a Walker, son. You were destined for a big life."

Perhaps. With a dad who'd fought in Vietnam and gone on to work as an ambassador and diplomat and a mom who'd helped start an international foundation, maybe being a Walker came part and parcel with lofty career goals. And maybe he would've ended up where he was now with or without Freddie's influence. But he certainly wouldn't have made it through Mom's sickness and eventual death without Freddie's intervention. Not that Logan hadn't had his family, but they'd all been grieving, too. Even Emma had seemed somehow . . . too close.

Freddie had stepped in right when Logan had needed him most. Given him an internship and later a job, a distraction.

And now he'd given him his legacy.

"As you should know from the papers I sent, Freddie was looking at selling the *News*. The flood last fall put him in a pretty bad financial hole. His insurance policy was a joke."

Logan forced himself to pay attention. He shouldn't have stayed up so late last night with his siblings. Definitely shouldn't have let Charlie stay up so late.

But even when he'd finally dropped into bed—in the bedroom in the house he'd grown up in—he hadn't been able to drift off to sleep. Not with so many racing thoughts about Charlie, the spontaneity of this trip, the newspaper, Roberta S. Hadley . . .

And that editor, Amelia, with the freckles and the tease in her voice. Somehow he needed to find a way to let her know *he* was now the owner of the paper she loved so much . . . and probably not for long.

"Freddie actually had a buyer lined up?"

"Cranford Communications. Tri-state media company."

"I'm familiar with them. They own the *Communicator*. Thing I don't get is why they were interested in buying the *News* if it's in such bad shape financially."

Hugh shrugged. "Because a bigger regional reach is a good long-term investment. The *Communicator* already covers three other towns in our county. Why not Maple Valley, too? They'd get our advertising, our subscribers, and our news without any of the overhead costs. They can sell off the building and the equipment."

Oh. Now Amelia's worry made sense. She wasn't just out to save the paper—she was out to save jobs.

"I've had a ridiculous number of calls from the Cranford people, by the way, since Freddie passed. They're still interested in moving forward with the sale. In fact, I've got a whole packet of paperwork I can give to you. Should've brought it in with me." Hugh rose. "I'll be back in a minute."

Logan stood, too, turning a circle in the office as he waited for Hugh to return. The room wasn't so much an office as a library—one with shelves that reached all the way to a ceiling supported by cedar planks and embellished with dark crown molding, its blunt angles matching the room's masculine feel— all browns and blacks and tans. A fringed rug with swirls of burgundy and blue provided the only splash of brightness.

Quite the contrast from his sparse office back in LA. Or Freddie's closet of an office at the *News* building.

"You were destined to live a big life."

Who knew what that even meant? But it couldn't mean holding on to a newspaper that was bleeding money. The sooner Logan got this whole thing off his plate, the sooner he could focus on earning that spot on Hadley's campaign.

He just hated the thought of hurting Amelia in the process. She seemed . . . well, nice. And she liked his speeches.

"I heard you were here."

He spun at the sound of the voice behind him. Not Hugh.

Jenessa? Of all the people to run in to in his first twenty-four hours home . . .

She stood in the doorway with her posture as rigid as a cement statue, lips pressed together.

"Uh, hi."

"Really? 'Uh, hi'? I thought you were a speechwriter." She pushed a sheet of coal-black hair over her shoulder and stepped into the room. "If that's the best you can do, I'm going to petition Maple Valley High to rescind that valedictorian title they gave you."

"If I remember correctly, you already tried that. Sixteen years ago, week or two before graduation. Didn't go over so well."

She brushed past him, tight black sweater emphasizing curves every guy in high school had noticed—Logan included. Until Emma had come along.

"You missed half the first semester of our senior year." She leaned against the desk that dominated the room's floor space.

"Yeah, because my mom was sick and—" He cut himself off. It was an old, pointless argument, and it wasn't what bothered Jenessa anyway. He knew that much. "Jenessa, about your dad—"

"Don't. There's not a thing you can say that could in any way make up for what you did." Her fingers tapped against the gilded antique globe propped on a stand next to the desk.

He dropped back into his chair, eyes on the globe spinning underneath Jenessa's red fingernails. "Why are you here anyway?"

"The firm's called Banner & Associates. I'm one of the associates."

"But I thought . . . didn't you and . . . ?" He sorted through high school faces, searching for the name.

"Gage Fellows."

Right. Baseball star in high school. Played in the minor leagues now. "Doesn't he play for some team out East?"

The tiniest chink marred her stern bearing as she slapped her palm over the globe. "We're still together. But during spring training and the rest of the season, he's barely around. He lives here during the off-season, much to my parents' chagrin. They've never been big fans of Gage. Not like with . . ."

You. She didn't have to finish it. He and Jenessa hadn't dated more than five months their junior year of high school, but he'd never shaken the feeling that he'd let down her parents as much as Jenessa when he'd broken things off. And that'd been just the beginning of his tumultuous relationship with the family.

"It's not only your shoddy reporting that lost you points around here, Walker."

He swallowed, sour memories stinging him. The article he'd never wanted to write.

"He could've been governor. He'll never get those years back, Logan."

He should stand. Look her in the eyes. Counter the attack. But how did a person argue when the opponent was the one with truth on her side?

"You ruined his career all for a stupid headline."

"That's not why—"

"And what really makes me sick is you're *still* the town golden boy while my dad's in and out of the hospital, forced into a retirement that's killing him as much as his disease you couldn't wait to publicize in a splashy front-page article."

No, that's where she was wrong. He'd cared. He'd hated

writing that story. Didn't matter that it was the truth, that Freddie had backed him, that voters deserved honesty. "He had a serious, congenital disease, Jen. A degenerative disease, and he purposely misled voters. He lied about hospital stays."

Why was he even trying to defend himself? Jen and her whole family had made it plenty clear years ago there wouldn't be any reconciliation. He'd written the story exposing her father's illness. Basically ruined the man's campaign . . . his entire career.

Interestingly, as much as he'd hated the experience, it'd shaped his future in ways he couldn't have imagined at the time. While covering that campaign, he'd gotten his first real taste of the political world. Had found himself reading press releases and listening to speeches and mentally rewriting them in his head.

And when his story about Jenessa's dad made national news, he ended up with connections that led to covering the Iowa caucuses for a couple national media outlets. By the end of that summer, he'd reconnected with Theo, an old friend from college—a California kid who'd never seemed to fit his poli-sci major.

But apparently he'd taken his studies seriously enough.

"Just stay away from my dad, okay?" Jenessa's voice jutted in. "Don't visit him while you're here. His health is getting worse, and the last thing he needs is to see you."

"Jenessa." This time it was Hugh's voice behind him, censure in his tone and pace swift as he entered the room. He strode past Jenessa and rounded his desk.

"Sorry, Hugh." Jenessa straightened the globe atop its stand, refusing to look at Logan as she marched toward the door, heels clicking as the rug gave way to hard flooring.

Logan rose to his feet. "Jen?"

Her footsteps paused.

"I'm only here a couple weeks."

She didn't face him.

"Last thing I'd want is to make anything worse with your dad. I'll . . . keep away."

No acknowledgement. Only the latch of the door.

⁓

Maybe—probably—she was a hundred kinds of crazy. But tonight crazy felt good.

Especially with the whole *News* staff gathered around the oblong table, their laughter mingling with the live music and buzzing chatter filling The Red Door, Maple Valley's newest and nicest restaurant. Outside its gaping front windows, another round of spring snow glistened under the light of lampposts that wrapped like a line of sentries around the town square.

Amelia set her last folder in front of Owen and returned to her own chair, her puffy winter coat slung over the back.

"Wait, you brought us all here to work?" Kat Chin, the ad manager, flipped open her folder. "I thought this was, like, staff party time. A morale boost or something."

Across the table, Owen fiddled with his straw wrapper, tearing the paper into tiny bits and letting them sprinkle to the tabletop. "You're not the only one who got blindsided."

Poor Owen. He'd been the one to suggest dinner at The Red Door before calling it a day. Hadn't known until everyone else showed up that Amelia had gone and invited the rest of the team—and decided to present her plan for saving the *News*.

A plan that just might work. And she had Logan Walker to thank.

His hypothetical answer to her not-at-all hypothetical question had crawled into her brain and stayed there, lulling her into her first good night's sleep since C.J. Cranford's visit. And this morning, she'd woken up with the idea in her head.

She might not know who owned the paper. But she knew how she'd save it.

Her gaze flitted around the table now. Kat and Mikaela and Abby from the ad department. Mae, who was whipping through the pages in her folder. Ledge, the quiet giant of a man who ran the press. Taylor, their subscription and delivery manager. And Owen, half scowling as he swept up the bits of his wrapper into a pile.

"I don't even want to know how much ink you used printing this." Mae flipped to the last page. "You could have at least printed double-sided."

Maybe Amelia should have left her a second plate of cookies last night. She might seem huffy now, but Amelia had seen her munching on one of the treats this morning. "The printer jams whenever I try that." Amelia propped her elbows on either side of her half-guzzled Diet Coke. "I promise, guys, this won't take long. We'll be done by the time the food arrives."

Like most nights since The Red Door had opened last summer, a local crowd filled the tables dotting the hardwood floor. The historic bank-building-turned-eatery boasted a perfect mix of trendy and downhome with its thick redwood beams overhead, dim lighting, and amber-colored walls. In the corner tonight, a fireplace crackled while Bear McKinley wooed patrons with his Martin and a voice smooth as velvet.

To think, Seth Walker—cousin to the Walker siblings—had started this place with nothing more than half a vision and a love for a decrepit building. Well, that and the old cobblestone he'd salvaged when the city had decided to pave Main Avenue. He'd used it to create the restaurant's counter in back. She'd written the front-page story herself, the one about how he'd stored the cobblestone for years in a shed on his uncle's property, never quite sure why, until he'd finally decided to pour his savings into renovating the bank building and opening a restaurant.

It must be a Walker thing—landing on a dream and making it happen. Look at Kate and all those movies she'd written. Logan and his success.

She cupped her hands around her pop glass. "This summer is the 100th anniversary of the paper. Freddie wasn't going to make a big deal of it because he wasn't sure he'd even be around. If he'd lived, the *News* would've been sold by now."

"So we're going to put out an anniversary issue?" Mikaela fingered through the pages in her folder.

"Yep. In May—exactly one hundred years after the very first issue. It's not our usual production day, but that's okay because this won't be our usual paper." She stirred her straw through her Diet Coke, ice cubes clinking as her excitement built. "Kat, Kaela, Abby—you guys are going to sell ad space like never before. Ledge, we're going to triple our usual print run. Everyone in town gets a copy, subscribers or not. Taylor, we'll need to line up extra delivery guys that week. I know it's almost three months away, but the lead time is good.

"We'll offer a special subscriber rate that week. Between the extra advertising and hopefully new subscribers, we'll convince the new owner we're worth hanging on to."

That is, unless the new owner swooped in and sold them off before they could get to the special issue. But whoever he was, he was taking his sweet time announcing himself. Maybe the lawyers hadn't even located him yet. Maybe it was some long-lost relative of Freddie's who lived off in Alaska or Hawaii or South America.

She could hope.

Their food arrived then—a still-sizzling burger and fries for her. Her stomach rumbled at the sight. Across the table, a waiter lowered some sort of fancy salad with a see-through dressing in front of Owen. He'd barely looked at her while they talked. Was he really that upset she'd invited everyone else along tonight?

The next few minutes passed in a blur of clinking silverware and satisfied eating. Until Ledge looked up from his plate. "I think it's a good idea, Amelia."

The burly older man, bald with ebony skin and kind eyes, rarely spoke up. The most noise he ever made was with the press. But his simple statement was enough to quiet the rest of the crew.

"You do?"

He nodded, then looked around the table and seemed to prompt everyone else into doing the same. Even Mae.

Except Owen, who lowered his fork and finally looked at Amelia. "Yeah, but what's going to actually fill this thing besides ads?"

"Stories about the paper's history. Old photos, maybe even some old articles."

"No actual news?" Skepticism clouded his tone.

"Oh, there's going to be news." She leaned forward, fingers lacing around her glass. Her favorite part, this. "I'm finally going to solve the Kendall Wilkins mystery."

She'd expected a few *oohs*, maybe some *ahhs*. Not the blank expressions that stared back at her.

"The town loner?" This from Abby. "Didn't he die?"

"He was more than a town loner. Half the buildings in town wouldn't have been built without him. He lived to be 101. He saw more world history than most of us have read about in textbooks."

He was Maple Valley's most famous citizen. Businessman, philanthropist, collector. He'd lived through the Great Depression, fought in World War II, and made millions after the war, which he then poured back into this community. In the seventies, he'd donated his mansion to the city. Now it housed the public library.

And perhaps the most interesting of all his stories—he'd been in Paris in 1927, stood on Le Bourget field as Charles Lindbergh made his historic landing. Even had a black-and-white photo of himself standing next to the record-setting aviator and the *Spirit of St. Louis.*

Logan had said to write a story she was passionate about. Well, she'd wanted to write Kendall Wilkins's story for years.

"He might've been an interesting guy, but no one ever knew him." Kat forked her grilled asparagus. "Believe me, I grew up here. The man was a legend, but not necessarily a well-liked one. For all his philanthropy, he never came to a single town event. Never got involved. And then he pranked the whole town when he died. I'm not sure putting his face on the cover of a special issue will do us any favors."

"But that's just it. I don't think he meant to prank anyone."

It was town lore these days, the story of Kendall Wilkins's will. Five years ago when he'd died, he'd left the contents of a safe-deposit box to the city of Maple Valley. The town made a big deal of it, gathered a crowd to open the box . . . only to find it empty. Everyone assumed it was the elaborate hoax of a hermit.

But they didn't know the Kendal Wilkins she'd known. Oh, she'd never met him in person, but she had . . . well, she definitely had insider knowledge.

"I think there was supposed to be something in that box. I'm going to figure out what it was and what happened to it. And that, my friends, will be our front-page story."

She could sense the skepticism threading through the group, but they were either too hungry or too nice to voice it.

Except for Owen, who pushed back from the table—abrupt, annoyed—and stood. "I'm . . . not hungry." He swiped his coat from the back of his chair and tromped away from the table.

The rest of the group looked as confused as she felt. "Owen," she called after him, the wallop of the closing door punctuating his exit.

She followed him outside, shrugging into her jacket as she stepped into the snow-salted outdoors. Moonlight slanted in to highlight the scowl on Owen's face as he stopped and turned under a flickering lamppost. She hurried toward him. "I know you're from the big city, Berry, but you can't dine and dash in a small town."

"I just needed some air." He huffed the words, crossing his arms and refusing to look her in the eye.

Her steps slowed as she reached him. "What's wrong with you? Do you hate my idea?"

"It's not that."

"Is it that I invited everyone else tonight?"

He peered down at her. "Yes. All right? Yes. Finally, after a year and a half of working with you, I go for it. I ask you out. And you invite the entire staff on our date."

"Date?" The word slipped out before she could stop it, enough disbelief embedded in it she couldn't have masked her surprise if she'd wanted to. "You thought tonight was . . . a date?"

And now it wasn't only irritation in his expression, but embarrassment.

"I didn't realize . . . we hang out lots."

"Rarely just the two of us. I went out of my way today to ask you and only you. You said, and I quote, 'It's a date.'"

"That's an expression." The reply did nothing to loosen his grimace. She lowered her voice. "You're twenty-four, Owen. I'm six years older than you."

"Which isn't exactly May-December."

A chilly breeze slinked through the fabric of her lightweight coat and scuffed over her cheeks. "I'm flattered, really. But—"

He cut her off with a raised hand. "Don't."

She barreled on anyway. "But even if I had known what this was, you know the two of us wouldn't work. You can't wait to leave Maple Valley. You're constantly saying you didn't go into debt getting a degree in journalism to write about Division III sports and Little League forever. Me? I adore it here. I never want to move away."

Snowflakes dusted Owen's shoulders and hair, disappointment lurking in his eyes. "Is it because of your divorce?"

The flinch cut through her. Ridiculous, really. This many years after, she should be able to hear the word without feeling like the stitches in her heart were coming loose.

"Is that why you've been oblivious to me? And the UPS man, who everyone knows is crazy about you? Oh, and that math teacher at the high school? You haven't been on a date in the whole time I've known you."

"You don't know what you're talking about."

"Of course I don't. Because I barely know you. Because as much time as we've spent together, you never talk about your past. It's all the paper and Maple Valley and how much you love snow and life in this weird town. I don't know why I thought you'd let someone close enough to actually take you on a real date." He turned.

"Owen—"

He brushed her off with a wave of his hand. Wind tugged strands of hair free from her ponytail as she watched him walk away, his steps scuffing through snow until he turned the corner.

Oh, Owen.

The sigh feathered through her. She'd hurt him. She'd hurt him, and she hated herself for it. He'd always been so sweet. Winsome. She'd just never looked at him like *that*.

But he was wrong about her. So she didn't talk about her life before Maple Valley. So what? She'd been a different person then.

"Amelia?"

She turned at the sound of Seth Walker's voice. He stood

just outside the restaurant's bright red door, the words *First National Bank* still etched in cement overhead. "Everything okay? I saw you standing outside by yourself . . ."

"Uh, Owen had to leave. I was just saying 'bye.'"

"Your burger's going to get cold. I can send it back to the kitchen if you want. Reheat it or get you a new one. I know how you love your burgers."

See, this was what she loved about this town. *You're wrong, Owen. People know me here.*

Seth held open the door for her as she reentered the restaurant. "So what's up with your whole staff being here tonight? You all planning a mutiny against Logan or something?"

She stopped halfway to her table. "What?"

"Trust me, if you guys are surprised about Logan being the new publisher, triple it, and that's how surprised he is."

Her brain fumbled to connect his words. "Logan . . . Logan Walker is the new owner of the *News*?"

Seth flipped a towel over his shoulder. "You didn't know?"

~

Amelia really did live in a barn.

Logan stared at the building set back from the road at the edge of town, where a residential neighborhood thinned out and gave way to sweeping fields. The Klassens lived in the last house on Second Street, and across the gravel drive that leaned into their yard, right next to a cascading willow tree, sat Amelia's home. Moonlight painted a blueish tint over its red paint and glowing white trim.

Logan cut the engine of his car and climbed out. He'd kind of thought Raegan was joking when she said Amelia lived in the barn on Lenny and Sunny Klassen's property. Figured he'd get here and discover the older couple had turned their basement into an apartment, like Dad had for Seth, or even that woodshop out back where Lenny worked.

But the barn?

An owl *hoo*-ed from the line of craggy trees, black in the dark and shivering in the wind behind the property. A yard light buzzed and flickered on as he approached the barn. Must be motion-sensored.

Hopefully Amelia wouldn't mind him showing up at this time of night—especially at her house. But when he'd gotten Seth's text, letting him know he'd accidentally spilled the beans about Logan owning the paper, he'd figured he owed Amelia an explanation. And with it being Friday night, it's not like he could find her in the office in the morning.

He knocked, cold raking over his cheeks. Snow shaven from a drift that edged up to the barn swirled around his feet.

A muffled voice sounded from inside. Did she say "come in"?

He knocked again, and this time the door cracked open. He stomped the snow from his feet and then pushed the door the rest of the way open, stepped inside, and—

Amelia's squeal about stopped his heart.

She stood in the center of what looked to be her living room, a towel slipping from her head and wet hair tumbling over her shoulders. Bare feet and legs whiter than the snow outside peeked out from underneath a pink robe.

The door thumped closed behind him. "You . . . you said . . ." Words, why couldn't he conjure any? "You said 'come in.'"

"I said 'just a minute.'" She flapped her hands in exasperation, the belt on her robe loosening with the movement until she flung her arms around herself.

Maybe he should just turn around and walk back out.

Or at least stop staring.

But it was like his feet had grown roots through her welcome mat. So he simply lifted one hand and covered his eyes.

Only to hear Amelia burst out laughing. "What are you doing?"

"Being a gentleman." And hopefully hiding the fact that his face had to be the color of her barn—er, house—right about now.

"I'm wearing a robe. I'm not naked, Logan."

"Please don't say the word *naked*."

She only laughed harder. "Man, you are easy to embarrass. Imagine if I'd been wearing this last night when you hugged me."

A rumble of laughter escaped, surprising considering how much that hug had bothered him as he'd tried to sleep. How could Emma still—and so swiftly—walk back into his brain? Not to mention the ache that came along with her.

Maybe he needed a break more than he realized. "Do you want me to leave?"

"No, but let me go change. I just ran down here to turn on the teakettle after taking a bubble bath. Not that you need to know that—or that I was taking a bubble bath."

He couldn't help a grin at her rambling, peeking through the crack in his fingers as she bent to pick up her towel and cinched the belt at her waist. She might've laughed at him, but he obviously wasn't the only one uncomfortable at the moment.

Still, he didn't drop his hand until she'd started up the boxy steps that led to an open loft.

"So what are you doing here, Logan?" she called down.

"Just wanted to talk for a few minutes. If that's okay." Her living room, with simple beige furniture and an antique trunk in place of a coffee table, spilled into a narrow dining room. "Charming house, by the way."

The ceiling overhead creaked as Amelia walked around the second floor.

"Cool dining-room table." Someone—probably Lenny—had crafted it from an old door. Two long benches sat on either side. A spread of papers covered one end of the table. Old newspaper clippings, scribbled notes. Logan picked up the top papers, ignoring the voice in his brain reminding him he'd already barged in on Amelia. Probably shouldn't go through her things, too.

But curiosity got the better of him. Why was she reading so many articles about Kendall Wilkins?

"What did you want to talk—"

The screech of the teakettle interrupted Amelia's question from above, so he dropped her papers and walked the rest of the way past her dining room into the kitchen. Steam hissed from the kettle as he pulled it off the burner. A canister of Nestlé hot chocolate mix sat next to the stove.

She was going to make hot chocolate with that? Instead of placing the kettle back on the stove, he moved to the sink and poured out the water.

By the time he turned around, Amelia stood behind him. She'd traded the robe in for jeans and an emerald sweater that made her eyes seem more green than hazel. Her hair still hung damp around her face, the scent of vanilla clinging to her.

"What are you doing with my water?"

"You can't make hot chocolate with this."

The freckles on her nose scrunched together. "Yes, I can. I do every night."

He moved past her toward the fridge. "You've got milk, don't you?" He pulled it open and found a half gallon of two percent behind a pile of Chinese takeout containers. "Good."

Amelia stood with her hands on her waist now. "Make yourself at home, why don't you?"

He opened a cupboard. "Spices?"

"Next one over."

Cinnamon and nutmeg. Perfect. He turned away from the cupboard. Couldn't tell if that was amusement or annoyance flickering in Amelia's smirk. Probably both. "My mom was very particular about hot chocolate."

"Clearly she passed on the trait." She brushed her fingers through her damp hair.

He ignored her wry tone. "Mom, however, used cocoa extract and sweetened condensed milk. We're going to do our best to re-create it, but it won't be exactly the same."

He found a pan under her oven and poured in a couple cups' worth of milk, then set it on the still-warm burner.

"You're awfully comfortable in my kitchen, Logan. Much more so than you were in my living room."

She stood beside him now, hands in her back pockets while she watched him work, and that vanilla smell—her hair, maybe—grew stronger as she moved close.

"Well, you know, you're wearing clothes now. That helps."

She had a nice laugh, low and lilting.

"So what's with all the reading material about Kendall Wilkins?"

She leaned over the counter, chin propped on her fists. "You barge into my house—"

"I knocked."

"—take over my kitchen, *and* you were snooping through my stuff?"

"I was admiring your table, and your stuff just happened to be there. Whisk?"

She pulled it out of a metal-ringed cylinder full of utensils. "If you must know, I'm doing a story on Kendall."

"A story about the dead town loner?"

"Why does everybody call him that?

Logan started scooping Nestlé cocoa powder into the milk. "Because he lived in a mansion and never participated in a single town event and—"

"—and donated ridiculous amounts of money to the town,

had a life history that belongs in a biography, met Charles Lindbergh, and paid for my college."

He set down the canister. "He paid for your college?"

She nodded. "He had a scholarship fund. Anybody in Iowa could apply, and you had to write an essay about something that made an impact on you when you were younger. I wrote about this Amelia Earhart picture book I checked out from the Des Moines library over and over, and how I used to lie about being named after her."

Logan *tsk*ed. "You lied?"

"Some kids lie about missing homework. I lied about a historical namesake. Weird, I know. But it did end up impacting me because that book spurred a love of history. So that's what I wrote about. And I guess Kendall Wilkins liked it because I won the scholarship and got to go to college because of him. He even wrote letters to me my first two years there."

Logan lowered the burner heat as the milk began to bubble. "No kidding?"

"Handwritten and everything."

"And here I always thought he was just a grouchy old man." The sweet smell of the cocoa glided up from the stove, tinged with the extra spice of nutmeg and cinnamon. "What's the story angle?"

"The empty bank box. I'm going to figure out what was supposed to be in it. Because unlike the rest of Maple Valley, I think he was actually trying to do something nice."

He flicked off the burner and turned. Her eyes twinkled with something like anticipation, maybe even mischief, as she waited for his reaction—lips pressed into a half grin that dared him to counter her.

Instead he moved the pan off the stove and pulled two mugs from the mug tree on her counter. "Marshmallows?"

A minute later, he handed her a mug, warm around its edges. "Drink up. You'll never settle for water and powder again."

He waited until she acquiesced, watched as the pile of mini-marshmallows bumped against her nose, and lifted his eyebrows when she swallowed. "Well?"

"Okay, it's good."

"Just good?"

"Fine. Kind of amazing."

He took a drink of his own. "It *is* amazing. You're lucky I happened by tonight, Miss Bentley."

"Yeah, about that . . ." She lowered her cup to the counter, blithe expression drifting from her face. "You came to talk."

He did. But sometime between seeing Amelia in her robe and right now, he'd lost the desire to talk business. Wanted, instead, to . . . he didn't know. Maybe talk more about that Wilkins mystery she couldn't possibly solve? Ask her how she'd ended up living in a barn in Maple Valley?

Maybe make her laugh again.

But those hazel eyes of hers brimmed with questions.

"Well, Seth texted. I guess he told you . . . that is, you know . . . I mean I only found out myself . . ." He looked down at the globby mess of melting marshmallows in his cup.

"Better at writing speeches than giving them?" There was kindness in Amelia's voice. But also a hint of pleading, too. And then she made the request he'd dreaded. "Please don't sell the paper, Logan."

5

"Release the ducks!"

The mayor's voice warbled through a megaphone from his spot at the foot of the Archway Bridge. The curving bridge reached over the Blaine River, where a splash of plastic yellow ducks rained into the cobalt water.

Logan shook his head. "This town is so weird."

Kate laughed as she slid her arm through Logan's, nudging him to join the crowd now migrating from the main bridge connecting both halves of town south toward a smaller bridge. "It's hilarious and fun, you mean."

Logan burrowed his chin into the high neck of the navy blue puff vest he'd found in the hallway closet at Dad's house. Probably Seth's. He should've packed warmer clothes for himself and Charlie.

Or skipped pilfering through the closet and stayed inside altogether. Figured out a way to let Amelia down easy so he could get the *News* off his plate and enjoy the rest of his time at home before falling back into the hectic pace that was his life in LA. He needed to call his in-laws, too. Let them know he and Charlie were in town. He should've contacted them by now.

It was just that he knew the second they found out, the tug of war would begin. He loved Rick and Helen because they were Emma's parents. But they'd never made a secret of resenting how far away he and Charlie lived.

Anyway, Kate had refused to let him miss the annual duck race. She'd practically dragged him from the house, insisting Charlie deserved to experience as much of Maple Valley life as she could while they were here.

Logan's feet sunk into patchy snow and damp ground as they walked along the riverbank. Cars packed the street that bordered the river.

"It's barely above freezing, and we're all standing outside, watching a hundred plastic ducks float down a river that's still half-jammed with chunks of ice." He buried his hands in his pockets. "I bet most of the people here don't even know what we're raising money for."

"I sure don't." Kate tugged her stocking cap over her ears. Or, rather, Colton's hat—the LA Tigers logo wrapped around its rim. She pointed a gloved hand up ahead. "But take a look at your daughter. Tell me that plastic duck wasn't worth twenty bucks."

Several clumps of people away, Charlie rode atop Dad's shoulders. She wore a pair of white earmuffs that were way too big for her head and matching mittens, along with a coat as bright pink as that robe Amelia had been wearing last night.

"Now you're smiling."

Yeah, but Kate only knew half the reason why. No way was he repeating the story of barging in on Amelia to either of his sisters. They'd never let him live it down. "Charlie's having the time of her life, isn't she?" His daughter turned her head to look back at him. Waved. The sunlight made her green eyes more luminous.

"I don't think she's the only one. Dad hasn't stopped beaming since you got here." Kate sidestepped a puddle of mud and melted snow. "He's got three of his four kids home and his granddaughter. If a miracle happened and Beck showed up, he'd be in heaven."

It *would* take a miracle to get Beckett here from Boston. He always said it was work that kept him away. But did any of them actually believe that? "So you're pretty confident you and Colton are sticking around the Valley?"

His sister's smile told an entire story, one he'd only heard about from afar but could actually take some of the credit for. After all, he was the one who'd asked Colton to come back to Iowa with him last fall after the tornado hit, stick around town and help Dad repair the depot when Logan couldn't stay himself.

He hadn't realized Kate would end up home from Chicago at the same time. Never would've guessed Kate and Colton would form the kind of friendship that shifted into love before they knew what hit them. They'd had a fair amount of bumps—one that had even landed Kate in the hospital—but looking at her now, watching the joy spread over her face, he'd bet she'd say it had been worth it, broken bones and all.

"I'm confident I'm sticking around. Can't speak for Colt."

"Ha, don't try to pretend you guys aren't a package deal."

She snickered and freed her arm from his. "I'll say this— twelve months ago if you'd told me I'd be moving back to Maple Valley early this year, I'd have laughed in your face. Now, I couldn't be happier, and it's hard to picture myself anywhere else. But Colton has a dream of eventually expanding his non-profit, and who knows what that could mean?"

Still hard to believe, sometimes, the same Colton he'd known back in LA—the one whose injuries had forced him out of the NFL, the one he'd had to pick up at a bar after a fight the week he'd announced his retirement—had now opened a transitional home for male teens aging out of the foster care system.

In fact, Colton was with one of the teens right now, a high school football player he'd started mentoring last year. Kate said they worked out at the community center every Saturday morning like clockwork.

"Duck number fourteen is in the lead now." The mayor's voice rasped as he walked and talked at the same time. "But seventy-six is right on his tail. As are forty-two, forty-eight, and ninety-one. But we all know how this goes. It can change as fast as the tide. Who will win this year? It's anyone's guess."

"Man, how badly does he want to be a sports announcer?" Kate waved at a friend. "Or a circus ringmaster. Or game show host. Oh, hey, look. Your paper's covering this shindig."

He followed her gaze down the river, its ripples marked by an almost pearl-white sun, to the bridge up ahead. On the other side stood Amelia Bentley with a long-lensed camera. She already had the camera to her eye, angling it down the river and back.

"You should've seen her last night, Kate. She was almost . . . desperate."

"Amelia?"

His hot chocolate had turned bitter as he'd swallowed after she'd asked about the paper. And for five minutes he'd just stood there, practically mute, while she pitched all the reasons he shouldn't sell. The jobs he could save. The legacy he could preserve.

"You don't even have to stay in town, if you don't want. I know enough about the day-to-day operations. Not that we don't want you to stay. If you did stay, it could be awesome. It'd be fun—you'd see. Have you thought about staying?"

Stay. Stay. Stay. How many times had she said the word?

Every time had felt like a pinprick. Did she think he'd just walk away from his life in LA to oversee a paper that was hemorrhaging money?

"She asked if I'd hold on to the paper, at least through June.

She thinks she can turn the numbers around by the end of the fiscal year."

"Do *you* think she can?"

Across the river, Amelia lowered her camera, leaned over to say something to the guy standing next to her. "I think if irrational love for a small-town weekly was enough to keep its heart pumping, she'd be the one to do it. But is it actually financially possible? I have my doubts. I mean, maybe if they got a website, then they could bring in some extra ad revenue."

And her idea for a centennial issue wasn't a bad one. Might actually give them a nice subscriber boost.

"So what'd you tell her?"

He shrugged. "She got a phone call, and I was saved from answering." Some guy named Owen. Was that the dude standing next to her now?

"So why don't you stay?"

He turned. That word again.

"Stay. Not forever, but longer than a week a two. Shouldn't that be one of the perks of being your own boss? Being able to take extended time off or work remotely? Take some time to make your decision."

"There's no decision, Kate. I'm selling. That money will be really helpful. Even with insurance, speech therapy for Charlie is expensive."

"But you could probably get a better deal for the paper if you take some time, make some improvements, start that website."

She had a minor point. He'd read the paperwork Hugh Banner had given him. The offer from Cranford Communications was lowball, no question about that.

"I can't just take a break from real life, though."

"Logan, this *is* real life. Real life isn't just your career or your everyday stuff. It's the surprises and opportunities and open doors you didn't see coming. Last year taught me that. You remember. I thought I was going to be writing another movie or going to Africa to work for Mom's foundation. Coming home felt like the hugest interruption—but it turned out maybe the interruption was part of some bigger plan all along."

Of course by *bigger plan* she meant God's plan. But he didn't know how he felt about the idea of God and his plans these days. Not if life interruptions like Emma's death could be considered part of "God's plan."

Or how about Charlie? Was it God's plan she grow up without her mom—her adoptive mom *and* her birth mom? And was it God's plan Emma's little sister get pregnant at nineteen while on drugs? Oh, she'd promised she was sober all the way through her pregnancy, but he'd started wondering lately if that had been a lie. If maybe Waverly O'Hare's addiction issues might've contributed to Charlie's not talking.

"We're getting closer. Eighty-four has captured the lead." The mayor's voice cut into his thoughts.

"Okay, I'll stop," Kate said. "I know that look."

"What look?" He scoped out Charlie again, still smiling atop Dad's shoulders. What was her duck number again? Sixty-five or sixty-six?

"The look that says I'm being pushy and you're the older brother. You're the one who's supposed to dole out advice."

An expectant hush fanned over the crowd as the bobbing ducks neared the bridge. "I don't mind your advice, sis."

"In that case, I'll say one more thing: You're burnt out, Logan. We all see it. You've got circles under your eyes, you've forgotten how to shave—"

"You really know how to make a guy feel good about himself, you know that?"

"Stick around for a while. We can help with Charlie. You could remember what it feels like to have a hobby. Go fishing. You used to love that. Or get out your guitar—"

"I don't play anymore." His voice came out sharper than he'd intended.

But Kate didn't seem to notice. "Besides, you might have fun playing newspaper publisher for a while. Write some articles, flirt with the cute editor—"

"Kate."

"Come on, admit she's pretty."

Maybe she was—something about those speckled eyes—but he'd shave his head before admitting it to Kate. She wrote romantic stories for a living, after all. She'd start playing matchmaker so fast he might as well write his vows already.

"Logan?" She'd stopped, the rest of the crowd continuing to move around her. "You'll do the right thing. Whatever you decide about the paper and selling and staying or not staying. You'll do the right thing. You always do."

But that was the problem, wasn't it? This time he honestly didn't know what the right thing was.

"And number sixty-six has taken a solid lead with only feet to go!"

Kate's eyes widened. "That's Charlie's, isn't it?"

Up ahead, Charlie was waving her arms from atop Dad's shoulders. Minutes later, they stood on the Peach Street Bridge, Charlie holding a wet duck and Logan holding Charlie. Dad grinning and Kate clapping. And somehow he heard the whisper in his heart even over the crowd.

Stay.

"Can I get a picture for next week's paper?"

Amelia. With her camera and her notebook and that hopeful expectation in her eyes. She lifted her camera, and Charlie held up her duck with a smile that could've melted the last of the ice in the river.

Sometimes it really stunk, being the only one in the office with both the gall and an arm small enough to battle the press machine. Amelia flexed her hand as she felt around inside the machine for jammed newsprint, inky fumes clouding around her from her perch on the stepstool. Great way to start off the week.

And Mae wasn't helping.

"This is exactly why you should be talking with my niece, Amelia. I can guarantee you *USA Today* doesn't have her fixing jammed machines."

It was at least the fiftieth time Mae had brought up her niece—a "real journalist." Apparently, she worked at *USA Today's* Chicago outlet. "You really want to get rid of me that badly, Mae?"

"I'm just saying, if you love the newspaper business so much, then why would you not take advantage of a connection at a major paper? Plus, Belle's part of this young startup thing on the side, which you, of all people, would love, and she's in town this weekend—"

Amelia huffed a strand of hair from her face. "Thank you, Mae, but I'm staying." If she wasn't willing to move an hour away to work for the *Communicator*, she certainly had no desire to traipse off to Chicago.

"Sorry about this," Ledge rasped behind her as the door signaled Mae's sulky retreat. Amelia had only recently learned the reason for the press operator's soft, throaty voice—the result of damage to his vocal chords in a house fire when he was a kid. It didn't match his frame—bulky enough for a spot on a football team's defensive line.

"Not your fault this equipment is older than dirt." Freddie had wanted to replace the pressroom's machines last year after the flood, but a flimsy insurance policy had left him cash-poor and forced into making lousy repairs instead. There, her fingers latched on to the source of the jam, and she yanked.

"Try it now, Ledge."

"Get your hand out of there first."

She hopped off the stepstool and backed away. Ledge hit the button to start up the machine.

It gurgled to life, rumbling enough to rattle the window in between the pressroom and newsroom. But a couple chugs later, the clunking started again, and then the flashing light alerted them to another jam.

As if the mangled paper shooting from its mouth wasn't sign enough.

Ledge released a sigh and switched off the press. "I don't know, Amelia. We might have to buckle down and call a repairman this time."

"Oh no. I have fixed this baby so many times. No way are we paying someone else to come in and do what I'm perfectly capable of myself." Never mind that she'd probably ruin her shirt in the process. She'd already accidentally smeared ink down her arm.

She climbed onto the stool again, buried her hand inside the machine again, and felt around for more bits of paper and the rod that always insisted on coming loose. The pressroom door whomped behind her. Owen, probably, coming to check on their progress. With production day tomorrow and the paper due to hit doorsteps on Wednesday, Monday afternoons were always busy.

But it wasn't Owen's voice that caused her to jerk, bumping her shoulder against the top of the machine. "Having trouble?"

She yanked her arm free and turned. Logan? He held a stack of folders under one arm, wore a gray, unbuttoned plaid flannel coat—looked like something he'd borrowed from his dad—over an untucked Oxford and tie, along with a pinched smile that told her he was trying to hold his amusement in check. Even from the stepstool, she had barely an inch on him. "Just . . . ah . . . a paper jam."

"You know, I fixed that thing about a thousand times back when I worked here. If you need help . . ."

She swiped the back of her hand over her forehead. "That's okay. I've got it." She turned back to the machine, trying to pretend the heat in her cheeks was from the effort of fighting the press and not the man standing behind her.

Please, it was thirty-five degrees outside, and this building was as drafty as an old garage.

She'd had the exact same reaction to Logan at the bridge on Saturday, when he'd held his daughter with the pride of an Olympic athlete's parent. And then Sunday when she'd spotted him in church with his family, way up front in the Walker pew. Had almost considered sticking around after church just to say hi. Almost. Would've been the first time in two years she didn't slip out during the last song.

She wasn't even sure why she still attended, really. Maybe just a stubborn hope that one of these days she'd be able to scrounge up some trust in the God who'd let her down.

Or who she'd let down. Could never quite decide which.

Aha. Her fingers brushed over a crinkled paper. She gave a hard pull, then felt around to make sure there weren't any more scraps jamming the inside. She slipped her arm free, bringing the paper with it. "Victory."

Logan had rounded to Ledge's side of the machine, and she could feel his eyes on her as she jumped down from the stepstool. "Try it again, Ledge."

This time when he turned on the machine, it chortled into a steady rhythm right away. "Yeah, baby."

She balled up the ruined paper and chucked it at the garbage can. Rim shot.

"Proud of yourself, are you?"

She turned back to Logan. "Well, we'll get the *Shopper* printed on time." The tab-sized advertiser they printed every

Monday afternoon was their one actual moneymaker. "So yeah, fairly proud."

"Can I tell you something?"

"That you're impressed with my mechanical skills?"

The corners of his eyes crinkled with his smile. "That there's a panel on the side of the press. You have to use a screwdriver to open it, but if you do, you can actually see what you're doing rather than feeling around blindly."

What she wouldn't give for the kind of poker face that would make him think she already knew this. Just happened to like squeezing her arm down the tight opening to feel for the jam.

"If not for the fact that Ledge didn't know it either, I'd feel totally idiotic right about now." Except, why was Ledge looking at her like that—all contrite? "You knew?"

He rubbed one hand over his bald head. "You're just so proud every time you fix it. You always hear it jam from the newsroom, come running back like it's on fire and you've got the only bucket of water." He shrugged.

And Logan just stood there, not even trying to hide his amusement anymore.

"Well, I still fixed it."

"That you did." His overly consoling tone might've been irritating if not for what might actually be a hint of impressed sincerity joining the humor in his expression.

And if not for the nerves that refused to settle. *Pull it together. You're thirty, not thirteen.*

It was all those articles and speeches of his she'd read. She'd let his words build him up too much in her mind. Couldn't separate the real deal from the writer up on a pedestal in her mind.

Didn't help that he somehow managed to look both rugged and polished at the same time. The shadow on his cheeks, the tie, that funny plaid coat.

The press machine's chugging snapped her to attention.

She was staring at him, wasn't she? "Uh, well, so . . . you're here."

"I'm here. Maybe we could talk in the newsroom?"

"Right. The newsroom. Of course. The press, it's loud." The words, they jammed. Worse than the decrepit machinery.

The newsroom was empty. Owen must've gone off to cover something or another. Maybe for the best. Things had been strained all morning. She'd apologized so many times for Friday night, but it didn't erase the awkwardness.

They were barely through the doorway when Logan stopped. "I'm not going to sell the paper."

She tripped over Owen's chair, caught herself on the counter. "What?"

"I mean, I probably *am* going to sell." He stuffed his hands in his pockets.

She sent Owen's chair rolling back to his desk with her foot and leaned against the counter. "You're confusing me, Logan Walker. You're not going to sell but you are."

"Just not right away. And there's more."

"There's more."

He stood next to her now, looking down, like he still wasn't sure about what he was going to say. He licked his lips, fingered the folder still tucked under his arm, flicking its corner up and down. "I think I might stick around for a while."

"You're going to stick around?"

"Are you going to repeat everything I say?"

"Only when I'm not entirely clear what you're saying."

He took a breath, stopped fiddling with the folder, and leaned his hip against the counter to face her straight on. "If you don't mind, if it's not intruding, I'm going to . . . help out, I guess. I still plan to sell . . . I need to sell. But I think I could do some good around here. Get a website going, help you with that centennial issue. It's partially selfish—the better shape the paper's in, the better price I'll get. But . . . well . . ."

She tried to ignore that last part. Latched on instead to the first part. He was staying. He was going to help.

"How long?"

"At least a month. Although after the way my partner reamed me out when I called him this morning, I'm tempted to stretch it into two. Besides, there's this speech therapist I really want Charlie to see, and the soonest I can get her in is three weeks from now. So I've got even more reason to stick around."

Two whole months? If he wasn't her new boss, she just might kiss him.

And oh, if that thought didn't make her stomach somersault. Then, in a move that surprised her and sent all her nerves fluttering to attention, he reached one hand out to brush his thumb over her cheek. "You've got ink . . ."

From her fight with the press, of course.

His thumb came away smudged. "So I was thinking as my first official act as publisher, I'd buy everyone coffee."

She had to blink and step back in order to actually hear him. "Brown-nosing?"

He glanced at her. "Or I'm just not ready yet to see Freddie's empty office."

His honesty shook her even more than his touch. "I'll come with. I know everybody's drink of choice."

They were outside and halfway to Coffee Coffee, quiet accompanied by the wind flapping through the awning over the flower shop, when Logan suddenly stopped. Sunlight tumbled like ribbons through cottony clouds. "I almost forgot." He held out the folder he'd been carrying. "This is for you."

A breeze rustled through the papers as she opened the folder, and she clamped them down with her palm. Handwriting—

Logan's, she assumed—filled the margins of Xeroxed articles and newspaper clippings, covered pages of lined notebook paper. "Notes about Kendall Wilkins?"

"You're not the only one who thinks he's interesting. Way back, I wanted to do an article on him, but he refused to be interviewed, so it never went anywhere. But Dad still has all my old boxes in his attic, and I found my notes."

She flipped through page after page.

Logan laughed, and she cocked an eyebrow. "What?"

"You gonna read it all right here in the middle of the side-walk?"

"Maybe. This is a gold mine, Logan."

"Yeah, but it's cold." Circles of red covered his cheeks, and specks of amber flickered in his dark eyes. He'd gone looking through his dad's attic just for these old notes? For her?

"He's the reason I live here, you know. I came to town a few years ago during a hard season in my life. Felt like so many people had given up on me. So on a whim, I decided to come and thank the one man who'd somehow strangely believed in me."

"But he'd already passed away by then?"

She nodded. "And yet, I ended up staying. I met Freddie that very first day and found out there was an opening at the paper. I ran across Sunny and Lenny Klassen's advertisement for the barn-turned-house on their property. There was some fair going on in the town square." She gazed over the street to where the river burrowed its course, sparkling blue under a matching sky. "I just stayed."

She looked up, suddenly surprised at where she'd let her words wander, the snippets of her past she'd let him see. He simply waited. Maybe she should tell him how lost she'd been in those months leading up to her arrival in Maple Valley. How a failed adoption and a broken marriage had shattered her.

Things she'd never even spilled to Raegan.

But no, it was too much. Too soon. Maybe it'd always be *too soon.*

So she shook her head and lightened her tone. "Tell me the truth—it's those emails I sent you weeks ago that really convinced you to come back to Maple Valley and stay, isn't it?"

He grinned. "Of course. You were just so persuasive. Not at all blunt or out of the blue or . . ." His words trailed as his focus flitted from her face. He looked over her shoulder, his expression shifting into concern. "I don't think she's okay."

"Who . . . ?" Amelia turned, seeing what he saw through Coffee Coffee's lanky windows. Megan, alone in the shop, gripped the edge of a table with one hand, holding her protruding stomach with the other, a broken coffee cup at her feet.

Logan was already moving toward the door.

"I'm sorry, but if you're not family, I can't allow you back." The woman behind the hospital's ER waiting room counter leveled Logan with a look that said she wasn't budging.

"You don't understand." Logan flattened his palms on the counter. Megan, still clutching her abdomen, had been wheeled away ten minutes ago. For all he knew, she was in some room down the hallway in labor, scared and alone. "She doesn't have any family in town. Isn't that what you said, Amelia?"

When Amelia didn't answer, he glanced over his shoulder. She'd taken a seat in a burgundy vinyl chair underneath a droning TV, face almost as pale as Megan's had been.

"You said your name's Logan Walker?"

He turned back to the woman behind the desk—nurse or receptionist, he didn't even know. "Is there a Katherine Walker with you, because if so—"

"I'm here!" His sister, out of breath and coatless, burst from the waiting room's revolving door.

The nurse tapped a file with bright red nails. "*Her* name is on the patient's medical file. I can let her back to see Megan."

Kate breezed past him. "Thanks for texting."

"But I didn't—" Oh, right. Amelia had his phone. She'd used it to call the hospital on their way. She must've texted Kate, too.

His sister disappeared down the corridor, and he walked back over to Amelia. "How'd you know to text Kate?"

She looked up, emotion in her eyes he could only describe as anguish. It was there and gone, chased away in a blink. And yet it pierced him all the same.

What's your story, Amelia Bentley?

Reporter's curiosity. He might've given up the profession years ago, but the side effects lingered.

Or maybe she's just the first woman to have piqued your interest since Emma.

A distracting thought. A ridiculous one.

Because he knew almost nothing about her.

"Kate took Megan under her wing last fall. I'm not sure she meant to. Just happened. But I'm pretty certain Kate's the closest thing Megan has to a support system."

He lowered into the chair next to Amelia. "I'm glad you knew to contact her."

An infomercial murmured on the TV overhead, and in the corner, a vending machine hummed against the otherwise quiet room. So different from his one experience in an ER in Los Angeles. Crammed with bodies and smells and voices. And the groan that had bullied its way through him over and over as he'd waited—five minutes feeling like five years—for a doctor to appear and tell him what he somehow already knew.

"We did everything we could do, Mr. Walker."

"You okay?"

At the sound of Amelia's voice, his focus lurched from his knuckles, white over his knees, to Amelia—brow pinched in concern. He forced his shoulders to relax, slid his hands over his jeans. "I was just wondering that about you a minute ago. I looked over and you had your head in your hands. Not a fan of hospitals?"

"Something like that."

He could tell there was something else going on behind her autumn irises right now. Maybe she was reliving a memory that stung as much as his. "Come on. Let's go."

"But Megan—"

"Kate's with her, and there's nothing we can do at the moment."

A languid sky brushed dusky shadows against the parking lot as they walked outside. Amelia sat up front this time. Didn't say a word until after he'd passed the turnoff for Main Avenue. "Aren't you taking me back to the office?"

"Ah, I can. Or . . ." The sliver of a low-slung sun glinted in his eyes, and he flipped down his visor. "The rest of my family's out at the depot now—where Dad works. You know that. The railway's opening for the season in a couple weeks, so everybody's helping out, getting it cleaned up."

It was pure impulse that led him to turn onto the road that led to the Maple Valley Scenic Railway and Museum, situated on the edge of town. But that fleeting trace of hurt he'd seen on Amelia's face back in the waiting room, the thought of him spending the evening with a passel of family while she hung out alone in her little house . . .

Didn't feel right.

"It's just painting and polishing woodwork. Nothing thrilling. But—"

"I'd love to." He slid her a glance. She held on to her seatbelt with one hand, earnest desire sparking in her eyes. "If you're asking if I'd like to hang out with you guys and help tonight, I'd love to."

Yes, there'd definitely been more going on in her head at the hospital than worry about Megan. He wanted to ask.

But she wanted distraction. It was obvious.

"All right, then. Word of warning, though—we're a loud crowd. I guess you saw that the other night."

"I did." Her eyes were on the windshield now. Ahead of them, the oblong depot building came into view, its pale blue paint silhouetted by a pastel sunset. Railroad tracks ribboned over gravel, reaching into the distance, where the landscape rose and fell in tree-packed ridges. Iowa wasn't all fields and flatlands.

Even now, with winter still clutching the landscape and only sparse hints of green grappling through muddy snow and wrinkled branches, this place had a beauty not even California and its beaches could rival.

He parked in front of the depot, gaze traveling over the train cars lined up on the tracks. One of Iowa's only heritage railroads, the fourteen-mile passenger ride helped make Maple Valley the tri-county tourist stop it was.

Amelia gasped as she got out of the car. "Wait, your notes. The Kendall Wilkins ones. I think I left them at the coffee shop."

He met her on the other side of the car. "Eh, we'll get them sometime."

"What if they're not there? What if someone throws them out?"

"They weren't that great of notes. Nothing you couldn't have learned with a little Googling."

He started toward the boardwalk that circled the depot, shovel tracks forming a path.

"But you went to all the work of finding them."

"It wasn't any work at all." Not exactly the truth. But she didn't need to know that.

Raegan met them outside the depot. "Megan's fine. Kate just texted. She was dehydrated, which I guess can cause early contractions. They've got her on fluids and are going to keep her overnight, but she and the baby will be fine." She glanced at Amelia. "Oh, hey, Amelia. I didn't realize you were . . . together."

He didn't miss the ragged relief in Amelia's sigh at the update about Megan. "Oh, well, Logan was at the office, delivering some notes, and we were getting coffee when . . ." .

What was with the look passing between Amelia and Raegan?

"He delivered the notes. Good. After making Kate and me help him look through the attic last night for hours. Needle. Haystack. Mission impossible. Come on in. We're going to order pizza."

He started to follow Raegan into the building, but Amelia's voice stopped him. "Hours? You said it didn't take long at all to find the notes."

He turned. "Relatively speaking."

"You made your sisters help."

"They love me. They miss me. They were happy to do it."

She stepped up to him, the scarf around her neck fluttering in the breeze. "You are just as curious about Wilkins as I am, aren't you?"

"I'm mildly interested."

"You think there's a story there." She hid her teeth behind a close-lipped, delighted smile. Her first since arriving at the hospital.

It shouldn't gratify him so much. "Or I'm just really nice and I'm humoring you."

"Maybe." The wind played with her hair. "But I think I just figured out how I'm going to convince you not to sell the paper. I'm going to remind you how fun it is to chase a story. Prove Maple Valley is full of interesting stuff to write about. Mystery, even. And we need a paper to preserve it all." She patted his arm. "Good luck withstanding my powers of persuasion, boss."

She waltzed past him into the depot, and by the time he'd blinked, swallowed something that tasted way too much like attraction, his family members voices were already drifting from the open door, welcoming Amelia and putting her to work.

6

The little desk wedged into the tight space at the back of The Red Door's kitchen wasn't the best place to have a business discussion. Not with the racket of banging oven and dishwasher doors and Southern rock growling from the radio.

But considering Seth Walker was giving up his Friday lunch hour to dole out free advice, Amelia wasn't about to complain.

"There's a bunch of stuff you'll need to prepare in advance to go along with your application." Seth pulled apart a cinnamon roll he'd swiped from a tray when they'd entered the room, despite the glare of his chef. The industrial kitchen gleamed with stainless steel and copper, Tuscan tile on the floor and walls adding flair to even this less-seen piece of the restaurant.

If anybody knew something about applying for a small-business loan—taking a leap of financial faith—it was Logan's cousin. Bold career moves seemed to be a Walker family trait.

Seth slid a paper toward her. "You sure you don't want a cinnamon roll? Shan, my chef, is a culinary genius."

"Nah, had two Pop-Tarts before coming over here. But thanks anyway."

"You realize my health nut cousin would break into tears if he heard you say that?"

"Says the guy currently licking icing off his fingers."

"Touché."

Seth was right, though. Two weeks of working with Logan and she hadn't seen him pop so much as a Lifesaver. One day, mid-argument about a headline—because apparently he *loved* to change her headlines, another thing she'd learned in their short time working together—he'd announced he was hungry for a snack. Came back from the office's kitchenette with a bag of baby carrots.

She'd teased him for days. Partially because anyone who legitimately counted carrots as a snack deserved to be badgered. But mostly because it was just so fun to fluster the guy.

Amelia scanned the list Seth gave her now. *Personal credit history. Business credit history. Financial statements.*

The crash of breaking glass tried to cut in, followed by Seth's voice calling to ask his chef if everything was okay.

"Just a broken plate. No biggie."

Detailed business plan. Cash flow projections. Personal guarantee from principal owners.

A groan worked its way up her throat. "I think I'll take that roll now."

Seth chuckled and stood. "You might need two. We haven't even looked at the application itself yet."

Owen had been the one to plant the idea of applying for a small-business loan in her head. Yesterday they'd watched Logan and Ledge mess with the binding machine in the back room through the horizontal window separating the space, Logan with his sleeves rolled up and his tie askew—he didn't seem to catch on that this was a casual office—and his brow knit. Owen had shaken his head.

"You've got about as much chance convincing that guy to

hold on to this paper as you do of stumbling upon the money to buy it yourself."

Logan had tangled his fingers through his hair. Scowled at the machine.

And she'd realized Owen was right.

Amelia swiveled in her chair now to face the rest of the kitchen as Seth pulled a plate from an open shelf, then used a pair of tongs to serve up her roll. Behind him, a waiter swept up shards of broken glass and the dishwasher rumbled. "I'm in over my head, aren't I?"

He plopped the roll on a plate. "Amelia, when I got the crazy idea to gut this place and turn it into a restaurant, I had exactly two thousand and nine dollars in my bank account. Plus eighteen cents. I remember it to the penny because it basically haunted me." He set the plate in front of her. "When I told Uncle Case about my idea, when I walked into that first bank meeting, when I met with the contractor . . . every time, I kept seeing two thousand and nine dollars and eighteen measly cents."

He lowered once more beside her, a tickly breeze from the open window over the desk ruffling his hair. "I thought I was in over my head until the day The Red Door opened. Half the time, I think I still am."

She dabbed one finger through the cinnamon roll's icing. "What helped you take the initial leap?"

There was that Walker resemblance again, this time in his grin. Almost a perfect match for Logan's. Except Logan's was always accompanied by those crinkles at the corners of his eyes. "I was on the verge of signing the loan papers when I reconnected with Ava."

His girlfriend. The one who'd finally moved to town last summer after a full year exchanging emails with Seth. Now she lived in the apartment over the restaurant and would probably be a Walker herself before too much longer.

A wisp of longing skimmed over Amelia, like a wayward feather she'd usually brush away. But today she allowed herself to grasp it. To think, just for a moment, about what it'd be like to have what Seth and Ava had. And Kate and Colton.

A love that supported and encouraged and inspired, as Ava had Seth, to reach for what could be.

Instead of one heavied by what couldn't.

"I'll admit, though, it wasn't only Ava's confidence that helped me. It was also the fact that Case co-signed my loan." *Amelia* ~~Ava~~ slouched in her chair. "And unfortunately, I don't have a Case. If I do this, I'm in it on my own."

"Look, you may be the only one personally absorbing the financial risk. That's true. But you're not in it alone." Seth took the list back from her and slid it under a stack of papers. "You've so firmly cemented yourself in this town, no one even remembers you're not a native. More than that, you've got the support of the Walkers. After all, we all kind of owe you. You've put articles about my restaurant and Colton's nonprofit on the front page. You're friends with Raegan, who is clearly the craziest of our clan. And you've spent how many evenings in the past couple weeks helping out at the depot?"

Three evenings. She'd spent three uncannily fantastic evenings with the Walker family over the past weeks—cleaning and painting and polishing the depot in preparation for its spring opening this week. She'd gotten to know Kate much more than she had before. Saw in a new light how much Rae looked up to her older siblings. Listened to Case's stories of his former life as an international diplomat.

And she'd watched Logan and Charlie together—the way he swung her onto his shoulders so she could "help" paint, his attention always drifting to her when he was in a different part of the room, how he communicated with his daughter even though she rarely uttered more than a word or two.

That first night, her thoughts had strayed back to Jeremy, how she always used to imagine him as a dad. But that was only imagination, wasn't it? Logan was the real thing. And he was good at it, no matter how much he doubted himself.

Yes, his doubts. Another thing she'd picked up on in just two weeks. He'd mentioned Charlie's upcoming speech therapy appointment earlier this week, his words weighty and worried. *"I should have done it long ago."*

"You're a good dad, Logan," she'd said. *"Charlie's lucky to have you."* No tease in her voice then.

"You've got a great family, Seth."

"Don't I know it." He straightened. "Now, let's look at the application. It's going to feel overwhelming, but I promise you, it'll impress the bank if you show up to that first meeting with the application complete and all the required attachments—"

The buzz of her phone on the desktop cut him off. The display lit up with a number she'd just called yesterday. Her attention perked. "Sorry, Seth, this is work-related." Her first official lead on the Kendall Wilkins story—thanks to Logan's notes. She'd found the name—Claire Wallace—scribbled in a margin, followed by a question mark.

"No prob. If you need a quiet spot . . ." He pointed to the doorway to the back stairway that led up to the apartment.

She nodded her thanks as she answered. "This is Amelia."

"Hi, this is Claire Wallace. Just returning your call."

"Yes, thanks so much for calling me back." Amelia passed through the doorway and closed the door softly behind her, blinking to adjust to the dim space, lit only by a wedge of light from the apartment door at the top of the steps. "I just had a few questions for you about your time working at the bank."

"You know I retired four years ago, don't you?"

Amelia lowered onto a step, feet propped on the one below. Why hadn't she grabbed a notebook or at least a piece of paper from Seth's desk? "Yes, the bank manager let me know that. I'm actually calling because I'm following up on a story about Kendall Wilkins and that safe-deposit box."

What should she make of Claire's stretching pause?

Finally, the woman spoke. "Sorry, just checking my calendar to make sure of the year." She chuckled. "We're five years past Mr. Wilkins's death. So I'm afraid I don't understand."

"Nobody ever solved the mystery of what was in his safe-deposit box. I know the odds are remote, but I'd like to figure it out."

"What's to figure out? He played a practical joke on a whole town. He was always a cranky-pants. It fits."

"He also donated a mansion to the library, built half the buildings in town, provided college scholarships . . . and never asked for anything in return." Had she let too much defensiveness into her tone?

"I'm still not sure how I can help you."

"I just wondered if you might remember anything that could be helpful. Did he ever hint at what was in the box? Open it in front of you?"

"Trust me, I answered these questions years ago. No, he never hinted. I was never in the room when he opened it. Up until that last time he came by the bank, just a week or so before he died, it was as much a mystery to me as anyone else. But that's bank policy—confidentiality."

Amelia ran one hand over the stairway bannister above her. She'd known the call might not produce any leads. But she'd hoped . . .

Wait.

Her brain snagged on something Claire had said. *"Up until that last time . . . just a week or so before he died . . ."*

"Kendall had access to his deposit box just days before he died?"

"He'd stop by every now and then. And yes, I saw him the week before he passed. I remember thinking he didn't look well. Wan and thin. Which made sense. He was pretty old by then. Amazing he was still out and about."

"If that box was meant to be a joke on the town, why would he need access to it? What would he be doing with an empty box?"

"Maybe it was a last-minute decision. Maybe he removed whatever used to be in it that day, so it'd be empty when he passed."

But according to the notes Logan had given her—color-coded and ridiculously, entertainingly organized—Kendall's will had been revised for the last time three years before he died.

Maybe he *had* removed whatever was in the box that day. But not because he'd made some last-minute decision to trick the town. If so, he would've called his lawyer and changed the will.

"I'm not sure why you're doing this story," Claire added. "Or what hope there could possibly be of finding out anything after all this time. But if you're intent on it, who you should really talk to is his nurse."

"His nurse?"

"The one who took care of him those last couple years. She's the one who'd drive him wherever he needed to go. The one who brought him to the bank that last time. She moved away several years ago, but with the Internet, anybody can find anybody these days, right?"

"Do you know her name?"

"Easy enough one to remember. Marney. Marney Billingsley."

Amelia stood, grinning at the empty hallway, excitement-fueled energy coursing through her. Maybe the whole town had made up its mind about Kendall and his intentions years ago. But they were wrong.

Something was supposed to be in that box.

And Marney Billingsley, wherever she was, might have the answer.

⁓

Two weeks in Maple Valley felt like two months.

"So you'll do it?" The sound of a football smacking as it landed in Colton Greene's hands accompanied his words.

The sound of Charlie's giggles as she ran toward them from the house filled the yard. Tiny pink buds peeked from the magnolia tree Mom and Dad had planted when they first moved here, and green had begun to take over the line of trees cordoning off the ravine.

Yes, this had been a good idea—to take the afternoon off after a morning at the office. Spend time with his friend and his daughter. Forget his overflowing inbox with emails from the LA office or the list of to-dos he'd made himself for the newspaper. Equipment to repair and a website to design and—

"Well?" Colton sent the football flying toward him, then bent over to tickle and chase Charlie while a gleaming sun showered the backyard in light. Near-spring warmth had long since lured away the last of the snow.

Not that Amelia wasn't still hoping for one more whomping visit from winter. She'd made that clear enough when she decorated her desk with homemade paper snowflakes. The whole office had laughed at her.

But then, later in the day, he'd seen Mae tack a snowflake of her own on the bulletin board when Amelia wasn't looking.

"Your dad's smiling." Colton swung Charlie into his arms. "That must mean a yes."

Logan caught the sailing football, the tie he still wore batting against his shirt. "Yes to what exactly? All you said was, 'Wanna do me a favor?'"

Charlie had hold of Colton's jersey now, her little legs pumping as she tailed him on his way to catch the football. Colton caught it with the ease of the practiced quarterback he was. "The question is, will you help with my fundraiser for the Parker House? It's coming up in a few weeks, and I'm in over my head."

Colton had just launched the nonprofit earlier this year—an effort to provide shelter and care for older teens aging out of the foster care system. The Parker House he'd opened in Maple Valley was first of what he hoped would be many.

Man, Iowa had been good for Colton. Kate was good for him.

Actually, Colton would say finding his way back to God was good for him.

"But I'm not an event planner, Greene. Besides, you want to talk about in over your head? I'm trying to bring an antiquated newspaper into the twenty-first century. I met with Freddie's old accountant this week and accidentally swallowed my gum when he showed me the numbers." He crouched and tossed the football with a light enough touch that Charlie could catch it. "Not to mention, I've got Amelia arguing with me constantly. I suggest the tiniest changes for headlines or articles or ad placement and she feels compelled to remind me I may be the owner, but *she's* the editor."

"You like it and you know it."

"I put up with it."

"You enjoy it."

"Whatever." He could argue all he wanted, but Colton wasn't an idiot. Two weeks of spending his Monday-through-Fridays at a slower pace, the smell of newsprint and ink sticking to his clothes, sparring with Amelia, it wasn't all bad.

Amelia wasn't all bad.

In another time and another place, he might've been interested in her in another way.

But not here and now, when he had a daughter who came

first and a life fifteen hundred miles away and a presidential candidate knocking on his door. At least he hoped Hadley was still knocking. Theo had called yesterday in a panic about the fact that they still hadn't heard anything.

But more than any of that was the fact that he still planned to eventually sell the *News*. And it'd break Amelia's heart when he did.

His phone dinged, and he pulled it from his pocket. A text from Amelia.

Got a new lead on the KW story. Be impressed!

"Colt, take his phone away," Dad's voice called from the deck. "You said you were taking a break this morning, son."

"Not work, Dad." Not exactly. The Wilkins story was Amelia's thing. He was just . . . playing along. Although, if she had a *real* lead . . .

I'll believe it when I see it. Hear it. Whatever.

He was baiting her. For no other reason than it was fun. And he could see her in his head, annoyance narrowing her eyes. He watched his phone, waiting for her reply. Until . . .

A crack and a cry tore through the yard.

His phone slipped through his fingers as he whipped around in time to see Colton bending over near a broken branch leaning into a bulky trunk. *Charlie* . . .

His phone hit a muddy patch.

"She wanted to climb the tree," Colton said as Logan hurried over, pushed in to see Charlie standing, shaking, a gash over her right eye. "The branch snapped."

He dropped to his knees. "It's okay, honey. Daddy's got you." Her tears wet his own cheek as he held her close.

"I don't think she's hurt too bad. I think she's more scared—"

"What were you thinking?" The words snapped from him, biting. "She could've broken an arm or leg."

She's okay.

No, she had a head injury. She was bleeding. He needed to look at that cut over her eye, but she'd buried herself against his neck.

"Daddy."

He inhaled so sharply at the shaken, whispered word muffled by his jacket, he could feel the cold air hit his lungs. *Charlie* . . .

He pulled back just enough to see her face. She'd said it, hadn't she? He wasn't hearing things?

"Daddy." She said it again, this time through a sniffle and a sob as she swiped her hand under her nose.

"Logan, I was watching her." Colton's football-player frame shadowed him. "I turned away just for a second to find the ball. But I saw her hit the ground, and it wasn't hard. I'm sorry, but—"

He interrupted Colton by standing, pulling Charlie with him, arms tight. He kissed her cheek. "Should we go inside and check out your forehead?"

He heard Colton's footsteps behind him, felt the tension lingering from his whipped words. Uncalled for, but the panic . . .

He took the deck steps two at a time, saw that Dad had gone inside, leaving the patio doors open. He toed off his shoes on the rug inside and hauled Charlie to the island counter in the middle of the kitchen. Dad was already running a rag under water, which he handed over as Kate walked into the room. "What happened?"

Colton explained to Kate while Logan dabbed the cloth over Charlie's forehead. He pulled it away in time to see another clump of blood push through her broken skin. With his other hand, he grasped one of Charlie's hands, and her fingers immediately tightened around his thumb. "Do I need to take her to the ER? What if she needs stitches?"

Kate leaned closer. "It doesn't seem that big of a gash."

"Walker, I am really sorry." Colton smoothed Charlie's hair, and her still-tear-streaked cheeks bunched with her smile.

He didn't have to look around to hear Kate's silent question. But she only rubbed one hand over Charlie's arm. "How about I take you to the bathroom and find a Band-Aid? I think we might have some pink ones." Colton left with them.

Leaving Logan to stare at the granite countertop, wet rag still in hand. And Dad, who faced him from the other side of the island.

"I should've been watching her more closely."

"Son, kids get hurt. I can't count the number of times your mother and I ended up in the ER with one of you. If it wasn't Kate with a concussion after dozing off in the hammock and tipping out, it was Beckett breaking his arm in a basketball game or Raegan falling off her bike." Dad rounded the counter. "Although come to think of it, you tended to escape those kinds of accidents."

Because he was the careful one. The responsible one.

He glanced down at the stained rag in his hand.

Yeah. Right. Charlie had spent too many days with a nanny back in LA. He'd waited too long to get her into speech therapy. And there'd been too many scares—that fire, today's accident . . .

Hearing her voice had been a gift, but it shouldn't take something like this to prompt it.

"I was a jerk to Colton."

"He'll forgive you."

He met his father's eyes. "Dad, what am I doing here?"

"Logan—"

But whatever Dad was going to say was cut off by the doorbell's chime. Frustration beat through him. Rick and Helen, here to pick up Charlie for an afternoon trip to the park. And they'd see her hurt.

So not what he needed right now. Not considering the weird vibe he'd gotten from them ever since coming home. But he didn't have time to dissect it now. He hurried through the living room, calling for Kate and Charlie as he did.

It was only Rick standing on the porch when he opened the door. "Hey, Rick. Charlie's almost ready to go."

His father-in-law's reddish hair had faded to a yellowy white in the past years. He wore a Notre Dame sweatshirt and a half grin that seemed trapped in the lower half of his face. "Morning, Logan."

Plastic small talk filled the seconds until Kate arrived with Charlie in tow. When had it become this way with his in-laws? So stilted. Uncomfortable.

"There you are, Charlotte." Rick looked past Logan, his smile dissolving as Charlie ran up to them. There was no missing the hot pink Band-Aid on her forehead. "What happened?"

"Little incident climbing a tree," Dad answered from behind.

"She was a climbing a tree? She's *three*."

Rick looked from Charlie to Logan back to Charlie. But he only sighed and picked up the backpack Logan had packed earlier this morning. "Helen's waiting in the car."

Logan bent down, zipped Charlie's coat, kissed her Band-Aid.

"She's okay, Rick," Dad added. "Logan made sure of that."

Rick reached for Charlie.

Logan followed him out the door, leaving Dad on the porch. He waved at Helen through the windshield, stood in the driveway as Rick settled Charlie in a toddler car seat in back.

"We have our first speech therapy appointment late next week," he offered. An attempt at smoothing rough waters. "And she said 'Daddy' a couple of times today."

"That's progress? And you're just now getting an appointment scheduled?"

"I called the therapist's office before we even made the trip home, Rick. This was the soonest we could get in."

"You better hope for quick results. Especially since you only plan to be here a month."

Was he imagining the accusation huddled in Rick's words? "There are therapists in LA, too."

Rick barely acknowledged the response—offering only a slight shrug before opening his car door and sliding inside. Logan watched as Rick said something to Helen. Even from here, he picked up on Helen's stiff reaction.

A minute later, as Rick's tires bounced over potholes left by the snowplow's frequent winter work, Dad came up to Logan's side.

"Something's not right." He felt his father's gaze.

"She's just fine, son. Give it a couple weeks and you won't even see where she got hurt."

"Not that. Emma's parents. I don't know what I've done to earn their disapproval, but clearly something's brewing."

"You're a wonderful dad, Logan. You're doing your best. That's all anyone asks or expects."

He tried to breathe in Dad's assurances. Believe them.

But they couldn't find space to settle, not with the unease expanding like a balloon inside him, arguing in taunting whispers that his best might not be good enough.

◦◦◦

Logan had been the one to send the SOS text message asking Amelia to meet him here. So where was he?

The thrum of an overzealous bass pulsed like the throbbing headache that'd nagged her all afternoon—ever since she'd taken a second look at those loan papers Seth had pulled together for her. The band squashed into the little stage at the corner of the restaurant floor, cleared of its front tables, didn't so much sing as screech.

"Hey, I didn't know you were coming tonight." Owen appeared at the table near the back she'd managed to nab.

"Wasn't planning to." Open mic night at The Red Door had become a monthly thing. She'd been a few times, but had instead planned to spend tonight scouring the Internet until she located Marney Billingsley.

And then Logan had texted—something about needing help with a project he hadn't asked for.

And within ten minutes she'd changed out of pajama pants into leggings and a jean skirt with a black-and-white-striped top. She'd left her hair in its usual messy bun but taken time to swipe on some eye shadow and mascara.

Told herself the whole time it was the event she was prepping for—not the man. Did lying to herself count as a sin?

Owen dropped into the only other chair at the table. "You should've called. You didn't have to come alone."

She had to strain to be heard above the music. If it could be called music. "Actually I'm meeting someone."

"Who?"

"Logan."

Owen didn't even try to hide his scowl. "He's stringing you along, Bentley."

Wait, Owen didn't think . . . "This isn't—"

"Not just you. Everyone in the office." Owen's voice rose as the music amped. "He might've put off the sale for whatever reason, might be having fun playing Perry White, but he's still going to sell."

The standing-room-only crowd in front of her parted just long enough to offer a glimpse of the restaurant's gaping front windows. A lone figure stood out on the sidewalk. Logan?

"Not Perry White."

"Huh?" Owen had to nearly yell the question.

"Perry White was the editor. *I'm* the editor." The figure outside turned. Definitely Logan. "Logan's the owner."

"The owner who's going to sell, no matter how friendly you guys get."

Amelia stood. "You can have the table, if you want." With that, she left Owen and his bad attitude, wound her way through the mostly teenaged crowd, and reached the door.

The day's earlier springlike warmth had given way to chilly night air that curled around her as she stepped aside. "Logan?"

The hazy light of lampposts that wrapped like a line of sentries around the town square spotlighted the tension coiling his features. The tick in his jaw. The clearly finger-raked hair. The shadow in his eyes. "Hey."

"Whatcha doing? I've been inside for ten minutes." And why was he still wearing this morning's tie? He'd loosened it at some point, untucked his shirt, but his attire still pushed the formal side of the scale.

"I . . . well, I was thinking about . . . wasn't sure I . . ." White puffs of air chased his sigh and unfinished sentences.

She leaned against the lamppost with one hand. "You were going to stand me up, weren't you?"

"I wasn't going to stand you up."

"You SOS-ed me—for what reason, I don't even know—and you were going to up and leave me here by myself with a bunch of emo teens and a growly Owen."

Logan glanced at the restaurant, uncertainty gliding through his expression. What had happened in the hours since she'd seen him at the office this morning? He looked back to Amelia. "Emo teens and Owen, huh? You're not doing much to convince me to stay." At least his tone had sloped into its usual ease. His postured loosened, too. "I just don't know how I let myself get talked into this stuff. I felt bad for snapping at Colton today, so

I agreed to help with this fundraiser thing for his nonprofit, but I had no idea how much work there is to do. Now somehow I'm basically in charge of cobbling together an entire event that's only three weeks away, and he told me to go to open mic night to find live music possibilities, and Charlie got hurt today and I have this feeling my in-laws think I'm a negligent parent and—"

"Whoa, Logan." She moved her hand from the lamppost to his arm. "Charlie got hurt? Is she okay?"

"She's fine. More than fine. Helen texted me a photo of her playing house in Emma's old room and . . ." Another sigh.

"And if I'm understanding right, you need to pick out a band or musician to perform at a fundraiser? And you SOS-ed me because . . . you trust my taste in music?"

"You have, like, three shirts of your favorite bands. Kat told me the office goes into collective shock if a week goes by without you wearing one of them."

"Which makes me a music expert?"

"Or I just didn't feel like hanging out at this thing by myself."

So he'd invited her. Best not even to acknowledge the flutter of pleasure that fact raised. So instead she patted his arm and reached for his tie.

"What are you doing?"

"Helping you loosen up." She tugged at the tie's knot. "You've dressed for the office, not a night of live music and appetizers."

"Sure you're not strangling me?"

She yanked the tie again. "You could help."

"Kinda more fun watching you try."

She paused, fingers still wrapped around the tie, and had to tip her head up to look up at him. "Boggles the mind, Logan Walker, how you can go from broody to mocking in the span of a few seconds."

"I am a man of many talents."

One of which clearly included dousing every last speck of

common sense from her brain. Because standing this close, invading his space . . . well, it probably wasn't the best idea she'd ever had. *He's your boss.*

"Amelia?"

She whirled, pulling Logan's tie—and him—with her. He exaggerated a choking sound that might've made her laugh if she hadn't suddenly gone jumpy.

No laughter from Owen, though. He stood just outside The Red Door's entrance, looking back and forth between them. "What's going on?"

"I was just—"

"She was just—"

They spoke at the same time.

Logan stuck one finger into the knot in his tie, gave a swift tug, and it slackened and fell into her hand.

"How did you do that?"

"I told you. Many talents."

"I've got a busy weekend, so I'm taking off." Owen lifted his hand in a halfhearted wave and started down the sidewalk before either one of them could argue.

Logan took his tie from her and stuffed it in his pocket. "I swear that guy does not like me."

"Owen is just . . . overprotective." And possibly still smarting from their failed date-that-wasn't-a-date.

"I'm the one who was out here getting choked by my own tie. Come on, let's go in."

A new band had taken the stage while they were outside—a trio—and they were just ambling into the first chords of a folk song as she led the way to the table her coat still reserved. Logan held out her chair, then pulled out his own.

They listened through one song, and then another. During the third Logan stood and disappeared into the restaurant kitchen. Being related to the owner apparently had its perks. By the end of the song, he'd returned—Diet Coke for her, bottle of water for him—and Raegan in tow. He gave his sister his chair and instead stood across from them.

"Didn't know you guys were here or I would've come down sooner." Raegan wore her hair in two short braids, a line of beaded bracelets stacked on one wrist. "I was upstairs in Ava's apartment. Been pretending for the past half an hour to be into some movie about some football team."

"I think she and Colton are on a quest to turn us from a basketball family to a football family." Logan uncapped his water.

"You guys are into basketball?" Come to think of it, she'd seen the hoop in the driveway.

Raegan held up three fingers. "Breakfast, basketball, and the big screen. Our family hobbies."

"Nice job with the alliteration."

"Mom's doing," Logan explained.

"Although speaking of hobbies . . ." Raegan turned to tug on Logan's arm. "You're going to get up there, yeah?" She nudged her head toward the stage.

The trio's song hit a minor chord. "Ha. No way."

Amelia slurped on her pop. "He sings?"

Raegan gave a proud-sister grin. "And plays guitar."

Logan shook his head. "I can pluck a few chords. That's it."

Raegan ignored him. "He's being modest. He sang at his wedding, at Mom's funeral, almost every Christmas Eve service I remember attending."

"I'm not playing tonight, Rae."

Amelia poked an unwrapped straw at his arm. "Come on."

"I don't play anymore."

"Log—" Raegan began.

But in a look that lasted less than a second, understanding seemed to flash between them. A conversation without words and one Amelia wasn't privy to. And before anyone could say anything else, a new voice drifted from the stage.

Raegan jerked, and at the sound of the smooth-as-velvet voice, Amelia knew why. Bear McKinley, an open-mic-night regular who could melt a girl's heart right into a puddle, him and that guitar.

And one girl's heart in particular.

She glanced at Raegan.

"Think I'll get going, guys." Raegan slid from her chair. "Working at the library tomorrow . . ."

Logan's brow furrowed in confusion as he watched his sister leave. "That was . . . sudden."

He didn't know? "Logan, that's Bear."

"As in Smokey the . . . ?"

"As in the guy Raegan's been half in love with since I met her. Something happened last fall, though. Not sure what, except I think Bear might be leaving town soon—some missionary thing in South America, I think. Should I be telling you this?"

He was watching the guy on stage now, dark eyes narrow and observing. Big brotherly and . . .

Cute.

"Maybe you shouldn't, but I'm glad you did. Now I know to scope out the guy. So they were a thing?"

"I don't know if it was ever official or not, but they were definitely . . . something." A love story waiting to happen, she'd always figured. Next in line after Seth and Ava, Kate and Colton. Something in the Maple Valley water, she'd thought. She looked toward Raegan pushing through the crowd to the exit. Obviously she'd thought wrong.

"I wonder why she didn't tell me."

"Maybe it was easier to talk to Kate." Because, unlike Eleanor, some sisters actually did that—talked.

"He better not have hurt her."

"I think whatever happened between them, well, it seems like it was mutual." Bear strummed into a new song. "But I guess it's good it happened now instead of later. Always better to know early than to find yourself later on wondering how in the world you got where you are. Letting go before you're completely invested, before . . ."

Stop.

She'd let too much weight into her tone, hadn't she? Said more than she meant to. The way Logan had turned his studying eyes back to her, patient and prodding and caring.

"It's just . . . better to know."

"Amelia."

All he did was say her name and suddenly she itched to answer the question he hadn't even asked. "Divorced. Going on three years."

If he was shocked, he didn't show it. Only capped his water bottle and glanced at the pop glass she hadn't yet touched. "I didn't know."

"It's not really my favorite topic of conversation. Don't know why I told you. I couldn't even say the word for the longest time. For a while there, I thought it might've been easier to lose Jeremy to death than—"

She cut herself off with a gasp, felt the burning regret of what she'd just said.

Who she'd said it to.

"Logan, I—"

"It's okay, Amelia. We've had different experiences, but we both know what it feels like to be one half of a whole one moment, and the next . . ." He shrugged. "I'm sorry either one of us had to go through it."

She traced a pattern in the ring of liquid at the base of her glass. How could he be so gracious when she'd just compared her divorce to the sudden and tragic loss of his wife? She glanced up at him, the restaurant's soft lighting brushing bronze hues into his brown eyes.

"Thanks for telling me. About the divorce, I mean." He reached for a napkin from the holder in the middle of the table. Wiped up the drips of water from her sweating glass. Unwrapped a straw and plunked it in her pop for her. "And for giving me the lowdown on Rae and Bear. And for insisting I come inside."

His words burrowed inside her, found a space she hadn't even realized was empty, and filled it with warmth. "Even if I nearly strangled you with your tie?"

"Even if."

He angled in his chair to watch Bear, and she followed suit. But she couldn't help one more glimpse his way. And then he did the same—angling his gaze in her direction. And . . .

"Amelia?"

She ripped her focus away at the sound of the voice and nearly tipped her cup. Shock spiraled through her. *Eleanor?*

Dear Mary,

If you were my daughter, I'd tell you about my fascination with history. And Amelia Earhart. And Charles Lindbergh. And how it all started because of a lie.

I have a twin sister named Eleanor. She was named after our grandmother—Eleanor Marguerite. Grandma died when I was little, so I never really knew her. But from what my mom says, she was strong. Confident. Full of personality.

My name was chosen from a baby name book. Nothing wrong with that, but I was always jealous Eleanor had a cool story, a cool figure, behind her name. So one day in elementary school, I lied. I told my classmates I was named after the only Amelia I could think of—Amelia Earhart.

And then I decided I'd better learn about this apparent namesake of mine. I found a picture book in the library and read it so many times the librarian laughed. Soon I started reading other biographies for children—Lindbergh, for one, but others, too. By third grade, I was the class nerd—evidenced by the fact that, while my friends spent the summer at the pool, I attended history camp.

7

An azure sky swam overhead today, no foamy clouds, no breathy gales. Clear and brilliant.

But not enough to chase away the fog of confusion still hovering over Amelia this morning. Hands full—coffee and pastries that'd filled her car with such tantalizing scents an animal's growl issued from her stomach—she used her foot to kick the car door closed behind her.

The cherry red of the barn and golden sunlight gushed through the bowing limbs of the willow. Amelia skirted around the tree and maneuvered her way into the house, ears perked for the sound of Eleanor's movement upstairs.

Nothing.

She moved into the kitchen, ignoring the sheet and blanket she'd left twisted on the couch when she'd awoken earlier, neck and back both protesting the night she'd spent pretzeled up.

She freed her hands in the kitchen, sat at the table, and tried to decipher for the hundredth time what Eleanor's sudden appearance might mean.

"How'd you know I was here?" It was the first question

out of the dozen scrambling through her that'd made it out of her mouth last night, when she saw her sister for the first time in—what was it? A year?

Whatever weightless, warm exchange had just happened between her and Logan curdled with the sight of Eleanor. Hair cropped to her chin, she had the reedy figure of a runner and a face more angular than Amelia's.

"I was driving through all three blocks of your downtown. Saw your car, saw the lights here, made an intelligent guess."

She'd introduced Logan to her sister, forced lightness into her tone as Bear McKinley said something into the mic about his last song of the set.

"What in the world are you doing here?"

"Is it so hard to believe I might want to visit you?"

Yes. Because in the two years she'd lived here, Eleanor had come to visit exactly once, and the only nice thing she'd had to say about the town was that she'd passed a cute B&B on the way in.

Because they hadn't been close since high school.

Because she was never quite sure her sister liked her all that much.

"Mornin'."

Eleanor stood in front of her now, red silk pajama pants and white cami, hair hardly mussed after a night of sleep. They'd barely talked when they'd arrived home. Had instead exchanged stilted updates about their past few months as they changed the sheets on Amelia's bed.

Amelia's work at the newspaper, her Kendall Wilkins story.

Eleanor's upcoming wedding. Date TBD. Still. Didn't she realize by now if she kept waiting to set a date until Mom and Dad got back together, she might never get married?

"I ran downtown and got coffee and pastries. Didn't think you'd appreciate my usual Pop-Tart and breakfast blend."

Eleanor took a seat at the table. "You didn't have to do that."

But she did. It'd been the only distraction she could think of to run off the memory of last time Eleanor was here, her hurled words before she'd left.

"It's your fault, Amelia. You made it look easy."

Those words threatened to sour and swallow her all over again. So she'd fled for town.

Eleanor opened the white bakery bag and pulled out a Danish. "I still can't believe you live in a barn."

"A renovated, remodeled barn that hasn't had a four-legged inhabitant in more than a decade." And Logan had called it *charming.*

"Still. We're eating where a horse or cow used to." Eleanor pulled a napkin from the holder in the center of the table. "And you know what else I can't believe? Technically, considering this place doesn't have much in the way of interior walls, we kind of shared a room last night. On different floors, maybe, but for one night, we were, once again, roommates. And we both survived. A feat, considering past experience."

Amelia took a long drink of muddy coffee. "One semester. We roomed together one semester our sophomore year. And if memory serves, neither one of us killed each other."

Eleanor grinned. "Yeah, but we came close, and who knows what would've happened if you hadn't up and eloped over Christmas?"

There it was—mention of the elopement. Never could get more than ten minutes into a family gathering without someone bringing it up. Not that they'd had much in the way of family gatherings since Mom and Dad had separated last year.

"El."

Her sister lowered her Danish to the napkin, pressed together lips still puffy from sleep.

"What are you doing here?"

Eleanor pulled the lid off her coffee, sniffed the blackened brew. "You wouldn't answer any of my calls."

"You called once. One time. I was in the middle of finishing a story on deadline. I figured you were calling about a wedding date and you'd leave a message." And had, frankly, sighed in relief when she hadn't.

Because a phone call couldn't hope to cross the gap their last interaction had forged.

"There's no wedding date."

Eleanor said the words with such finality that Amelia couldn't help honing in on her left hand.

"The ring's still there. Just haven't pinned down a date. Trevor's getting antsy. And I'm . . ." Eleanor took a sip of coffee, wrinkled her nose. "I'm having doubts."

Oh. Something fragile and fragmented splayed over her sister's face—usually so confident, so set. Eleanor had always been that way. Grades, athletic ability, ribbons and awards, and always the one with the handsome date. Trevor had come along their freshman year of college.

But unlike Amelia, who'd so swiftly and fully dropped everything else to marry Jeremy—the charismatic, older guy she'd met through a church ministry on campus—Eleanor had held back. She and Trevor dated off and on through college, amicably parted after graduation when Eleanor decided to go to grad school. Got back together a few years ago.

In other words, she'd done things the "right" way, the expected way—school and career, *then* love life.

"El, I—"

Eleanor abruptly unfolded from her chair, knees knocking into the table and coffee slurping over the edges of her cup. "You know what, I don't really want to talk about this."

Her sister left the kitchen, taking the stairs two at a time for the loft bedroom.

Amelia downed another drink, indecision swirling with the warm liquid in her stomach. Maybe Eleanor needed space.

But wasn't space all they'd had for nearly a year now? And El had made the first step, hadn't she? Driven from her cushy apartment in Des Moines to Maple Valley?

Maybe now wasn't the time for space. Maybe—if she ever hoped to have the kind of relationship with Eleanor that Logan and his siblings had—it was the time for effort, for crossing gaps, even uncomfortable ones.

Amelia climbed the steps to her bedroom, Eleanor's half-eaten Danish on a napkin in her hand. Her sister slid something— a book, looked like—under the sheet on the bed as Amelia emerged into the room. She stopped at the foot of the bed. "Thought you might want the rest of this."

Eleanor's half smile paved the way for Amelia to sit on the bed. El's toes—painted turquoise—peeked out from underneath her pajama pants. "We don't have to talk about Trevor if you don't want. But if that's why you came, if you need a listening ear, I'm here."

Her own gentle words surprised her. But it was the kind of thing Logan would've said to his sisters. Probably *had* said to Raegan last night, considering what Amelia had spilled about Bear.

El's gaze was fixed on the striped bed sheets. "I just keep wondering what our chances are. I look at Mom and Dad—thirty-five years and one day they up and separate. You and Jeremy."

She clamped her lips around a sharp inhale. Had to force herself not to clench the sheet beneath her.

"And yet, the thought of breaking up with Trev . . ." Her voice faded until she looked up at Amelia. "Look at you, though. You've bounced back, haven't you?"

She couldn't stop the tightening of her throat this time. Did a person really *bounce back* from an unwanted divorce? From a husband who couldn't even wait one month after the greatest hurt of his wife's life to call it done?

She closed her eyes against the memories—the social worker's apologetic tone, the smell of the hospital OB wing, the glimpse of the girl in the nursery and the baby in her arms. The realization . . .

"Jeremy says it's possible to move on without falling apart and—"

Her attention whipped to the present. "What?"

Eleanor's hand rested on the outline of the book under the sheet. Amelia pulled back the sheet only to see Jeremy's face grinning back her. Bleach-white smile and airbrushed skin. The title of the book, splashed in garish orange, like a mocking voice: *How I Moved On.*

"Amelia, try to forget he's your ex-husband for a minute."

She clambered to her feet.

"He's a respected life coach," Eleanor added. "His books—"

Amelia was at the stairs in two steps, shambling down as if distance might soften the shock of her sister's betrayal.

Was that too strong a word?

Maybe.

No.

Eleanor's voice followed her down. "I needed to hear from someone who managed to move on after a big breakup."

Amelia spun. "It wasn't a big breakup, El. It was a divorce. One I didn't want." But one all the arguing and pleading in the world hadn't been able to salvage.

The oval mirror hanging over her couch reflected the hair trickling from her ragged ponytail, the granite in her eyes.

"I'm just saying, he got through it," Eleanor said, arms swinging as if that helped make her point. "His career took off. And if I'm going to break things off with Trev, I want to know that's possible for me, too."

"Jeremy's career took off because he turned me and our marriage into a talking point. Every time he stands on a stage or writes in a book about how he got through such a horrible hurdle in his life, the *horrible hurdle* he's talking about is me." Her voice cracked despite the flint hardening it. "What you called easy—"

Eleanor lifted one hand. "You can't honestly still be upset about that."

"You told me my divorce looked *easy* and that's why Mom and Dad separated. Because somehow marital failure must be contagious."

"Amelia—"

"No, no, I can't . . ." She didn't stop for her purse or phone or jacket. She reached the front door and hauled it open. "I can't do this."

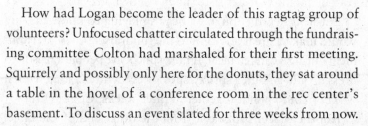

How had Logan become the leader of this ragtag group of volunteers? Unfocused chatter circulated through the fundraising committee Colton had marshaled for their first meeting. Squirrely and possibly only here for the donuts, they sat around a table in the hovel of a conference room in the rec center's basement. To discuss an event slated for three weeks from now.

Colt was a good guy. But event-planning? Clearly not his thing.

Logan's pen clunked to the table. "Maybe it's time to adjourn."

"But it's only been an hour." Kate, his one attentive ally.

"Yeah, but we've covered the basics. We've got a venue, an emcee, an advertising budget." One he was going to make sure went toward at least a half-page ad in the *News*. Conflict of interest, perhaps, but hey, that's what Colt got for roping him into this. "I think that might be as much as we can hope to accomplish today." Because half the group had stopped paying attention ten minutes ago when Colton and Raegan started a game of table hockey. With a donut.

"What about music?" Kate pointed to the last item on his meeting agenda. The one they'd all teased him for preparing. At least he'd prepared at all.

At the end of the table, Raegan let out a whoop as she flicked a donut past Colton's makeshift goal—two Styrofoam cups. Behind them, muted sunlight attempted its way in through a recessed window at the top of the wood-paneled wall.

"I've got an idea for music but gotta make sure Rae won't hate me first."

Bear McKinley may not have had his full attention last night—not with Amelia at the table. Not with the peek into her past she'd offered. Like peering through a keyhole, seeing just enough of a room to want to barge the rest of the way in. And he might've if her sister hadn't shown up.

But he'd heard enough of Bear's playing to know the guy would make a great addition to the fundraiser. Live entertainment during a catered meal. A fancy one. Give people a reason to dress up and go out, a spritzy, springy event after a long winter.

They could pull it together in three weeks. Couldn't they?

Another cheer broke out from the other end of the table. Colton, apparently, with the winning goal.

Okay, *Logan* could pull it off.

"I may have officially retired from the game of football, but at least I can still champion one sport." Colton stood, looked to Logan. "So we're done."

"Sure."

"He says with a sigh of resignation." Kate patted his arm. "Don't worry, brother. Last fall Colton conjured a last-minute fundraiser at the depot. You heard about that, right? City was talking about closing it after all the tornado damage. Colton got some of his NFL friends to come and do a train pull with the football team. On less than a week's notice. Raised enough for the repairs."

"Colton did that, huh?"

"Fine, I might've helped him. A lot. And Seth and Rae and Ava and everyone else. But still, it all came together. This thing will too."

He wanted to believe her. And if he was honest with himself, it wasn't really this fundraiser poking his mood today.

It was the lingering anxiety from Rick O'Hare's consternation yesterday.

It was missing Charlie her first full night away from him.

It was Amelia. It was the fact that he'd spent half a restless night thinking about her. And thinking about how he shouldn't be thinking about her.

The scraping of metal chairs jabbed into his attention. "Maybe if we'd met at Dad's, we would've been more productive. Or at the Parker House itself."

Kate tugged him out of his chair. "Yes, but Dad already has three adult children, one adult nephew, and a grandchild crashing at his place. And the Parker House is getting new carpet today. Only on the second floor, though. My man listened to my advice and restored all the original hardwood downstairs."

Her man. Logan draped his arm around his sister. "You're happy, yeah?"

"Like a bookworm in a library."

"You know if you and Colt hurried up and got married—"

"We've been officially dating all of two months, bro."

"I'm just saying, then Dad wouldn't have such a full house."

"Yeah, but Colton's smarter than to propose when I'm in the middle of rewrites on a book. He'll wait until after deadline, when I'm sane enough to enjoy it." Kate snickered, but the way she looked at Colton, now talking to a teenager in the corner, Logan guessed she'd marry the guy tomorrow if he asked.

"Hey, that's Webster, right?"

"That's him."

The lanky high schooler with Colton wore sweatbands on his wrists and baggy shorts. Logan had heard plenty about the young wide receiver and foster kid Colton had trained with last fall. Training turned into mentoring, which had turned into the inspiration for the Parker House.

"I snagged a good one, didn't I?'

"You did. Although I don't know why he's doing this fundraiser in Maple Valley when he could've done a golf tournament back in California or something. Reeled in a few celebrities and made five times what he'll make here."

"Because he's not after money so much as community support. Wants each town he builds a house in to really take ownership. This is a way to spark that."

Logan glanced at the scribbled notes he'd taken during the meeting. "I wish The Red Door did catering, because that'd make it easy and—"

Kate tugged the notes from his hands. "It's Saturday. It's sunny and warm. Go pick up Charlie. Take her to the park or something. Colt took me on a picnic in that old corncrib in Millers' Field last fall. Remember when we used to play there? Charlie would love that—"

"That rusty old thing? That's just asking for tetanus. And possibly a rat sighting."

"Let her experience true Iowa playtime. Make a day of it. Ask Amelia along."

"Why would I ask Amelia along?"

Kate rapped his notes against his chest. "Raegan once told me I'm no good at playing dumb. Same could be said of you, big brother."

She closed the half-empty box of donuts and pushed in her chair, then gave him a grin packed with cheeky implication and bounded off toward Colton.

Kate could infer whatever she wanted about his friendship with Amelia. And maybe she wasn't entirely off base with whatever conclusion she'd drawn. Maybe they did have a surprising connection, enigmatic. Maybe, definitely, that's what'd kept him awake last night.

But a couple weeks, a penchant for banter, a temporary working relationship . . .

Well, it was just that: temporary.

And he wasn't about to open himself up to any kind of possibility that already had a built-in expiration date. Not with Charlie to think about. Not with his career on the brink of really taking off.

Kate helped him clear the remainder of the napkins and cups, flicked off the lights on their way out. Outside, the April day beckoned. Sunlight skated over the lineup of buildings, brick and pastel—the *News* office, the coffee shop, the bridal store. Across the street, the river rested still and blue.

And down the block was the person he'd managed to avoid ever since that morning in the lawyer's office. Jenessa Belville carried a paper bag in each arm, clipped stride accented by her heels.

The second she saw him, she grimaced, her glare like Barbara Stanwyck's in that one film noir flick Mom loved. The one where Stanwyck plotted to kill her husband. Jenessa looked away, crossed the street, made for the riverfront walkway.

"Not my biggest fan."

Kate gave a *hmm* and a shake of her head. "Her dad's awfully sick. Her mom's an alcoholic. Her husband's only home a few months of the year."

He turned to his sister. "I didn't realize about her mom."

"One of those things everybody in town knows but nobody talks about. She's got a lot on her shoulders, though."

A clatter sounded across the street, and they both turned to see Jenessa bending, broken grocery bag and items scattering over the sidewalk.

Kate started forward, but he stopped her. "I'll go."

He jogged across the street, but by the time he'd reached Jenessa, she'd already re-piled almost all the groceries in her ripped bag. He knelt anyway, rescued a rolling can of soup.

"I don't need your help."

Surely not even Barbara Stanwyck could've pulled off the spite bulleting from Jenessa's expression. Black hair in waves and milky white skin marred by the faintest red marks on her cheeks. Had she been crying?

"Jen, that bag isn't going to hold."

He tried to reach for it as they straightened, but she jerked it away, ignoring the bag of spaghetti that toppled out. "Leave me alone, Logan."

"I'm just trying—"

"What don't you understand here? I don't want your help. I don't need your help. Go away."

She whipped around, the too-sweet scent of her perfume jarring against the malice lingering in her wake. And something else.

Hurt. He'd seen it in the tear streaks on her face. The sag in her voice not even her anger could hide.

"I could give you a ride," he called after her.

She didn't even acknowledge him. Just kept walking.

He bent to pick up the spaghetti. Carried it back across the street and dropped into his car with a sigh. This week felt like such a mess. Broken equipment at the paper. Charlie getting hurt. Jenessa. And of course, Theo's never-ending slew of check-in emails. It was as if he was convinced Logan wasn't coming back.

He leaned his head against the headrest. Wished for a redo on this morning. Maybe this whole week. *Except for last night.* The open mic night. Amelia.

But no, last night, too. Because it might've been fun, but was it really worth the unsettling eddy swirling in his stomach now?

Why does every move I make lately feel like the wrong one? I thought coming home was the right thing, God, but now . . .

Now he was sitting in his car half-praying to a God he'd pretty much ignored for years. Why, he didn't even know.

All he did know was he'd come home to sell a newspaper and spend time with his daughter. And he wasn't making progress on either.

The disquiet stayed with him, a second passenger in the car, as he drove to Rick and Helen's. The neighborhood thinned out as he reached the border of town. His in-laws lived on the last stretch of street before the city limits gave way to sweeping fields. He parked in their driveway.

Put it all away for now. The newspaper, the fundraiser, Jenessa. Amelia.

And focus on Charlie. Just for today, just for now, just be a dad.

He turned off the car.

But he hadn't even climbed out before Rick emerged from the backyard. His father-in-law waited beside the car as Logan unfolded from the driver's seat. "Hey, Rick."

"You're here earlier than planned."

"I seem to remember getting the opposite charge back when Emma and I were dating." He said the words with intentional lightness, hoping the memory might erase some of yesterday's rigidity.

Rick offered a slight smile. "Yes, though you only missed curfew once, I'll hand you that. Listen, I'm wondering if you'd mind if we kept Charlie the rest of the weekend."

An instant *no* jetted up his throat, but he clamped his lips around the instinctive response. "I was hoping to spend time with her this afternoon."

"She's had such a good time the past day. You wouldn't even know she fell out of a tree yesterday."

There it was again, that undercurrent of accusation. "She didn't fall—"

Rick waved off the argument. "I'm just saying, I think it's been good for her, this past twenty-four hours. And we've enjoyed it. We hardly ever have the chance to be grandparents in person." He stepped closer. "You went to Boston at Christmas instead of coming home. We barely saw her when you were here in February."

Why did he get the feeling he was being railroaded?

"Logan, I haven't seen my wife this happy since Emma died."

The clincher. Everything in him argued. This was supposed to be *his* time with his daughter. But he read the words Rick wasn't saying.

Logan had taken Emma to California.

He'd kept Charlie in California.

Least he could do was let her grandparents spend a weekend with her. His nod was heavy with resignation.

She didn't know why she was here.

Amelia's gaze hooked on the sun-drenched yard that unfolded into a rolling field opposite Case Walker's house. Black soil turned and ready for seed. She breathed in spring and expectation, the scent of freshly mown grass and white cherry blossoms.

"I thought I saw someone out here."

The sound of a screen door tapping shut followed Case's voice. His shadow poured over the porch steps.

"Hey, Mr. Walker. Sorry to camp out on your steps." She laced her fingers over her knees.

"I seem to recall telling you to call me Case." He lowered beside her. "Probably about three hundred times."

"Sorry." It was something about the man. He gave off a regal vibe. Somehow commanding and mild all at once.

"You apologize a lot, you know that?"

"Sor—" She caught herself with her first grin since this morning. Since walking out on Eleanor.

"So which of my kids are you waiting for? Few weeks ago I would've guessed Rae, but lately you and Logan are together more than you and Rae."

True. So true, in fact, she'd gotten used to seeing him on a daily basis. Maybe, probably, that's why she'd come here, a mix of whim and desire. She'd never made a friend this quickly, not one who managed to draw out her secrets.

Well, not all her secrets.

"Waiting for Logan. Although he'll laugh at me when he finds out why."

"Good." Case drawled the word, the creases bracketing his smile deepening at her raised eyebrows. "He doesn't laugh enough, my son. So you go ahead and say whatever you came to say and make him laugh."

And there was Logan's car now, plodding around a curve, tires kicking up gravel and dust. "Even if it's crazy?"

"Especially if it's crazy." Case stood. "Besides, half the time crazy is just another word for bold. Or grand. Or adventurous. All of which I generally support." He patted her shoulder as Logan's car came to a stop underneath the basketball hoop in the driveway. "And Amelia?"

She tipped her head.

"Don't forget to laugh yourself."

How was it possible, in one little sentence, one look, to feel as if Case Walker saw all the way inside her? It was as if he'd overheard her argument with Eleanor this morning or, even more, knew the floating fragments of her story she'd never allowed to bob to the surface.

He waved at his son, then slipped inside the house.

And Logan's gaze connected with hers from behind his windshield.

No wonder Logan was such a good listener, with a dad like Case. No wonder this was the place she'd ended up today, when the past she'd worked so hard to confine inside a vault blasted its way into her present.

Logan walked toward her now, sleeves of his plaid shirt rolled to his elbows. He stopped in front of her. "Hey."

"Hey." She rose, wedged her hands into her back pockets, felt the wind working tangles into her hair.

"Where's Charlie?"

"How's Eleanor?"

Their questions collided as she took in the faint circles under his eyes. Had he had as restless a night as she had, folded onto the couch while El slept a floor above? "I'm just going to say it. You look as ragged as I feel."

"Yeah?" He rubbed one hand over his unshaven jaw.

"Which makes why I'm here all the nuttier."

"I'm getting used to your brand of nutty, Amelia Bentley. What's up?"

"I found Marney Billingsley, Kendall's old nurse." She took a breath. "Want to go to South Dakota with me?"

8

I can't believe we're really doing this."

Stars glittered in clusters across the stretch of sky, like sequins on a satiny black dress. Shadowed fields reached to the north and south on either side of the highway, the lights of Logan's Ford casting the only color out the front windshield. In the rearview mirror, the lights of Maple Valley paled with every mile.

If the GPS on her phone was right, they'd reach the roadside lodge where Marney Billingsley apparently lived and worked by the time sunshine bathed the Black Hills.

"We're really doing it." Logan sipped from the travel mug she'd handed him when he'd come to pick her up. Midnight. Not a minute late. Because that was Logan. "You know, this tea isn't that bad."

"Told ya. Enough caffeine to keep you alert for a few hours. Not so much it'll keep you from getting some shut-eye later when it's my turn to drive."

"Speaking of which, Super Sleuth, you're supposed to be trying to sleep now."

"Can't. I'm too excited." Did she sound like a five-year-old on the first day of school? Because she felt like one. The dancing thrill of chasing a story—literally—all the way across state lines rollicked through her.

And she was still in shock that Logan had agreed to come.

They'd stood on Case Walker's porch, a breeze brushing dust and a few of last fall's leftover leaves across the steps. The swing in the corner had tapped against the side of the house while she'd explained how she'd spent the afternoon using the Internet to track down Kendall Wilkins's old nurse. Found her in South Dakota.

"I tried calling the lodge's number, but I keep getting voicemail. I sent an email. But I just . . . don't want to wait."

Because she needed this.

She couldn't deal with Eleanor. Didn't know how things would turn out with the paper. Felt a pit in her stomach at the thought of her meeting at the bank next week.

But this one thing—this story and its latest lead—was a clear bull's-eye amid a blur of moving targets.

Logan had thought about her request for seconds that stretched and rolled like the afternoon's pallid clouds. And then, a simple nod and two words. *"I'm in."*

They'd decided to drive through the night. Had agreed to go home and take naps, with the goal of hitting the Black Hills by morning.

"Then we can Woodward and Bernstein it up for a few hours and head home by afternoon." Exhilaration had trailed into Logan's voice, steady and building, until she was convinced he needed this impulsive road trip as much as she did.

She glanced at him now. For once, no sign of a tie or suit jacket. Only a dark-colored Henley and worn jeans. Instead of his usual tempered hair, it looked like he hadn't bothered with it after his nap. Still with the unshaven cheeks and jaw.

And glasses in place of his usual contacts.

He wasn't a bad-looking man any day, but tonight . . . well, he looked good, that's all. If *good* meant a hundred kinds of attractive. The glasses only added to the appeal.

An instant fog of warmth enveloped her, and she unzipped her hoodie, struggled to pull her arms free.

Logan set his travel mug in the cup holder, then leaned over to help her out of the hoodie. "Too hot?" He knocked the heat down a notch.

The faint scent of his cologne lingered even when he straightened. Something spicy, masculine. *Enticing.*

"You okay, Amelia? You've got a funny look on your face."

"I'm fine."

"What'd your sister say about our road trip?"

The silhouette of a line of silos rose on one side the road. "Didn't get a chance to talk to her."

Because when she'd finally returned to the house, Eleanor hadn't been anywhere around. Her car, her suitcase, gone. Only the echoes of their argument loafing in the empty space.

Hurled words had accomplished nothing other than to dredge even deeper the cavern that'd separated them all these years.

"I left a note for her." She'd stuck it behind an *I <3 Iowa* magnet on the fridge, certain Eleanor would never see it. She'd probably already left for Des Moines. "How about your dad?"

"He said something about you taking his definition of crazy to heart."

She grinned at that. What was it he'd said? *"Half the time, crazy is just another word for bold. Or grand. Or adventurous."*

"And your in-laws have Charlie for the weekend?"

Impossible to miss his frown, fleeting as it was. And the apprehension in his single-word answer. "Yes."

She shifted underneath the hold of her seatbelt, pulled her feet up to the edge of her seat, knees nearly knocking against her chin. "She's adorable, by the way."

"She's the best thing in my life."

His eyes were on the road when he spoke, but clearly his mind was elsewhere. Back in Maple Valley with little Charlie, or even farther in the rearview mirror of his life? Back to when his wife would've been the one seated next to him?

"Logan?"

One hand slid down the steering wheel. "Yeah?"

"What was she like? Emma."

His quiet pause dawdled so long, only the puff of the heater filling the silence, she thought maybe he wasn't going to answer. But then he nudged his glasses up and spoke. "She was incredible. Beautiful. So ridiculously talented. And intelligent. She actually turned down Yale. They offered her a free ride, and she said no."

"What made her do that?"

One hand slipped lower on the wheel. "Me. I didn't ask her to, told her we could long-distance it. But she insisted. Not sure her parents have ever forgiven me for that, really."

"She must've loved you."

"Guess so."

Amelia knew the pull of first love, remembered the lengths a heart could go to just to hold on to it. She'd given up a scholarship, hadn't she? Would've followed Jeremy anywhere. And did until he'd decided love and loyalty weren't enough.

When she hadn't been able to give him what he wanted, he'd lost patience.

And she lost him.

"Thing about Emma was, she was with me . . . in everything. Even when she wasn't so sure—when I reconnected with Theo and he talked me into moving out to California to work on a campaign—she had this sort of 'take one for the team' mindset and jumped in. And then later . . ." Distance crawled into his expression. "I remember holding Charlie for the first time, looking at this little bundle in my arms and thinking, 'What have I gotten into?' A second later, I look up, and Emma's watching me, and she says, 'You're going to rock this fatherhood thing.' And instantly what felt for a second like the scariest moment of my life became the happiest. She grounded me."

Amelia couldn't look away from Logan as he spoke. She saw the tick in his jaw. The glaze in his eyes he tried to blink away. Felt her heart twist and her own emotions well.

And for moments that spread in a hushed stillness, he wasn't Logan Walker the award-winning writer she'd idolized or the owner who might sell the paper out from under her or even the newfound friend caught in her web of story-hunting.

He was just a man who'd lost something precious.

And who was doing everything he could to hang on to what he had left.

Understanding unfolded inside her, leaving her strangely breathless.

And she couldn't help it. She leaned over the console separating their seats, laid her hand on his arm. The curve of his muscle ticked at her touch.

He looked over, moisture gone from his eyes but something heart-tugging still resting there. "I . . . I hate the thought of you going through that."

He'd said something similar to her last night, hadn't he? Was that really just last night? When she'd told him about the divorce?

Logan opened his mouth, closed it. Looked from her hand back to the road.

Had she said too much? Steered the conversation places he hadn't wanted to go?

She let her hand drop.

But before she could fully lean back to her own side of the car, he let go of the wheel with his right hand and reached down to grasp hers. He squeezed and then released it, words he didn't need to say captured in the gesture.

"You should get some sleep, Bentley. It's going to be your turn to drive in a few hours."

The heater's rasp and something new, a bond so real she could almost hear its whisper, curled in the space between them. Her lungs tightened.

"Here." Logan shrugged out of his vest and held it out to her. "You can use it as a pillow."

She bunched his vest into a ball and leaned it against the window. It smelled like Logan, the scent encasing her as she laid her head against it. She closed her eyes, heard a rustle of movement, and felt Logan lifting her hoodie over her, spreading it over her shoulders like a blanket.

"Sweet dreams, Hildy."

Sleep held tight as sunlight tried its best to lull Logan into consciousness—sunlight and someone tugging on his arm, pulling him from a dream in which he and Charlie were back in LA, sitting at the breakfast bar inside his apartment.

Only it hadn't been Emma flipping pancakes over the stove.

"Logan, wake up."

He opened his eyes one at a time, the flood of morning light as jarring as the memory of the face in his dream. Hazel eyes, freckles . . .

"Hey, sleepyhead, you're finally awake." Too much perk lilted in Amelia's voice.

"Barely." He croaked the word, uncoiling from his position in the passenger's seat. Muscles groaned at the movement as his brain pilfered through scraps of recollection to piece together the past twenty-four hours.

That meeting. Jenessa. A few hours at Rick and Helen's house with Charlie before reluctantly agreeing to let them keep her until Monday morning.

And then he and Amelia taking off at midnight, sights set on the Black Hills of South Dakota and a story he still wasn't convinced was a story.

What had he been thinking? What if Charlie got tired of being at her grandparents'? What if this trip was one more notch against him in Rick and Helen's view?

And why weren't they moving now?

"I almost woke you up three hours ago to see the sunrise," Amelia said now. "It was like a watercolor painting, all these pastel smudges, and I kept thinking I should wake you up to see it, but you needed your sleep, and then I started wishing we had time to stop by Mount Rushmore because I've never been . . ." She stopped. "I'm talking too much. Jeremy used to hate it when I talked too much in the morning. He said—"

She cut off so swiftly it was enough to shatter the last of Logan's fatigue. He straightened in his seat, the vest they'd both used as a pillow dropping to his lap. "He said . . . ?"

"Never mind. How'd you sleep?"

Surprisingly well. There'd been something about last night—moonlit fields and the low drone of talk radio, Amelia's soft breathing. He'd agreed to wake her at four-thirty but had instead waited until almost a quarter past five. She'd looked so comfortable, face mashed into his vest and legs curled up to her chin. He'd hated rousing her.

When he'd finally taken his turn in the passenger's seat, he'd expected to have trouble falling asleep. But the warmth from the heater, the rhythm of wheels on pavement, the lingering scent of vanilla on his vest . . .

He'd drifted off in no time.

"Why are we stopped?" He looked out the window, car pulled

onto the shoulder, an orange sun brushing tawny strokes over black fields. And in the distance, shadowed ridges—the Black Hills. They were close.

"Well, that's why I woke you." Chagrin stilted her words. "We're out of gas. We passed a station a while ago, but I thought stopping would wake you up, and we seemed so close, I thought we could make it."

"You're kidding." He leaned over, elbows propped on his knees, fingers rubbing his forehead.

"I never kid when stranded in a different state with a man in the car who may or may not handle this kind of situation well. I know your writing style, Walker, but not your emergency-situation style. Not that this is much of an emergency. My GPS says we're less than a mile from the turnoff for the Glorietta. That's the name of the lodge."

He lifted his head. "You really do talk a lot in the morning." More amused observance than accusation, but what he wouldn't give for a mug of Dad's swampy coffee right now. Most the time he had to add water to get it down, but today he'd have gulped it as is just to keep up with Amelia. "You said we're only a mile away?"

"Right, so . . . we walk?"

He nodded.

They got out of the car, the morning breeze brushing cool air over Logan's cheeks. He pulled on his puff vest, zipped it up, and burrowed his chin inside. He looked across the car's hood at Amelia. "Where's your coat?"

"Didn't bring one. It was so warm in Iowa yesterday."

South Dakota wasn't exactly a frozen tundra at the moment, but she needed more than that flimsy hoodie. "Pop the trunk. I've probably got something in there you can wear."

He rounded the car and found a fleece jacket as she came up beside him. "Here you go. You'll drown in it, but it'll keep you warm." He helped her into it, reached for the zipper, and pulled it up to her chin before realizing what he was doing. "Sorry. Habit. Charlie."

Except standing this close to her, the wind blowing her hair in his face, well, those weren't exactly paternal feelings pooling inside him. He stepped back, but she only stared, a hint of a grin tugging at her lips.

"What?"

"Just thinking about what a good Boy Scout you must've been. Look at this trunk. Emergency kit. Blanket. Jug of water. Tool box. Extra jacket." The sleeves of his jacket flopped over her wrists as she spoke. "It's like whoever came up with the 'Be Prepared' motto was picturing you."

"I can't tell whether you're mocking or complimenting me."

"Good. I like retaining a hint of mystery about me."

"That's very Lauren Bacall of you."

"Now *that* is a compliment."

He closed the trunk. "But don't think for a second I need you teaching me to whistle."

Her nose wrinkled at the comment, and he could almost see the cogs in her brain turning. "Reference?"

"You'll figure it out. But I'll give you a clue: Humphrey Bogart was in it, too." He pulled the keys from her hand, locked the door, and started walking.

She hurried to catch up. "That's not a clue. They were in, like, twenty movies together."

"They were in three movies together."

"Showoff."

They walked in silence for a few minutes, accompanied by only the sound of their shoes on gravel and the swish of grass. In the distance, a bird's *caa* pealed through the air. If they had to finish the trek to their destination by foot, this wasn't such a bad day to do it. Cold, maybe, but the fresh air filled Logan's lungs with something fresh and energizing.

He pushed up his glasses with one finger. Was he smiling? He felt like he was smiling.

"Oh, I almost forgot." Amelia reached into the bag slung over her shoulder and pulled out a silver package. "Pop-Tart? I saved you one."

"I haven't had a Pop-Tart in fifteen years." A gravel turnoff came into view only yards ahead.

"Well, you're missing out."

He took a bite. Admittedly, not the worst thing he'd ever eaten. "Clearly you've never experienced a Walker breakfast. We do it right. Everyone in the family has a specialty."

"What's yours?"

"Omelets. Not going to lie, they're amazing."

"What do you do? Stuff them with kale and tofu?"

"Joke all you want, but I'll make you one someday, and you'll eat your own words, somewhat literally, and—"

He broke off at her sudden stare—past him, down the lane they'd reached.

He followed her gaze to see what had to be the Glorietta. The lodge was carved into the side of a hill, two stories that jutted out from a tree-lined ridge. And it was . . . bright.

Teal siding encased the rectangular structure. Dirt-caked windows were framed by peeling pink shutters. "Holy 1980s comeback."

More details came into view as they approached. The dilapidated balcony poking out from the north end. A lone car in the parking lot. An unfilled outdoor swimming pool hardly larger than a bathtub.

It only got worse inside. Mustard-yellow shag carpet and brown walls, the scent of potpourri both overwhelming and yet not enough to cover the lingering smell of cigarette smoke.

"And we've gone back another decade." He whispered the words—not that he needed to. The woman with peroxide-blond hair behind the check-in desk had earbuds in both ears, magazine open in front of her.

"Who leaves Maple Valley to work in a place like this? And why go from nursing to . . . whatever she does here?"

"Didn't you say her family owned it? People have made bigger career and geographic moves for family." Look what his dad had done for Mom. When she got sick, he'd given up an office at the U.N. building and moved their family of six back to small-town Iowa. "Anyway, we've got a source to find and another nine-hour drive back home, so let's do this, Nancy Drew."

She rolled her eyes at the nickname but approached the desk. When the receptionist didn't acknowledge them, Amelia tapped the Ring for Service bell.

The woman's head jerked up, mouth dropping open and bubble gum landing on her open magazine. She pulled out her earbuds, then unpeeled her gum and stuck it back in her mouth. "I didn't hear y'all come in. Need a room?"

"No, actually, we're looking for Marney Billingsley. We understand she works here?"

Amelia's tone was pure business. Did she have any idea how comical she looked, trying to play serious reporter with her hair windblown and static-y from his fleece jacket hanging past her waist?

"That's my sister. But she's not on shift now."

"Any chance we could talk to her?"

The woman blew a bubble with her gum. "I don't know who you are. I'm not inclined to go looking all over the place for her on account of a couple strangers."

"Maybe you could call—"

"This is the boonies, honey. Cell phone reception is still five years away."

"LillyAnn, is it?" Logan interrupted, clued in by her nametag. "That's a pretty name."

She stopped chewing her gum and closed her magazine. "Thanks."

"Look, I know it's probably annoying—us showing up and asking for a favor. But we drove nine hours to get here just to talk to your sister. If there's any way you could help us out, I'd be so far beyond grateful, you wouldn't even believe it."

LillyAnn hopped off her stool. "Okay, then. I'll see if I can find her."

She disappeared from the desk.

"Flattery? Really?" Amelia flatlined the words.

"Got results, didn't it?" He gave her his best self-satisfied grin.

"Is that how you win elections, too? Bat your perfect eyelashes at female voters, sweet talk 'em into voting for your candidate?"

"You like my eyelashes?"

"It's not even that great of a name. LillyAnn." She jerked the zipper of his fleece. "Like someone couldn't make up their mind which name to give a baby so they just smooshed two together, and—" She broke off.

"What?"

"*To Have and Have Not.* That's the movie you were referencing. Where Lauren Bacall tells Humphrey Bogart how to whistle—that iconic line. Can't believe it took me this long."

"Maybe you were too distracted by my eyelashes to think of it."

Man, he liked it when she attempted to glare at him. And completely failed.

"Here she is." LillyAnn ambled behind the desk, an older woman trailing behind her. Oh yes, he recognized Marney Billingsley. She'd been a nurse at the clinic when he was a kid. Unlike her sister, she hadn't tried to hide the gray of her hair, nor the lines on her face. Her pink cardigan ended at her elbows, purple-ish veins extending down her wrists.

"How can I help you?"

"Hi, Marney? I'm Amelia, and this is Logan, and we're here to talk to you about Kendall Wilkins." Excited energy fueled Amelia's hurried words.

Confusion tinted Marney's expression. "Kendall Wilkins? From Iowa?"

"I know it's going to sound crazy, but we're following up on that safe-deposit-box mystery, and I thought you might be helpful."

"You came all the way from Maple Valley?"

Amelia's nod was eager.

But Marney only sighed. "Then I'm afraid you've come all this way for nothing."

※

"Wow." A single word released in a whispered gasp. Amelia couldn't stop staring.

A lazy sun crouched behind the ridges of Mount Rushmore, craggy orange light rimming the etched faces and reaching into the sky in a blaze of sizzling color. She stood beside Logan on an outlook that gave a panoramic view of the full landmark.

"I can't believe we're here." Wind and dust had caked her hair into stringy waves, and fatigue pulled at her limbs. But wonder awakened her senses. A husky breeze marked trails over her cheeks even as Logan stepped closer, his warmth and shadow like insulation against a day that'd ushered in a returning cool.

"We had to do something to cheer you up after that interview."

The interview, he meant, that shed little light on Kendall Wilkins's life or death or that empty bank box. Marney had the same impression of the man as everyone else did: prickly, aloof. And not above taking a shot at the town on his way out.

"Sorry we don't have time to do a full tour or eat in that cafe."

"Logan, you agreed to an eighteen-hour round-trip drive. Humored my wild goose chase. Sat through a pointless interview. Brought me to Mount Rushmore. And you're apologizing?"

He blinked against a piney breeze, one that billowed through the oversized jacket she'd worn nearly all day. They started walking again. "But it wasn't entirely pointless. You found out Kendall Wilkins belonged to some society or other. What did she call it?"

"The Elm Society."

"Right. You learned he did have at least one long-time friend. Harry Somebody-or-other."

"Wheeler."

"And you learned he was buried with an aviator's helmet from his childhood."

Yes, that'd been the one part of the interview during which she'd felt like she'd gotten at least a glimpse into the man she'd thought she'd known.

"So you didn't have any clue what was in that box? What it might've had to do with Lindbergh?"

"We weren't close. I took care of him. Drove him around. Ran his errands. But he didn't talk to me. He didn't really talk to anyone. Do you know the only true time I felt in any way a significant part of his life is after he died, when I helped . . . prepare him?"

Marney had shaken her head. *"He truly didn't have a single family member, so it fell to me to follow the instructions he left. He wanted to wear a particular suit, so I had to search around. When I went looking, this old aviator helmet came tumbling out of his closet. From his childhood, I'm sure. He used to talk about watching barnstormers, you know. It was the one personal touch I felt like I could give him, including it in his coffin. But other than that . . ."*

"It just doesn't match up."

Logan's arm brushed against hers as he led the way around a curve. "What doesn't?"

"The man Marney describes. The man everyone else in Maple Valley knew. Or didn't know. I don't see how he can be the same man who wrote me all those letters when I was in college. He was funny and personable and wise." A little laugh escaped. "He even had this love for anagrams. You know, where you take a word or phrase and change the letters around to see what other words and phrases you can come up with?"

The sun was barely a shaving now, wedged behind rock.

"I wish somebody else could've seen that side of him."

Logan's gaze dipped, and his steps slowed. "Maybe somebody did. Maybe that Harry Wheeler guy. Or maybe it's enough that you did. For some reason, he connected with you. It's kind of cool if you think about it—you sorta filling a place in his life no one else did."

Yes, but look what she'd gone and done with that cool thing. Drifted away. Got so caught up in her romance with Jeremy that she'd slowly stopped responding to Kendall's letters. Hadn't even finished the education he'd paid for.

She'd let him down.

And by the time she'd thought to go to Maple Valley, find the man, both thank him and apologize, it was too late.

A sigh trundled through her, but she cut it off. She could think about this later, back home. This moment should be for awe and remembering and . . .

She looked at Logan again.

Gratefulness.

Truthfully, it wasn't even the splendor of Mount Rushmore that impacted her most—but the fact that Logan had remembered what she'd said this morning about never having been here.

While she'd been rambling, he'd been listening.

"Want to know something? I haven't been to the Grand Canyon, either."

"Angling for another road trip next weekend?" The scarlet sunset turned his skin tawny and his eyes golden.

"I traveled all the time in my other life. But not lately."

"Your other life? Actually, yeah, Rae mentioned something about how you used to be in marketing?" He paused in the middle of the trail, turning away from the landmark to face her. "I meant to ask you about it."

Normally she'd skirt the question. She hadn't even listed the job on her résumé when she'd gone looking for new employment after the divorce.

But now? Under the glow of dusk, in the middle of a path cut into a ridge, only strangers, rock, and soil for company, something inside her loosened. Maybe because he'd told her about Emma last night. Or carted her across state lines. Or brought her here to see a sight that had taken her breath away.

Whatever the reason, her reserve felt as thin as spring's hold.

She stepped off the path, Logan following, and paused near a wilty evergreen, its branches bowing in the wind. "I was the marketing manager for Jeremy Lucas. Early on in his career."

"Why does that name sound . . . wait. *The* Jeremy Lucas? The one with all the books and the radio show?"

"That's the one. I didn't just work for him, actually. We were married."

He tried to hide his shock, she could tell. But didn't quite manage to. "Jeremy Lucas is your ex-husband. The 'Live the life you've always dreamed' guy."

Oh, how she hated that tagline. "Yeah, but the life he dreamed included kids. Which I couldn't give him, at least not after seven years of trying. So he . . . decided he wanted to end things."

She shrugged as if this were a room in her life she invited

anyone into, rather than a cordoned-off chamber of secrets. And she waited—waited for the questions he had to be mentally asking. Why couldn't she give him children? What about adoption? Had she argued—fought the divorce?

But instead he only looked at her as if she were one of those presidents' heads on the mountain, worthy of unhurried scrutiny. And then he took a step toward her. He pulled her into a hug, arms reaching all the way around her and her head landing against his chest.

"Clearly the guy is an idiot and doesn't deserve you." He spoke the words over her head.

"Thank you." Her heart stumbled over the effect of his comforting hold.

"And I've seen the photo on his book jacket. Fake tan and teeth way too white to be real."

"Thank you again."

"And I bet he wears too much cologne."

She tipped her head up. "It's true. Honestly, sometimes getting in his car was like walking into a teenage boy's bedroom."

Laughter rumbled from Logan's chest until he stilled, breathing steady and rhythmic and . . .

She closed her eyes against the cotton of his shirt. And it suddenly wasn't all she'd lost churning through her in disarray. But what she had right now. A friend. One who'd glimpsed more of her heart in a couple days than . . . honestly, than anyone she could think of.

There was something sheltering and so very wonderful about this man.

It scared her.

It thrilled her.

"Amelia—"

But his phone stole whatever he was going to say next. He pulled away, the last sliver of sun now hidden. "It's Helen. I'd better take it." He lifted his phone to his ear. "Hi, Helen. How's Charlie?"

She tried to snub the rise of desire—to know what he'd planned to say, to go on with this side trip uninterrupted. But how did a person disregard what felt like cool water for a soul she hadn't even realized was thirsty?

One look, though, at Logan's face as he listened to whatever his mother-in-law was saying pulled her out of her daze. And seconds later, he'd pocketed his phone and sprung into action.

"We have to leave. Charlie's sick. Spiking fever and coughing."

The worried look on his face pelted her heart, and she started for the trail.

"They wanted to know if she'd had a flu shot." He froze. "I couldn't remember. What kind of dad can't remember . . . ?"

Amelia gripped both his arms. "Logan, it's probably nothing more than a little cold." She rubbed her hands down his arms. "It's going to be fine. And I'm going to drive. I just need the keys."

9

Logan hit *Ignore* on his cell phone for the third time today. He didn't have time for office catch-up with Theo. Not when Charlie was three days into the flu.

He leaned his head against his bed's headboard, Charlie snuggled against his torso, and his legs outstretched in from of him, sheets tangled.

A cartoon character blathered on the computer screen propped on his old desk. The one that still displayed framed photos from his high-school years, a bending lamp, a speech trophy. He'd kept Charlie in here while she was sick instead of Beckett's room, served her chicken noodle soup in bed, and kept her sippy cup filled with 7-Up.

He laced his fingers through his daughter's curls, now sweat-dampened and flat. Almost twelve hours since the last time she'd thrown up.

Most days it amazed him how quickly she was growing—scared him, too. But this week, she'd seemed tiny. His little girl, wracked by a bullying flu.

His phone dinged. Another voicemail. He closed his eyes.

"Son?"

At the sound of Dad's voice, Logan opened his eyes and lifted his head. His father stood in the doorway. "How's she doing?" Dad entered the room and pulled the chair from Logan's desk. He sat backward in it, legs straddling either side, and then leaned over the back.

Logan palmed Charlie's forehead. No fever. "I'm hoping the worst is behind her."

"I can't tell you how much I've loved having her around. Reminds me of when you kids were little."

Logan's arm was asleep behind Charlie, muscles numb. He toed away the navy blue comforter. "You ever start to feel like you're running a hotel here? Rae and Seth and then Kate and now Charlie and me?"

Dad fingered the gold ring he still wore on his left hand. "I'd rather have a full house any day than swim in empty rooms."

Logan looked to the largest of the framed photos on his desk. A photo of him and Mom in Washington, D.C. She'd taken each sibling on a trip on their thirteenth birthday—he'd picked D.C. The picture beside that one showed him and Beckett on Logan's graduation day. "Think you'll ever get Beck back here?" Nearly six years and counting since his little brother had returned to Maple Valley. Not for the first time—and certainly not for the last—concern for Beckett needled him.

"That lawyer thing keeps him busy." The smile dissolved from Dad's face. "If there's one thing I've learned after having four kids, it's each of you has your own timing." He let out a long exhale. "Beckett will come home when he's ready."

Logan glanced at his sleeping daughter. "That's what I keep trying to tell myself about Charlie. She'll talk when she's ready."

"Can I ask something, son? Do you pray about it? About Charlie talking?"

If anyone else had asked this, Logan might wave off the question with an easy "sure." Because, yeah, now and then in fits of frustration he rattled off quickie prayers. Ones with less thought behind them than the simple press releases he could whip out in his sleep.

But he couldn't fool Dad. His inner turmoil was like old glass to Dad—transparent, cracks visible. "Not really."

He smoothed Charlie's hair, felt the sting of hollow whispers. How could he not pray for his daughter? He loved her more than anything in the world. He should be on his knees every day, begging God to keep her safe and healthy, to fill in the gaps created by Emma's loss, to right anything Logan might be doing wrong.

To help her talk.

But what was the use in praying when he wasn't sure anyone was listening?

He waited for Dad to say something, anything, in that firm but gentle way he had—to scold him or challenge him or . . . something.

But when silence lingered, Logan spoke again. "After Emma died, I . . . I tried to cling to faith. The way you're supposed to. I pretended I knew what people were talking about when they'd go on about 'peace that passes all understanding.' But I didn't feel peace, Dad. I didn't feel anything. And so I prayed about that, too. Prayed God would let me sense him or feel or hear him. I wasn't asking for a burning bush or an audible voice. Just something to convince me he was there, that he heard me. And . . . nothing."

The numbness in his arm spread. "And all I could think was, if I can't trust God to meet me in my deepest pain, how can I trust him at all?"

He'd never given his doubts such an open stage. Maybe because he worried if he gave them a voice, they might finally drown out the last fragments of his faith. The piece of him still clinging to the beliefs he'd grown up with.

That there was a God who cared.

That he wasn't alone.

I'm still holding on. I don't know why, but I'm still here. Barely.

Dad pulled his arms away from his chair's back, lowered his hands to his knees, and breathed deep. "Thank you."

Logan lifted his head. "For what?"

"For telling me the truth. It is a privilege to be your father, Logan, and to be entrusted with what's going on in your life and in your faith."

"Even if my faith has been reduced to crumbs lately?"

"Even if."

"That's it? You're not going to try to steer me back to the straight and narrow? Give me a magic Bible verse so I'll stop feeling the way I feel?" He hated the derision in his tone. It smacked of immaturity, and probably simple exhaustion. Three days of jetting back and forth between the office and home. Pretending to be mentally present at another meeting for Colton's fundraiser. Waking up every couple hours at night when Charlie moaned.

But Dad didn't even flinch. "You're thirty-four, Logan. You don't need a sermon, and you definitely don't need me telling you how to feel."

"I wish I knew what I needed." At least back in LA, he'd been busy enough to avoid the cavern inside where his faith used to be. Work had made the grief easier, too. It wasn't denial, just a coping mechanism.

But here, even with the newspaper and the constant activity of family and . . . and Amelia . . . avoidance felt impossible.

"When your mother's cancer came back the third time, I'll never forget . . ." Dad picked up the photo on Logan's desk of him and Mom in D.C., a soft smile tugging at the lines in his face. "The oncologist gave us a few minutes in his office alone after he gave his prognosis. And I slipped back into my soldier days for a moment because I looked at your mother and said, 'We aren't going to lose hope, Flora. We aren't going to despair. We're going to fight this together and win.'"

Dad set down the photo. "And she looked back at me, straight in the eye, and said, 'Liar.'"

Logan gave a mangled laugh, and Charlie stirred at his movement.

"She shook her head. 'We are too going to lose hope,' she said. 'We're going to despair. We're going to feel things this time around like we've never felt before.'"

He stroked Charlie's hair. "She was blunt." And the best mom. Just . . . the best.

Dad's eyes turned glassy. "She said, 'We might even break. Because we're humans and we're allowed. And because . . .'" Dad's voice cracked, and he rubbed a tear from his cheek. "'And because I'm dying.'"

She *had* known. Maybe they all had. And they'd all dealt with it in different ways. Kate had written a book. Logan had proposed to Emma. Beck had run away, and Rae had vowed never to leave.

And Dad . . .

He'd seemed so strong at the time, but look at him now. In the privacy of his own heart, even while taking care of his adult kids however they needed, his soldier father had broken just like Mom had predicted.

"I didn't know it at the time, but Flora was giving me a great gift. Permission to feel. If I couldn't feel grief and despair and anguish, then how would I recognize peace and healing and even joy later on?" Dad cleared his throat, straightened. "She gave me something else that day, too. She reminded me that there'd always be someone hoping for me, when I couldn't hope. And loving me, even when I couldn't see it. And waiting for me, even when I didn't believe it."

Charlie shifted against him, burying her face against his chest.

"He'll wait for you, Logan. Just like you're waiting for Charlie to talk and I'm waiting for Beckett to come home. God will wait for you."

⟢⟋

He'd been quiet for days.

Amelia tapped her pen against her chin, facing away from her desk, an unfinished city council article languishing on her screen behind her. Through the window of Freddie's office, the one Logan had been reluctant to settle into at first, she could see his profile. Stubbled cheeks and hunched shoulders, elbows bent and fingers curving around the back of his head to massage his neck.

He hated Charlie being sick, she knew. Worried about his in-laws' reaction to his spontaneous out-of-state trip. Too, his business partner back in LA kept calling. That presidential candidate seemed to have forgotten them.

Was there more he wasn't saying?

Or was she reading into his exhaustion? Using her concern for Logan to distract her from the fact that Eleanor had retreated from her life as quickly as she'd shown up?

Amelia had made only one feeble attempt to call Eleanor since their argument—sighed in relief when she'd gotten her sister's voicemail.

Maybe they simply weren't meant to share the kind of closeness Logan did with his siblings.

"He's going to sell, you know."

She hinged toward the sound of Owen's voice.

"The stuff he's doing—the ads, the website, everything—it's just so he can get a higher price when he does sell." Owen clicked his mouse, attention on his monitor.

Amelia stood and swept up the pile of last week's area papers cluttering the countertop. "Maybe, but it's only late April. I still have a whole month to convince him."

"Except I don't see you doing much convincing. Road-tripping to South Dakota and pretending you're part of his family, maybe. But that's it."

"Owen."

The bite in her tone was enough to make him turn. "He's humoring you, Amelia. And you're getting attached. But you know Cranford has called at least three or four times since he's been here. Meanwhile, have you even asked Kat and Mikaela how we're doing on ads for the centennial issue? Have you bothered looking at Abby's web banner mockups? You're the one who came up with this plan that basically doubled our workload, but what are you doing to help out?"

He'd risen halfway through his lecture, reached around his computer to turn it off, and grabbed his leather messenger bag from a hook on the wall. Numbing surprise at his hostile words crushed any response.

"What do you think my trip to South Dakota was for, Owen? It was for the cover story for the centennial. I'm not ignoring it." Not that she'd gotten anywhere on it since. She'd Googled the name *Harry Wheeler*, and the results had numbered in the millions. Searching *The Elm Society* hadn't gotten her anywhere, either.

What if this story really wasn't going anywhere? What if Kendall Wilkins really was just a cranky old man?

"All I'm saying is, you'd be a lot smarter focusing on that—or better yet, spending this time polishing your résumé and looking for a new job—instead of flirting with a guy who's already got one foot out the door."

She smacked the papers in her arms back to the desk, grappling for words. "Owen, we've been friends first and coworkers second for a long time now. But you're stepping over a line."

He slung his bag over his shoulder. "If we're really friends, then it's a line worth stepping over." With that, he pushed through the newsroom door, skulking past Mae, who filled the doorframe after he left.

"He's in a hurry." Mae's eyebrows lifted behind her bifocals.

"He's mad at me."

"He's just sore because he likes you. He's jealous."

"He's not—"

Mae cut her off with a droll eye roll. "I may sit in a different part of the office, but I'm not blind, Amelia. Anyway, you've got a call. It's my niece, actually. The one I always tell you about."

Right, the one who worked at *USA Today*. The "real journalist" Mae had brought up again just a few weeks ago.

Mae must have read the direction of Amelia's thoughts now. "Don't worry, she's not calling to recruit you. She's calling about . . ." Oddly, Mae seemed to soften. "Well, anyway, she'll tell you."

Amelia glanced in Logan's office on her way back to her desk. Had he even moved in the past five minutes?

She lowered to her chair and picked up her phone. "This is Amelia."

"Amelia Bentley? Hi, this is Belle Waldorf with *USA Today*, the Chicago office, and I can barely believe I'm making this call. Or, rather, that I'm making it to my aunt's office, of all places." She laughed, a tinkling sound that seemed to fit her name. "I knew your name sounded familiar when I was doing my research, and when I Googled you and realized why, my jaw dropped and my bubblegum fell out of my mouth and—"

She finally paused to take a breath.

Amelia twirled the phone cord around her finger, waiting for the moment when this call might make any kind of sense.

"Anyway, I'll just get to the point. Were you married to Jeremy Lucas?"

The phone cord snapped against her finger. "Excuse me?"

"Actually, I don't really need to ask. I have the information right in front of me. I'm nothing if not a good researcher. But Aunt Mae acted surprised when I told her why I was calling, like she didn't know and—"

"Why *are* you calling?"

Belle laughed again, completely oblivious—of course—to the tension her question had invited into this conversation, so thick it was like a third person on the call. Amelia stared at her computer screen, now asleep.

"I write personality profiles, and my editor has been after me to get an interview with Jeremy Lucas for months. You'd think his publicist or manager or whoever would be better at responding to inquiries from the press."

"He's picky about publicity." It slipped out. Present tense. As if she'd just seen him yesterday and talked about it.

But it'd certainly been the truth years ago. He was so picky that if he couldn't micro-manage the story, he simply said no to the interview request. He had eagle-eye focus, knew exactly the direction he wanted to steer his career.

And nothing—not an uncooperative reporter or a wife who couldn't cordon her hurt—would get in his way.

"I just thought, maybe a personal call from someone he knew might help me nab an interview. So I started looking for any kind of connection, found out he had an ex-wife—"

"Belle—"

"I realize this is probably completely uncomfortable, but seriously, picture an alarm clock that just keeps buzzing no matter how many times you hit snooze. That's my editor nagging me about this story. And anyway, I just couldn't believe it when I realized the Amelia Bentley who used to be married to Jeremy Lucas is the same Amelia Bentley my aunt's always telling me about."

This conversation was giving her a headache. "You mean the Amelia Bentley she's always trying to pawn off on you?"

"Ha! She thinks you're great."

"She thinks I'm a joke."

"That's just Aunt Mae. The more she likes you, the more she grouches at you. It's her love language. Anyhow, if there's anything you can do to help me—make a call or write an email—I'd really appreciate it."

"The thing is, I'm not in touch with Jeremy. It's been almost three years since we divorced." And even if she did call, what were the chances he still had the same number?

Or that he'd even answer?

"I'd do whatever I could to return the favor. *USA Today* has openings all the time, and I've got friends at other papers if you're looking to move—"

"I'm not." She twisted in her chair, wishing for a way to escape this call, the intrusion of her past.

Logan came into view once more—Freddie's tattered old chair, the cubbyhole of an office. *Wait a second.*

"You said you do personality profiles?"

"Yep. It's my bread and butter."

"You ever interview political speech writers?" The question came out of her mouth while the idea was still percolating.

Logan and that partner of his were frustrated because whatever presidential candidate they'd hoped to work for seemed to have forgotten them. Well, could being featured in a national publication get Logan back on the candidate's radar?

In other words, you want to help him leave Maple Valley?

No. But she did want to help him. And after all he'd done for her . . . besides, maybe Owen had a point. Maybe she was getting overly attached.

Distance. That's what you need. Distance and space to get your head on straight.

So she'd meddle in Logan's career not only to help him, but also as a reminder to herself that his life wasn't here.

"There's this guy." She started in, told Belle all about Logan. His work at the paper, his success in California, his ridiculously good writing. "People don't really know what speech writers and political consultants do, you know?"

"Yeah, but do they want to know?" Belle's skepticism traveled through the phone line. "I mean, most people I know were jaded by politics long ago."

"Trust me, I'm one of them." Unfair as it was, life with Jeremy had soured her to most kinds of public-platform individuals. "But Logan's different. He's one of those sincere people who really wants to make a difference. He takes such care with his writing."

"So he's interesting?"

"Oh, he's interesting."

"Is he single?"

She spun back to her desk. "Uh—"

"I'm just saying, the way you said *interesting* makes me think you might have a few synonyms for the word other than Webster's standard definition."

Amelia's feet flattened on the floor. "Would you ever consider doing a story on him?"

"Straight-up avoidance. I like your style." Belle paused. "Look, I can't guarantee it'd make it into the print edition. But it could make it onto the website, and I've got a blog that my editor gives me pretty much free rein with. So I could feature him there."

Oh, she hoped Logan would like this. He was so reticent about ever being in the spotlight. Look at the way he'd reacted that night at The Red Door when Raegan had asked him to sing.

But if it could help his career . . .

"But just so I'm understanding," Belle said, "I do a story on Logan and you get me an interview with your ex-husband?"

Amelia let out a sigh and then turned at the sound of Logan's office door opening. He held his cell phone to his ear, his expression harried. Yes, for him, she could call Jeremy. "I'll do my best, Belle."

They exchanged contact information, and she hung up as quickly as she could. "Everything okay, Logan?"

He dropped his phone into his pocket. "I have to go. Kate was going to watch Charlie tonight for me—I had . . . plans— but apparently Megan's in labor and Kate needs to be there, so I guess—"

Amelia stood. "I can watch Charlie."

"Really?" Relief and reluctance mingled in his expression. "She was pretty sick. There could still be germs—"

"I've got a great immune system. Do whatever you were planning to do tonight. I'll head over to your house right now."

She could kick herself for the way her heart tilted when he smiled at her and when he spoke. "You're the best, Amelia."

The best or just plain crazy. She'd just agreed to call Jeremy solely for Logan's sake. And for the sake of distance.

Her gaze snagged on the gratefulness in his magnetic eyes. Distance. Yeah. Right.

He couldn't believe he'd actually hoped Jenessa would answer the door.

Or that he was even here, really. The brick two-story home where the Belvilles resided, once one of the grander houses in Maple Valley, seemed to sag with age. The cement steps leading to the front door were crumbling, the black metal railing rusty and crooked. The lattice that used to climb one side of the house was a knotty tangle of stripped stems.

He balanced the carefully piled stack of cake pans in his arms and used his elbow to ring the doorbell. A battery of storm clouds gathered overhead, weighty with rain that threatened to fall any minute. Oh, he should've warned Amelia—let her know Charlie hated thunder.

Maybe he shouldn't be here at all.

Too late, though. The door swung open, and Jenessa appeared. Cheeks gaunt and sweater hanging from bony shoulders. "What are you doing here?"

He hardly knew. She'd made it clear twice already that she didn't want to see him. And the glare in her eyes told him the third time wasn't the charm in her case.

Still. He must be a glutton for punishment because he had to at least try. "I brought some meals. I've had some extra time at home because Charlie's had the flu. Raegan and Kate helped and—"

"You think I want flu-contaminated food?"

"Jen." A few pans of lasagna and chicken casseroles shouldn't be so heavy, but the muscles in his arms pinched.

The glower didn't leave her face, but at least she stepped aside, beckoned him in. "I don't know why you felt the need to do this. I'm capable of feeding my family."

The inside of the house was as shabby as the outside. Not dirty, just aged. The faded fabric of the couch had once been a country blue, and the blinds on the windows hung at an awkward angle. He followed Jenessa past a dining room table that looked like she was using it to dry laundry—shirts and jeans hanging over each chair. Didn't she know her wet clothes would leave rings around the wood?

In the kitchen, one of the bulbs was burnt out in the light fixture overhead, and the dishwasher gurgled under the counter. "Fridge or freezer?"

She answered by opening the freezer. Empty save for a few ice-cube trays and a stack of one-person frozen dinners.

He slid the pans in. "Kate wrote the oven temps and times in Sharpie on the tinfoil." So awkward, this whole thing.

"We're not a charity case, Logan."

"I know that. I just . . ." A dish clanked inside the dishwasher. "I just wanted to help somehow. And I don't know—in rural Iowa, help tends to look like food even if you don't need it. I know you're taking care of both parents right now and working full-time and—"

"Jenessa, who's here?"

Logan closed his eyes at the sound of the barking voice. He should've skipped the rambling explanation. Better yet, just handed Jenessa the pans at the door and turned around.

Brigg Belville appeared on the opposite side of the galley kitchen, at the top of a stairway that probably led down to a basement den. Gone was the brawny stature he used to wear like a uniform, though his chest seemed distended—a symptom of his emphysema? The years had paled his skin and whitened what thin hair remained.

But his voice still carried the imperious edge it had back when he was a candidate for governor and Logan a small-town reporter just beginning to develop a taste for politics.

"What. Is. He. Doing. Here?"

The window over the kitchen sink ushered in a sticky breeze, air thick with cloying moisture. "He's just leaving, Dad."

"I don't want him in my house."

Any ire Jenessa had hurled his way the couple times he'd run into her was nothing compared to the malice in Brigg's yellowed eyes. "Brigg—"

He didn't know what he was going to say. Didn't have a chance to say it anyway. Because a fit of coughing wracked through the narrow kitchen—harsh, cringing.

"Dad, let's get you back downstairs."

"You ruined my life, Walker." Brigg forced his words through rasping coughs. "Ruined all our lives. You're just like all the other media people. Dirty, rotten."

The man doubled over with another fit of coughing, and Jenessa hurried to his side, held his arm, and turned him to the open door at the top of the stairway. "Please just go, Logan."

He heard Brigg's coughing holler through the house as he turned, pace nearly a jog to escape the house. But another voice stopped him, this one from the open stairway at one end of the living room.

He turned to see Mrs. Belville, straggles of stick-straight hair and a flimsy nightgown that gaped below her neck. "Who are you?" She slurred the question, the veins in her hand purple where she gripped the banister. A line of framed photographs—buildings and scenery he might've stopped to admire at any other time—tipped and shook as she rocked against the railing.

"Logan Walker, Mrs. Belville. I was just leaving. Sorry if I disturbed you."

"Walker? Why do I know that name?" Each word seemed to tip into the next, her voice tinny and her gaze distant.

Oh, Jenessa.

"Where's my daughter?"

"Uh, she's downstairs. Looking after your husband. He was coughing—"

"Of course. She's always with him. Always the dutiful daughter where he's con . . . concerned." She swayed with the words.

And he had no idea what to do. Help her before she fell?

But then she seemed to right herself, turned as if she'd forgotten he was even there, and climbed back up the stairs.

He just stood there, sick inside, the casseroles he'd stuck in Jenessa's freezer feeling suddenly paltry and pointless. No wonder she'd practically scoffed. His gaze returned to the photos hanging along the stairway wall. They seemed almost too bright, too alive for this house.

"Logan?"

Jenessa walked into the living room.

"Sorry, I was just leaving. Your mom—"

"I heard." She brushed past him, and instead of marching to the front door to hurry him out, she lowered—slowly, tiredly—onto the worn couch. "Now you've seen it all. How the Belvilles have fallen."

"Don't say . . . you haven't . . ." He felt like a tree or something, planted in the wrong place but rooted to the floor. "You shouldn't have to deal with this alone. Does your husband know how bad it is? He should—"

A scathing laugh ripped through his words. "He's not my husband."

"What?"

"We aren't married. Never were." She flicked her wrist as if the revelation was as trivial as the weather. "We ran off the night of high school graduation. Went to Vegas. I thought we were going to get married, but Gage, not so much. But I'd left a note for Mom and Dad saying we were eloping, so . . ."

Despite her father downstairs who wanted him out and her mother upstairs who . . . well, who knew what . . . he went ahead and sat in the recliner next to the couch, its leather webbed with cracks. "You've been pretending you're married all this time?"

"Trust me, it was easier. Gage got a kick out of fooling everyone, and frankly, I think he was scared of my dad. Plus, you remember his family. He had six younger siblings. Pretending to be married to me meant my parents paid for an apartment for us during college semesters and let us stay here during summers."

"Yeah, but . . ." He had to count. "Sixteen years of pretense?"

"I guess if we'd actually lived together all those years we'd have a common-law marriage. But he's on the road most of the time, and I stay here, and nobody's ever had reason to question."

She laughed—a nonsensical, dry laugh. A laugh that said she found this anything but funny. "'Course it's ridiculous to think about now. I didn't want to tell them I'd run away with a guy who had no intention of marrying me because I didn't want to ruin their fine, upstanding image of our family. Eloping might be impulsive, and I might've been young, but better that than running away with a guy who has no intention of marrying you. But if I'd known then how they'd turn out . . ."

She laughed again, but this time it was almost a cry. He couldn't help it. He abandoned the recliner and moved onto the couch. "Jen, is there anything I can do?"

"Can you rewind time to back before my dad tried to lie his way into the governor's seat and my mom decided alcohol would solve her problems? Before Dad got sick . . ." Her eyes were dry, but her voice clogged anyway. "You could drag Gage home."

"Why? He's a jerk."

"My dad's going to die, Logan. And my mom, best case scenario, she finally listens to me and goes to rehab. Worst case, she gets sick of my nagging and throws me out. Gage is all I've got." She leaned her forehead into her hands. "He's all I've got."

Her shoulders shook with silent cries he didn't know how to soothe. Why couldn't he be like Dad in this moment? Say the right thing, find the perfect words . . .

The sound of coughing rose from the floor below, and outside a tree branch rapped against a window. Or maybe that was the first tapping of rainfall.

Jenessa stilled.

"He's not all you've got, Jen."

She didn't acknowledge him, didn't even raise her head.

"Listen, there's a fundraiser next week I'm helping with. Colton Greene—I don't know if you've had a chance to meet him. But he's opening that transitional home for teens, and I'm helping with this event, and . . ." Where was he even going with this? "Why don't you join us? I know you're busy. I know you've got a lot to take care of. But it's a fun group of people working on it."

She finally looked up, maybe—just maybe—faint interest playing over her face. "What day?"

"It's on Saturday. We'll be setting up that morning."

Her nod was so slight he might've imagined it. But something had shifted. "He shouldn't have said those things, Logan." She swallowed. "My dad, what he said about you ruining all our lives. He made his own choices. We all did. And it was just easier to blame you."

She stood then, and he did, too. Followed her to the front door. But he paused before moving outside. "Hey, those photos hanging around the stairway. Did you take those?"

"Yeah, actually I did."

"They're good, Jen. Really good. You're talented."

It was as if he was the first person who'd ever acknowledged it—the lifting of her shoulders, the shadow seeping from her eyes.

"I'll be there Saturday."

Dear Mary,

If you were my daughter, I'd tell you about my faith. Because if you were my daughter, I think I'd still have some.

But maybe that's where I was most wrong as a hurting young adult.

My parents would disagree. Eleanor would disagree. They would say dropping out of college and eloping and following Jeremy blindly were my biggest failures. Old church friends might say not being able to fix my marriage was my hugest mistake.

But I'm starting to think maybe the worst was abandoning God when I needed him most. Thinking he abandoned me the day I lost you.

If you were my daughter, perhaps I'd still be the same devout follower I used to be. But only because I'd placed all my rickety hope and shallow faith on circumstances going my way.

But real faith is bigger than that. Deeper.

And maybe it can find you again, even years later, after you've let it go. And you can welcome it back— tentatively, perhaps, but with a hopeful sense that maybe, just maybe, it might be stronger this time.

10

"Hey, bro."

The singsong voice of Raegan Walker hauled Amelia from sleep. *Wait . . . Rae?*

She opened her eyes, sight hidden by the mound of pillows and heavy navy comforter huddled around her, a nest of warmth and comfort and . . . confusion. Because the striped sheet around her smelled like a man—and not just any man, but . . .

Where in the world . . . ?

"I have to get ready for work, but I wanted to check on Charlie first." Raegan's voice came closer. "She's finally all better, yeah? If you need someone to stay with her today, I might be able to get Roxie to cover my shift."

Charlie . . . last night . . . Logan's bedroom.

Amelia shot up, hair flopping over her face and Raegan's shriek joining her own gasp.

"You are not my brother!"

Hands pressed into the mattress on both sides of her, Amelia whipped her gaze around the room. She'd been in here last night, babysitting a sleeping Charlie, dozing off and on as an old movie she'd found on a shelf in the living room played on the computer. Had felt the satisfied sigh of every maternal instinct inside her as Charlie nestled into her. She'd closed her eyes. *"I'll just nap until Logan gets home . . ."*

"Amelia?" Logan's sister stood with her hands on her waist, spicy glint in her eyes. She held a towel over one arm, wet hair draped around her face.

"This isn't what it looks like, Rae."

"What do you think I think it looks like?"

Amelia dropped her feet to the floor. "Don't."

"I mean, I did find you in my brother's bed."

"I was babysitting last night." Light spouting through half-open blinds drew lines on the opposite wall—the one with the bulletin board still packed with old photos and ribbons from Logan's high school years.

"Then where's Charlie?"

Amelia wrangled her fingers through snarled hair. "I don't know." A whine rippled her voice. "I'm very confused right now."

She still wore the jeans she'd slipped on before heading to work yesterday and the baseball-jersey-style shirt, now wrinkled from a night of sleep. The smell of coffee and breakfast food drifted in from the open bedroom door behind Raegan, mingling with that piquant evergreeny, minty, mannish scent she'd come to associate with Logan.

She hadn't even seen him last night, though, had she? Yeah, that was one of his dress shirts swathed over the desk chair and his laptop bag hanging over the knob of the closet door. But . . .

"Well, if Logan isn't in here, where is—"

"Hey, guys, thought I heard voices." Logan appeared in the doorway. Collared light-blue shirt unbuttoned and white tee underneath. Tie draped over one shoulder. Khakis. "Amelia, I'm making omelets. Do you do onions? Mushrooms?"

She couldn't make last night come into focus—nothing past the movie and Logan's daughter snuggled up to her.

"I promise, no kale or tofu. Rae, do you have time before work? Want me to make you one?"

"Sure, but only if you can make it fast. Work in an hour." She rubbed the towel through her damp hair.

"Can do. Amelia, you didn't answer. You okay with the works?"

Raegan turned to Amelia. "Let him do the works. He makes the best om—"

"What am I doing here?" She finally made it to her feet as the question squeaked from her, flustered and shrill. She must look and sound ridiculous.

"Um." Raegan stopping drying her hair. "I'm going to go change." She disappeared.

Leaving Logan to step the rest of the way into the stripey light of the room, a look of pure delight passing over his way-too-awake face. "Memory a little jumbled this morning, is it?"

"I feel like I was drugged."

"You never caught up on sleep after South Dakota, did you? I told you to stay home from work and nap on Monday." He stepped closer and patted her head. "You should've listened to your elder, Amelia Anne."

Why did he have to stand so close? Close enough he could probably smell her morning breath and hear her heart trying to punch its way out of her chest. And not because she was confused about why she was here, but because the moment she'd seen Logan in the doorway, everything she'd decided yesterday afternoon—distance, focus, detachment—slipped through the crack in the open window, where last night's rain still dripped from the eaves and tapped against glass.

"You still look confused." Logan's lips stretched. "Okay, you were sound asleep when I got home last night. So I picked up

Charlie and the two of us bunked in Beckett's room. No biggie. That's where she'd been sleeping anyway before she got sick."

Amelia dropped her arms. "W-why didn't you wake me up? Send me home? Do you know h-how it looks, me waking up in here?"

"I already told Dad and Seth why you're here. Would've told Rae too if I'd gotten to her first. No one thinks anything untoward about you." He over-exaggerated the word *untoward*, unable to hold back another smirk. "Besides, I tried to wake you up. You mumbled something incoherent and pushed me away."

"Don't you dare laugh, Walker." Her eyes narrowed, but Charlie came bustling around the corner before she could say anything else, curls sticking up every which way and wearing zebra pajamas Amelia had changed her into last night. At least she remembered something.

Logan swung her into his arms. "Char-lie." He drawled her name as she looped her arms around his neck. "I was wondering when you were gonna wake up."

She planted a kiss on his cheek, then looked to Amelia. Recognition landed in her eyes, and she wriggled out of Logan's arms to instead hook a hug around Amelia's leg.

Logan lifted his eyebrows. "So? Omelet?"

"I don't know. I feel weird about going down there with your family and all."

"Well, we're on the second floor. You can't exactly climb out the window."

Wasn't there a drainpipe or tree branch she could climb down?

"Come on, Hildy. Let me introduce you to a Walker breakfast."

It did smell amazing. And there was Charlie, beaming up at her, those emerald eyes repeating Logan's request.

"Could I at least brush my teeth first?"

Logan grinned. "Bathroom's across the hall. The drawer at the far right has extra toothbrushes." He reached for Charlie's hand and started for the door. "Oh, and in your omelet?"

"Go ahead. The works."

He tapped the doorframe on the way out. "You won't regret it."

In the bathroom, she found the drawer of toothbrushes and a tube of Crest in the medicine cabinet. *Please tell me the light in this bathroom exaggerates the smudges of day-old mascara under my eyes.*

She ripped her focus away from the mirror and looked around the bathroom instead. A pair of pink little-girl slippers—Charlie's, of course—had been abandoned in the corner. A hunter-green robe hung on the back of the door. She could see a couple bath toys on the tub ledge where the shower curtain had been pushed aside. And an electric razor sat on the counter next to Logan's glasses.

All the signs of a shared family bathroom. Voices and laughter drifted through the vent in the floor. A pang bolted through her, sharp, carrying with it desires she'd thought she'd packed away long ago. She turned.

"Our guest is here." Case Walker's voice caught her on her way down the stairs.

"Hey, everyone." She gave a tiny wave to the family gathered around the table—Case, Seth, Charlie propped in a booster seat. Raegan must still be getting ready. Logan stood over the stainless-steel stove in the kitchen. But no Kate . . .

Oh! "Megan's baby?"

Case stood and pulled out a chair for her. "Born about an hour ago. Six pounds, which apparently is really good for how early she is. Both mom and baby doing good. Did I forget anything?"

"Name's Delia." Logan turned at the stove, spatula raised. "Omelet's ready."

The next twenty minutes passed in a blur of storytelling and laughter, arms jutting into the center of the table for more food, pitchers of orange juice and chocolate milk passed in a circle. Her self-consciousness dissolved as she ate her omelet at a turtle's pace. Partially in order to savor each bite, but mostly to stretch out these few perfect moments.

She felt a tug on her arm and looked over. Charlie held out a grape.

She accepted it and popped it in her mouth. When she lifted her gaze, it was to see Logan watching. Smiling.

Until the chime of her phone ruined the moment. *Trevor?* Eleanor's fiancé.

"Sorry, but I'd better take this." She rose, padding into the kitchen, hope trailing that this family—this perfect family—wouldn't think her rude.

"Amelia, thank God you answered. I don't know why I didn't call you sooner. Actually, I do know why. It's not like you and Eleanor are close, but—" He halted. "Have you heard from Eleanor in the past week?"

She moved farther into the kitchen. "I've more than heard from her. She was here."

"There? With you? In Maple Valley?"

The refrigerator's ice machine clunked. "She stayed overnight on Friday." She stepped closer to the refrigerator, gaze meandering over the photos covering it like a collage. The four siblings in goofy candids. Logan, Seth, and who she assumed was Beckett, high schoolers with arms slung around each other. Several of Charlie. Kate and Colton.

"But she's not there now?"

"No." Her focus slanted to a photo at the far edge of the fridge. Logan and . . . that had to be Emma. The woman's strawberry-blond hair flowed over her shoulders, and her smile was bracketed by twin dimples. Sleeveless dress.

And suddenly she could hear Logan's whispered voice again his first night home. *"Emma."*

Her stomach churned.

"I just stopped by her apartment for the third time this week. She's not answering my calls. I don't know what to think."

She turned away from the fridge, the panic in Trevor's voice finally registering. "Wait, Eleanor's not back in Des Moines?"

"Amelia, I'm worried."

It didn't make sense to be nervous about this. It wasn't like this was the first time.

But parked here, alone, in the center of a plush red leather couch that was probably supposed to make this waiting room feel homey and comfortable, anxiety scratched under Logan's skin. Behind that redwood door flanked by twin ficus plants with slick plastic leaves, Charlie was under a therapist's microscope.

For the fourth time in the past forty-five minutes, he rose from the couch and walked to the room's one window, tilted its bamboo blinds, and looked out on the parking lot without really seeing it.

What if the therapist determined something was seriously wrong with Charlie?

What if her language delay wasn't fixable?

What if he'd waited too long?

Please, God, don't let me have waited too long.

It was as close as he could get to a prayer. But if Dad was right, if God was waiting for him—had been all this time—then maybe, for now, this was okay. A start. A tentative testing of the waters.

He let the blinds drop back into place and fished his phone

from his pocket instead. He'd tried focusing on emails earlier—no luck. But why not call Theo, check on the office?

Theo answered on the second ring. "What do you know? Walker's still alive. I was about to send a search party into the boonies for you."

Theo had every right to scold. Logan's voicemail was crammed with messages from him. Same with his inbox. "Afternoon to you, too."

"Nope. Still morning here in LA. You've got two hours on us, remember?"

"Right, the time difference." Though lately California seemed a lot farther away than just a couple time zones.

"How'd you know to call? I've got news for you. Was just trying to decide whether there was any point in calling or if I should go old-fashioned instead. Send a telegram or transport a letter via stagecoach."

"Carrier pigeon would've been acceptable." The couch sighed when he dropped back onto it. He propped his feet on the coffee table. Why hadn't he thought to call Theo earlier? Could've saved himself an hour of pacing or trying to force interest in any of the outdated waiting room mags. "What's your news?"

"Roberta S. Hadley. We're in."

Logan's feet dropped to the floor. "We're in?"

"Well, close to in. She wants to meet us. Wants to fly us to D.C."

"Whoa." For the first time since he'd walked into this office an hour ago, something other than apprehension grabbed hold of him. "Whoa."

"I'll say it a third time just for good measure. Whoa."

He tried to straighten, but the couch cushions made it impossible. He finally let himself flop back, head tipped, eyes on the ceiling fan spinning overhead. *Who would've thought back when we first went freelance?* "A presidential campaign."

"Yeah, and not some piddly third-tier candidate who won't make it past Super Tuesday. Hadley's an actual contender." The sound of Theo's pen, tapping frenetically against his desk, came over the phone—his personal tick. "So we need to talk dates. She's suggested May 1—"

"Can't." He hauled himself from the couch's pocketing hold. "I've got something that day."

Theo's pause was a reprimand. One he followed with an incredulous tone. "You've got something that day?"

"Yes, you know Colton Greene. He lives in the Valley now. He's got a nonprofit, and there's this fundraiser, and I got roped into basically coordinating it because organization and focus aren't exactly anyone's strong suit around here, and—"

"Logan, this is Roberta S. Hadley. You don't say no to a meeting with her so you can put on a bake sale in Iowa."

"I'm not saying no, I'm saying pick a different date." Logan leaned over to re-fan the magazines he'd fingered through earlier on the coffee table. "And it's not a bake sale. Give me a little more credit."

"I don't care if it's a black-tie affair at the governor's mansion. Get out of it. It can't be more important—"

"It can." Now he did straighten. Stiffen, actually. He faced the couch, where his indentation still marked its cushion. "It is more important. I made a commitment."

Another pause. Another wordless reproach. "Yeah, well, you made a commitment to me, too. We have a business together. You remember that, don't you? And with no warning, when we were on the brink of our biggest career opportunity, you stretched what was supposed to be a two-week break into a two-month disappearance."

"Theo—"

"How do you think that's going to look to Hadley? If you manage to even get around to meeting with her, that is?"

He turned at the sound of the office door opening, the therapist's assistant's footsteps. "Mr. Walker, if you'd like to come in now—" She broke off when she realized he was on the phone. "Whenever you're ready."

He mouthed an apology. "Look, I need to go."

"Logan—"

"I will get on a plane to D.C. any other day you or Roberta S. Hadley want. Just not May 1."

He heard Theo's pen clunk to his desk. "I'll see what I can do."

"And Theo?" He placed a pillow he'd moved out of the way back onto the couch. Straightened his tie. "I want this. Just as much as you. I'm not flaking on you."

"I want to believe that."

"Believe it."

Charlie spotted him as soon as he entered the now-open office. She ran toward him, carrying a book, the barrette in her hair crooked and dangling. And oh, he could feel his heart constrict. That mix of drenching love and care and concern and the weight that always came along with it. The responsibility. The worry that, on his own, he wasn't enough for this treasure of a person.

"Logan, thanks for your patience." Lacey White couldn't have more than a few years on him—if that. She wore a pink sweater over a simple yellow dress—like something Emma would've worn. She had an easy smile and confident handshake. "If it's all right with you, I'll have Charlie hang out with Patience for a few minutes while we chat."

He unclipped Charlie's barrette, pocketed it, and palmed her little head like a basketball. "Sure thing. You cool with that, Charlie-pie?"

She didn't even hesitate—ran straight to Lacey's waiting assistant, who ushered her out the door.

"Have a seat, Logan." Lacey motioned to two chairs edged up to a table that matched the redwood of the door and the bookshelves carved into one wall. "And try not to be so nervous."

He sat. "It shows that much?"

"You're a single dad. It's only your second experience with speech therapy. And you want to know if your daughter's okay and is ever going to start really talking. It doesn't have to show."

He could kiss her feet for that.

She settled across from him, crossed one leg over the other. "First of all, Logan, you have a wonderful daughter. Charlotte— you call her, Charlie, yes?" At his nod, she continued. "Charlie is bright. She's very aware and attentive. She's communicative in her own way. And I agree with the two other doctors she's seen. Cognitively, mentally, physically—she is developing at what's considered a typical rate."

He rested one palm flat on the table. "She just . . . doesn't talk."

"But you said she says single words now and then, correct?"

"It's rare, but yes. Honestly, it's usually when she's tired or upset or impatient. She'll say 'Daddy' or 'book' or 'water.' She talks in her sleep, too."

"And when she says words, they come out clearly? She doesn't have trouble getting them out?"

"Yeah. I mean, clearly for a toddler, that is. But she doesn't stumble or stutter, really."

Lacey nodded thoughtfully. "So it does very much seem like she *can* talk. She's just choosing not to. Or simply doesn't have a great desire to."

His fingers fisted atop the table. "She's spent too much time alone with a nanny. She hasn't been in playgroups or . . . or what's that thing everyone does now? Playdates? We go to church, but she usually sits with me instead of going to a nursery or anything and—"

"Logan." Lacey leaned forward, her knees nearly touching his, waiting until he looked her in the eye. "Charlie's speaking delay is not your fault. If you hear nothing else I say, hear that. The fact that you've got her here today proves that you're an attentive, caring, and supportive father. She clearly adores you."

Those words—the assurance embedded in them—they slicked over him. Like aloe over sunburned skin. Quenching and more needed than he'd even realized.

"I . . . she . . ." Whatever grateful reply he meant to give stalled in his throat. He swallowed around a lump, vision blurring as hot, embarrassing tears pooled against rapid blinks. "Sorry. I don't know why . . ."

Emotion pressed at him from all sides. And the urge to escape collided with the need to stay here and lap up the promise of help and hope for his girl.

"It's all right." Lacey offered a simple smile and opened a folder she'd carried with her to the table, moving on as if he wasn't sitting next to her attempting not to fall apart.

Thank you, God.

There it was. Another one-line prayer. And he meant it, didn't he? He'd needed an inch of reassurance and, in the form of a kind professional, he had been given a mile of encouragement.

"Now, what we're going to work on in therapy is helping Charlie *want* to talk." Lacey pulled out a sheet of paper with scribbled notes. "We're going to work together to develop some prompts and some very specific activities meant to stimulate her interest in verbal communication. Something as simple as playing with puppets can be incredibly helpful."

Puppets. He could do that.

The Everwood Bed & Breakfast stared Amelia down behind pearl-white shutters—strangely the only pristinely painted piece of the old Victorian's exterior. Its weather-stripped siding and a rickety porch appeared more gray than white. The gnarled branches of blunt-cut bushes edged the front, and a narrow walkway cut through sparse grass.

And there on the porch, curled into a sun-faded rattan loveseat—Eleanor.

Amelia closed her car door and started up the sidewalk to the forlorn structure. It'd hit her halfway through the workday that, if by some curious chance Eleanor was still in Maple Valley, she'd have come here.

Jaundiced floorboards creaked, and a thin breeze slithered through wind chimes as she climbed the porch steps. Not until she stood in front of her did Eleanor finally look up.

"How'd you know?"

"I knew to come looking for you because Trevor called. I knew to come looking *here,* because you love B&Bs. Always have. And the one other time you came to visit me in Maple Valley, the only good thing you had to say about town is that we've got an intriguing B&B."

Eleanor closed the book she'd been reading—not Jeremy's this time. She dropped her feet to give Amelia room to sit. "Now that I've actually stayed here, I might use a different word than *intriguing.*"

"Such as . . . creepy?"

"If I had my realtor hat on, I'd say *eclectic,* but honestly, your adjective's better. There's this paisley-print wallpaper in the room I'm staying in that's so dizzying it should come with a doctor's warning. Oh, and the lady who runs this place carries her cat with her everywhere—just draped over her arm like it's a fur stole or something."

Her sister combed her fingers through her unruly tangles—so

different from her usual tamed hair. She wore a light sweatshirt over yoga pants. Circles under her eyes suggested restless nights.

A weary wind jostled an empty flower basket hanging from a hook in the porch ceiling. Eleanor's gaze settled on a magnolia tree in the B&B's yard—the property's one cheery feature. But with each cascading gale, cotton-white blooms were stripped from its branches in waves. "Remember how we had one of those trees in our old house? Mom used to lament how quickly it lost its blooms each spring."

"Looks like snow when it falls like that." Amelia shifted to tuck her feet underneath her. "Speaking of which, they're actually saying we're supposed to get another round of snow next week. Can you believe it? Snow in May. You gotta love it."

"Actually, I think maybe you're the only one who loves it." She said the words without any hint of criticism. Only mild tease.

"You didn't have to leave, you know."

Eleanor turned her head to look straight at her. "I did. I needed . . . to think, I guess. And I felt awful about the way I showed up without any warning, interrupted your date—"

"That wasn't a date." And was it really only a week ago she'd sat in The Red Door, listening to live music and telling Logan about her divorce?

"Well, I interrupted either way. And then I took your bed. And worst of all, Jeremy's book. If it makes you feel any better, I quit reading it. I considered trashing it, but it's a library copy."

"You didn't have to quit reading it."

"Thing is, I think I wasn't just reading it because I wanted a life coach's thoughts on love or whatever. I thought maybe there'd be a chapter in it that explained why things went wrong for you two. I thought it might tell me all the things you never did."

Cool air brushed circles of pink over Eleanor's otherwise pale cheeks—no makeup today. "We've never been close like that, El."

Eleanor's hands flopped to her lap. "I know. And that's the thing that's so sad. We're twins. Shouldn't we have, like, ESP or something? And it's just one more thing that has me terrified about marrying Trevor. It's not just seeing other marriages fall apart that scares me—it's realizing I don't even have a good relationship with my twin. How in the world can I expect a marriage to work?"

She'd never seen her sister like this. Not confident, organized, Type-A Eleanor. The one who always knew what she wanted. The one who'd chosen the practical college major. Who'd earned a grad school fellowship. Who'd put off her love life until she was ready for it.

Except listening to her now, maybe she wasn't ready for it.

Then again, was anybody ever ready?

"So was there?"

Eleanor's eyebrows dipped into a *V*. "Was there what?"

"A chapter on why we broke up?"

"Not in what I read. And I flipped through the rest of the chapters just in case. Didn't see anything that looked too tell-all-y."

"Well, that's good, at least." She slipped her feet to the floor and leaned over, elbows on her knees. A chug of wind sent petals from the magnolia tree dusting over the porch floor. "We broke up because he said I was too much for him."

She felt the force of her own surprise, heard the prodding of Eleanor's silence.

"All those years of trying to get pregnant took their toll on me, I guess. And then when the adoption fell through . . ."

For a naked moment she was there again. In the hospital, staring through a nursery window, watching her whole world fall apart. Knowing before the social worker even said the words . . .

"Maybe I *was* too much. Maybe there were too many nights of tears and too many days of existing like a zombie. I don't know." But her eyes were dry now, her words listless. "All I know is, Jeremy couldn't put up with it anymore. How was he supposed to go out and speak and inspire people when his own home was in such emotional distress? I told him I could go to a doctor. Maybe I had a chemical imbalance. He said, good, go for it. But he still wanted the divorce. Because how would it look, a motivational speaker with a depressed wife who couldn't keep it together?"

Eleanor's inhale was sharp. "What a jerk."

She glanced over. "I think he wanted out for a long time. And I think I knew it. I was hoping the adoption might save the marriage. But, well, it is what it is, right?" She'd closed the door on that chapter in her life. Told herself over and over her new life in Maple Valley was enough to fill the blank spaces. Even believed it often enough. Especially here lately.

If only she hadn't promised that reporter she'd call Jeremy.

She straightened. "You know what's weird? I've talked about Jeremy and the divorce more in the past two weeks than I think I have in the almost three years since it all went down."

"I'm sorry I wasn't there for you, Amelia. You needed a sister and instead you got platitudes."

Genuine regret filled Eleanor's eyes. Understanding, too. The kind Amelia had been so desperate for in those days and months after the divorce. The kind she'd finally found in Maple Valley.

"And I'm sorry I wasn't there for you last weekend."

Eleanor gave a half smile. "It's hardly the same level of sisterly infraction."

"But still. You drove all this way. You obviously needed someone to talk to." She lightened her tone. "You know, Trevor sounded crazy with worry when he called."

"He did?"

"You love him, El. And he loves you."

"That's not always enough."

She leaned her head against Eleanor's arm. "Maybe there's more going on than I know about, but I can tell you this: You can't see into the future. You can't control what changes are going to come into your lives. You can only control *your* choices. You know what kind of man Trevor is. Is he a person you can see yourself choosing to love, day in and day out, even when it gets hard?"

"Yes." Not even a moment of hesitation. And then, stronger, "Yes."

"Well, then." Amelia straightened and reached for the bag she'd dropped on the porch floor next to the loveseat. She towed it onto her lap and opened the top flap. "I may have stopped at a convenience store on the way here. Just in case." She pulled out a stack of magazines.

"Bridal magazines? Really?"

"I know you probably still need to think and pray. And you definitely need to talk to Trevor." She set the magazines in Eleanor's lap. "But for this afternoon, let's just put all that aside for a while and look at pretty dresses and take a quiz on whether you should be a spring, summer, or autumn bride."

"Not winter?"

Amelia couldn't help a grin. "No, because if I ever get married again, I get the winter wedding."

Eleanor opened the top magazine. "Speaking of, tell me about the guy at open-mic night." No missing the glint in her tone.

"Nothing to tell." Lie. Except . . . "Actually, there's this call I have to make, and it has to do with him. It's not going to be fun." Apprehension flooded in. "I could use a sister to get me through it."

Eleanor met her eyes, a new and comforting softness there. "You've got one."

11

*S*ix hours. Logan had six hours to turn the high school gymnasium into a fundraiser venue for tonight's event. Catered dinner. Live music. Candlelight.

Half an hour ago, he'd thought it impossible. But now—perched three-fourths of the way up a rickety ladder and surveying the circus of activity in the room—his confidence buoyed. Music pumped through speakers, drumbeats reverberating off the gym walls while the bump and clatter of round tables being rolled and set up joined the noise.

They might actually pull this together. As long as the fluke May 1st snowstorm that had all the meteorologists in a tizzy didn't come to fruition.

"You're doing it wrong, Logan." Jenessa Belville's voice climbed over the ruckus from her spot below.

Logan tugged at a pleat in the draping that would provide the backdrop for the raised platform serving as a stage. "I've hung pipe and drape plenty of times. I know what I'm doing."

"You should've slid the curtain on before you got up there."

He was still halfway in shock Jenessa had even shown up today. He hadn't seen her since that discomfiting night at her house last week. Had tried calling once, but she didn't answer. He'd thought maybe she regretted spilling so much to him, planned to go back to avoiding him.

But no, she'd been the first one to arrive today.

"Anyway, aren't you in charge of this thing? Shouldn't you be roaming around with a clipboard making sure everything else is getting done?"

"Not a clipboard guy, Jen. And I'm not in charge. Colton is."

He could hear her *tsk* even from up here, over the music and the racket. "I think we all know Colton's the queen of England here. It's a title. You're the prime minister who's getting everything done."

"Wouldn't he be the king?"

Jenessa laughed—and not a dreary, end-of-her-rope laugh today, but the real thing. "Fine, I'll go help with decorations." She almost waltzed away, a lightness to her step. Hardly seemed like the same Jenessa from last week.

Maybe she'd just needed someone to listen. To hear her. And he'd been in the right place at the right time.

So much of these past weeks in Maple Valley felt that way— right place, right time. The way he'd been able to step in and help with this event. That opening with the speech pathologist.

The newspaper, too. They should be able to launch the website in a couple weeks, and advertising for the centennial issue was coming together. He'd even written some articles here and there, actually enjoyed himself. It'd been a long time since he'd written in his own voice rather than the voice of whatever candidate or committee or foundation hired the firm.

"Logan!"

Amelia's voice carried across the gym, and he leaned over the hanging curtain to see her mazing through the tables. A belted tan coat, unbuttoned, flapped behind her, and a newsboy hat bounced at an angle on her head. And was that a bag of Twizzlers in her hand?

She stopped in the center of the room, scanning the space. "Up here, Nellie Bly."

She cocked her head to find him, his arms resting on the top of the curtain piping. He waved with one hand. She made it to the foot of the ladder in seconds. "Logan, you will never guess what I just discovered." The ladder quivered as she stepped on the bottom rung.

"Careful, this thing's rickety."

She ignored him and climbed the other side. "I was at the office, researching this Harry Wheeler guy."

"Not a word about the nickname? Nellie Bly? I was proud of that one, especially with your hat and coat. You're very reporterly today."

Her package of licorice crinkled against the ladder as she clambered toward him. She stopped when she was face-to-face with him across the top of the ladder. "Did you know Nellie Bly married a millionaire who was almost forty years older than she was? He was in his seventies when they got married." She held out the bag of Twizzlers. "Licorice?"

Her cheeks were flushed, and please tell him those weren't specks of snow in her hair and on her hat. The high school was located six miles out of town. If they really got that blizzard the forecast called for, would people still come tonight?

"What're you doing here, Amelia? I thought you were in Des Moines?"

She'd taken the day off yesterday, something about wedding dress shopping with her sister. The office had felt . . . empty. But there was a new lightness to her steps ever since she'd reconnected with her sister.

Not unlike his own calm lately. Something about this town, his family . . . the woman facing him across the ladder.

195

"I came back early this morning 'cause everyone was talking about a snowstorm, and obviously I didn't want to miss tonight because I never miss town events, and besides, I promised Charlie I'd sit by her and—" She bit into a piece of licorice. "I think you're doing the curtain wrong."

"Why doesn't anyone trust my curtain work?"

She leaned to the side, reaching for the curtain he'd just arranged, the ladder wobbling beneath them both.

"Hey, careful."

"You scared of ladders, Logan?"

"No, only of crazy women who climb up and feel the need to undo my work." This close to her now, he could smell her hair. Like honey or vanilla or coconut or he didn't know what, but it was nice.

"I'm not undoing your work. Just perfecting it. The way you feel the need to perfect all my headlines. And switch up my ad placement. And—"

A voice came over the mic—"Testing, testing"—followed by the static-y screech of an amp. Amelia jerked at the sound, dropping her bag of licorice to the ground, as the ladder trembled again. She let go of the curtain, grabbing for the top of the ladder, where Logan's hands found her arms and held them both steady until the ladder stabilized.

He loved the sound of the spooked laugh that chased out her "whoa," her nervous smile. "That could've been bad." Her hat had gone even more crooked on her head.

"We could've fallen off this ladder and broken all kinds of bones all because you didn't trust my curtain-hanging skills." He still held her arms, and for a breath of a moment, couldn't make himself let go.

Because Amelia was . . .

Fun and funny and charming and . . .

Enticing.

He swallowed—more like gulped—suddenly recognizing the pulsing under his skin for exactly what it was. Pure, unmistakable desire.

"Logan?"

"Tell me about Harry Wheeler." His words toppled, his voice choppy to his own ears.

Her focus was on his hands, securing her to the ladder. "How about down on the floor? Where it's safe?" She looked up, and the amber flecks in her eyes told him she hadn't missed a thing.

And that maybe he wasn't the only one who'd felt the surprise, magnet-like pull.

He let go of her arms, used the seconds climbing down the ladder to steady his staccato-ing breath. He pretended to take stock of the progress in the gym instead of looking at Amelia. Colton was rolling in a rack of folded chairs. Jenessa and Rae and others were draping tablecloths into place, and Kate was following around behind them, arranging centerpieces.

Whoever had been testing the mic had finished, and the music was back on. A slower song now, some jazz thing.

"Harry Wheeler was with Kendall in Paris."

He exhaled, tried to focus. "In Paris when?"

"When Lindbergh's plane landed. In 1927. They were both there together. And it gets way better than that."

He let himself look at her then—the ruddy excitement in her cheeks from whatever discovery she'd made. Or maybe, like him, the lingering effect from whatever had just happened on top of that ladder.

The lilt of a saxophone slid in.

"When Lindbergh landed, he was rushed by a crowd and practically dragged from the plane. It was chaos, and in the craziness, someone else ended up being mistaken for Lindbergh. He was hoisted onto people's shoulders and carried through the crowd, and it actually worked out well because it allowed Lindbergh to make it to the French Ambassador."

He reached down to pick up her bag of licorice. "You really have been doing your homework."

"Some sources say the accidental decoy was an American journalist. One random newspaper says he was a fur trader. Several others say he was a Brown University student." She pulled her hat off her head, hair a static-y mess. "Guess what his name was."

Honestly, he didn't even care. Not nearly as much as he cared about the fact that here, right now, in the same gym where he'd danced at Homecoming with Emma and posed for a graduation photo with her—the one that still sat in a frame on Rick and Helen's fireplace—he wanted to kiss Amelia.

With her tangled hair and her hat in her hand and those eyes that couldn't decide what color they were. Just . . . kiss her.

Because he'd missed her yesterday. Because she'd promised to sit by Charlie tonight. Because she'd come running to him with her latest story development—and he loved it.

"Harry Wheeler, Logan. Kendall's friend was the Lindbergh decoy. They were both students at Brown together. Do you know what that means?"

"I'm not sure . . . I guess . . ."

But before he could force his common sense into actually, like, working, a ringtone blared from her coat pocket. She pulled it out, blanched. "Um . . . I better take this."

Colton's voice jumped in from behind as she walked away. "Well, that was just adorable."

Logan turned. "What was?"

"You. Amelia. The top of the ladder. Like a moment in one of those old movies your whole family loves."

Logan reached for the ladder, pushed it closed with a clack. "Don't know what you're talking about, Colt." Except that he did, and it stirred him, and he couldn't decide if it was a good stirring or bad. Just a month ago, he'd had a moment of missing Emma so immensely he'd made a fool of himself in front of Amelia. And now he was close to making a fool of himself for an entirely different reason.

"Don't worry, your sisters were too busy to notice. Pretty sure I'm the only one who saw."

"I don't know what you think you saw." *So not true.* An unsettling lump clogged his throat.

"That tackle last year might've killed my knee and shoulder and career, Walker, but my eyesight's just fine."

"Whatever." He hoisted the ladder under his arm, Colton's laughter following him across the gym.

Everything in Amelia wanted to ignore Jeremy's call. After all, she'd left him the message last week. Passed on Belle Waldorf's request. Wasn't that enough? Couldn't he take it from there?

But Belle had called Logan earlier this week, done an interview and everything. Amelia had heard the whole thing from her desk, along with the follow-up call Logan had made to his partner afterward. *"I have no idea how she even heard about me, but there's going to be a story or something. Next week, I think. Think it might get Hadley's attention?"*

Belle had done her part. The least Amelia could do was answer her phone now and make sure Jeremy had listened to her voicemail, responded to the reporter's request. Even if her stomach clenched at the thought.

She escaped the noise of the gym, the strains of the jazz music, and the hype in the air and forced herself to answer the call. "This is Amelia."

Jeremy's voice was exactly as she remembered. Tenor and honey-smooth. "I didn't think you'd answer."

She didn't have a response for that. For anything, really. Amelia slumped against the high school's wall, a line of mustard-yellow lockers ogling her across the hall.

She used to imagine what it might be like to talk to Jeremy again. Would she yell at him or cry or don a mask, pretend all was well and she'd completely moved on?

But haven't you?

Hadn't she just minutes ago lost herself in another man's deep russet irises and wondered, for seconds that stretched with tension, if he might actually lean across the ladder and kiss her?

No, not just wondered. Hoped.

"I was surprised to get your message last week," Jeremy finally went on.

So he had listened to it. "Well, if you got it, then you've already got the reporter's info. Did you accidentally delete it or something? Need her email or phone—"

"No, I've already talked to her."

"Then why . . . ?" An *Exit* sign at the end of the hallway cast a shadow of red over the gray tile floor. Outside the door, a flurry of white whipped in the wind. Were they really in for a May blizzard?

"I'm calling about Dani."

She pushed away from the wall, shoes squealing, still damp from her walk across the parking lot. "I don't—"

"I know you don't, but Ames, she's been trying to get ahold of you for months."

"Don't *Ames* me, Jeremy." The force in her own voice surprised her. But he'd lost the right to a nickname the second he'd called it quits on their life together.

And as for Dani . . .

Her heart threw up barricades as fast as the memories flew at her.

"She said she's sent two or three letters and you've returned them all."

"Jer—"

"I saw her at church last Christmas when I was visiting my parents. She's still in Des Moines. She asked if I could help her get in contact, and I told her I was probably the last person you'd listen to."

Darn right.

"But after you called last week, I thought maybe things had changed and enough time had passed and maybe I *could* help. I at least had to try. You should see her, Ames—Amelia. She hardly looks like the broken-down teen we knew, and Mary is—"

"Stop." Her voice echoed down the hallway, the beat of music drumming from the gym and a throb beginning in her head. "I don't want to hear it."

Someone walked past the gym opening, glancing out at Amelia.

She paced farther down the hall, saw a door marked *Janitor's Closet*, and yanked it open. Inside, she pulled on a string, a dangling light bulb buzzing to life.

"Don't shut Dani down because of me. You used to be so close to her. She looked up to you. She needed you then, and she might need you now. I'm not sure. She didn't say why she wanted to talk to you, but—"

"Jer, what about, 'I don't want to hear it' don't you understand?"

"I understand perfectly fine. You're being as emotional and rash about this as you were three years ago."

The sting lanced through her. She shouldn't have answered the call. Should've known.

But how could she have guessed he was calling about Dani? *Dani and Mary.*

The heady smell of bleach and other cleaning materials twisted in the air around her, suffocating. And in a flicker of a moment, time reversed and Amelia was back in the hospital in Des Moines, standing outside the nursery, looking through a gaping window at the empty bassinet. At the name card written in a nurse's scribbled handwriting: *Mary Danielle Malone.*

Lucas, she'd thought. *Her last name is Lucas now.*

All the paperwork had been signed. And more than that, they'd already bonded. In nine months of doctor's appointments and hovering over Dani. In days spent picking out colors for the spare bedroom at home, setting up the crib and changing table and rocking chair. In minutes right here in this hospital, cradling Mary in her arms just last night. Cleaned and swaddled and tiny and perfect. *Her Mary.* Even Jeremy had given in to the haze of wonder as he'd held her after Amelia.

And in that one flawless moment, all her worry about their marriage, all her disappointment, eroded into dust. Later, back at home, for the first time in so long, Jeremy had held her all night, whispered his love like he used to when they were first married. She'd woken up curled against him and so very, very happy.

But movement caught in her periphery, and she lifted her gaze from the empty crib. There, in the corner of the nursery . . . Dani. She sat in a rocking chair, hospital gown draping over her form, and in her arms, a bundle of blanket and baby, Mary's tuft of black hair peeking out.

Why . . . ?

Hadn't Dani said she wasn't going to hold her? Thought it'd be easier that way?

Dani leaned over to kiss Mary's cheek, her bangs flopping over her face. And when she lifted her head, pushed her hair away from her own cheek, her eyes met Amelia's through the glass. They brimmed with apology and something else.

Decision. Certainty.

No. Please, God, no.

The hurt was sharp, sudden. Numbing. She couldn't move. Just stood there, staring, watching a wounding flood she hadn't seen coming sweep away her future as Dani shook her head.

And that's when she'd heard the footsteps, Jeremy's rising voice, and the social worker's futile attempts at calming. *"I'm so sorry, Mr. and Mrs. Lucas. Unfortunately these things happen more than we'd like."*

Voices sounded outside the closet, and Amelia jerked, the flashback over as quickly as it'd begun.

And then Jeremy's voice—unwelcome, mollifying, and almost professional. "Why don't you let me help you, Amelia? Obviously you're still struggling. I've helped a lot of people dealing with things in their past and—"

"You can't seriously be trying to counsel me right now." For the first time in years, she almost wished he was standing right here with her. Because then she could reach for a bottle of Windex from the janitor's shelf and spray it at him. Make him stop.

Instead, impulse wrangled her into doing the next best thing. She jerked her phone away from her ear and sent it hurtling into the mop bucket next to her feet. It plunked in the water with a tiny splash.

What. Is. Wrong. With. You?

But before she could register what she'd just done, the closet door swung open.

"There you are. Some kid said you were in here, and I didn't believe him. What are you doing—" Logan cut off at the sight of her. Trembling. Probably looking like an idiot. "Amelia, what's wrong? Did you just get bad news?"

"It's nothing."

The closet door banged shut behind him as he crossed the narrow space toward her. "It is, too. You're white as a ghost, and you're shaking. Who was that on the phone?"

She didn't want to tell him. Or maybe she did. Oh, why was she reacting like this? Like her past was a haunted house and she was a little kid, lost. "Jeremy."

Logan stilled. "Your ex-husband?"

She nodded.

"Why was he calling?"

Even with only a flickering bulb for light, she could see the billows of compassion in Logan's eyes, the concern. It was the same look he had given Charlie the other day when she'd been running around the office and knocked into the edge of Owen's desk. Or when he'd told her about Jenessa and her parents.

"Maybe we could have Jen take some photos for the paper. She's good, Amelia. And I think she could use the boost."

How did he do it? Hone in on people's hurt and know just what to do? As if he'd refined the craft of compassion as much as he had his writing.

"There's a girl named Dani. Before Jeremy was as big of a name as he is now, we helped with the youth ministry at our church. Dani was a high school senior. Bad home life, tough childhood. We—especially I—mentored her. We got pretty close." She took a breath. "And then she got pregnant."

The rest of it rushed from her. "I'm not even sure how it happened, but somehow I talked to Dani about her options, and by the end of the conversation, I'd asked if she'd consider letting Jeremy and I adopt her baby. We'd been trying for so long . . ."

She could see the pieces coming together in Logan's eyes.

"Jeremy thought it was a bad idea, but I talked him into it. Turns out he was right, though. Dani changed her mind the day after she had . . ." She couldn't even say the baby's name.

Maybe she was over Jeremy. Maybe that one piece of her heart had glued itself back into place.

But she wasn't over everything.

"Amelia."

"I think I hated Dani almost more than Jeremy for a while." The confession came out a shaky whisper.

Logan stepped toward her, but she backed up, knocking into a shelf behind her, wrapped rolls of toilet paper wobbling. No, she didn't want his comfort right now. Not after the ugly truth scraping through her, the lingering effect of Jeremy's voice.

"Jeremy was calling about Dani?"

She nodded.

"I didn't realize you were in touch with him."

"I wasn't. Only called him last week because of that reporter. The one who interviewed you. She contacted me looking for help getting ahold of Jeremy, and I told her no but then she said she'd do whatever she could to return the favor and . . . well."

Understanding dawned on Logan's face. "You asked her to do a story on me?"

The first twinge of something other than heartache slipped in. "Well, yeah. I thought it'd help you. National exposure . . . that candidate you want to work for . . ." She shrugged.

Logan just stared at her.

And then, before she could think or respond or resist, she was in his arms and he was kissing her. Like . . . like she'd gone and righted his entire world rather than made a simple call. Like a man starved.

Or maybe she was the one starved. Because she was the one threading her arms around his neck and pressing all of herself into all of him. She hardly heard the rolls of toilet paper hitting the hard floor as he backed her into the shelf or his foot knocking into the mop bucket where her phone sunk.

She couldn't breathe.

She didn't want to breathe.

But then the door swung open once more, assaulting them with light. Logan broke away with a gasp. And Colton's voice. "Uh, I . . . whoa . . . sorry. But Logan, you have to come see this. The blizzard. And the caterer just called to cancel."

⁓

"I think I might literally be in shock."

The blizzard furled in twirls of white, like a thousand tiny sandstorms swaying from the ground. All these people should be tucked in their homes, under blankets and in front of fire-places, laughing about Iowa and snow in May.

Instead, it looked like half the town of Maple Valley had come out for the relocated fundraiser. The one Amelia had saved with a fleet of last-minute changes and slew of phone calls.

He'd been ready to cancel. "I didn't think this was possible."

She stood beside him now, huffing into her cupped hands next to him, lantern light sparkling in her eyes. "Anything is possible when you call in enough favors."

"But I don't understand. How did you . . . we only had a few hours . . ."

Bear McKinley's voice crooned over the snow-covered yard that stretched outside the Maple Valley depot. A train car anchored to its track served as the stage, side door pulled open and strings of Christmas lights adorning its insides. Outside, community members tramped through still-falling snow, um-brellas for shelter, and dozens, maybe hundreds, of paper bag lanterns for light.

No catered meal like he'd planned, but Seth had pulled through to provide enough dessert offerings to put the whole town on a sugar high. The employees of Coffee Coffee—minus Megan, who was still at home with a newborn—had assembled to serve coffee, apple cider, and cocoa. Bear, apparently, had a cold, but he was pressing through anyway up on the makeshift stage.

"Did Seth ever tell you about the day before his restaurant opened, Logan?"

His gaze wandered to the lit-up depot building, like a light-house in the white-out. "I couldn't come home for it, but I remember him saying it got crazy."

Amelia nodded. "Raegan told me that the day before he realized he didn't have any chairs—not a single one. He started to panic, but eventually he and Rae got on the phone, starting calling folks. And by the next day, he had all the chairs he needed." She looked out over her handiwork. "That's just how things work in Maple Valley."

He turned to face Amelia now. She'd traded her newsboy hat for a knit cap, and it flopped over her forehead. The scarf around her neck matched the hat, her hair spilling between the two.

And for what had to be the thousandth time since this afternoon, he replayed those heated minutes in the closet. Had he seriously done that? Him, the guy it took six dates to as much as peck Emma on the cheek on her parents' porch steps? He'd practically tackled Amelia.

Yeah, well, it's not like she didn't kiss you back.

"You're grinning. You think Colton's happy? We did good?"

"*You* did good." The end of her scarf batted in front of her, and he reached to wind it back in place.

"Wasn't just me."

No, but she'd had all the ideas. She'd made it happen. "I can't believe people showed up, though. I mean, in a blizzard."

"I have lived in this town for a few years now, Logan. I know people. They loooove to complain about snow and the cold. But offer horse-drawn sleigh rides, and they can't dig out their long johns and boots fast enough."

The lineup of sleighs waited off to the side of the depot, horses covered with blankets. "But where'd you find the sleighs and horses?"

"I did a story on J.J.'s Stables last summer, and it helped out their horse-boarding business. J.J. owed me."

She shrugged as if her efforts amounted to nothing more than a last-minute dinner party for friends. "It may not make as much money as Colton hoped for, but then again, I'm not sure money was his end goal so much as moral support for the Parker House. It's not the sit-down fancy dinner you'd planned. No spinning glitter ball, either."

"There was never going to be a glitter ball." He couldn't stop smiling.

"No? I'm strangely disappointed by that." A snowflake caught in her eyelash, and she blinked it away.

He remembered the umbrella hooked around his arm. In a spurt of movement, he lifted the thing and popped it open. "Here, you're getting pelted by snow." He lifted it over their heads.

"So where's Charlie tonight? I've been looking for her."

He took a steadying breath. "When Rick and Helen heard we moved this thing outside, they didn't like the idea of Charlie being out in the storm. Maybe they had a point."

"Are you kidding? You would've bundled her up, and she would've had a blast. She would've loved a sleigh ride."

She would've especially loved that. One of the puppets the therapist loaned him was a horse, and she broke into laughter every time he fake neighed for her.

"I don't know, things are weird with my in-laws right now. I don't know if they're just sore that they don't get to see her more or think I'm a bad parent or what. But something's off."

Charlie's fall from the tree a couple weeks ago and Logan bringing her home when she had the flu last week instead of letting Helen care for her at their house had only made things worse.

"If they think you're a bad parent, Logan, they're the ones who are off. Charlie couldn't ask for a better dad."

Was she *trying* to get him to kiss her again? And shouldn't they talk about that at some point?

He turned away from the stage to face Amelia. "Hey, so about this afternoon . . ."

Her eyes were still on Bear, but he had a feeling it wasn't just cold rosying her cheeks now. Snowflakes tapped on the umbrella above them.

"If that was, like, in any way inappropriate or . . . well . . ." Maybe he should've figured out what he wanted to say before opening his mouth and botching this.

She bit her lip over an amused half smile. "It wasn't inappropriate, Logan."

"We were in a supply closet, though. Like it was high school or something."

Now she turned to him. "It *was* in a high school."

She was laughing now, and he was too, and oh, maybe they didn't need to talk about this. Analyze what had happened or define what had changed in their relationship this afternoon or what it meant for tomorrow or next week or whenever. Maybe tonight, for now, they could just enjoy this bubble of time.

Bear's song slid to a close.

"Hey, there's one thing I haven't told you about tonight. One other change I was thinking we could make."

The wind shifted direction, and he tilted the umbrella to shield her. "What's that?"

"Come with me."

She started for the depot, hair bouncing against her shoulders underneath her cap. He followed.

They reached the shoveled boardwalk that circled the depot,

snowdrifts packed against the building's baseboards and their steps pounding on the wood underfoot. Amelia pushed her way in, the warmth of inside reaching out to pull him in behind her.

He blinked to adjust to the lighting, gaze roaming the space. It still shone with new paint and gleaming displays after the renovation following last summer's tornado—not to mention their cleaning a couple weeks ago.

Amelia disappeared down the hallway, moving in the direction of his father's office. She reappeared seconds later carrying . . . a guitar case?

Not just any guitar case, he realized as she came closer. *His* guitar case. The one from high school and college, covered with stickers from his favorite bands, most peeling and some faded. She held it out to him upright. "I saw it in your room the night I babysat Charlie."

"And it's here because . . . ?"

"Bear's got a cold. He's not going to be able to do more than a few songs."

"Amelia, I haven't played for years."

"I'm sure it's like riding a bike. Just sing a song or two. People will love it."

The wind pushed against the building, shaking the hinges of the depot's doors and rattling its windows. "Sorry, but no."

"I know you haven't had time to practice, but—"

"Amelia." He didn't mean for his voice to sound so sharp. Hated how it made her wince and step back. But there wasn't any arguing this. "I'm not singing tonight."

"Well . . . okay then." She didn't meet his eyes as she lowered the guitar case. "Guess I'll go put this back."

Regret bobbed through him as she turned.

He heard the door open behind him, felt the whoosh of cold air barrel over him even as he overheated under all the layers he wore.

"What are you doing in here, son? Party's outside." Dad.

He spun. "Why'd you save it? The guitar?"

The bridge of Dad's nose pinched under his stocking cap. "I think I missed something."

"I said you could sell it or give it away or even trash it."

Dad stomped the snow off his boots. "I thought you might change your mind and want it eventually. What's wrong with you?"

He didn't know.

Okay, he did, but . . .

Amelia.

No, he couldn't play. But he could at least apologize for biting her head off when there was no way she could've known what she was asking him. He muttered an apology to Dad and took off after Amelia, trailing down the hallway.

Except she wasn't there. Only the telltale puddle of melted snow that must have drifted through the back door when she exited. And there, leaning against Dad's office door, his guitar case.

12

The gray walls of Jonas Clancy's office were like a mirror into Amelia's spirit this Monday morning—and a perfect match for the sky outside his window, cloud-laden and drab.

"Sorry about the smell," the bank's senior loan officer said as he lowered into the angular chair behind his glass-top desk. Grayish hair and kind eyes above a crease-lined smile. "Whole place got a fresh paint job last week."

And they couldn't have picked a cheerier color? The paint's cloistering smell had knocked into her as soon as she'd walked into the bank. If she hadn't already woken up with a headache, the heady air inside the building would've done the job.

But she pasted on a smile as artificial as the Sweet'n Low Jonas tipped into his coffee now. "Are you sure you don't want a cup?"

If she downed any more caffeine this morning, she could add a stomachache to the pounding in her head. This was why a person shouldn't wake up before five a.m. Way too much time to drink way too much coffee before an important meeting.

"I'm good, but thanks anyway. I think I've downed half a pot already this morning."

"Nervous?" Jonas pushed aside the empty sweetener packets.

"That obvious?"

"More like, that normal. Most folks waiting on a bank loan deal get a little edgy when it's time to talk numbers."

So she wasn't ridiculous for feeling like jitters had taken over her body. Truth was, it wasn't only the possibility of a *no* from the bank that'd rumbled around in her brain all night, even when she was asleep.

It was Saturday night. It was the look in Logan's eyes that went so far beyond annoyance.

It was the gnawing realization that she'd hurt him without even knowing how. The fact that she hadn't heard from him since. And that kiss . . . she'd relived it how many times now?

"Now, then." Jonas tapped the stack of application papers against his desk to straighten their edges, then laid them in front of him. He scanned the cover sheet, licked his finger, and then flipped to the second page. Third, fourth. "You've done your homework, Amelia."

"I'll admit I had help. Seth Walker."

"Ah, hard to believe it's already been a couple years since I signed off on his loan." The furnace kicked in, the movement of air just enough to sway the potted fern at the side of Jonas's desk. He continued through the application, fingering his burgundy tie, the one streak of color in a suit ensemble that otherwise matched the walls.

Silent minutes ticked by—only the hum of the furnace and swishing papers filling the quiet as Amelia's hands knotted in her lap.

Finally, Jonas reached the last page. He once again lifted the stack, straightened it into a neat pile, and re-secured it with a binder clip. "Well, I commend your attention to detail. You wouldn't believe how many people come in here, hoping for ten, twenty, a hundred thousand dollars but haven't even managed to complete the application in full or, just as bad, it's full of typos and errors. Never bodes well."

She should've taken Jonas up on the coffee offer, if only for something to keep her from fidgeting. "You can chalk that up to my slight compulsion when it comes to proofreading." Logan had taken to teasing her about it every production day. Said he couldn't believe they ever managed to get a paper out the door.

"You'd go on editing forever if there wasn't such a thing as a deadline."

That'd been just last week. Before in one innocuous request—or apparently the opposite of innocuous—she'd ruined things.

"You've done a wonderful job prepping for this, and no one would doubt your zeal for the *News*—or this town, for that matter. Hard to believe you've only lived here two years."

"Almost three."

"One would think you'd been born here, considering what a part of Maple Valley you've become. I still remember Lenny and Sunny Klassen talking about the girl who wandered into town and showed up on their doorstep. 'Just the right tenant,' they called you."

They'd also called her an answer to prayer. The daughter they'd never had. Where she'd seen simply a classified ad and an affordable place to live, they'd seen a hurting heart and a chance to help.

"It's people like Sunny and Lenny who make me so passionate about why I'm here today. Did you see the story last summer about Lenny crafting his five thousandth chair in his woodshop? A small-town newspaper captures not only the personality of the community, but the people who live in it. It chronicles all the little things that make a place like Maple Valley so special." Amelia leaned forward in her chair. "If the *News* is sold off to a chain, chiseled down to a little section in a larger regional publication, we lose the chance to preserve the legacy of people like Sunny and Lenny in print."

"And you're certain Logan Walker's going to sell?"

Yes. No. She didn't know. Just like Owen had said, she'd become so caught up in chasing the Kendall Wilkins story, had sunk so quickly and easily into a friendship with Logan that just felt *right*, that facing their cross purposes when it came to the *News* faded more and more from her radar.

Then Saturday, he'd kissed her. And for a few dizzy hours she'd started to think . . .

Well, she didn't know what she'd thought. Except that she'd started to wonder if she really needed to go through with this bank loan application after all.

But the reality had come pummeling in later—when she'd upset Logan by asking him to sing. After the fundraiser, she'd gone home and finally finished the loan application.

"Yes, I'm pretty certain he's going to sell," she said now.

"I appreciate what you're trying to do, Amelia. And I have no doubt that if we secure financial backing, you'll pour yourself into this."

She heard his *but* before he went on, breathed in the sour disappointment that came with it in a long inhale tainted with paint fumes.

"But I have to be honest with you: the numbers simply may not add up. You don't have much in the way of collateral. You don't have any experience owning and managing a business. You don't have a college degree." He pushed her application aside.

"But I worked closely with Freddie for two years. And even in just the past couple months, I've learned a lot."

"There's also the fact that the paper doesn't have much in the way of a profit margin. That doesn't mean it can't turn around. But what we like to see in these cases is someone with a track record in fixing what's broken."

Fixing what's broken.

No. No, she had no track record there.

"So, you're saying no?"

"No." His tone was soft, compassionate. "But unfortunately, I'm not saying yes, either. I need more time to study the numbers, confer with colleagues, see what options we might have."

The tiniest murmur of hope feathered in. And Jonas must've seen it on her face because, as his fingers curled around his coffee mug, his expression suggested caution.

"I'm not going to tell you not to be optimistic, Amelia. But, well . . ."

He didn't have to finish. "Is there anything else I can do to boost my chances?"

He took a long drink of coffee. "Yes. Find someone to co-sign the loan. Someone with collateral."

Jonas saw her out of the office minutes later, a disenchanted weight dragging her steps. Find someone to co-sign her loan, he'd suggested. As if it were as easy as picking a dandelion from a wide-open field.

As if she weren't . . . alone.

She stopped at her car, a prickly wind sharpened with sleet gusting around her as the truth settled in. For all the friends she'd made since moving to town, all the ways she'd worked to become a part of this place and these people, she was still just . . . Amelia.

On her own.

Seth Walker had his uncle to support his dream.

All the Walkers had each other.

Eleanor had gone back to Des Moines, once again wearing her engagement ring. Sure, Amelia had heard from her a couple times since last week. They were tiptoeing their way back into a real relationship.

But she wasn't here.

And ironically, the one person who'd somehow rummaged his way deeper into her life than anyone else in Maple Valley was the same person on the brink of selling out her dream.

⁓

"You have to be on cloud nine. Tell me you're not on cloud nine." Theo's ecstatic voice bounded through Logan's speaker-phone as he pulled up in front of Rick and Helen's Tudor-style house—brick exterior and sloping roof. Since when had they uprooted the giant maple tree that used to slant through the front yard? Why hadn't he noticed that last time he was here? "Hey, where'd that expression come from anyway? Cloud nine."

"Probably meteorologists. They used to number clouds depending on altitude, and nines were high in altitude." He mumbled the explanation while he watched Rick O'Hare clear a path down the sidewalk in front of the house. Even with the car still running, he could hear the jagged scraping of a shovel against cement.

Like the grinding of his nerves ever since Rick had called Sunday night, asked him to stop by this morning. Without Charlie.

Actually, no, that wasn't right. He'd been on edge long before Rick's call. Ever since he'd been a jerk to Amelia Saturday night.

"Trust you to know the origins of an overused cliché."

"'Overused cliché' is redundant." And now he was being a jerk to Theo. He turned off the car.

"I'm going to ignore that because *USA Today* just called you—and I quote—'as winsome as he is enigmatic.' How old was this reporter anyway? Because I'm thinking maybe it's more than your speechwriting savvy she liked."

Logan glanced at the copy of the newspaper in his passenger's seat. Dad had gone and bought a copy—ten copies, actually—before Logan had even finished his first cup of coffee this morning. He'd forced himself to read it, tried to muster the pleasure he should be feeling at how well it'd turned out.

At least Theo was happy.

"You weren't just calling about the article, were you?" Outside, Rick perched his shovel against the side of the house and went inside.

"No, just wanted to make sure you're really going to be on the plane this Thursday. Because—and I quote—'Walker is equally at ease in his LA office, penning winning words that eventually end up on a teleprompter screen, as he is back in his hometown, where'—and this is where it really gets good—'kin and kindness, family and fellowship take top priority.'"

"She likes her alliteration."

"To be sure. But read the article a second time and there's a pretty clear underlying question. She paints you as a man torn, Walker."

Yeah, he'd picked up on that, too. Read the question she didn't spell out: Which world did he really belong in?

"She writes personality profiles, Theo. She was just looking for a way to make me more interesting than I am." The curtain at the O'Hares' front window swooped. If they hadn't known he was here before, they did now. "Don't worry. I'll see you in D.C."

He hung up seconds later and let himself out the car. Anxiety weighed each step as he walked to the house where he'd spent so many evenings through the years. Dinners with Emma's family when they'd first started dating. Rotating Thanksgiving and Christmas gatherings once they'd married. Weekend trips home after they'd moved to California, doing their best to squeeze in time with both families.

He passed the blunt, snow-covered stump where the old maple tree used to stand.

Helen opened the front door as he climbed the steps. Her red-tinted hair—so like Emma and Charlie's—was pulled into a braid. Her smile was genuine, if not entirely relaxed.

"Good to see you, Logan. We missed you in church yesterday."

Yes, because he'd skipped. Frustrated at the night before. Sleepless from the memories it summoned. Emma. Amelia.

Helen took his coat inside the entryway, then beckoned for him to follow. The house smelled of lavender and vanilla, like always, and also like always, it was spotless. Vacuum tracks still trailed the carpet.

Rick was already in the living room when they entered, settled on a flower-printed couch with a beige blanket draped over the back. He leaned forward to shake Logan's hand as Logan lowered into the wingback chair opposite the couch. An oval coffee table filled the space between them, a display of nature magazines splayed over its surface.

Helen moved aside a throw pillow and sat next to her husband, but then popped back up. "I'm sorry, I should offer you something to drink before we . . . talk. Coffee?"

"No thanks. You've had my dad's coffee before, right? He makes it so strong, one cup lasts an entire day."

Helen nodded and lowered once more, her obvious unease feeding his own. Was something wrong here? Was one of them sick?

Or maybe they'd heard from Waverly.

On instinct, he glanced to the wall, where a collage of photos surrounded a large family portrait. Probably nearly a decade and a half old now, it displayed a beaming Rick and Helen standing behind their daughters—Emma with those luscious curls and the braces she'd hated in high school, and a six- or seven-year-old Waverly, whose smile bent more toward a smirk even then.

Charlie's mom.

No, her *birth mother*. Emma had been Charlie's mom from the second she'd held her.

"How's Waverly?" He couldn't stop from blurting out the question. He knew Rick and Helen didn't like to talk about her. Getting pregnant in high school, frankly, had been only the beginning of Emma's sister's troubles. There'd been alcohol-infested parties, drugs, a couple arrests.

Last he'd heard, she was staying in a halfway house down in St. Louis. Did she ever think about the daughter her brother-in-law was now raising alone?

Rick's long exhale made Logan regret the question. "We tried to call her about a month ago, and the number was disconnected."

"I'm . . . sorry."

"We pray for her every day," Helen added softly. "One day . . ." She let the sentence trail.

Rick cleared his throat. "Of all the bad decisions Waverly has made, though, giving Charlotte up for adoption wasn't one of them. We're very glad she went through with her pregnancy, and well, that leads into what we'd like to talk to you about." Rick and Helen shared a look before Rick went on. "Logan, you've done a fine job with Charlotte. Many men would've buckled under the pressure of single fatherhood and a rising career."

"We saw that *USA Today* article," Helen interjected, forced cheer in her voice. "We're very proud of you."

"Thanks." Kind words, but they did nothing to quell his rising tide of concern.

"It mentioned something about you being vetted as a possible staffer for a presidential campaign. Is that true?" Rick, too, seemed to intentionally inject his tone with plastic interest.

But the pit in Logan's stomach only grew. "It's looking that way. Roberta S. Hadley's flying Theo and me to D.C. this week."

Why did it feel like a confession? "That's not public information, by the way."

Helen and Rick exchanged glances again, and no, there wasn't a chance he was imagining the resolve in their silent conversation. He'd just confirmed something for them. But what?

"There's no use talking around this, Logan." Rick folded his hands as he leaned forward. "I respect you, so I'm going to lay this out on the table, straightforward-like."

"I appreciate that." The words were robotic as the buzz of his dread heightened.

"We think you should consider letting Charlotte stay here."

Relief escaped in an exhale. That was all? "I know you offer your guestroom every time when we're in town, but it just wouldn't feel right not to stay at Dad's—"

"No, I mean, we'd like her to live with us permanently."

His mental reprieve cut off—jarring and abrupt. "I don't understand."

"You're so busy, Logan," Helen said, an overly gentle lilt to her words. "You're successful, moving up in your career. But where does that leave Charlotte?"

"What do you mean, where does it leave her?" His volume lifted. "It doesn't *leave* her anywhere. She'll be with me, like she's always been. Whether it's in LA or somewhere else, she'll be with me."

"Or a nanny." Rick dropped the statement with a thud.

Logan could only stare, disbelief slicing through him. Were they really asking what he thought they were? He tried to straighten from his sunken position in the overstuffed cushions of the chair.

Helen tried again. "We can give her a home with a mother and a father figure—"

"*I'm* her father."

"And we're her grandparents," Rick said with force. "And

221

we're concerned she needs more attention than you're able to give her. I'm sorry if this sounds harsh, but we have a right to state our opinion. Yes, you're her adopted father, but we're blood relatives—"

Logan pulled himself free of the plush chair and jumped to his feet. "I can't believe I'm hearing this."

"Logan, we just want what's best for her." Helen's gaze was rimmed with anxiety. Perhaps apology, too.

But it wasn't good enough. They couldn't actually think he'd agree to this. "Charlie is *my* daughter. She belongs with me. I am doing the best I can—"

"We know you are." Desperation clung to Helen's voice.

"And I will not for one minute consider abandoning her."

Rick shifted. "You wouldn't be abandoning—"

"She's already lost one parent." Hurt strangled his voice. "I can't believe you'd even ask . . ." He jabbed his fingers through his hair, focus shooting to that portrait again, to Emma's teenage smile. "The answer is no."

His feet carried him to the door, shock still coursing through him along with a lurching need to see his daughter.

"What about the fact that she won't talk?"

He turned to see Rick standing.

"What about the fact that she's almost four years old and has yet to form an entire sentence?"

"We're seeing a speech pathologist. You know that. It's going well."

"So what happens when you pick up and leave? Disrupt the routine Charlie's forming? You're just going to let it go? Don't you think settling in one place could help?"

"She's not the only therapist in the world." He heard the dark tenor in his voice. "I'm not letting anything go, Rick."

He grabbed his coat from the coat tree and walked out the door.

He didn't know why he was here.

Slushy snow, dirt-stained and slickened by the layer of sleet, spit out from today's melancholy skies, chomped under his feet, pushing against the night's frosty quiet. The third of May, and winter held on. Dogged. Cold.

Logan rubbed his palms against the ribbed sweater that did nothing to ward off the crisp air. He should've grabbed his coat.

He should've done a lot of things today after stalking away from his in-laws this morning. Shown up at the office, for one.

Instead, he'd spent the day helping Dad fix a broken pipe at the depot, shoveling snow back at the house, attending therapy with Charlie.

Pretending Rick and Helen's—what? request? offer? demand?—hadn't shaken him to his core.

And now he stood outside Amelia's house, shafts of moonlight breaking through the cloud cover and skimming over the angles of her front door. The muffled buzz of a table saw drifted from Lenny Klassen's workshop. Amelia would probably close the door in his face after the way he'd spoken to her Saturday night.

"You gonna knock or what?"

His gaze jerked upright at the sound of Amelia's voice. He stepped back and tipped his head until he could make out the open loft doors above, Amelia sitting at the edge, legs dangling over.

"What in the world are you doing up there?"

"Just thinking. What are you doing *down* there?"

Wasn't she freezing? And how had he not noticed her?

Probably the willow tree had blocked his view as he'd parked. And during the short trek from his car to the barn, his eyes had been on the ground as he'd asked himself for the fiftieth time why he'd come here.

"Can I come in?"

"It's unlocked."

He opened the heavy door and stepped inside, warm air tinged with a cool from above and a sweet smell that reminded him of . . . camping?

He stopped in the middle of the living room, suddenly feeling intrusive. A cast-off pair of shoes lay in the middle of a rug. An open book on the coffee table. A sweater over the edge of the couch. An empty cup on the desk. Only a small lamp, antique-looking, with beads dangling around the shade, lit the space with dim, ocher light.

And then she stood in front of him, her footsteps on the stairs having barely registered as he gulped in the very Amelia-ness of this house. It shouldn't feel so . . .

He didn't have the word for it. Comfortable? Soothing? *Needed*.

Her brow pinched as she studied him now, hazel eyes locked on his and probably wondering why he wasn't saying anything. She wore pajama pants and a sweatshirt, hair in a wind-ruffled ponytail, and slippers on her feet.

"I think you need a s'more."

He blinked. "Excuse me?"

"You look like I felt today. Only one cure for that in my book. Or if not a cure, at least a pretty good pain reliever."

She turned to the kitchen, and like a man dazed—or maybe just hungry—he simply followed.

She was already pulling open cupboards and twisting the dial on the stovetop. "I know you Walkers consider yourselves the experts on breakfast. Well, what you can do with eggs, I can do with marshmallows."

"Amelia—"

She lifted a fork from a drawer and pointed at the kitchen table. "Sit."

He sat.

"I don't know why other people don't get more creative with their s'mores. There's a whole world of possibilities out there, and we settle for Hershey bars? No thanks." She opened another cupboard.

He gasped. "You have an entire shelf of candy bars?"

She angled so he could see her smirk. "Two shelves. Don't sell me short, Walker. Now what's your damage? Reese's Peanut Butter Cups or Milky Way?"

He only stared.

"O-kay. Both." She stuck two marshmallows on two different forks. "Actually you can help. Hold these over the burner for me?"

So this was what he'd smelled when he walked into the house. For the next couple minutes, he stood next to her at the stove, watching shades of brown curl over the marshmallows as Amelia prepared the rest of her ingredients. She used a spoon to flatten the mini Milky Way atop a graham cracker. Set the peanut butter cup on its own cracker.

The smell, the warmth of the stove, Amelia's ease with him in her kitchen . . .

He could almost forget he'd launched angry words at her Saturday. Had his feet knocked out from under him today.

They don't trust me. Rick and Helen don't trust me to raise my own daughter.

"Amelia—"

"Ooh, careful, they're about to go black." She pulled the forks from his hands, slid the marshmallows free, and squished them into graham cracker sandwiches. She held the plate to him. "Here you go. My version of a nightcap at the end of a bad day."

"How do you know it was a bad day?"

"You didn't show up at the office. You haven't shaved. You're not wearing a tie. You didn't even scold me for my candy stash."

She waited until he took the plate and then brushed past him. "Come on."

And then he was following her again, practically mute. Past her desk and up the stairs and into her bedroom, where a blast of chilly air churned from the still-open loft doors. Unmade bed with pink-striped sheets. Bookshelves spilling paperbacks. White shag rug and a wooden wardrobe Lenny had probably handcrafted.

Amelia was already sitting at the window. He moved to her side, lowering to the cold floor. Faint moonlight traced the willow tree's drooping branches and shimmered over snow-covered fields.

"Nice view. But don't you freeze when you sit up here like this?"

"Sure, but cold air helps me think. Has this way of helping me mentally and emotionally declutter. It's refreshing. Besides, I've got blankets." She pointed to a stack beside him.

He bit into the first s'more. "You weren't kidding. This is amazing."

"Glad you think so. I know it's no fancy omelet, and it's sticky and messy to eat and—"

She cut herself off, laughing as he pulled stringy, melted marshmallow away from his mouth.

This. This was why he'd come here. Because in two years of burying himself in work and fatherhood, of feeling alone in every scarce moment in between, somehow with Amelia, the isolation crumbled.

Oh, he'd always had Theo and his wife. Colton had been a good friend. He saw his sisters often enough, and Beckett was only ever a phone call away, even if he hardly ever saw him. And there was Dad . . .

But Amelia was different. He didn't know how, but she'd tunneled her way past the confident, hold-it-all-together exterior he wore like a suit of armor, his way of convincing the world—or maybe just himself—his wife's death hadn't shattered him.

"Amelia." He set down the plate, needing to say these words before he finished eating. "On the day of Emma's accident, the day she died, I was at a friend's recording studio."

Amelia opened her mouth, maybe to ask why he was telling her this, where it'd come from. But she must've changed her mind, because she only pressed her lips together and waited.

"I played in high school all the time and even in college. Fiddled for a while with trying to actually do something with music. Kind of unrealistic, I guess, and Emma encouraged me to pick a focus and stick with it. I picked writing." A bristling wind sluiced past the window. "Anyway, I'd been missing playing and got this impulse to pick it up again. I didn't tell Emma. I don't know why I didn't tell her. Maybe I was embarrassed or thought she'd think it was childish. I don't know."

A shiver vibrated through him, urging him on. "The point is, I held a piece of me back from her, and she died not knowing. I was carelessly strumming a guitar while she was pinned in her car." The image—one he'd never even seen with his own eyes but that had fully formed all the same in years of tormenting imagination. "And when the police called, I was so into what I was doing at the studio, I didn't answer."

"Oh, Logan." Her voice was barely a breath.

His own, strangled. "She died an hour after arriving at the hospital. I got there minutes too late. If I'd just answered that call, I might've had time to . . ."

He couldn't say any more, lost in the pain that racked him. For once he let the anguish heave against his ribs and escape in quiet shudders and hot tears he couldn't see through. All he could do was feel—grief and release.

And Amelia's hand sliding over his back and her face burying in his neck.

"I'm sorry—"

She cut him off with a shake of her head, his tears landing in her hair. Her other arm wound around the front of him.

And he didn't know how much time passed—five minutes, ten, maybe more—as two years' worth of heartache and remorse poured from him until he felt emptied. Bereft and undone.

Still.

Save for Amelia shivering against him but still holding on. Tight. As if this loft floor might tilt, and she alone would keep him from falling.

With his free hand, he reached for a blanket, orange and wooly. Managed to drape it over their huddled form and then kept his arm around her. Waited until he could push words from hollowed lungs. "I'm sorry about Saturday night."

"No, I'm sorry. If I'd known . . ." Her breath was warm against his neck.

"But you didn't."

Maybe he should feel embarrassed at the way he'd broken down, cried in front of her. But somehow there wasn't space for humiliation now.

Only . . . understanding.

The blanket slipped from her shoulder, and he tugged it back into place. "You're right about the loft and the cold."

"I know."

Silent, steadying moments ticked by, and only when Amelia shifted, moved her head to his shoulder, did he speak again. "Hey, Amelia?"

"Hmm?"

"I have to go to D.C. later this week." He paused. "Want to come with?"

"To Washington, D.C.?"

"I want to bring Charlie along, but I've got a big meeting."

Was he making it sound like he only wanted her along as a babysitter? So not even close to the truth of it.

"But the Maple Valley Market is next weekend. First big event of the spring."

Right, the one when all the businesses in town set up booths in the town square. This town would use any excuse for a shindig.

"I always help with it."

Because she never missed a town event. And for the first time since he'd met her, that particular quirk seemed less charming and more . . . unsettling.

This is her home. Everything she loves is here.

Still, he couldn't help himself. "You'll be back in time for the Market. Promise."

She glanced up at him, moonlight-speckled eyes he could lose himself in.

"Come along?"

Dear Mary,

If you were my daughter, I'd tell you about Kendall Wilkins. I've told a few people about how he paid my college tuition for the couple years I attended. How he wrote me letters.

But I haven't told them how he helped me stand up to my family. My parents, you see, were not fans of my decision to major in history. "You'll never find a job with that degree," they said. "Why can't you find a useful major like Eleanor?"

I told this to Kendall in one of my early letters my freshman year. And you know what he wrote back?

"Poppycock, Miss Bentley." (Yes, he actually used the word poppycock.) "I'm not paying for your education so you can study something 'useful.' I'm paying for your education because I felt your passion in that essay you wrote. The way history enchants you. To you, it's more than dates and facts—it's stories and lingering mystery and legacies.

"Don't settle, Miss Bentley. Nurture your passion and, I promise, one day you'll discover its purpose."

He was right.

I just wish I'd held on to that advice later.

13

I can't believe we're here."

Amelia basked in the white light cratering down from the ceiling of the Boeing Milestones of Flight Hall in the Smithsonian's National Air and Space Museum. In front of her, the silver wings of the *Spirit of St. Louis* reached outward, its body tilted up, as if ready for flight.

Charles Lindbergh's plane. Right in front of her.

"I've heard you say that before." Logan stood next to her, Charlie sitting atop his shoulders. "At Mount Rushmore."

Twice now Logan had escorted her to a sight that took her breath away. "Can you believe how small it is? Can you imagine flying more than thirty hours over a crystal ocean, by yourself, in something so little?"

"And I thought our coach seats were cramped this morning."

She turned to Logan. Speaking of things that took her breath away . . .

They'd gone straight to the hotel after landing in D.C. While she and Charlie had jumped on the bed in her room as a cartoon played on the flatscreen, she'd heard the splatter of Logan's shower next door, the buzzing hum of his razor.

Thirty minutes later, he'd knocked on the door joining their rooms, and she hadn't been able to stop the "whoa" that'd slid out. Perfectly fitted metallic-gray suit and pale plum tie—the light colors making his eyes and hair seem even darker than before. Gone was the hint of a beard that usually stubbled his cheeks, and maybe she would've missed it if not for the alluring spice of his aftershave.

"Do I look worthy of a presidential candidate?"

She'd had to cough to make her voice work. *"I think she'll find you passable."*

He'd grinned then, and she'd suddenly loved and hated Roberta S. Hadley all at once. Loved because without the politician's summons, she wouldn't be here with Logan and his daughter, a part of their world, however temporary.

Hated because Hadley's interest meant Logan wasn't long for Maple Valley.

But no. She'd promised herself she wouldn't think of that now. Just like they'd apparently made an unspoken pact not to talk about that kiss last Saturday in the janitor's closet. And anyway, Logan had whisked them to the museum for a hurried visit before his one o'clock meeting. She wouldn't ruin this surprise with thoughts of the future.

"You do know this makes the four-thirty a.m. wakeup entirely worth it."

Logan's hands held Charlie's legs in place over his shoulders, apparently no care to the way his daughter mussed his rakish hair. "I just wish we could see more of it. I've only got fifteen minutes before I need to catch a cab."

She turned back to the plane. "This is enough." To think, this small aircraft had survived not only a historic flight across the ocean, but the swell of the 150,000 people who'd rushed the French field after Lindbergh landed.

"We're lucky to be visiting when we are." Logan followed

her around the plane. "It's usually suspended overhead. Only reason it's down on the floor is because of renovations."

Amelia pointed. "See how the fuel tanks are ahead of the cockpit? That was for safety, but it meant Lindbergh couldn't see directly in front of him without using a periscope. Or he'd just turn the plane and look out a side window."

"Just how many Lindbergh biographies have you read, Bentley?"

"You saw the bookshelves in my bedroom. At least one is dedicated solely to Lucky Lindy."

"Did you ever think of doing something with your slightly over-the-top love of this stuff?"

"What, like work in a museum?"

Charlie's feet knocked against Logan's blazer, and he crouched to let her down. "Or write for a historical magazine or become a biographer or . . . I don't know. Just makes me a little sad that you're stuck in Maple Valley writing about street repavings and the occasional petty crime instead of indulging your . . ."

"History geek side?"

He grabbed ahold of Charlie's hand. "You said it, not me."

"Well, I appreciate the concern, Logan, but what I write about back home is important to the people who live there, my friends and neighbors. So it's important to me, too. It may not be the kind of stuff that's immortalized in museums and books, but it matters." She paused. "I'm not discontent."

She meant what she said. And yet, she couldn't deny the flicker of passion this museum had flamed to life. There was an aura here—something both mysterious and satiating.

How much more amazing would it have been to witness history in real life? Like Kendall Wilkins had, watching this plane land, experiencing the throng and thrill at Le Bourget Field.

And he hadn't been alone. There'd been somebody who'd shared the memory.

"You're thinking about Kendall, aren't you?" Logan asked

"I'm thinking about Kendall and Harry Wheeler. And how crazy it'd be to be mistaken for someone like Charles Lindbergh. For a few minutes, to have so many eyes on you—to feel that kind of adoration. If he'd ever felt small or unseen, I bet he didn't in those moments."

Even as Charlie tugged on his hand and tourists filtered around them, Amelia could feel Logan's gaze on her.

"But the adoration wasn't meant for him." Thoughtfulness layered his comment. "They weren't really seeing him, only who they thought he was."

"I guess . . ."

He shrugged. "I just think one person seeing you for who you really are is better than 150,000 people who've got it wrong."

But what if that one person chose to stop seeing you? What if you could feel yourself disappearing from his world? "I thought Jeremy saw me," she said. She hadn't meant to let it out. Hated that she did.

But Logan would've heard it even if she hadn't said it.

"I'm going to make a guess that Jeremy only ever saw himself." He tipped his head to one side. "Because when you really let people see you, Amelia—all of you, not just the snow-obsessed reporter—it's impossible to look away."

Her breathing hitched, his sincerity, the depth of what he'd just said . . . the way he looked away when he said it, as if surprised by his own honesty.

"Daddyyyy. Swim." Charlie's voice poked in then, not breaking the moment so much as adding to it. Because at the sound of her voice, Logan's eyes filled with delight. She wasn't speaking in sentences yet. But clearly just a couple weeks in therapy was already helping.

"You'll get to swim soon enough, Charlie. First we need to let Amelia *ooh* and *ahh* a little more over the plane."

"See how the window curves over the cockpit? Even though it was cold and icy during his flight, Lindbergh kept it open to help him stay awake." She circled the plane a second time, stopped at its nose and lifted her phone to take a photo. "Thirty-three hours of flight. What if he'd dozed off?"

"You must've read those Lindy books as many times as my last editorial."

She snapped a photo. "I never should've told you about that."

"Don't be embarrassed. You know good writing when you see it, that's all."

He twirled Charlie in a dancing turn with one arm as he teased, and oh, those crinkles at the corners of his eyes could set aflight a thousand butterflies in a girl's stomach. "I wonder when he finally got to get some rest. When he landed, he was immediately whisked off. Later, he came back to look at the plane to make sure the crowd hadn't destroyed it. The plane survived, but it was definitely damaged—that's why he looks so unhappy in some of the photos taken the next day."

"Or maybe he was just jet-lagged." Charlie had clamped onto his leg now, sitting on the museum floor.

"Your poor daughter is bored to death. And you've got a meeting. We should get back."

"You don't have to leave. I was going to catch my own cab. Stay here. See the rest of the museum. There was another plane you wanted to see. What was it? Long name, starts with a *T*."

"Ting-miss-ar-toq. It means 'one who flies like a bird.' It's the plane Charles and Anne Morrow Lindbergh flew together. It had pontoon floats so it could land in water."

"Is your brain a flytrap for Lindbergh trivia?" He dragged Charlie with his foot, stepping closer to Amelia. "But seriously, go ahead and stay. Charlie will be fine. She'll behave." He looked down. "Won't you, kiddo?"

"Maybe."

Amelia grinned. "She's honest. I'll give her that. But no, we'll go back with you. We can come back another time."

Her breath caught on those last words, the realization of what she'd said—*we*—and all the hope huddled in those two little letters she hadn't let herself fully acknowledge until right now.

She was falling for Logan Walker.

So very hard and so very completely.

But if he'd heard the assumption in her comment, he let it slide and instead swung Charlie into his arms once more. "Let's get a picture before we leave."

He tapped a nearby tourist, made the request, and handed over his phone, then moved to scrunch in closer to Amelia.

"I'm going to look ridiculous in this photo. You in that suit and me in airplane clothes."

Charlie perched on one side of him, he draped his other arm around her shoulder. "You look perfect."

The tourist snapped the photo. "Safety shot," he called out, then snapped a second. "Good-looking family," he said as he returned Logan's phone.

And oh, if she didn't foolishly love the fact that Logan didn't correct him.

The wonder of the museum stayed with her as they exited, hailed a cab just outside the National Mall, squeezed into the backseat, and traveled the cramped streets of D.C.

She'd said *we*.

He pushed into the Hyatt Regency Hotel, just across the street from the Marriott where he'd left Amelia and Charlie, Amelia's words still echoing through him even as he summoned the focus for what might be the most important meeting of his career.

We can come back another time.

"Walker!"

He heard Theo's voice before the hotel's revolving door had even spilled him into the lobby. He hurried forward, no reservation in the hug that followed, the sound of rolling suitcase wheels and the ding of an elevator accompanying Theo's slap on his back.

He stepped back, taking in his friend's surfer hair, now gelled into cooperation, and a dark suit that contrasted with his own.

"You look good," Theo said.

"You look tan."

"I forced myself to take a Saturday off last week. Jill and I went to the beach."

"I think I hate you. We got a blizzard on the first day of May."

Theo reached for the Starbucks carrier on a marbled ledge behind him. "Here, your usual afternoon decaf chai."

He accepted the warm cup. "Believe it or not, I've given in to all-day coffee."

"You? What happened to 'I can't drink caffeine after one o'clock 'cause it'll keep me up all night'?" Theo's voice pitched to a whine as he mimicked Logan.

He swallowed a hot sip, the sweetness of the chai a shock after getting so accustomed to Dad's daily muddy brew. "I've changed."

He said it with off-hand nonchalance, but Theo regarded him with a serious glint in his eyes. "You *have* changed."

"Don't look so baffled. I welcomed caffeine into the afternoon portion of my day. Didn't shave my head or pierce my eyebrow. Oh man, you should've seen my parents' reaction the day Raegan came home with a pierced eyebrow."

Theo shook his head, still peering at Logan over the rim of his cup. "It's not that. You're . . . I don't know, calm or something. Less frazzled. No circles under your eyes."

"Well, I've always slept best at Dad's."

Theo took another drink, then lowered his cup, studying gaze still in place. "So you brought Charlie and who again? One of your sisters?"

"Amelia. I've mentioned her."

"In one of the four or five oh-so-wordy emails you've sent in the past month? Sure. She's the editor, right? Interesting choice for a babysitter."

Yeah, well, *babysitter* had been a convenient excuse, hadn't it? Not that he would've considered leaving Charlie in Maple Valley, not after Rick and Helen's pushy request. But he could've asked Kate or Raegan to come along. Even Dad. They could've made a trip of it—gone to see Beckett in Boston afterward.

But no. He'd wanted Amelia.

And Theo saw the truth written all over his face, didn't he? His partner peered at him over his Starbucks cup. "Poor Alena's going to be disappointed."

"Shut up, Theo." And shoot, he hadn't checked in with their intern in days. She probably wondered if he still existed—if she still had a job. "So where's this meeting actually happening?"

Theo checked his watch. "Room 1316. Apparently they want to keep it on the down-low—no dining room or lobby meetings."

Which made sense. The senator hadn't formally announced her campaign, hadn't even made a statement about forming an exploratory committee. But if she was seen meeting with potential staffers, speculation would run rampant.

They passed a sign for the pool as they moved toward the elevator. Amelia would remember to bring those floaty arm things along when she took Charlie to the hotel pool, wouldn't she?

Inside the elevator, Theo punched the button for the thirteenth floor. "Back to the editor—"

"Not going there."

"Jill's been asking me if you're ready to, like, you know . . . date or whatever. She's got a couple friends. I've been saying I didn't think you were there yet, but . . ." He drew out the last word.

"We're about to meet with a presidential candidate. I'm not having a discussion about my love life right now."

"But there is, in fact, a love life to be discussed?"

The elevator dinged. *Saved.* He practically barreled from its moving doors.

"Fine, avoid the conversation. But you know Jill's going to pummel the truth out of you at dinner tonight."

He stopped in front of the corridor's brass-framed mirror opposite the elevator, straightened his tie. Right, dinner tonight. He'd forgotten he'd told Theo they'd join him and Jill tonight. Sorta wished he hadn't.

Sorta wanted Charlie—and fine, yes, Amelia—to himself tonight.

Theo eyed him in the mirror. "Ready?"

"Let's do it."

They covered the distance to the hotel room in seconds, stopped outside the door. Theo looked to him. He knocked.

And Senator Roberta S. Hadley herself answered.

"Right on time, gentlemen."

She looked much the same in person as she did on C-SPAN: auburn hair twisted into a light updo, reserved blue suit—about the same color as the furniture in the room behind her—and tall. He'd heard she'd played basketball back in college. He could believe it.

"Come on in."

Lofty windows magnified the space of the suite and offered a gaping view of the D.C. skyline. Logan had expected a full room, but only one other person waited in the seating area that circled around a glass coffee table. He stood as they approached.

"This is Gaius Jefferson. He'll be my campaign manager once I technically have a campaign."

They shook hands and exchanged greetings, then sat. And the next fifteen minutes passed in a pattern of light chitchat as they established rapport. The senator asked about Theo's wife, Logan's daughter. They took turns inquiring about her family, recent Senate activities, her home state.

Finally, she steered the conversation to the campaign. "I plan to announce by the end of June. I need a deputy for Gaius"—she eyed Theo—"and a communications coordinator." And now Logan. "I've been watching the two of you for a while. I like your style. And I love the fact that you're not Washington insiders. Just so you know, we've vetted you up one side and down the other in the past few weeks. And I'd like to get to know you more in these next few hours. But first, I'm correct in understanding this would be your first presidential campaign, yes?"

Did Theo's nod feel as weighty as his own?

At a glance from the senator, Gaius leaned forward. "Then we need to make sure you understand the realities of what you'd be asked—expected—to commit to. I've done four presidential campaigns. It's why I'm bald now and wrinkled as a prune. From the minute Senator Hadley announces her candidacy, this race becomes a 24/7 job for her, for me . . . and for our team. Campaign work can be grueling—I'm sure you know that from your past experience. But anything you've put in before will be nothing compared to this. Our headquarters will be in the senator's hometown—Allentown, Pennsylvania—but you'll be on the road more than you'll be there. Logan, you're a single dad. Have you considered what life on the road means for your daughter?"

He wouldn't be here if he hadn't considered it. He'd need to find a nanny willing to travel. Find a way to continue Charlie's speech therapy. He'd told himself it'd work.

But here, now, sitting across from the woman he'd researched and come to respect, a woman who could end up being one of the most powerful people in the world, reality rose like a heavy fog. This was everything he'd worked and hoped for.

But Charlie . . .

What would it mean for her? Life on a campaign bus?

Or worse, staying behind with a nanny, only seeing her daddy in the snatches of time he could finagle away from work.

His gaze went to the window, the shape of the Capitol Building just visible in the distance.

It's one thing to sacrifice a year of your own life. But your daughter's?

Theo shifted on the couch next to him, probably an effort at stirring some kind of answer from him. But he didn't even remember the question anymore. "I'm sorry, I—"

"Oh, and the other thing," the senator cut in. "We'd need you in Allentown in three weeks."

Three weeks. The remaining air seeped from Logan's lungs.

∽

Amelia had never felt so very Midwestern as she did now, sitting across from Jillian Tompkins in the hotel restaurant's booth, hair still damp from an afternoon of swimming with Charlie, her coral top and favorite jeans a sorry contrast to Jillian's black sundress and turquoise jewelry. Next to Jillian's sun-kissed skin, she wanted to slither out of her own—pasty, with the clingy smell of chlorine.

Why hadn't Logan told her to bring clothes for dinner out?

But maybe this was exactly what she needed. A wakeup call. A reality check. Hadn't she decided this afternoon she had to do something about the feelings spinning inside her like yarn on a loom, weaving together a tapestry destined to go unfinished?

He's got a new life in front of him. Your life is in Maple Valley.

Amelia poked at the grilled asparagus that'd come with her

salmon. She didn't even know why she'd ordered the entrée. Seafood was not her thing. But after Jillian had ordered the prosciutto-wrapped cod, she'd panicked and ditched her previous pick of a burger and fries.

"I'm serious, though—there's basically no point in throwing a dinner party anymore if Logan's not there." Jill held her fork in the air, a cooked baby carrot on the end. "We tried to play Speeches on our own the other night and just ended up boring each other."

The soft, moody notes of a jazz piece flitted in, along with clinking dishes and the hum of conversation at nearby tables. At least Jill and Theo were nice—funny, too. Turned out Jill was a genealogist, called herself a nerd, and declared she could be happy living in a dungeon as long as she had a computer with Internet access. Logan had already made her promise to help Amelia find Harry Wheeler's family.

The Tompkinses both clearly adored Charlie, too—and she, them. She'd insisted on sitting by Jill.

And Amelia had swallowed something that tasted a little too close to jealousy.

Which is silly. She lifted her water glass. *It's not like she's . . . yours.*

And of course, then Jeremy's voice crowded in. *"She was never ours, Amelia. You should've never thought of her as ours. You got way too far ahead of yourself."*

A chip of ice lodged in her throat, and she sputtered, coughing until Logan patted her back and the ice scraped the rest of the way down.

"You all right?" Logan still wore his suit, though he'd long since lost the tie and loosened his collar. In the dusky light of the restaurant, his eyes looked almost black . . . exotic.

Like this whole town. New and captivating and exciting. An enthralling mix of history and energy. And for snippets of time today, she'd let herself imagine living here. A part of Logan's world-to-be.

"*Way too far ahead of yourself.*"

"I'm fine," she rasped. Took another drink. Grasped for composure. "Um, what's Speeches?" And why was Logan looking at her like he'd heard every scattered thought knocking around her brain?

"Oh, it's this game we made up just for Logan." Jillian finished her last bite of fish. "Theo was joking once that Logie can write a speech about literally anything."

"Logie?"

"Another thing she made up just for me." Logan rolled his eyes, then moved a handful of his fries onto Amelia's plate while Jill kept talking. He leaned in. "You've been eyeing them for twenty minutes."

God bless him.

" . . . and I said, 'Okay, Logie, make up a speech right now about that ugly vase my great-aunt gave us for our wedding.' And just like that, he starts waxing eloquent."

Theo put his arm around his wife. "So now it's a thing. Anytime we're out for dinner or at a party with friends, we inevitably end up playing and making Logan give a speech about a light fixture or a doorknob or whatever random object we spot."

"Emma was the best at it. She made him give a speech once about her overbite."

The mention of Logan's wife invited a hush over the table. Nothing heavy. Logan didn't even stiffen. But still, it was there . . . a shared quiet.

"She was good at it," Logan finally said. And then he slipped his last fry onto Amelia's plate.

Thirty minutes later, they stood in the lobby once more. Amelia held Charlie now, her little arms and legs draped over her,

her breathing heavy. Amelia shouldn't have felt such a spark of victory—almost maternal pride—when Logan's daughter had reached for her as they'd left the restaurant. She'd even whispered a shortened version of Amelia's name—Lia. She felt perfect in her arms now, head tucked into the pocket of Amelia's neck.

"Well, we've got a crazy-early flight tomorrow," Theo said. A valet rattled past with a luggage cart. "We better hit the hay. Logan, let's touch base on Monday."

"And Amelia, I'll start investigating this Harry Wheeler guy as soon as I'm home." Jill leaned in for a light side hug. "If he's got descendants, I'll find them."

"My wife, the Sherlock of family trees." Theo patted Logan's back and then moved away with Jill.

Logan glanced down at Amelia. "Arms numb yet?"

"Not enough that I'm willing to hand her over. If you haven't noticed, I've gotten a bit attached to your kid."

They trekked through the lobby and into a waiting elevator, its closing doors too much of a metaphor for this long, luscious day. Iowa seemed a million miles away, but in less than ten hours, she'd be on a plane, landing in Des Moines. And tomorrow she'd work in the office and then help set up for the Maple Valley Market.

The walk to their adjoining rooms was hushed, the hallway lights low. Logan stuck his key in the door, pushed it open, and turned. "Do you mind carrying her to the bed?"

She shook her head, trailing through the room to the bed closest to the window. The D.C. skyline glittered in a puzzle of lights and stars. Logan pulled the covers back, and she bent over to lay Charlie in the queen bed. Charlie barely stirred, sinking into a pillow, her hair fanning around her face. Logan tipped off her shoes before covering her with the sheet.

"No pj's for her tonight," he whispered, then bent to kiss his daughter's cheek.

And something in Amelia's tattered heart pieced itself back together.

In too deep. Pull back.

Logan straightened.

"Hey." His voice was a whisper. "Thanks for coming."

"Thanks for asking me. It was . . . kind of the best day." But also devastating. Because here, away from the pull of Maple Valley and the cares of running the newspaper, she hadn't been able to hide from the truth any longer.

I'm in love with you, Logan Walker.

Not like she used to be back when he'd been a faceless name whose words and awards she pored over.

She was in love with the real thing. The man whose love for his adopted daughter was written into his every move and thought and decision. The man who'd kissed her in a janitor's closet and held her in her loft window. Who helped his dad and supported his sisters and clearly worried about his brother.

Whose past, even with its hurts and regrets, had only deepened his character. He was real, genuine. The whole package.

I really think I love you.

What if she just said it?

After all, his languid gaze hadn't moved from her face in a minute. Maybe she wasn't the only one whose heart was turning inside out.

"I have to be back in three weeks."

Her rambling emotion froze. "What?"

"If I take the job with the campaign, they want me in Allentown in three weeks." He raked his fingers through his hair. "Theo's going to say yes, of course. Jill's all for it. I just keep thinking about Charlie."

"You want to do it, though, don't you?"

"Yes." No hesitation. "The more we talked today, the more I

could feel the energy. The buzz. It'd be such an incredible thing to be a part of."

"Being a part of something . . . it's important." *Until it's taken away.* For once, it wasn't Jeremy's image filling her mind at the thought.

This was why she belonged in Maple Valley. She was a part of that town, the people. And it wasn't going anywhere.

"Sleep on it, Logan. Pray. Maybe it'll feel clearer tomorrow."

He nodded, walked her to the door in between their rooms. And then, just like he had the other night in her loft, tucked her against him for a hug.

But she didn't let herself linger this time. Forced herself to pull away before the buttons on his shirt left an imprint on her cheek and his chest felt too much like home.

She closed the door between them. Dragged herself to the bathroom and changed into pajamas. Washed her face. Brushed her teeth.

And then paused outside the bathroom door as Charlie's voice drifted in. "Daddy?" A muffled whine.

She padded to the door between their rooms, listened to Logan's muted voice settling his daughter back down. And then—*oh*—then he sang her a couple lines. Just like he had that first night home. Soft, faint words she couldn't make out.

But it was enough to magnetize Amelia. Pressed against the door, she lowered to the floor, knees bent to her chin. He sang another line. She closed her eyes.

And maybe she would've fallen asleep there, listening to him sing, balled against the door closing her into a room way too big for just her . . . if not for Logan's voice once more. Closer now.

"Amelia?"

He was back at the door? "Yeah?"

"I'm weirdly not tired." Even with the door between them

muffling his voice, she could feel his closeness. "Want to see if there's a late-night movie on or something?"

Yes.

And no. Because any later, any longer . . . and she'd lose whatever last hold she might have on a heart that'd already broken too many times.

"I'm already in my pajamas."

"I've seen you in pajamas before."

"I already washed my face."

"I've seen you without makeup, too."

For a tempting second, she considered it. Why not open the door and find some classic movie on TV that reminded him of his mom? Sit on the bed and munch on vending-machine snacks and . . .

No.

Because he was going to leave.

And the sooner she accepted it, the better.

"I just . . . don't think it's a good idea."

His pause was long enough she almost changed her mind. And then, "Maybe we could just talk? Just for a few minutes. Right here." His voice had moved downward, as if he, too, had lowered to the floor. And there, through the crack under the door, she could see his shadow.

Tell him you're tired. Tell him you should both get some sleep before tomorrow's early flight.

Tell him you can't spend any more time exchanging pieces of your heart because it's getting too hard to tell yours from his.

"What do you want to talk about?"

"Anything. I just like talking to you."

She leaned her head against the wall. And couldn't even attempt to lie. "I do, too. Okay, then, so tell me what's so great about Roberta S. Hadley."

14

*J*ust when I think Maple Valley can't get more bizarre,
it does."

A laugh tracked Logan's words as he hoisted one end
of a six-foot folding table. Across from him, Raegan lifted her
end. "You know you love it here."

"We're setting up for an outdoor event under clouds so black
they could rain soot." All around the town square, activity
whirred as community members readied for the day's event—
setting up tables and booths, unfolding tents and awnings.

Like one of Charlie's pop-up picture books. And it wasn't
even seven in the morning yet. The stocky clouds blurred the
blush of sunrise and daubed a greenish tint over everything
below.

"Remember for a second where you are, brother. This is
the town that went on with its live nativity even after one of
the wise men burned down the stable. We had a parade last
year just a few days after a tornado." She stopped right in the
middle of Main Avenue, letting her end of the table conk the
cement. "And, if you'll recall, just a couple weeks ago we had

a fundraiser during a blizzard. So I don't think a little rain is going to deter our first festival of the summer."

"Clearly." Not if the citizens of Maple Valley could help it. Because apparently nobody cared that the forecast called for a ninety percent chance of thunderstorms, complete with lightning and hail.

And here he was out with all the rest of them, helping set up a booth where Seth would serve The Red Door's sliders and strawberry lemonade. Such a contrast from a few days ago, when he'd sat on a chair across from a senator with her eye on the White House, imagining a life he'd dreamt of for years but that was only now coming into focus.

How could two such vastly different worlds both feel . . . right?

A gust of wind carried Charlie's giggle across the square from where she played in the band shell with several other kids under a couple parents' supervision. He'd debated bringing her, especially considering the coming storms. But it wasn't supposed to get bad until lunchtime.

His gaze roved over the green space, hooked on Kate and Colton walking down the sidewalk, Coffee Coffee drinks in hand. Dad was around here somewhere—he was helping man a booth for the church. All the antique shops had sale racks and tables set up outside their stores, and over in the corner of the square, a bouncy castle was swaying its way into existence.

"She'll show up."

He turned back to Raegan. A stack of beaded bracelets cuffed both her wrists, and since when had she added pink and green streaks to her hair? "Who?"

"Men aren't supposed to play coy, Logan. That's for girls."

"Whatever." He hefted the table once more, and Raegan followed suit.

To be fair, he didn't blame his family for the curiosity that had revealed itself in hints and subtle questions ever since he'd returned from D.C.

Subtle? Yeah right.

Last night Seth had just come right out and asked. *"All right, we gave you forty-eight hours. Long enough. What's up with Amelia?"*

He'd mumbled something pathetic about friendship and working together and just when he'd run out of lame, stock explanations, Charlie—that little apple of his eye—had asked for another glass of milk. He couldn't have timed it better.

Thing was, he couldn't have answered Seth's question with anything concrete if he'd tried. He didn't know what was up with Amelia. One minute they were kissing in a closet or knotted together in her loft window or posing like a family for a photo at the Smithsonian. The next she was practically fleeing from a simple hug and hiding behind a hotel door.

At least she'd talked to him. One hour had stretched into two and then three Wednesday night as they'd whittled away the remainder of their time in D.C. The floor had grown hard underneath him and his throat was dry, but he hadn't been willing to peel himself away. Not until the red numbers on the hotel alarm clock let him know it was after two.

He might've slept all of three hours before rising to catch a cab to Dulles.

"Where are we going with this?" Raegan's arms strained at the weight of the table.

"Other side of the square, but we can take another break." He should've waited for Seth to get back instead of enlisting Rae's help. She was no weakling, but this table could've been made of lead.

"Uh, can I help?"

A shadow flickered in Raegan's eyes as she looked over Logan's shoulder. He angled to see Bear McKinley, the guitar player whose name matched his appearance. Coal-black hair, granite eyes, tattoo visible under the edge of one sleeve. He rounded the table as if to take over for Raegan.

"We've got this, Bear." Raegan's voice was as wooden as her posture.

Actually, no, they didn't. At this rate, it'd take them half the morning to make it across the square. No way was he arguing with Rae, though. "Thanks, anyway."

Something of a pleading expression crossed Bear's face as he looked from Logan back to Raegan. "Rae."

And that, apparently, was enough. His sister shoved her hands in her pockets. "Fine. I'll go help Ava with the lemonade."

"I didn't mean—" Bear started to call after her, but the drop of his linebacker shoulders signaled his defeat. His sigh dragged as he gripped the table, lifting it up as if it weighed as much as a puppy.

Logan nudged his head toward the table's designated spot in the park.

"For the record, I never wanted to hurt her."

They wedged their way around a red-and-white-striped tent. "For the record, I believe you." He'd heard enough from Kate to get the picture. Bear had no more blown into town before Raegan had latched on. They'd become fast friends on their way to something more before Bear had pulled the brakes—not because he didn't care, but because he did.

"She's my sister, though."

"I get it. Team Raegan."

"There really has to be teams?" They reached the section in the grass reserved for The Red Door.

Bear looked back to the spot on the road where Raegan had stood a minute ago. "Rae and I . . . I'm a leaf blowing in the wind, and she's got roots so deep, there's no pulling 'em up."

"Quite the metaphor."

"Quite the truth. I'll be in South America this time next week. Raegan made it clear she's staying put in Maple Valley. Wasn't meant to be, I guess. Or whatever other relationship-ending cliché works."

But if the outright longing in his expression was any indication, the man didn't feel nearly as nonchalant as his words sounded. Ledge walked past with a couple folding chairs under each arm, and in the slot beside them, Webster Hawks and others from the high school football team were setting up a face-painting booth.

Bear ducked under the table to secure its legs, then rose, tucking a shaft of hair behind his ear. "Look, I really have been trying to stay out of Raegan's way. Don't want to make anything worse—for either of us. But when I saw her arms about ready to fall off carrying this thing—"

"I know." He glanced at Charlie again, still playing in the band shell, chasing a kid he recognized as Nick Sheffield's son, the pastor of Dad's church. He'd attended almost every Sunday since coming home, just like he did back in LA, telling himself he was doing it for Charlie.

But there was a piece of him—wasn't there?—still hoping for a spiritual second wind. A voice or even just a whisper from the God who'd gone silent the day Emma died.

"Can I ask you something, Bear? How do you know going to South America is the right thing? You're in as deep as anyone here in the Valley. You sing in church and at Seth's, you've got friends, you're out here playing along even though this thing's doomed to get rained out." Even as he said it, a stray raindrop landed on his cheek. "And then there's Rae." He turned from the square back to Bear. "How do you know it's the right thing to do?"

Bear appeared to consider the question. "It's interesting you'd ask that. I talked to Kate once last fall when I couldn't figure out what to do about Raegan. She asked the same question about South America. I told her it came down to doing the next right thing, walking through the open door, you know?"

"So what if several doors open? How do you know which is the right one? How did you decide to choose the door to South America over my sister?" Another raindrop. But it wasn't supposed to storm until later. "And, man, forget all that for a second—how do you know it's even God opening any of the doors?"

Finding any kind of spiritual foothold was like trying to pin down spring in Iowa, when rain and snow and sun and clouds turned everything unpredictable.

Bear leaned against the table, arms folded, thoughtful. "Man, I don't think God is out to confuse us. When multiple doors open up, maybe there's not a right and a wrong one. Maybe sometimes God says, 'Dude, choose.' That whole free will thing."

Yeah, well, then Logan was right back where he was after Emma died. Looking to God for answers and getting only silence in return.

"Suppose I shouldn't say this to a soon-to-be missionary, but I'm not sure what I believe anymore."

Errant raindrops had turned into a near-drizzle now.

Bear straightened, seemingly nonplussed by Logan's confession. One he didn't know why he'd made to a guy he barely knew.

"I think sometimes believing is a matter of deciding. Deciding who you're going to trust and what you know about who you trust. And once that decision starts sinking into your bones, the wide-open spaces of your future get more invigorating than intimidating. Doesn't mean the choices suddenly get easy. But it does mean we stop worrying so much that we're going to mess up and pick the wrong door, as if we could possibly out-wander God."

Dad's voice slid in then, his words mingling with Bear's. *"He'll wait for you."*

And as the rain slicked over him and all the voices and noise of the Market faded, Logan's heart hooked on something solid.

Because if that was true, then maybe it wasn't about what he chose for his future—a campaign, a move, a relationship—but *Who* he chose. And how he trusted.

"Logan!"

His father-in-law's call cut in, an intrusion. Because here, under rolling clouds and a waifish rain, something was reawakening.

Maybe God had been silent two years ago, or maybe Logan simply couldn't hear. Maybe it didn't even matter, not today. Because in many ways, Logan was a different man now.

"Sometimes believing is a matter of deciding. Deciding who you're going to trust and what you know about who you trust."

"Logan, where's Charlie?"

The question knocked into him. *Charlie* . . .

A rumbling overhead. Thunder. He looked to Rick. "She's playing in the band shell." And she hated storms. If those clouds were going to break early—

"No, she's not."

He whipped around, only to see an empty shell. And in the millisecond it took to turn back to Rick, the sky broke loose. "I . . . she was just . . ." He blinked against the rain, now falling in sheets, concern that threatened to crest into fear rivering through him. He looked around, gaze weaving through booths and tables.

"You seriously don't know where she is?" Rain streamed down Rick's face.

"Don't worry, Walker," Bear said. "We'll find her."

Another groan in the sky.

Probably this was one of the more idiotic things she'd ever done. Especially considering the intermittent lightning strobing around the edges of storm clouds. But Amelia threw the pebble anyway, aiming for Owen's window—second floor of the only apartment complex in Maple Valley that'd gone to the effort to add a buzz-in security system.

The pebble thwacked against the glass, but the only response she got was a murmur of thunder. She crouched, felt around for another pebble and sent it sailing.

Seconds later, Owen's face appeared at the window. He pushed it open. "What?"

Mission accomplished. "You didn't answer when I buzzed." She'd hit the buzzer three times, shifting her weight from foot to foot, excitement whittling away every last crumb of patience.

"Because it's seven on a Saturday morning."

"I've got news." Raindrops bounced in the grass around her flip-flops.

"And it couldn't wait two more hours?"

She held up the bottle in her non-throwing hand. "I brought OJ. The kind you like, with the pulp."

"Fine." The window slammed shut.

With a grin, she dodged more raindrops and dashed her way to the front door, just in time to hear the latch release. Up on the second floor, Owen was waiting in his doorframe, ISU tee above Nike gym shorts, folded arms.

"I've never seen you this dressed down."

He held out his hand.

She gave him the bottle of OJ. He let her in.

"I don't know how you can drink it with the pulp. It's like little hairs floating around—" She stopped barely two feet into his living room. Bare walls—none of the framed pictures or baseball posters she was used to seeing—and boxes scattered around the room. "You're . . . packing?"

The news she'd been so antsy to share trickled into a puddle.

She turned back to Owen and waited as he capped his juice bottle and rubbed the sleep from his eyes. "Yep." He moved into the kitchen.

"That's it? 'Yep'? Were you going to tell me?"

He yanked a cereal box from a nearly empty cupboard. "Of course I was going to tell you."

"When? When you'd already switched zip codes?"

Bowl, spoon, box. He clunked each item onto the island counter. "I've still got three and a half weeks until I leave. I'm just getting a head start on packing. I was going to tell you Monday. Or maybe today at the Market."

He poured his cereal—some kind of oat and granola concoction she would've made fun of any other day—and scooted onto a stool. "I've got a letter of resignation written. Wasn't sure whether it went to you or Logan."

"Owen."

He looked up from his bowl, and from the twist of his face, she knew he'd heard the petition in her voice. The need for an explanation, but even more, the regret over how off-course their friendship had veered these past weeks.

He abandoned his stool and disappeared into the bedroom off the side of the living room, returning with a piece of paper. It was creased with the faint smudge of inky fingerprints, as if he'd folded and unfolded the letter for multiple readings.

She flattened it now while he poured milk into his cereal, didn't have to read more than a line to understand. She lifted her eyes. "You got into grad school."

"Three of them, actually, but this is the one I'm going to accept."

"When? Why didn't you tell me?"

"There was never a good time. Somebody else was always around."

He meant Logan, of course. But it wasn't true. She'd hardly seen Logan in the last two days. When he was in the office, she found excuses to flit off—photos to take or interviews to do. She'd turned skittish.

Scared of her own heart and the things it wanted.

The things it couldn't have.

"I'm crazily happy for you, Owen. And not at all surprised. Even when your sports pieces made zero sense to me, I knew the writing was good. You're going to have an awesome career."

He crunched a bite and swallowed. "And you're not mad at me for leaving?"

"Nope." How could she be? He knew what he wanted, and he was going after it.

That's what she'd thought she'd been doing all this time in Maple Valley. Especially these last two months—trying to salvage the paper any way she could. Begging Logan. Begging the bank.

Because she'd been so sure. Of course it was the right thing to do. The obvious thing.

Like Dani and the baby, the adoption.

Everyone had tried to tell her it was a bad idea, but she'd barreled on, convinced the adoption would save her marriage and maybe somehow complete her at the same time.

And look how that had turned out.

"So what's your news?"

Owen's question jarred her into focus. Her news. Yes, the email. She'd read it a dozen times already. And all she'd wanted to do was call Logan. Better yet, drive out to his father's house and join their family for breakfast and watch Logan's imagination dance as he read the email.

She'd come here instead.

"Remember how Logan's friend's wife is a genealogist? She found Harry Wheeler's granddaughter. I emailed the woman yesterday and already heard back. The history lover in me about freaked out when I read it."

It was her turn to pull out a folded sheet of paper. She'd half-memorized the email already.

Dear Amelia,

What a pleasure to meet you via email. I'm not sure how you found my address, and it's rather fortuitous I received your message so quickly after you sent it. I check my email perhaps once a month, twice if I'm feeling ambitious.

You're correct about my grandfather. He is the Harry Wheeler who was at Le Bourget field when Lindbergh landed in Paris. And yes, he was mistaken for Lindbergh. He told us the story over and over when we were children. How he was hoisted onto shoulders and carried through the field. How his clothes were tattered and he got separated from his friend.

And yes, his friend was Kendall Wilkins. I heard about him as a child, too. Only it was a different story Grandfather told whenever he talked about Kendall, though one that also took place in France. You said you've researched Kendall, so perhaps you know he fought in WWII?

According to my grandfather, they lost touch after that day in 1927 . . . but met again in France in 1944. Kendall Wilkins saved my grandfather's life on a battlefield somewhere in France. Grandfather was tangled in a barbed-wire fence, gunfire all around. Kendall rushed into fire to help him.

Grandfather used to say that was the moment that changed his life forever. He'd prayed, you see, to a God he wasn't sure he believed in. Kendall was his answered prayer.

To thank Kendall, Grandfather sent him a memento from the day Lindbergh landed, something he'd brought home with him in 1927. I wish I knew what it was. Perhaps it's the item missing from the safe-deposit box you mentioned. Grandfather said he used to believe it brought him luck. After being spared in

WWII, he no longer needed luck. He had something better . . . a Savior.

And also, a friend. I believe Grandfather kept in touch with Kendall until he passed away in 2001. He was 92, and even fourteen years later, we still notice the hole in our family.

Please feel free to email any other questions you might have, although I'm afraid this is the extent of what I know of your Kendall Wilkins. I never had the privilege of meeting him. But in a small way, through Grandfather's stories, I always felt he was a part of our family.

Best wishes with your story.

—Annalise Wheeler James

Owen looked up. "He was a war hero?"

"I knew he fought in World War II, but not this. And the extra awesome thing is this email supports what I've said all along: There was supposed to be something in that box. I just know it." She held up the page. "This is proof."

"Too bad you don't know what."

"But see, I'm realizing maybe I don't need to know. The real story is that Kendall Wilkins tried to give us something special—the same thing Harry Wheeler gave him. He wasn't playing a prank on the town, Owen."

And, too, there was something comforting in the thought that maybe Kendall hadn't been so family-less, after all.

"Yeah, but if you're right, what happened to whatever was supposed to be in the box? Did it get stolen? Did he just forget to put it back in the box the last time he stopped by the bank?" Owen's spoon scraped against his bowl, and he chewed on another bite before saying anything more. "And the biggest question I've got: Why'd you come to me with this?"

"What do you mean?"

He set down his spoon. "I mean, I'm happy for you. It's fun.

Your detective work paid off, and you'll probably write a great article." He pointed at the printout. "But I'm not the one you want to show this to."

She looked down, his implication perfectly clear and her next words quiet with admission. "You were right. I got too attached, but he's going to leave. So call this a first attempt at detaching."

She waited for him to say he'd told her so. "Dumb move, Amelia."

Her gaze shot up. "Excuse me?"

"I've worked with you for two years. I've watched you be all perky and plucky and flit from town event to town event. Friends with everyone. The opposite of old Wilkins." He tapped his spoon against his bowl. "And yet, not. Did you know I didn't even know until just now that you consider yourself a history lover? And until a few weeks ago, I had no idea you have event planning and marketing in your background. And man, Mae says you were married to Jeremy Lucas. Jeremy Lucas?"

Great, she'd spread that around? "What are you saying, Owen?"

"I'm saying, Logan Walker got past a wall with you that none of the rest of us could, and now you're trying to put it back up for a dumb reason like geography?"

"It's more than geography. What about the paper? You might be going to grad school, but other people actually need their jobs. And doesn't this town deserve a newspaper? I should just drop that and—what?—follow Logan to whatever coast he ends up on?"

Owen added more cereal to his bowl. "You're putting words in my mouth, Amelia. I'm just saying, let go of the need to protect yourself and you might be surprised where it gets you. Besides, you should know, no one's going to blame you if the paper folds. And it might be worth asking yourself why you'd rather fight for paper and ink and other people's futures than your own."

Don't panic.

But with the wind rattling through tents, and swaying tree branches batting against a now-steady rain, alarm choked Logan. He threaded through the square, Rick on his heels.

"Where did you see her last?"

"I told you, she was playing in the band shell. I just saw her five minutes ago." Or had it been longer? He and Bear had been talking . . .

Rick's steps crunched over a fallen branch behind him. "Who was she with?"

"Several kids. A couple moms were watching them—"

"Names, Logan." A crack of thunder punctuated Rick's demand.

And Logan's heart thudded at the thought of Charlie cowering against the sky's growl. Without him. He turned a circle in the middle of the lawn, rain now trailing down his face in rivulets.

Surely she was with one of those parents. With . . . someone.

He scoured the groups of people huddled under awnings—most of them laughing, shaking their heads, this almost-storm a joke.

"Logan!" Rick yanked on his arm, fingers digging into his flesh.

Logan spun at the pull. "You're not helping." The words came out tense, tight, as he looked past Rick.

"Neither are you, running around half-cocked. Maybe if you'd been watching her in the first place—"

"Don't."

"What were you thinking bringing her? You knew it was supposed to storm."

"I didn't think it would roll in so fast." But he should've

known. As soon as the clouds had thickened, he should've loaded Charlie back into the car so they could sit out the storm at home, where he could rock away her fear.

But no. He'd wanted to be here. Wanted to be a part of the event.

Wanted to see Amelia.

Rick stepped closer. "You didn't think at all."

"Logan?" Dad's voice barely registered as he jogged over.

"*This*," Rick said, tone black. "This is why Helen and I asked what we did. About Charlie living with us."

"I don't have time for this now." Did Rick really think they were going to argue this out in the middle of the square, in the rain, when he didn't know where his daughter was?

He pictured her then, back in LA, in the walk-in where she always hid. In the tulle of Emma's wedding dress. And the urge to start running, calling for her, nearly overcame him.

Rick was only inches from him now. "She deserves more than a dad who would lose her in a storm."

Something snapped in Logan then. Something untamed and unchecked.

Something scared.

And he punched his father-in-law, hand connecting with Rick's cheek in a flash that rivaled the lightning. He felt the jolt of his own shock, the flinch of his anger . . .

And Dad pulling him backward. "What in the world is happening here?"

"I can't find Charlie."

Rick just stood there, working his jaw, one hand on his cheek, the other balled.

"She's terrified of thunder, Dad."

"We'll find her." Dad eyed Rick as he spoke, tone even. "We'll start spreading the word. Get out your phone. Text your sisters."

His knuckles stung as he dug into his pocket. Oh Lord, he'd *hit* his father-in-law, let his fear turn into anger and just completely lost it.

Concentrate on Charlie. Worry about Rick later.

"She was playing in the band shell. There were a couple parents . . ." *Names, like Rick had said.* All he could find were faces. "The p-pastor's wife, she was there. And that teenager Colton mentors—his foster mom was there, too."

"Laura Clancy. I've got her number." Dad pulled out his own phone. "Rick, you might want to get some ice."

But no sooner had Dad lifted his phone to his ear than Raegan's voice carried above the wind and the crowd. He swung around, focus panning for the sight of her. And there, underneath the shelter of a jacket Bear held over their heads, was Raegan with Charlie in her arms.

Logan's feet carried him through the grass, relief like the wail of the wind, and it was all he could do not to wrench Charlie from Raegan's hold when he reached her.

"When the lightning started, Laura got worried, but she didn't see you." Raegan's explanation tumbled out. "She took Charlie to The Red Door."

"Thanks, Rae." Lightning jagged through the sky. "Hey, sweetheart."

Charlie reached for him, but nowhere were the tears he'd expected. She wrapped her arms around his neck as he ducked under a tent.

"You've been on a bit of an adventure, haven't you?"

"I'm wet, Daddy."

The thrumming in his heart slowed. "What's that?"

She palmed his hair. "And you're wet."

He hadn't imagined it. Six little words. Two little sentences. He could kiss the rain.

"We are wet. We should get home and change, yeah?" Her

hands slid from his hair to his cheeks. She always liked it when he didn't shave. "I love you, Charlie, you know that, yeah?"

Sometime in the past few seconds, Dad had joined them under the tent. He met his father's eyes. Read the delight there.

But Rick had followed them over, too. He stood at a distance now, watching. And even from where Logan stood, even through the rain, the red of his cheek smarted Logan's conscience. Dad followed his gaze.

"You'll apologize, Logan. He'll realize you were just worried."

"I don't know," Logan replied when Rick turned and walked away. "I have a feeling this could be bad."

15

Logan assumed the footsteps swishing through wet grass belonged to Dad. After all, Dad was the one who'd stuck the fishing pole in his hand and sent him down here to the little bridge at the bottom of the ravine, where a wandering creek rustled against the quiet.

"Go on down to the creek, son. That bridge is this whole family's thinking spot."

If it could be called a bridge. More like a few boards nailed together that had somehow survived last year's tornado. Sturdier than they looked, he supposed.

But when the steps paused behind him, and he towed his gaze from where his rod's weighted hook bobbed in the murky water to the surface of the bridge, it wasn't Dad's Reeboks he saw.

"Hey." Amelia's greeting was soft, landing just as he looked up.

She'd left her hair free today, and it billowed around her face, caught—like reeling leaves and grass and reedy branches—in the windy wake of this morning's storm. "Hey."

She sat down beside him, folding her legs and wrinkling

her nose as she settled on wet wood. "Glad I'm not wearing white pants."

The storm had left a tinge of cool air behind, and it sifted over him now. "Whatcha doing here, Amelia Bentley? I thought you hadn't missed a town event since the day you moved here?"

"There's a first for everything."

"How are we doing on headlines for next week? You skipping the Market might belong on the front page."

She drew her cloth bag onto her lap. "Wanted to bring you this." She pulled out a bag of frozen peas. "Makeshift ice pack."

He didn't know whether to laugh or sigh or just lean in to the concern in her eyes and spill every detail of this morning and every anxiety that'd choked him since.

Instead, he asked, "How'd you know?"

"It's Maple Valley, Logan. You can't pick a dandelion without someone seeing and finding a reason to spread the word. You go and throw a punch in the square and you're looking at five minutes—ten minutes, tops—until the news reaches the county line." She held up the bag. "I know it's been a couple hours already, and this is barely even cold still, but . . ."

He set his fishing pole on the bridge and accepted the limp bag, settling it over his fist.

A leftover drop of rain from a bending tree landed on her cheek, and she brushed it away. "Now I feel like I did something helpful."

Didn't she know just finding him here was helpful? Hadn't she felt the same blah-ness as he had in the past day of barely seeing each other? "I was freaking out because we couldn't find Charlie. Rick said things. And really, this has probably been building a long time. But I've never just . . . hit someone like that." Except Beckett when they were kids and playing superheroes.

And it wasn't just Rick that had set him off, if he was honest.

It was realizing the full cost of his D.C. dream. Having exactly zero clue what to do. Knowing how many people were waiting on him—Cranford and Hadley and Theo.

It was wanting so desperately to do the right thing for Charlie but not knowing what the right thing was.

It was Amelia. Even now, with bruised knuckles and the clock ticking on his time in Maple Valley, he couldn't deny his desire any longer.

"Confession," she said. "I tried to conjure the image of you punching someone on my way over. Couldn't exactly picture it."

He mustered a half-smile. "If I thought things were bad with Emma's parents before . . ." The perspiration from the bag of peas seeped through his fingers and onto his jeans.

Emma. Did it bother Amelia when he brought her up? If so, she didn't show it. Only tipped her head toward his pole. "You were fishing?"

"Uh, kind of. The creek's pretty shallow, so there's not much to fish for. Crappies are the best bet, a stray bluegill here and there. Mostly the pole's just an excuse to come down here and . . . I don't now, fish away my frustration, I guess. Kate always came down with a book. Raegan with her iPod."

"And your brother?"

Now he did grin. "Beckett always brought a girl." A twinge accompanied the memory. Man, he missed his brother. Didn't always realize how fully, but it grabbed hold of him now. "Mom and Dad came here more than anyone, though. This is where they had their first date, where Dad proposed. And when we moved back to Iowa, they jumped at the chance to buy the land."

"I forget sometimes you guys lived out East."

"Yep, 'til I was eight. Feels like a different life sometimes." Sorta like LA felt now. Had it really only been a couple months since he'd been there?

"I've never been fishing before. Can you believe that?"

"Never? Didn't you grow up in Iowa? What'd you do in the summer?"

She shook her head. "I'd say, but you'd never let it go."

"Now you have to tell me." He leaned closer to her. "Tell me, and I'll teach you to fish."

"Fine, but only because some Huck Finn piece of me thinks fishing could be fun." She reached around him for his pole. "History camp. Grades three through nine, I went to history camp every summer."

His laugh cut through the trees, his first since walking away from the square today, Charlie in his arms, wondering how he could've messed things up so badly. "Only you, Hildy."

"No, not only me. There were always at least five other kids there." She jiggled the line dangling from his rod. "So I just drop this in the water? Don't I need a worm?"

He caught the hook midair. "Nope, I'm just using synthetic bait. If we were really doing this right, I'd teach you to thread the end of the line through your hook, make a clinch knot, and dig for a worm to impale. But you're gonna get off easy since I already did the prep work. As for casting, this is a push-button spinner reel, so it's easy." He pointed out the pieces of the reel. "Pushing this releases the line, letting go stops it."

"Push to release, let go to stop. Got it. I wish I had a fishing vest. And one of those hats." She waved the pole as she talked. "And waders, because how cool are waders?"

He closed his hand around hers to still the pole, his smile traveling through him. "For never having gone fishing, you've got a handle on the style."

"I'm well-read, Logan."

"Hey?"

She inspected the reel. "Hmm?"

"I've hardly seen you the past couple days. You sorta disappeared after D.C. You didn't show up at the Market this morning. I thought maybe . . ." Well, he didn't know what he'd thought.

Only that he'd missed her.

She met his eyes. "I guess I . . . let go of something today."

It was all she said, but the release—maybe even peace—in her voice made it enough for now. Hand still covering hers, he guided her thumb to the button. "Okay, when you cock the rod back, push the button. When you point, release."

But her focus had landed on his bruising knuckles—faint reddish-blue, the hint of swelling—and before he could make any move to help her cast, she looked up at him. "Does it hurt?"

Not his hand so much as the reminder of Rick's words. *"She deserves more than a dad who'd lose her in a storm."*

Instead of waiting for him to answer, Amelia lowered the pole, set it on the bridge beside her, and reached for his hand. She held it in hers—her touch light, her thumb brushing over its ridges—and in a move that made him catch his breath, she lifted it to her lips. One by one, she kissed each knuckle—*one, two, three, four.* Lips feather-soft and delicate, and together with the coconut scent of her hair and the care in her every movement, it was enough to hush every harried voice inside him.

She turned his hand over, pressed a kiss to his palm. *Five.* And everything stilled.

When she lifted her head, he moved his hand to her cheek.

"I let go of something today."

Maybe that was what he was doing now, as his fingers grazed her cheek, her hair tickling over his skin. He could lose himself in the copper warmth of her eyes.

Except, no, this wasn't losing himself.

This was finding something precious.

And so he kissed her. Not like last time, as if he was desperate and it was his only chance. But soft. Slow. Once, twice, and then—when she leaned in—again. No counting, no sense at all of time or anything beyond her lips and his fingers in her hair and now her palm on his chest.

And only when he was breathless did he pull back, just barely, to whisper, "I'd have gone and started punching people a lot earlier if I knew it came with this kind of consequence."

He could feel her smile.

"And if I'd known kissing you was like this, I'd have gone and done it that first night you came home, even if you did criticize my snowman."

He touched his forehead to hers, laughing. "Although if you'd kissed me when I thought you were Emma . . ."

"Good point." The wind brushed through her hair again. "Now, are you going to teach me to fish or what?"

"One condition: Go on a date with me tonight?"

Maybe Eleanor hadn't been the right person to ask for fashion advice, after all. Amelia glanced down at the burnt-orange, beige, and cornflower-blue pattern of her summer dress—then at the spot Logan had apparently picked for their date. The Kendall Wilkins Library.

"Logan, it's after five on a Saturday. The library's closed. What are we doing here?"

"Patience, Curious George." He patted her bare knee. "Wait here."

Rain fell in sheets from a blanket of clouds so thick it made the evening seem later than it was. But at least the sky had cleared out long enough this afternoon for the Market to continue. Spring had finally settled in and, for once, she didn't mourn the end of winter.

They'd had lunch with Case and Charlie at the house before

heading downtown, where big-band music piped through the band shell speakers and the smell of popcorn and sweets hovered over the square. Logan had held her hand as they'd wandered through squishy grass and a maze of booths and tables and then stood outside the bouncy castle while Charlie jumped around inside. He'd bought Amelia a handmade necklace at one table. She'd watched him ogle an antique typewriter at another.

And then, about ninety minutes ago, he'd dropped her off at her house. Told her he'd be back for her at six.

She'd spent the next hour on a video chat with Eleanor, trying on one outfit after another. *"You can't go wrong with a sun dress, Amelia. Dress it up with some jewelry. Wear sandals and bring along a jean jacket in case you end up somewhere more casual."*

It'd sounded like good advice at the time, but the library? She could've stuck with cargo shorts and a tank top.

Logan was coming around the car now, opening an umbrella and then her door, that Walker grin of his just oozing charm as she slid out. The tips of his hair were still wet from a shower, and the smell of whatever rustic cologne he wore was downright intoxicating.

"Won't the library be locked?" Did her voice seriously just squeak? She reached down to grab her purse, and when she rose, Logan and the still-open car door blocked her from going any farther.

"You underestimate me, Miss Bentley." He dug into the pocket of his khakis and came up with a key.

"How'd you get that?"

"So many questions."

"I'm a reporter. That's what we do." Although he was standing so close, she couldn't have eked out another question if she'd tried. Rain pattered over the umbrella like music.

Logan's fingers curled around hers. "Well then, if you'll recall, my little sister happens to work here." He tugged her away from the car, careful to keep the umbrella over her.

"Raegan gave you a key? I bet she could get fired for that."

"I bet not. I saw the library director talking to my dad at the Market. I think she might have a crush on him."

Not hard to believe. Not if the old "like father, like son" adage had any truth to it. And for the hundredth time today, pure, unadulterated delight whisked through her—fluffy and as sweet as the cotton candy Logan had bought her at the Market. Poor man had cringed as she and Charlie had eaten the whole bag, rambled on about sugar and artificial flavoring.

And she'd stood there wondering how in the world she'd gone thirty years without knowing this man . . . and how Maple Valley was ever going to feel right again when he left.

Don't think about that now. Not tonight.

Somewhere down the line, it'd become her mantra. *Don't think too far ahead. Pretend he's not leaving. Enjoy this while you can.* Not nearly as hard to do when his palm was glued to hers under the rhythm of rainfall.

Logan handed the umbrella to her when they reached the front entrance, unlocked the door, and let them inside.

"What if there's a security system?"

"Then we get arrested, and in one fell swoop get a great first-date story and something to put on the front page next week. Win-win." He retrieved the umbrella, shook it off, and leaned it against the wall, then grasped her hand again. "Now, pizza is getting here in half an hour. I know it's not fancy—"

"I love pizza way more than I love fancy."

"I know you do." He nudged her toward the stairs leading down to the children's department. "And plus, I was busy getting some other things ready, so dinner wasn't the main priority for this date."

Their footsteps rapped against the marble steps, the shadows of bookshelves and tables rising from the basement, only the red of an *Exit* sign and impulsive darts of lightning through recessed windows bouncing against the dark.

She huddled closer to Logan, and he surprised her with a kiss on the cheek.

"What other things?" Her voice was breathless around the question, her curiosity about tonight and her fear of some vague tomorrow when, in one direction or the other, Logan would wind up half a country away, suddenly taking a backseat. "What other things did you have to get ready?"

"Again with the questions."

"Just call me Barbara Walters."

He wrinkled his nose. "I just kissed you, Amelia. And I'm pretty sure at some point tonight—possibly multiple points—I'd like to again. I'd rather not have the picture of you as an eighty-year-old in a pantsuit in my head when I do."

"Fair enough. But what other things?"

He steered her toward the east end of the children's library, where the circulation desk and librarian's office were set up to look like a treehouse. "You'll know soon enough. But I have to show you something else first. I think Raegan said it was down here."

"You're very mysterious tonight, Logan Walker." They stopped at the desk. "I like it."

He released her hand and rounded the desk, gaze skimming over the shelves lining the wall behind it.

"And just so you know, I'm totally holding back right now from asking what you're looking for. Because if I do, you'll make a twenty-questions crack or worse, start picturing me in polyester and then you might never kiss me again."

"Found it." He whipped around, a flat picture book in hand.

It took a second to sink in. The salmon-pink cover, plastic curling at the corners. The '70s-ish cartoon picture of a plane. The title written in clouds. *Amelia Takes Flight.*

273

"My book?" The one about Amelia Earhart, the one she'd checked out so many times as a kid. The one she'd written about in that scholarship essay. "How . . . where . . . ?"

He circled the desk once more and handed it to her. "I called the library in Des Moines last week. I didn't think they'd have it anymore, but I thought they might at least be able to look up your name in the system and tell me the title. Which they could, and even better, they were able to tell me it was sold— along with a bunch of old books—to a library that was just getting started in a small town right on the border of Iowa and Nebraska. So I called that library, and lo and behold, they found it on the shelf."

She flattened her palm on the cover. "Wait, this isn't just a copy of the book? This is *the* book?"

"Yeah. Chalk one up for interlibrary loan. Raegan called me yesterday to tell me it came in. Oh, and get this: I asked the librarian in Des Moines if their system tracked how many times you checked it out as a kid—and it does. Thirty-seven times. And here I thought you were exaggerating."

She cracked it open, the pages faded with age and stained with fingerprints—some probably her own. She knew each line on each page before she even turned to it. "I was so fascinated by this book."

"Not going to lie, I'm a little fascinated at how fascinated you are."

She looked up, met his eyes. "You interlibrary-loaned a book for me, Logan Walker."

He shrugged. "Some guys buy flowers, some guys track down picture books."

She hugged the book to her chest. "This is so much better than flowers." And he was so much better than anything she'd imagined back when he was just a name and a legend.

He stepped closer to her, another flash of lightning giving

her a glimpse of the warmth in his brown eyes. His hands went to her bare arms, still clutching the book between them. "Hey."

Goosebumps trailed over her skin. "Hey what?"

"You being worried I'd picture you in a polyester suit and never kiss you again?" His fingers slid down her arms to her waist. "Not gonna happen."

"No?" She wriggled the book free, set it on the desk, then leaned into Logan, arms tucked under his.

"Not a chance."

And then he proved it by kissing her. No quick peck on the cheek this time. This was the real thing—soft and slow and perfect. And when a growl of thunder interrupted, scared her into jerking away, he only pulled her closer, hold tightening and another kiss that turned into another . . . and another . . .

Her head spun. Or maybe that was her heart. Or everything.

She couldn't get enough of him. "Logan." It was almost a gasp.

He barely pulled back, just as breathless as she was. "Too much?"

"No." The opposite, really. Not nearly enough. "You're leaving."

She felt his hands slide down her back. "Let's not talk about that. I haven't even bought a return ticket."

She laid her head on his chest. "But it's happening. Los Angeles or D.C., doesn't even matter which. The point is . . ." She couldn't make herself ignore it anymore. Not when with every passing minute any possibility of *not* falling apart when he left became less and less likely.

"Amelia . . ."

When he didn't go on, she tipped her head. His gaze was a mix of intense and uncertain. As if he knew what he wanted to say but wasn't sure he should.

"I'm sorry. I shouldn't have brought it up."

He shook his head and stepped back. "I've been telling myself not to think about it."

"Same here."

"Let's make a pact: We'll talk about it tomorrow. Tonight, we'll do our best to forget. Deal?" He held out his hand.

"Deal." She placed her palm in his.

"I can think of better ways to seal the deal than a handshake, but honestly, if I kiss you again, we might never get to the rest of the evening."

"Right, the other things you apparently got ready." She grabbed the Earhart picture book and let him lead her upstairs to the adult department. They walked through the center aisle. Lightning pulsed in flashes overhead through the domed ceiling. They wound up near the back, where a long glass window and an open cherrywood door peeked into a small study room.

"Here we are."

She stepped into the cramped room—only space for a couple chairs and a table covered with . . . wait . . . her laptop? She hadn't even noticed it was missing when she was at the house. But that wasn't all. All her Kendall Wilkins notes were spread over the table's surface. Her folders. Photos. Newspaper clippings.

"How . . . when . . . ?"

"Raegan played errand girl for me this afternoon. She got your house key from Sunny Klassen."

"You guys are sneaky."

"I thought we'd make it a working date—at least for some of the night. You should've seen the way your face lit up at the bridge when you told me about Kendall and Harry's war experience."

"It adds a whole new angle to the story." She'd recited the email from Harry's granddaughter for him as he'd taught her how to cast the fishing rod.

"And I know you're a little disappointed that you still don't know what was in that safe-deposit box. But do you really need to know? You've pretty much proven your point—there was supposed to be something in there. He wasn't pranking the town."

"Right." True. She *could* write the story without solving the mystery of the box's missing contents.

"And you said you've never been more excited or more nervous about a single story, that you weren't sure how to even get started. I thought maybe I could help you do that. Get started, I mean. I know it's work, but the whole writing, wordsmithing thing—we both love it. Could be fun." He lifted his eyebrows in question. "And there will be pizza."

And there would be him. Which was so, so clearly the best part.

"If you'd rather not—"

"Are you kidding? Write a story with *the* Logan Walker?" She leaned up on her tiptoes to kiss his cheek. "Best." His other cheek. "Date." His nose. "Ever."

He backed her into the room with a kiss of his own. "I think we might be lucky if we get a single word written."

⤜⤛

The clang of a door closing wrenched Logan from a hazy sleep. One arm numb, the other spread out beside him on . . . the floor? He was on a floor? And not alone, either.

It registered at a turtle's pace—the library, the date, Amelia. They'd worked for a couple hours on her story, eating slices of pizza while they took turns typing. They'd taken a break around nine, roamed around the dark library, wound up down in the children's department again in the storytime room, where plastic glow-in-the-dark stars were stuck all over the ceiling.

He'd coaxed Amelia to the floor, made up stories about made-up constellations to make her laugh.

And now . . .

She curled against him, her head tucked against his chin, her arm over his chest.

"Logan?"

He blinked, tried to focus. The clatter of footsteps sounded in the distance, and was that Raegan's voice?

"I saw your car, so I know you're still here."

Oh man . . .

He wrenched free from his sleepy daze and jerked upright. Amelia tumbled over, her head hitting the floor as she gasped awake.

"Sorry, sorry." He leaned over her, an apologetic laugh toppling out. "Your poor head."

She dragged her eyes open. "What . . . where . . . ?"

"Logan!" Raegan's voice again.

Now Amelia's eyes were open . . . and wide. "We fell asleep? What time is it?"

He combed his fingers through his hair. "No idea."

Raegan flew into the room. "There you are. Logan—" She cut off, glancing at Amelia, then back to him, thinking who knows what about how she'd found them. But she only shook her head. "You need to come, Logan. Charlie's on her way to the hospital—"

"*What?*"

"And the police need to talk to you."

16

"Okay, what we're looking at here is an incomplete fracture. That's good news."

Logan was sitting in a hospital room, holding Charlie's hand—the one not propped on a pillow and ice pack—while a police officer waited outside the room to question him.

About an assault charge.

Filed by his father-in-law.

Sorry if *good news* felt like a stretch.

"What's that mean exactly, an incomplete fracture?"

The doctor turned off the light on the X-ray viewer. "It means the bone didn't break completely. Children have softer, more flexible bones than adults—sometimes they bend and crack instead of breaking. She'll still need a cast, but probably only for four or five weeks."

Charlie whimpered, and he lifted his other hand to smooth her curls. *Oh, baby.* . . . Her My Little Pony nightgown had still been wet from her own tears when he'd arrived.

"In other words," Dr. Lewis continued, "if you have to fall out of a bunk bed and break an arm, this is the best-case scenario."

Best-case scenario—no. Best-case scenario would've been

Logan being the one to comfort her on the way to the hospital and sit with her through the first round of X-rays instead of showing up just five minutes ago.

Even better, Logan being the one to put her to bed so he could line up the wall of pillows and stuffed animals he usually did to make sure she didn't roll out.

Neither of those two scenarios included Logan on the other side of town being woken up to find out his daughter was at the hospital. Or arguing with a police officer in the ER parking lot.

"Assault? You've got to be kidding me."

"We just need to talk, Logan. Get your side of the story. Make sure we've got our facts straight."

He'd thrust his arm toward the hospital's fluorescent lights. *"The facts are going to have to wait. My girl is in there."*

Dr. Lewis wrote something in a file, then closed the folder. "Typically with children this young, we sedate them for the realigning and casting. And we'll want to take another X-ray once it's casted to make sure everything's lined up. We should have you out of here by midnight."

Midnight on a day that felt like it'd begun a month ago. Such an awesome high sandwiched between such incredible lows.

The next twenty minutes passed in a blur as they transferred Charlie to a different room, sedated her, and started the casting process while Logan waited in another hallway. Sans cop, at least. His reflection stared back at him from the glass window looking into the room. The bright light of the corridor highlighted the ragged pull of his fatigue, the beginning of a beard, the rumpled shirt.

"Logan?"

Dad. He walked toward him, Styrofoam cup in each hand. "It's basically water and some grounds. Probably been sitting on the burner all day. But it's something."

Logan accepted the cup but didn't take a drink.

"Amelia's still out in the waiting room. Raegan, too."

Oh right. Amelia had ridden to the hospital with them. Tried to encourage him from the backseat. Offered to come with him to the room where Charlie waited.

He didn't know why he'd said no.

"Raegan should take Amelia home. It's going to be a while longer. You should go, too, Dad."

"Then who would take you and Charlie home?"

"Oh yeah." He finally forced down a drink of stale coffee. "Not thinking so clearly."

Through the window, he could see the doctor and nurse at work, wrapping strips of white around Charlie's arm. Her curls hung over the edge of the table, and one of her shoes dangled halfway off her foot.

"Well, this is number six."

Logan turned. "Huh?"

"Six broken bones in the family. Beck broke his leg when he was eight and then his wrist when he was twelve. Rae fractured her collarbone that time she fell on the ice. And just last fall, Kate broke an arm and a leg at the same time. Charlie makes six. Although come to think of it, I think Kate had some fractured ribs last fall, too."

That had been one the scariest phone calls of his life—the one about Kate and Colton's backroad scare last year. Considering how Emma had died, the words *car accident* were enough to churn his stomach into losing its contents.

But Kate had recovered. And Charlie would, too.

He wasn't so sure about himself.

"This isn't me, Dad." He slumped against the wall. "This reckless, impulsive person. It isn't me. I don't leave my job for two months. I don't put off important decisions. I don't hit people."

And he sure as anything didn't go around falling for women

whose livelihood he was one sale away from ruining. Not when it distracted him from his daughter, his obligations, his future. If it wasn't for his feelings for Amelia, he might've sold the paper weeks ago. Told Hadley *yes* on the spot last week. Returned to LA already to prepare himself and Charlie for their new life.

Not fair and not true.

Because hadn't he also stayed in Maple Valley for Charlie? Been hesitant to take the Hadley job because of Charlie?

"She fell out of her bunk bed, Logan. Nothing you did— reckless or otherwise, today or any other day—caused that." Dad's hand rested on his shoulder. "She's going to be just fine, son. And so are you."

"Even if I get arrested for assaulting Rick O'Hare?" He wished he were joking. But the footsteps sounding down the hall belonged to the cop—he knew without even looking up.

"I don't know what Rick was thinking."

"He was thinking, *here's another notch in the O'Hare column when it comes to custody of Charlie.*" Logan's anger pitched. "I don't understand. He's not the same man who welcomed me into the family like the son he never had when Emma and I got married."

The police officer approached.

"One daughter has died, Logan. The other is in a halfway house four hundred miles away."

The reminder stung.

"Logan?" The officer stopped in front of him. "Can we talk now?"

He recognized the policeman. Stan Whitmore. Used to lead the drug and alcohol prevention program at the junior high. He'd grown around the middle, lost most of his hair. But he had the same calm voice, the one that'd made Logan wonder as a teen how someone so placid had gone into law enforcement.

But all the kind tones in the world weren't enough now to still his nerves. "Do we have to?"

"I'm afraid so. Normally I'd ask you to come down to the station, but under the circumstances . . ." He glimpsed past Logan into the hospital room. "If it were something else, I'd wait until morning. But with assault, it's policy to follow up immediately."

Dad stiffened. "Don't you think *assault* might be overstating things? He threw one punch. It de-escalated in less time than it took to escalate."

"And that's why I'm here. I need to hear Logan's take on what happened. As for assault, that's simply the verbiage of the charge brought forward."

"So I am being charged? Are you going to arrest me?"

The officer took a small notepad from his pocket. "Not at the moment. As for charges, that's what this conversation will help decide. But that's not up to me. I just need to know what happened."

Logan folded his arms. "Half the town saw what happened. Can't you talk to any of them?" Maybe someone who didn't have a daughter's arm being wrapped in a cast?

"Half the town doesn't have a police report in process. Do I need to ask you to come down to the station, after all?" The first hint of irritation tinged Stan's voice.

Frustration twisted so thick it threatened to clog Logan's throat. "No. No, I can . . . talk."

He relayed the story in fits and spurts. Couldn't find Charlie. Panicked. Exchanged words with Rick. Lost his temper.

"Where'd you hit him?"

"His cheek, I think. I wasn't really aiming for anything in particular."

Amelia appeared at the end of the hall, saw him talking to the officer. He could read her concern all the way from here.

"One punch?"

"Just one. Uh, my dad intervened. Brought me to my senses." He nudged Dad. "Hey, could you tell Amelia she can go home? Tell her I'm sorry about how tonight ended."

Stan lifted his pencil. "We're almost done here, if you want to tell her yourself."

No, it was better this way. She'd ask questions he couldn't answer. Like how he was doing and if there was anything she could do to help. She'd turn those warm eyes on him and reel him in until he honestly believed everything was going to be okay. Just like Dad said.

But it wouldn't be. Not until he found his way back to solid footing. Tonight was a wakeup call. *You could lose your daughter if you don't pull yourself together.*

He'd lost focus—but no longer. "Go ahead, Dad. Please." He lifted one hand in a limp wave, then turned back to Stan. "Any other questions?"

∽

Why didn't he call back? Or at least text?

Amelia sat in her car in the parking lot of the Maple Valley Community Church just like she did most Sundays. Refusing to be on time. Muted voices drifted from outside, where sunlight tunneled through yesterday's leftover clouds. She'd called Logan last night after Raegan had driven her home. And then again this morning after a wilted night of little sleep.

She'd almost driven out to the Walkers' house instead of coming here. But the same stalwart murmur that coaxed her here week after week, even when she was sure her days of steadfast faith were behind her, had beckoned again. So here she was.

But if her conscience could be stubborn, so could she. She'd walk in her usual five minutes late. Sit in her usual seat in the back. Stay invisible.

Amelia nearly jumped at the knock on her window.

Jonas Clancy? The loan officer had ducked down to look inside. He wore clip-on visors over his glasses and a gray suit.

So much for being inconspicuous. She glanced at her phone one more time, as if she somehow might have missed a ring or buzz or something—anything—from Logan. Then sighed and got out of her car. "Hi, Mr. Clancy."

The banker waved a teenager on toward the church—Webster, the high schooler Jonas and his wife had adopted after he'd come to live with them as a foster kid. The one who hung around with Colton Greene all the time.

"We're not in the office, Amelia. Call me Jonas."

Music drifted from the church, and a car's tires sputtered over gravel behind him. "All right. Jonas."

"I know it's Sunday, and if we don't get inside soon we'll miss the best donuts, but when I saw you in your car, well . . ." He straightened his tie, then flipped up the visors from his glasses. "Figured maybe I could save you a trip to the bank. It's about your loan application."

Oh. He shifted his weight from foot to foot, his regret so clear that the nice thing to do would be to save him from saying the rest. Tell him she understood and insist they go in for those donuts.

But something in her needed to hear the words. So she simply waited, her greenish-blue skirt ruffling around her ankles.

"We have a pretty firm threshold for financial risk. If ever I wanted to ignore the threshold and take a risk on someone, it's you." Beads of perspiration appeared on his forehead despite the cool morning. "I really mean that. I read the *News* each week. Love seeing photos of Webster in the Sports section."

She should feel something more right now than vague

disappointment. But hadn't she sensed this was coming? She'd known what a long shot the loan truly was.

And perhaps, too, Owen's words yesterday had burrowed farther into her heart than she'd realized.

"It might be worth asking yourself why you'd rather fight for paper and ink and other people's futures than your own."

Maybe it was time to let the desperate push for the newspaper's future rest.

"I really appreciate you letting me know."

Jonas looked almost relieved at her even-keeled response. "I do wish we could do something to help you out. There are some government small-business-loan programs. I can get you information on any of that, if you like."

"I'll let you know if I decide that's something I'd like to look at."

"Dad, Mom wants to know where you are!" Webster yelled from the church entrance.

Jonas grinned. "We never asked him to call us Mom and Dad, you know. All of a sudden, Christmas Eve last year, it just popped out of his mouth."

"Thanks again, Mr.—Jonas."

She watched him walk to the church, then reached back into her car for her purse. But instead of walking toward the entrance, she moved in the opposite direction. Away from the parking lot, across the road, down a cracked sidewalk toward a grassy knoll—finally green with spring and home to rows of stones that stretched from the ground.

She passed under the arched wrought-iron entrance of the Maple Valley cemetery, the bustle of the church parking lot fading and a choppy wind breathing through the field.

She didn't know why she went looking for it, didn't even know if she'd find it.

But minutes after the church service would've already started, she found herself standing in front of a granite stone with a beveled edge, well-kept and surrounded by flowers, silver lettering glinting.

Emma O'Hare Walker
1981–2013
She lived and loved well.
Isaiah 43:19

Logan's wife. Had he placed one of the wreaths or flower urns that adorned the surface around the gravestone? Would he come here in a couple weeks on Memorial Day?

A twig snapped behind her, footsteps rustling in the grass. She glanced over her shoulder. Case?

Logan's father ambled along the sandy path leading toward where she stood now. He lifted one hand to wave as he approached, and she offered a hello in return. Shouldn't he be in his family's regular row in church?

And what would he think of the fact that she was standing here, staring at his son's dead wife's grave?

He stopped beside her. "I thought that was you. Late to church and saw you from the road."

"I was just . . . well, skipping church, I guess."

He glanced at Emma's tombstone. "It's a lovely statement, isn't it? 'She lived and loved well.' You never had a chance to meet her, did you?"

She shook her head. Sunlight filtered through tree branches and streaked in goldish shards over the ebony-hued stone. "Actually, I think I moved to town right around the time she passed away."

Case sighed. "It was traumatic, that's for sure. For the whole of us, but of course, Logan most of all."

"I, uh, don't know the verse."

"It's an odd one for a gravestone, truthfully. All about God doing a new thing. Apparently she once made Logan promise if she died first, he'd make sure that verse was on her stone— because death would be the greatest new thing she'd ever experience."

"Whoa. That's . . ." She couldn't find words.

"A promise he probably thought he'd never have to keep," Case finished for her.

One quiet moment passed into another, broken only by the faint rhythm of a woodpecker in another corner of the cemetery and a tangled medley of questions and emotions, until . . .

"I don't know why I'm here." Abrupt. Off-key.

But Case seemed unfazed. "Because you love my son."

The wind whipped her hair against her cheeks and stole any response from her lungs. He'd said it so simply. As if it were just plain fact. Not at all surprising or ridiculous or life-altering.

"You love my son, and you're naturally curious about the woman he used to be married to." Case put his arm around her shoulder, like she'd seen him do so many times to Kate and Raegan. "Emma was wonderful. Bright, fun, creative. Somewhat cautious. Pretty. Even though she was technically Charlie's aunt by birth, I have a feeling if she'd lived, no one ever would've guessed she wasn't Charlie's birth mother. Those are some strong O'Hare genetics."

"I wonder if Logan sees her when he looks at Charlie." She tucked a strand of hair behind her ear.

"Maybe sometimes." Case grinned. "But I have a feeling more often than not, he just sees his daughter who he adores."

"He does." And if Case hadn't already seen right through her before now, he would've at that. She could hear the affection packed into her voice. "How's Charlie doing, by the way?"

Case steered her away from the gravestone, and they ended up on the path that cut through the cemetery. "She's taking it like a champ. Probably would've loved showing off her neon cast to everyone in church if Logan hadn't insisted on keeping her home."

"And Logan? I tried calling."

"He's . . . all right."

She didn't miss his pause, but he went on before she could ask for a more detailed explanation.

"And how about you?"

"Me?"

"I found you in a cemetery on a Sunday morning."

She couldn't help but laugh, even if it was tinged with something bittersweet. "Oh, I don't know. I just found out the bank is turning me down for a loan. I'd kind of thought maybe I could buy the newspaper from Logan. Now I have a feeling that despite my best efforts and even with the centennial issue we're running this week, we may be looking at a buyout. I could very possibly be out of a job before long." She slid him a glance. Would he offer words of advice? She hesitated. "I'd like to believe the whole 'when God closes a door, he opens a window' thing, but . . . well . . ."

It was Case's turn to laugh. "I think that's a ridiculous phrase."

"You do?"

"Yes, although if my wife were still alive and making me watch *The Sound of Music* twice a year, I would never admit it. I got really good over the years at holding in my groan when the Reverend Mother says that line." They stopped under the gated entrance. "Way I see it, doors and windows are two different things entirely, with completely different purposes."

"I can appreciate that."

"I'll tell you this much, though, Amelia. Don't confuse your career with your life. Your newspaper means a lot to you. You love your job, and that's special—it's not something everyone

289

can say. And losing it would hurt. But not nearly as much as missing out on your life." He stuck his hands in his pockets. "Well, I'm headed to the church. You could come with. We'll have empty room in our row without Logan and Charlie. You could even stay all the way through the last song."

He winked on that last part, and she felt her jaw drop. But why was she surprised? This was Case Walker. Where did she think Logan got his observant nature from, anyway?

She walked with Case back to the church and sat in the seat Logan would've if he'd been there. Listened to the whole sermon and stayed all the way until the pastor dismissed them at the end.

Might even have stuck around to talk to the people who sat near her, if not for the text from Ledge.

Stopped by the office on the way home from church. It's not good. You need to see this.

⁓

The sight of his bruised knuckles was almost enough to convince Logan not to knock.

Do it. You've been dragging your feet for too long about too many things.

He knocked.

Rick answered.

Smudges of blue and purple rimmed the ridge of his father-in-law's cheekbone, and a flint edge hardened his eyes. No invitation to come in. "What do you want?"

"To talk." Yesterday's storms had lapped all the moisture and warmth from the air, leaving an arid cool that felt more like autumn than spring. He should've grabbed a hoodie, especially if this conversation wasn't going to move inside. Which, judging from Rick's rooted stance on the welcome mat, it wasn't.

"I said all I had to say down at the police station last night."

"Rick, who is it?" Helen's voice drifted from the second floor.

"No one." He called the reply over his shoulder, then pinned Logan with a leaden glare, as if daring him to counter.

This was pointless, wasn't it? Futile. He'd debated it all day—first this morning as he'd made waffles for Charlie while the rest of the family was at church, and then all through an afternoon of Disney movies and glances at the neon pink synthetic cast on his daughter's arm, already half covered in signatures and drawings.

But he'd had to at least try.

"You know Emma wouldn't have wanted this."

"Emma's not here."

He could taste the sour resentment in Rick's tone, hear the bitter words his father-in-law didn't need to say. *Because of you.*

He didn't know when it'd happened . . . but it *had* happened. Somewhere along the line, Rick's hurt had morphed into blaming Logan. Maybe it'd been there the whole time and he just had never been home long enough to realize it. Didn't really matter when, though, did it?

"I'm sorry about yesterday, Rick. I overreacted, I panicked. I know that's no excuse, but please hear me when I say I am very sorry." He'd rehearsed the words the whole way over, but they came out flat now. Unconvincing.

"What's done is done."

Apology acknowledged, then, if not exactly accepted.

Rick unfolded his arms. "I might have overreacted myself—filing that police report."

"Well, it doesn't sound like there are going to be any formal charges." At least, that was the impression the officer had given last night. Although the report would still be filed. If someone did an extensive enough background check on Logan, they could come across it.

Hadley's people could come across it. Who knew what might happen then?

All Logan knew was that if he were advising a candidate in the process of assembling a team of staffers, he'd recommend pristine backgrounds all around. Not even a whiff of trouble. *The last thing you want to do is hand the other side any kind of ammo, real or perceived.*

But that was exactly what he'd done with Rick and Helen these past couple months. One misstep after another. He was practically building for them their argument for why he should let Charlie stay with them.

But something firm stitched through him now, sharp and unwieldy. "Charlie's my daughter, sir. I know better than anyone I'm not a perfect father. Don't think that fact doesn't hound me day in and day out. But I *am* her father." He walked down the cement stairs as the flag jutting from the house slapped against the siding.

"Logan, you should know I'm talking to a lawyer in the morning."

He froze on the sidewalk, halfway to his car.

"He specializes in custody issues."

He veered around. "There's no issue here. I'm legally her father."

Rick grasped the door handle with one hand. "I'm just giving you a heads-up." With that, he closed the door.

The trek to his car was a near-stagger, last night's too-few hours of sleep not nearly enough to combat the weariness slogging through him now, nor the alarm at Rick's words. He didn't honestly intend to sue for custody, did he? Did Helen support this?

Logan's anxiety only built as he drove toward Dad's house, the residential neighborhood tapering as he neared the edge of town. He never should have come back to Maple Valley.

He should've just let the lawyer handle the sale of the news-paper and stayed in LA. None of this would be happening right now.

But you would've missed out.

On what, the first fist fight of his adult life?

On all this time with Charlie.

On seeing her blossom with the speech pathologist. She wasn't babbling his ears off, but they'd had an entire audible conversation this morning. And Jenessa—a rift he'd once as-sumed irreversible had not only begun to mend, but he felt like he'd actually helped her some. Ever since the fundraiser, she'd been taking photos for the paper and spending time with Abby building the website.

He'd tried to encourage Raegan the couple times he'd seen her upset about Bear, and it'd been a blast seeing Kate and Colton together, and hanging out with Seth.

And Amelia.

He closed his eyes, only for a fleeting second but long enough for his tire to slip off the gravel road. He jerked his eyes open and steered back into the center of the narrow road.

Amelia.

God, I don't know what I'm supposed to do.

Was it a prayer or just a frustrated declaration?

Do you do signs, God? Is that still a thing? Burning bushes and talking donkeys? Dad said you'd wait for me, but I don't know how much longer I can wait for you.

Dad's house came into view, a blazing dusk throwing scarlet hues against its rustic exterior. He pulled in, recognizing Ame-lia's car parked under the basketball hoop—same spot she'd parked that first night he came home. How could that only have been a couple months ago?

She was sitting on the porch swing, Charlie by her side. They both waved when he approached, Amelia with a Sharpie in hand. A breeze clattered through the wind chimes in the corner, and he climbed the steps, a chary slowness to his movement.

"Hey, Logan." Amelia seemed subdued, maybe even upset. Because he hadn't returned any of her calls or texts, perhaps. Or had something else happened in the time since he'd brushed her off at the hospital?

You could've at least said goodbye to her last night. Or responded to any one of her messages.

He just hadn't been able to get over the feeling that in the past few weeks he'd done all over again what he did right before Emma died. Let himself get distracted. Something as innocuous as music then, and it'd cost him the chance to say goodbye to his wife.

And getting lost in this thing with Amelia now? It'd sidetracked him from his career and, even worse, from the gravity of his in-laws' mistrust. Maybe if he'd been paying more attention, he'd have realized how serious they were about their doubts in his capability as a father. How far they were willing to go.

"Look, Daddy." Charlie jumped off the swing and ran to him before he'd even reached the top of the steps. She held out her arm. Amelia had signed not far from his own name, the stem of her *A* wrapping around the rest of her name to form a heart.

"You're going to have that cast full in no time."

"I know."

He lifted her up, pressed a kiss to her cheek. "Do me a favor, Bug? Go find Grandpa and see if he wants to make popcorn for dinner? Sunday night tradition."

He let her slide down him and held the front door open for her to run inside. When he turned, Amelia was standing.

"You're a hard one to get ahold of, Logan Walker."

"Yeah, sorry about that. It's been . . . a day."

"I didn't mean to be a bother—"

"You weren't a bother." He hated that his silence had made

her feel that way. Hated his own reticence now, the space he couldn't bring himself to fill.

"At first, I was just checking in, but then . . ." She let out a breath, one heavy with distress. Something else *had* happened. "I stopped by the office after church today. Ledge texted—he'd left a coat in the pressroom on Friday, and he went by to pick it up and said as soon as he walked in he knew something was wrong." She'd started pacing in front of the porch swing but stopped now. "Logan, we think the office was hit by lightning. The server's down, all the computers. None of that's such a huge deal, but the press is dead. Not jammed or in need of a new part, but completely dead. You should see the cord. Ledge says we're lucky a fire didn't start."

Oh great. He pinched the bridge of his nose, so far from frustrated he didn't even have words.

Maybe it would've been better if a fire had started, burnt the whole place down and left him with an insurance check instead of a newspaper on life support. Except no, because Freddie's useless insurance policy was part of what had gotten the *News* into such a hole to begin with.

"What are we going to do? I think the machine is beyond fixing this time." She hugged her arms to herself. "Maybe we could call the *Communicator.* Maybe they'd print for us. I know they contract with some other area papers and—"

"Amelia." Her name escaped in a murmur. "I can't . . . I can't think about this right now."

"But we don't have time not to think about it. We've got the centennial issue this week *and* our regular issue."

He crossed paths with her, dropped into the swing. "They may not be able to come out."

"Logan, what are you—"

"They're just papers." Exasperation budged into his tone.

295

"I asked for a sign. Maybe this is it. Lightning strike—sounds about right."

She stood in front of him, silhouetted by the setting sun. "What are you talking about?"

"I need to sell, Amelia. I need to go back to LA."

"But the paper, the centennial. The article we spent months on."

He looked up at her, rubbing his stubbly cheeks, trying to convince himself it was just mild disappointment on her face—not heartbreak.

"It's not just me and my job at stake here. Think about Mae—she acts like a grump, sure, but I think the staff is the closest thing she has to family around here. And what about Jenessa? You said yourself that she's a different person since she started taking photos for us." She sat beside him, the swing's hinges creaking. "I know you've had a hard weekend, Logan, but to make a snap decision just like that—"

"It's not a snap decision. I've been poring over the numbers for two months now, you know that. I've met with a financial advisor, a lawyer. I've talked to insurance people. I even got ahold of a former paper owner who sold to Cranford last year, just to get his take." He ran one hand over the swing's wooden armrest. "I told Dad last night this isn't me—this guy who stalls on decisions and sabotages his own career prospects. It's just . . . not me."

"And at the library, or yesterday at the bridge—that wasn't you?"

He reached for her hand. "That was me." She looked up, and oh, the hope in her eyes killed him. "But it was me getting ahead of myself."

She lowered her gaze, slid her hand free, and after a painful moment, stiffened. "Just tell the truth, Logan. You're scared."

"Amelia—"

"You don't want to take a risk. Not on the paper. Not on me."

If she'd meant for the words to sting, they did the job. Enough that he couldn't stop his biting reply. "What about you?"

"What about me?"

"You want to talk about not taking risks? Who's the one who insists on staying in Maple Valley even when multiple opportunities have landed at her feet? Did you ever even consider Cranford's job offer? Or how about all the times Mae has said her niece could get you a spot on a national paper?"

She stood, the swing jostling at her movement. "What's so wrong with being content where I am? Not everyone has crazy-big dreams."

"No, everyone doesn't. But *you* do. Kendall Wilkins saw it in that essay you wrote him. I see it every time you talk about the Wilkins article. I saw it when we were in D.C. You want something different. Not better or more—but different. And you can tell yourself all you want that you're content here. But content isn't the same as stagnant."

She turned her back on him. "You don't know what you're talking about."

"I do because I know you." He stood. "You're scared of leaving the comfort of what you know for the possibility of what you don't." He stepped closer, hurling the words over her shoulder. "And you're so scared of becoming Amelia Earhart, disappearing or being forgotten, that you insist on staying in a small town where everyone knows you, everyone sees you."

She whipped around. "Stop it, Logan."

"You're scared of leaving the safe little world you've created here, and you're constantly scared that people will let you down."

"Maybe that's because people *do* let me down."

"Forget Jeremy—"

"I'm not talking about Jeremy."

Her words parked in front of him, sour and choking. How had they gotten here? Tension suffocated the air between them. If he could take it all back—

"Well, good for you, Logan. You finally gave me one of your famous speeches."

"Amelia—"

But she was already on her way down the steps, posture not nearly rigid enough to hide her hurt.

Dear Mary,

If you were my daughter, I'd tell you about how I met your birth mother.

She was quite possibly the most sullen person I'd ever encountered. I'd say "chip on her shoulder," but it was more like a boulder. Tough home life. Bad grades. Few friends.

I have no idea why she came to the youth event at church that first time. A desperate grasp for something, anything, perhaps. But she showed up, and we met, and something clicked in my heart. I watched her blossom in the coming months. She'd found a place to belong, a makeshift family. On nights when her home life got unbearable, she stayed with Jeremy and me.

I think I pridefully thought we'd saved her.

Then she made a mistake at a party one night. Woke up the next morning not even certain who she'd been with. Didn't take long to discover she was pregnant. And it was as if all the hope she'd breathed in seeped from her lungs.

So we stepped in again. Tried to save her again.

Only I'm realizing now, the one I was really trying to save was myself. Dani might've stumbled in a one-night stand. But I'd been crumbling slowly for months.

And it was never fair to blame her decision to keep you for my own broken dreams and misplaced hope.

17

melia Bentley. I was almost sure you were going to turn down a job offer from me a second time."

C.J. Cranford's clipped pace and sleek silver blazer matched the glass-accented lobby of the downtown Dixon office building—fluorescent lights overhead, vertical floor-to-ceiling windows, slate-hued paint. Metallic letters spelled the words *Cranford Communications* on the wall behind the receptionist's desk.

What Amelia wouldn't give to be facing a disgruntled Mae in the closet-sized lobby of the *News* office instead. To hear the clunky chug of their old, half-broken—no, now completely dead—press instead of this quiet hum. She could barely even pick up the smell of ink over the bowl of flaky potpourri on the receptionist's desk.

She accepted C.J.'s handshake. "Well, last time I already had a job. This time . . ."

This time the *News* was on its way to nonexistence, and Amelia to unemployment.

Had it really only been a week and a half since Logan had stood in front of their staff and announced his decision? The cost of fixing the press was simply too steep. And it was both too last-minute and too expensive to find another area printer to churn out this week's paper.

The lightning strike had aided the decision he was probably eventually going to make all along.

Far as she knew, the sale to Cranford hadn't been finalized yet. But he'd left for LA two days ago anyway, Charlie in tow, along with her last fragile piece of foolish hope that he might still change his mind.

He might as well have left the night they argued on the porch. Nothing had been the same since then. Didn't matter that she actually understood why he'd made the choice he did. That somewhere, behind the cracks in her heart, she'd seen this coming.

The logic of his decision couldn't come close to catching up with the ache wheeling through her. Oh, she missed him. Missed Charlie.

"I know this isn't what you wanted. I get it." C.J. pushed her low, russet ponytail over one shoulder. "You had an attachment to that paper. But I hope you'll at least consider my offer. Let me show you around."

Logan had cornered Amelia in the office after everyone else had left. Told her he'd asked Cranford to offer her a job once the sale was complete. *"Even if they do permanently dissolve the News, they'll still be covering an additional town. So it makes sense that they'd add a position. Obviously it should be you."*

If he'd expected her undying gratitude at that, he hadn't gotten it. *"Thanks, but I already had the opportunity to move to Dixon once, Logan. Maple Valley is home."*

His shoulders had dropped, as if she'd stuck the last pin in an already deflated balloon. *"Home or just a hiding place, Amelia?"*

The overly sweet mocha she'd downed on the forty-five-minute drive to Dixon churned in her stomach now. C.J. led her through a glass door and into a white-lighted open room with desks displaying oversized monitors that couldn't be more than a couple years old. A whir of activity enlivened the space, fingers tapping on keyboards, the purr of printers—all of it both familiar and foreign at once.

"This is our ad and graphics department, as I'm sure you can tell by the mockups hanging everywhere. Our bread and butter, just like most papers." Her heels clicked as she pushed through another door. "And this is where you'd spend your time."

The *Communicator's* newsroom had to be four times the size of the *News's*. New Macs on every desk. A couple reporters looked up as she and C.J. wound through the room, but most were busy—on the phone or typing with earbuds in.

At the back of the room, they pushed through a final door, leading into a hallway of offices. C.J. let Amelia pass into her office first. None of the gleaming white of the outer offices. Instead, redwood furnishings offset mint-green walls.

"Used to be my dad's office," C.J. explained as she sat behind the desk. "Modern wasn't so much his thing."

"I like it." Reminded her a little of Freddie's office—not in size so much, or even décor. But in personality.

Funny how she'd never thought anyone else could ever quite fit in Freddie's space—and how wrong Logan had proven her. He'd seemed so right in that office. So at home.

"Home or just a hiding place?"

Why couldn't she stop hearing his voice? And would she ever get over the ache of missing him? Missing Charlie? Wishing she could hear Charlie call her *Lia* again?

"So." C.J. flattened her palms on her desk. "We could do the regular old job-interview-type questions, but to be honest, this job is yours if you want it. You're qualified. You've got the experience. I'd rather talk about what the transition is going to look like."

"All right."

"This is a full-time reporting position. We can throw as many of the Maple Valley–specific stories your way as possible, but you will need to help cover events or news in other communities, too. I think you'll find the salary package satisfactory."

C.J. kept talking about the job duties—scheduling and digital news and photographers. The minutes passed in a misty blur.

"Okay, I'm just rambling now. Let's switch gears. Do you have any questions for me?"

Amelia rubbed her hands over her pants, mind clamoring for focus.

Pay attention. Whatever she'd said to Logan, the truth was, she needed this. Needed a job and a paycheck.

C.J. tapped a pencil against her desk. Right, a question.

"Well, I guess I've got one question. There's a story I've been working on for a couple months. It's actually been percolating for years, but I just recently got serious about it." For the first time since she'd arrived in Dixon, something close to enthusiasm fought against her apathy. She told C.J. about the Kendall Wilkins story—how it'd started out as a search for a missing safe-deposit-box item and turned into a story about Paris and World War II and a friendship that spanned decades.

When she finished, C.J. stood. "Coffee?" She walked to the Keurig machine sitting on a corner counter. "Even Dad, in all his disdain for modernity, couldn't deny the thrill of a fresh cup of coffee in thirty seconds."

"I'm good. Thanks."

C.J. started the machine, its gurgle filling the space until she turned. "How many words?"

Amelia blinked. "Thirteen hundred."

C.J.'s laugh overpowered the Keurig's noise. "You're kidding, right? You know how much column space that is?"

"It was originally going to go in our anniversary issue." The one that should've come out last week. Instead, she'd spent her days going from business to business, apologizing that none of the scheduled ads would run in the special issue . . . because there wasn't going to be a special issue.

"Even if it was normal length, I'm not sure how it's a story. You didn't figure out what was supposed to be in the box and where it is now?"

"That's kind of the point of the story—we started out looking for one thing and realized the story was more about friendship and heart and community." Maybe it sounded sappy and saccharine. But Amelia had poured her heart into that article.

"But there's nothing that makes it newsy, relevant."

"There was when it was part of an anniversary issue." She couldn't manage to keep the frustration from her voice.

C.J. retrieved her coffee mug and circled her fingers around it, then studied her for a long moment. "Amelia, why did you come here today?"

"I don't know." Her words were soft and quick, out before she could tug them back.

"You don't know?"

"I really don't." She stood. "And I'm really sorry, C.J. Thanks so much for giving me a chance—a second time. But I don't think I'm the right person to work here."

C.J. set her cup on a coaster, nodded. "Fair enough."

Amelia started for the door.

"Amelia?"

"Yeah?"

"That girl from the coffee shop who was going to have the baby. The one all the people were wearing ribbons for. Did she have the baby?"

Amelia glanced over her shoulder to see C.J. holding two ribbons—one green, one yellow. Of course. She'd voted for twins.

"They're my Maple Valley souvenirs."

"Yeah, Megan had her baby. A girl. Healthy and big despite being a bit early."

"Glad to hear it." C.J. closed her fingers around the ribbons. "See you around, Bentley."

"What on earth possessed you to make that call?"

Theo's voice sounded distant with the hum of Logan's fridge in his ears. Logan reached past a jug of milk that'd expired so far back he couldn't bring himself to empty it out. Forty-eight hours back in LA and so far he and Charlie had existed on pizza and takeout.

"You could've at least given me some advance warning."

He found a lone bottle of water near the back, then closed the refrigerator door and held the bottle toward Theo.

Theo only crossed his arms. Fine. Logan uncapped the bottle and took a swig. He didn't have time for this. He needed to get groceries and clean and unpack their suitcases.

Find a way to settle back into life in LA. Pretend the good-byes he'd said in Iowa—one in particular—hadn't cut clean through him.

"Talk to me, Walker."

"I had to do it, okay? It was the right thing to do."

Making that call to Senator Hadley's campaign manager had been a thousand kinds of uncomfortable. *I just think you should know there was a police report filed on me a couple weeks ago. Alleged assault.*

And oh, by the way, he might be facing a custody battle against his in-laws in coming months. Just saying the words had sent anxiety clawing through him.

The open patio doors off his apartment's kitchen ushered in

the sounds of his busy street—cars motoring down the road and kids playing in the complex's outdoor pool. And heat—sticky and baking. He should be running the air-conditioner.

But something about closing up the place—shutting windows and sliding the patio doors—made him feel hemmed in. And it wasn't only that. It was the constant noise, the claustrophobic traffic, that always-in-a-rush feeling that'd swept over him as soon as he and Charlie had stepped off the airplane into the crush of LAX.

In the span of two months, LA had stopped feeling like home.

But he'd had to come back. It was the only thing that made sense. He just wished he could've brought a piece of Iowa with him.

Theo was right, though. He could've given him some warning. "I'm sorry I didn't tell you first."

"You weren't even formally charged. We don't know that it ever would've come up if you hadn't said anything."

"But if it had? If it was primary season and the other party was looking for something, anything, to use against Hadley, and they dug deep enough? Do you know how awful I'd feel?"

"So what happens now? Do we still have a job?" Theo leaned one hand on the peninsula counter that divided Logan's kitchen from the living room, where Charlie sat at the coffee table coloring. Poor thing, her cheeks were red from the apartment's warmth.

Logan capped his water bottle and crossed over to the patio doors, sliding them closed. He tapped the A/C on his way to the living-room window.

"You have a job no matter what, Theo. Even if the campaign decides I'm not a good fit, that doesn't mean you're out."

"But . . . we're partners. I guess I always pictured us doing this thing together."

Logan closed the window and turned his gaze to his daughter. The curls that'd stopped at her chin two months ago now reached nearly to her shoulders. Freckles dotted her cheeks from so many afternoons out in Dad's backyard, and she wore a series of too-large bracelets on one arm—Raegan's.

"Theo." Logan lowered his voice. "You know if . . . if I end up having to go to court, I would've had to back out anyway." How he hoped he didn't. He hadn't heard from Rick and Helen since leaving Maple Valley, didn't have a clue if Rick had gone through with his threat to meet with a lawyer.

But the threat was enough.

"It was the right thing to do." He said the words again, a sigh stitched in. Maybe he was trying to convince himself as much as Theo. Not just about calling the campaign manager, but—he glanced around his apartment, dusty and unkempt after two months away—about this, all of it. Coming back so quickly. Leaving home.

Leaving Amelia.

It killed him the way they'd left things. The way he'd hurt her. The papers for the sale of the *News* sat on the peninsula counter even now, just waiting for his signature.

"When are they going to let you know what's happening?"

The water bottle crinkled under Logan's fingers. "Dunno."

Theo sighed and crossed the room. He paused by Charlie to muss her hair. "Take care of that arm, Little Charlie."

She saluted with her un-casted arm. "Aye aye, captain." Who'd taught her that? Seth or Colt?

And had she noticed how much quieter their apartment was than Dad's house? Because he sure did.

He saw Theo to the entryway. "I am sorry, man. I never meant to mess things up."

Theo pulled open the apartment's front door, someone else's footsteps from down the hall sounding behind him. "I know you didn't. Jill and I are heading out to Allentown this weekend, by the way. We're going to try to get a townhouse or apartment. We'd rather do that than camp out in a hotel for a year and a half. We can ask around for you, too, if you want."

"Sure, go ahead." What would it hurt?

They parted, and Logan started toward the living room, only to hear another knock on the door. He angled back around. "Forget someth—"

Only it wasn't Theo standing on the other side of the door. He gasped. "Beckett?"

His brother's form filled the doorway, his rumpled clothes evidence of a cross-country plane ride.

"I heard you might need legal counsel."

An honest-to-goodness laugh erupted from his lungs, hearty and homesick all at once. "Get in here." He grabbed his brother by the shirt and pulled him into a hug. When he stepped back, he studied his little brother. His hair was longer than when Logan had seen him last, and the circles under his eyes deeper.

Either his little brother was working sixty-hour weeks . . . or the ghosts that'd chased him from Maple Valley haunted him still.

Very possibly both.

"Seriously, what are you doing here?"

"Don't I get to see Charlie first?" He strode past Logan and into the living room. "Hey, kid, your favorite uncle is here."

Charlie pushed away from the coffee table and met him half-way across the room. Beckett swung her into his arms, ruffling her hair. "I hear you've gotten talkative. And what's up with that arm?"

She held her pink cast out like a display of show-and-tell. "You need to sign it."

"That I do."

"And then your uncle has to explain to his older brother what in the world he's doing here." But at the moment, Logan didn't even care. He'd wished for a piece of Iowa, of home. And unlikely as it was, he now stood right in front of him.

The next two hours passed in a blink. He ordered pizza. Beckett played with Charlie and even helped Logan give the apartment something close to a real cleaning. By eight, Charlie had conked out on the couch, and Logan transferred her to her bedroom.

When he came back, it was to find Beckett looking through a scrapbook Logan usually kept stored on the shelf under the coffee table—clips of newspaper articles about candidates and speeches, all with his name somewhere in the story.

"That's Emma's doing, originally. Alena, our intern, insists on adding to it these days."

Beckett flipped to a page with a photo of Logan standing with the governor. "It's like when you were in high school and Mom saved all the school newspaper articles, all the ribbons and photos and whatever. Man, you drove me crazy back then."

Logan reached for a piece of now-cold pizza from the box still sprawled atop the coffee table. "Gee, thanks."

"No offense, but you were so stupidly good at everything. Perfect GPA. President of the student council. Valedictorian. And then to top it off, the guitar player who made all the girls swoon."

"Uh, one girl. Emma." He dropped into the recliner—the one Emma had called ugly and promised to eventually ban from the apartment. "You were the basketball star with the constant gaggle of cheerleaders around you."

"That's the other thing. You use words like *gaggle*." Beckett grabbed the last slice from the pizza box.

"I've got a good vocab. So shoot me."

"Yeah, well, I'm a lawyer now, which means I speak legalese, which means I can out-dictionary you any day."

They ate their cold pizza in quiet minutes while Beckett continued looking through the scrapbook. Only when he'd closed it did Logan ask again. "So you're here because . . . ?"

Beckett tossed his pizza crust onto the cardboard box like he would've a basketball, his expression finally turning serious. "Because you've never once not been there when things got messy for me."

Messy—the perfect word. Two months ago, life had been tidy. Maybe not perfect—there were hidden dusty spots, he knew that. Lingering hurt crouching behind a busy work schedule.

And to think he'd accused Amelia of hiding.

But at least he'd had some sense of direction before going back to Maple Valley.

"It's just weird," Logan said. "I've always had a plan, you know? Even if it was a halfway-iffy plan like staying in Iowa for a couple months to fix up a newspaper before selling it off." But now? He still hadn't signed the sale documents, and he could get a call any day from Hadley's people, rescinding the job offer. He didn't know whether to find a new nanny and a speech therapist here in California or wait to see if he ended up transitioning to Allentown.

And he'd left a huge chunk of his heart in the Midwest.

"I keep waiting to feel grounded." Like when Emma was alive. Back when he'd been able to picture so clearly what the future looked like.

"Maybe you're not supposed to feel grounded." Beckett had shifted so he leaned forward now, folded hands dangling over his knees.

Logan lifted his head, let his expression ask his question for him.

"Maybe there comes a point when God doesn't want you all grounded and secure and confident in your plans. Maybe he wants you churned up and uncertain for a while. So you'll look to him, depend on him instead of your usual got-it-all-together Logan Walker roadmap."

Logan's conversation with Bear that day in the square came back. Bear had said something about the wide-open spaces of his future—that when you knew who you trusted, the openness became invigorating instead of intimidating.

Beckett straightened and rubbed his palms over his jeans before settling back against the couch. "Then again, maybe I don't know what I'm talking about, and I'm the last one who should be giving advice, and you should hash this out with Dad."

"No, you're . . ." He met Beckett's eyes. "You're more right than you know."

The foggy lemon smell of the Pledge they'd used to dust all the hard surfaces in the living room nearly masked the faint lingering smell of smoke damage. Somewhere a car honked.

Okay, God. If you need to take everything off my plate in order for me to hear you, go for it. If a clean slate and an invisible roadmap means I'll learn how to trust you, then all right.

The lazy whir of the overhead fan and the distant moan of traffic settled into silence.

"Just a sec." Beckett stood. "I left something in the hallway."

His brother returned seconds later, Logan's guitar case in hand.

"What? How did you get that?"

"Kate called the other night. Told me everything that'd happened recently and basically ordered me to get on a plane. And then Rae got on the line and said she'd already found a flight with a layover in Des Moines. They both met me there."

And gave him the guitar. But why?

"Raegan said to remind you that you're the one who told her it's okay to have varied interests, multiple dreams, and change paths as many times as she needs to."

He had said that, but he'd been talking about her part-time jobs . . . not his old love of music.

"And Kate said she's not going to let Colton propose until you're playing again, because she wants you to sing at their wedding."

"Do we have pushy sisters or what?"

"And I say the least you can do in exchange for me coming all this way is promise me you'll open this when you're ready."

He eyed the case. "That thing was out in the hall for two hours. What if someone had stolen it?"

"Then I wouldn't have mentioned it, and you wouldn't have been any the wiser." Beckett set it aside. "When you're ready, Logan. Oh, and one more thing."

Beckett reached into his pocket and pulled out a flat, square paper envelope.

New guitar strings.

Three years of motherhood had aged Dani Malone, but in a good way, a graceful way, Amelia decided. Gone were her dark, waist-length curls, and in their place, a stylish pixie cut framed her face. Her cheeks were fuller, sprinkled with freckles and a few faint lines that made her seem older than her twenty-one years.

But there was a peace in her eyes that Amelia had never seen back when she was a scared barely-eighteen-year-old. High school senior. Pregnant. Desperate.

"Amelia?"

Amelia stood on the front steps of the miniscule bungalow home on 31st Street in Des Moines. Hadn't even had to look up the address after writing it on so many unmailed envelopes, the letters to Mary she'd never sent. She'd simply ignored the turnoff for Maple Valley on her way back from the Cranford offices and found herself here.

"I know I should've called."

Dani's smile shifted out of surprise and into something warm as she ignored Amelia's hesitance and lunged for a hug. "Are you kidding me? I've been waiting for this." When she stepped back, there were tears in her eyes. "Come in. You've got good timing. My aunt watches Mary a couple days a week while I'm in class, and she just dropped her off ten minutes ago."

Mary.

Weirdly, her heart didn't even lurch at the thought of seeing the baby—no, now a three-year-old, just like Charlie—she'd once considered her daughter. Instead, a humming curiosity had settled in someplace between Dixon and here.

She followed Dani through the modest living room. Futon in place of a couch. Old fireplace that must not be usable considering the candles crowded into its base. A pile of textbooks on the coffee table.

"You're taking classes?"

"Yep, summer courses just started. I'm finishing up my gen eds this summer at the community college and then transferring to ISU this fall."

"What are you studying?"

Dani stopped near the kitchen. Its appliances looked like remnants of the seventies, the gold refrigerator crammed with crayon pictures. "Actually, you kind of helped me choose without realizing. I don't know if you'll remember this, but before I even got pregnant, when I'd only been coming to church a couple months, we were talking once after youth group about going to college and picking a major and all that. And I told you I had no idea what I wanted to do, that I didn't think I had any major skills or talents, and all I knew was I didn't want to end up living on welfare like my mom. I wanted to have a dream, I just couldn't find one."

Amelia did remember that. They'd been sitting on one of the ratty couches in the church youth room. Just that night Jeremy had told the group of kids it was his last night. His speaking career was getting off the ground, and he'd just landed his first book contract.

"I'll never forget what you said. You said, 'Dani, if you really want the dreams and desires in your heart to come into any kind of focus, maybe start by getting to know the one who gives us dreams in the first place.'"

"I said that, huh?" And she'd probably believed it, too. A wistfulness crept in then—for the faith she used to cling to.

"When Mary turned one and I started thinking about finally doing the college thing, it came back to me. I realized I wanted to do for other kids what you did for me—help them get to know God, I guess. But I'd like to do it outside church walls, so I'm double majoring in nonprofit administration and social work with the hope of eventually working for a youth organization."

Could this really be the same kid who'd shown up at church an angry teenager, sullen and sick of her life? Amelia couldn't find the words to express the mix of disbelief and pride and yes, even joy warming through her.

So when Dani turned toward a hallway, she just followed, wordless.

"Hey, Mare, I hope you finished picking up your bedroom like I asked, because we've got a visitor." She turned to Amelia. "Just a warning for when you see her: She got this new bike helmet last week, and for the life of me, I can't get her to take it off. She begged to wear it to bed last night." Dani paused. "You knew I kept the name, right?"

Amelia nodded, gaze caught on the collage of photos hanging in the hallway. Photos of Mary as a baby, as a toddler, in a kiddie pool, going down a slide.

"It worked out well, actually," Dani continued. "Mary is my grandmother's name. She thinks Mare is named after her, of course, and she's the only one I've never corrected. I tell everyone else the truth, though—that it's Amelia Earhart's middle name. Which always gets me funny looks from anyone who doesn't . . . know."

Dani's explanation had slowed to a crawl before it stopped, probably because she'd seen what photo Amelia stared at now. The one of Dani holding Mary in the hospital—in that rocking chair in the nursery. Might have been snapped at the very moment the social worker had told Amelia and Jeremy the adoption wouldn't be moving forward.

"I'm so sorry, Amelia." She took a step closer. "Not sorry that I kept Mary because . . . because she's my world, you know? But sorry it hurt you so much. After all you did for me, helping pay for all the medical bills, taking me to appointments when my mom refused to have anything to do with it all, everything. That's why I've been trying to contact you. I just . . . wanted to say sorry."

This time when Dani hugged her, Amelia let herself lean into it. She soaked up the apology, but more than that, the healing that came along with it. "And I'm sorry for holding it against you." Tears stung her eyes. "I'm sorry for not responding when you called and wrote and . . . I'm just sorry."

She'd turned into a weepy mess. A weepy but suddenly so very liberated mess. "I actually wrote letters to Mary. For years, I wrote letters, things I'd tell her if I were her mother. But . . ." She stepped back. "But I realize now that I was writing them for me. She doesn't need them. She has a mother."

Dani's eyelashes batted at her own tears.

"Moooom."

The voice came from behind, and they both turned.

Mary wore a polka-dotted shirt and pink jeans with an elastic waistband . . . and a bike helmet, just like Dani had said.

"I cleaned. Do I get a snack? Can I have a popsicle?" She stuck her tiny fists on her waist. "Who's that? Do you have to study tonight?"

Dani's lips tipped into a smirk. "She's talkative."

"Clearly." Same age as Charlie, but so different. Cute, though. Amelia crouched. "Hey, Mary. I'm Amelia. I . . . well, I'm your mom's friend. I even helped pick out your name."

"Do you want a popsicle?"

Dani laughed and reached for her daughter's hand. "We might be able to offer her something a little more substantial."

She watched mom and daughter walk down the hall in front of her.

"If you really want the dreams and desires in your heart to come into any kind of focus, maybe start by getting to know the one who gives us dreams in the first place."

That was where she'd gone wrong, she knew now. And Logan was right. She'd chosen a hiding place over a home. Chosen to let her life widen rather than deepen. Not that there was anything wrong with the town and job and people and events that filled her days.

But they couldn't take the place of old dreams . . . or the one who'd planted them in her heart.

Dani stopped at the end of the hallway. "You coming?"

She picked up her feet. "Coming."

"You planning on wearing your helmet all night again, Mare, or—?"

Amelia froze, brain snagging on the word *helmet*.

"Oh my goodness."

Dani looked back. "Amelia?"

Kendall Wilkins. Buried with an aviator's helmet. That photo

of Kendall and Harry, where Harry looked so much like Lindbergh, helmet and all.

Could it really be?

"You all right, Amelia?"

She blinked. "I might've just solved a five-year-old mystery."

Except that wasn't quite true. If what she was thinking was
correct . . . well, try a nearly ninety-year-old mystery.

18

"Are you sure you want to do this? Because now would be the time to back out, Jen."

Logan held his phone to his ear while he crossed his nearly empty office. Just one more desk drawer to empty and pack away in a bank box. He could hear Charlie chattering from the reception area, where she hung out with Alena on her last day. She spoke in bare sentences in short spurts, but those words were like splashes of ocean water against his face on a hot day.

Or an Iowa breeze brushing over prairie grass.

"I'm sure." Confidence anchored Jenessa Belville's voice. "I've already got the check written. Fax me the papers and it's a done deal."

The papers Jenessa was talking about were spread over his otherwise empty desktop. He fished in one of the boxes he'd already packed for a pen and resisted the urge to review the documents one more time. He'd scanned them at least half a dozen times already, and Beckett had stuck his lawyer eyes on them.

It was time.

Logan bent over his desk and signed his name. "All right, it's done."

Jenessa's whoop sounded over the phone. He hung up seconds later, the first real peace he'd felt in weeks settling over him.

Or maybe not the first, because there'd certainly been something easing about seeing Beckett three weeks ago. And even talking to Senator Hadley two weeks ago.

The senator had made the call herself. "*I want you on staff, Logan. I want you working with me. But a police report and a potential custody suit, it's too much for a lead position. I'll need communications people in several key cities, though. So once I've got a new communications coordinator on board, we'll be in touch.*"

It should've ripped through him. Instead, all he'd been able to feel was relief.

Not too long after that, he'd had the conversation with Theo, sitting on the patio outside his apartment, after he'd realized he didn't want to keep their consulting firm going without his partner.

"*We ran a great business for almost six years, Theo. It's okay to let it go now. You go to Allentown. Maybe we'll meet up in D.C. eventually.*"

Then just last week, the call from Jenessa. The one that had left him slack-jawed and stunned, but . . . strangely certain this wasn't just chance. God had just whisked the last thing off his plate, leaving him with a wide-open and plan-less future.

Probably right where he wanted him.

Logan pulled the last drawer from his desk, and instead of carefully pulling out each item and arranging it in his last empty box, he simply dumped the thing over and then reinserted the drawer. There. Done.

He grabbed the signed legal docs off his desk and roamed into the reception area. "I'm about to admit something horrible,

Alena." Charlie sat on his intern's desk, legs dangling as Alena arranged a necklace made of paperclips around her neck.

"What's that, boss?"

"I never once learned how to use the new copier-faxer-printer thing we got after the new year."

Alena spun. "You're kidding."

"You always jumped in when I was on my way to the machine and did it for me." Like Amelia jumping in to un-jam the press.

He could still smell the ink she'd smeared all over her arms and face that day in the office. Picture the blush she'd tried to pretend away when she'd realized Ledge had known all along she was fixing the machine the hard way.

Alena stood and plucked the papers from his hand. "You do know you owe me an explanation, right?"

He fingered the paperclips around Charlie's neck. "Cute necklace, Bug." He trailed Alena to the copier. "An explanation about what?"

"The girl. I asked before Theo left for Allentown last week why you weren't keeping the business going on your own. He did it for a couple months."

"Yeah, there's a difference between a couple months and a couple years." More than a couple years, really. Even if Hadley didn't win the election, Theo would most likely end up doing something much bigger than freelancing from a tiny office in LA.

"You were destined for a big life."

That lawyer back in Maple Valley had said those words the second day Logan was home, and at the time, Logan had agreed—easily and maybe even a little pridefully. Because hadn't he chased after big career goals? Hadn't he been on the brink of seeing his hard work pay off?

But *big* had begun to take on a new meaning lately. And his dream, a new shape. Even if it didn't have clear lines just yet.

"Well, anyway," Alena continued, "when I asked, Theo said you were closing up because of a girl."

The rat. "Not because of a girl."

But because of a prayer. One he'd prayed more than once since that night with Beckett. *If you need to take everything off my plate in order for me to hear you, go for it. If a clean slate and an invisible roadmap means I'll learn how to trust you, then all right.*

Alena stopped at the machine. "Fax number?"

Logan held out his hand, where he'd scribbled the number Jenessa had given him.

Alena punched in the number. "Well, you can deny there's a girl, but I'm not going to believe you. You wouldn't be grinning like you are right now if there wasn't."

He set the papers in the tray at the top of the machine. "Of course there's a girl. She's sitting over on your desk wearing your office supplies."

"You know what I mean."

"I do, and you don't seem to understand that I'm politely ignoring it."

Alena waited until the machine hummed to life, then turned to him. "Well, I'll tell you this: You aren't doing Charlie any favors by ignoring your own heart."

He stared at her, felt his forehead bunch and a whisper just lately becoming familiar trek in. *Listen to her.* "Say that again?"

"You aren't doing Charlie any favors by ignoring your own heart." She sing-songed it this time and rolled her eyes. "You want to be a good dad? Kids need to know what love looks like."

"Whoa, I didn't say anything about love."

The fax machine spit out the last page, and Alena pulled it from the side tray, smacking the original against Logan's chest. "You didn't have to."

"Amelia, this is some incredible writing."

Eleanor's voice drifted from outside the changing room in Betsy's Bridal. A mauve curtain separated Amelia from her sister and provided a backdrop for her reflection in the full-length mirror. The bridesmaid dress, a fallish shade of amber, had sheer straps that bunched over her shoulders and a form-fitting bodice. The skirt bowed at her waist before reaching to her knees.

"Did you hear me?"

Amelia pushed aside the curtain and stepped into the dressing room's lounge area.

Eleanor dropped the flat electronic tablet she'd been reading from into her lap. "Oh my word, it's perfect."

"I like it. Very autumn-y." Just right for Eleanor's October wedding.

"It looks amazing with your eyes." She rose from the tufted circular cushion in the middle of the room.

"Will all the bridesmaids' dresses be the same?"

Eleanor reached out to adjust one of Amelia's straps. "What other bridesmaids? You're my maid of honor. Trev's brother is his best man. Skipping the rest."

Amelia fanned her skirt around her, the tulle underneath scratching her knees. "Really? After all those years of scolding me for eloping and missing out on all the hoopla of a big event, I'd have thought you'd go with a massive wedding."

Eleanor laughed and stepped back, giving the dress one more once-over. "Nope. It's taken us too long to finally make this happen as it is. We're keeping it simple."

The store's owner slipped into the room. "Ah, it's gorgeous on you. And you were worried the style would make you look short."

"No, she was worried I'd think it made her look short and then force her to wear high heels," Eleanor corrected. "Amelia would rather roll into the church on skates than wear heels."

"Truth." Amelia nodded into the mirror. "But you were right, Gabrielle. It's a good fit."

The woman *tsk*ed. "Never doubt me again."

At the sound of the bells over the shop's entrance, she disappeared again.

"Question." Eleanor dropped back onto the circle couch. "If her name's Gabrielle, why's the store called Betsy's Bridal?"

"I asked her that very thing when I did a story on her grand opening a year ago. She said it was because she wanted alliteration in the name."

"She didn't think of Gabrielle's Gowns?"

Amelia laughed. "I don't know. But you chose to shop for a dress in Maple Valley, El. You were basically asking for quirky."

"Well, there's nothing quirky about that dress. We're getting it." She poked one finger at the iPad on the couch. "And this article—you have to do something with this. It's not just the writing, but the whole feel of the article. There's heart and depth, and your voice just shines."

The Kendall Wilkins story. Amelia had thought it was dead after the newspaper's centennial issue failed to happen. Two months of following the story through history and even across state lines, for nothing.

Except not for nothing. Because even if it never saw print, that story had changed her. Reminded her of her love for history. Pulled out her taste for a different kind of writing—the kind fueled by mystery and research and even a little investigative journalism.

If it had stopped there, it would've been enough.

But it hadn't. That day two weeks ago in Dani's house, laughing at Mary's refusal to take off her bike helmet, the pieces had finally come together in her head.

The Elm Society. Kendall Wilkins's The Elm Foundation. Harry Wheeler's The Elm Company.

The luck of Lindy.

Kendall's love for anagrams.

And that nurse who lived in South Dakota now. That last story she had told about Kendall and his burial. *"This old aviator helmet came tumbling out of his closet. From his childhood, I'm sure. He used to talk about watching barnstormers, you know. It was the one personal touch I felt like I could give him, including it in his coffin."*

T-h-e E-l-m.

H-e-l-m-e-t.

Charles Lindbergh's helmet.

She'd about dropped the popsicle in her hand in her excitement at Dani's. She'd asked to use a computer, Googled her way into discovering Lindy's helmet had indeed never been recovered. In the chaos of his arrival in Paris, someone had pulled it off his head.

And it'd ended up on the head of his accidental decoy, Harry Wheeler.

She plopped onto the couch next to her sister now, the thrill of the possibility swelling through her all over again. The bridal shop's air-conditioning pulled goosebumps from her arms.

Eleanor held the iPad in her lap now, tapping her way back to the beginning of the article. "My favorite part is how you left it a little open-ended. Like, hey, Charles Lindbergh's helmet might be buried in little old Maple Valley, Iowa. As if, I don't know, just thinking about it is stimulating enough. Like what other treasures are around us in our everyday lives that we don't even realize?"

"That's exactly what I was going for." She spread her skirt out around her. "Plus, I kind of had to leave it open-ended. Unless someone exhumes Kendall's body, we won't know for sure."

"But you're going to send out it, aren't you? Find a magazine or something to print it?"

"Yeah, I think so. I've got a list. I need to figure out how that works, probably write a query letter or something." The only thing she knew for sure was that it wouldn't end up in the *News*. Though there was still no word on whether the sale to Cranford Communications had ever been finalized.

But she fully expected the silver letters on the building just a few doors away from the bridal shop to come down soon. And for the *Communicator* to begin appearing in more mailboxes and newsstands by the end of the summer.

She glanced at Eleanor. "Thanks for being an early reader."

Her sister tapped out of the Word doc and set the iPad beside her. "Thanks for letting me. Am I really the first one to read it? You haven't even showed it to Logan?"

Logan. One of these days her heart might stop pinching whenever she heard his name. Or ran into one of the Walkers around town. Or drove past the library. "No, I haven't."

"But you want to." Not a question.

"I want him to know all the time he spent helping me paid off. Sure."

"Amelia."

"Eleanor." She whirled toward the dressing cubby. "I should change out of this dress."

"Ignore me all you want, but I'll get you to talk eventually."

Amelia stopped before hiding behind the curtain. "There's nothing to talk about. Logan went back to LA. I'm here." *For now.* "And I'm focusing on other things at the moment. Like your wedding. We only have a few months to plan it."

And trying to decide what to do now that she was no longer a newspaper editor. Go back to college and finish her history degree? Take a page from Raegan Walker and find a couple part-time jobs to tide her over?

She didn't know. The only thing she did know was that maybe it was okay not to rush it. That there was truth to what she'd told Dani all those years ago. Instead of falling into a hurried search for what came next, she would allow herself to linger . . . think . . . pray.

Even start trusting a little. *See, I am doing a new thing . . . a river in the wasteland.*

It was that verse—the one from Emma's grave.

Maybe her wasteland wasn't a place, and her river wasn't a job or person or plan.

But simply a hope.

Her phone cut in then, and she reached into the changing room for her purse. She didn't recognize the number. "Hello?"

"Hey, Amelia? It's Belle. Belle Waldorf."

"Oh, right. The *USA Today* reporter." Mae's niece from Chicago.

"You were holding out on me."

"Excuse me?"

"Here you get me to do a story on a guy who, sure, is nice and interesting and whoa, his headshot? Not bad. But all along you've got a sweet story of your own in the works."

Eleanor glanced at her watch. "It's been two hours since I had coffee. I'm going to run a couple doors down to that little coffee shop."

She waved her sister off while trying to land on whatever Belle was talking about. "A story of my own?"

"This piece about this guy and this other guy . . ." The tapping of computer keys sounded over the phone. "Kendall and Harry. Two friends who saw history in the making and then went on to become part of history and yada-yada. This is some stellar writing."

"I don't . . . how did you . . . I'm confused." This didn't make sense. She hadn't sent the article to anyone. "You have my Kendall Wilkins article?"

"Uh, yeah. Came from, let me see, publisher@maplevalley news.com."

Publisher?

No. Logan?

"You should know I'm not calling as a *USA Today* reporter right now. My aunt's told you I'm part of a startup publication, right? Just something fun I do on the side, not even part-time really. Right now it's just an online magazine, but we've talked about adding print someday."

Amelia bent over to scratch her knees. Annoying tulle. "A startup?"

"It's about the nerdiest thing you've ever heard of—grew out of a podcast actually. Best way to describe it is, we try to take historical events and stories and especially things like this Lindbergh deal and make them relevant for today."

This was what Mae had been trying to get her to check out?

Belle was still talking. " . . . totally a niche thing, and I don't think any of us ever expected it to go anywhere. But about six months ago, NPR featured our website, and after that the History Channel actually ran with one of our stories. Ever since then, we've had steady advertising."

"That sounds cool." Amelia wandered to the high table at the opposite end of the changing lounge and snatched a butter mint. "And you're interested in my article?"

"Yes." Belle drawled the word. "But we're also interested in you. Now that we've got somewhat of a revenue stream, we're looking at actually hiring a writer-copyeditor-marketer-slash-someone-to-take-us-to-the-next-level. Not sure if it could be full-time yet, but maybe." Belle took a breath.

And it was just long enough for the realization to sink in. "You think I might be—"

"A good fit? Oh yeah. Aunt Mae says you have a background in marketing. Obviously you can write, and you have an interest in history. I don't know how you'd feel about relocating to Chicago—and who knows, maybe there'd be a way to long-distance it—but that'd almost be sad because we are a fun, fun staff and . . ."

Her article. Logan. Chicago.

Her brain spun.

"My aunt also says you make amazing cookies." Mae knew about the cookies?

The call ended minutes later, with Belle promising to email her and Amelia promising to check out the website. And somehow she found herself outside the bridal shop, standing on the sidewalk and staring at the river, late-June air tickling over her bare skin and Eleanor's shoes clicking toward her.

"I haven't paid for that dress, Amelia. This might be considered shoplifting."

The dress. Her regular clothes still sitting in the dressing room. What was she doing?

"I just . . . that phone call . . . Logan."

Eleanor's eyebrows popped up. "Logan? That was him?"

"No. I . . . he . . . I think he sent my article in, but it must've been the earlier version because he doesn't even know . . . and now they want me to go apply for this job, and . . ." She wasn't making any sense.

Eleanor held out her coffee cup. "Clearly, you need this more than I do." She took ahold of Amelia's arm and steered her back into the shop. "Talk."

19

*B*rother, I love you, you know I do." Kate handed Logan
a red plastic cup filled with ice and cherry Coke. "But
this is a weird party setup. Newspaper on the tables?
A disco ball?"

Logan sat atop a picnic table, feet on its bench and guitar in
his lap, and looked to the band shell where Colton was hanging
the silver ball, his laughter punctuated by the thump of the A/V
system as someone plugged in a cord.

"Amelia would call it a glitter ball." He took a sip of pop, his
swallow turning into a grin as he looked around Maple Valley's
town square. So many people already milling around. Twinkle
lights circling lampposts. An indigo sunset accompanied by
rolling clouds.

The risk of rain couldn't come close to dampening Logan's
spirits tonight. He had no idea what Amelia's reaction might
be to all this. But anticipation glided in every breath.

And somehow, a knowing.

He went back to loosening the tuning keys of his guitar until
he was able to unwind each string from its peg.

"You really going to play that tonight?"

"Maybe."

"You realize every unmarried girl in Maple Valley save me and Raegan is going to swoon?"

He used the string winder to remove the bridge pins. "Yeah, I'm really only concerned about one girl."

He didn't even have to look up to know Kate was probably beside herself at that remark. She and Raegan both had been the definition of giddy since he and Charlie had showed up yesterday. He'd immediately warned his sisters to keep their presence on the down-low.

I want it to be a surprise.

A gravelly voice belted over the speakers—some nineties band Amelia loved—as Raegan moved toward them. Charlie came bounding over then, Colton not far behind. His daughter had been such a trooper these past few days of packing and driving the rental car back to Iowa. He'd tried to explain, but she didn't even seem to care. She'd heard Amelia's name and started bouncing off the walls.

This is *the right thing, isn't it?* He wasn't letting impulse and desire cloud his common sense?

"I am so proud of myself." Kate held out her hand so he'd drop in the pins. "Just think, if I hadn't called you to let you know that Raegan let me know that Amelia was heading off to Chicago, you might not be here right now."

He pulled the low-E string from the paper envelope and unwound it. "Yes, clearly, I owe my entire future to you. But let's not forget, you wouldn't have met Colton if not for me."

"Touché, my brother. We're even."

He inserted the metal nub of the guitar string into the hole in the bridge, pushed the pin through to lock it in place, and then strung the other end through the tuning peg. Five more to go.

Colton held up his ink-stained hands as he reached them. "Tables are covered, and here's the proof."

They'd borrowed tables from the church, and instead of tablecloths, Logan had insisted on covering them with back issues of the *News*. He finished stringing the guitar and played a chord, the bronze metal harsh under his uncalloused, unpracticed fingers . . . and yet, familiar. He looked up to see Kate sporting a grin.

One he couldn't help matching.

Oh yeah, this is right.

Kate's gaze shifted over his shoulder then, and she bit her lip. "Hmm. Did you invite them?"

He followed her line of sight to see Rick and Helen getting out of their car at the curb.

"Yeah, I invited them." Reluctance lodged in his throat. "I've been dreading this." But he had to do it. "Watch my guitar?"

With Kate's "good luck" following him, he moved across the lawn, a firefly whirling past his ear and the mouth-watering smells of Seth's industrial-sized barbeque wafting over him.

Rick nodded as he approached, one arm around Helen. Logan had grabbed his sweating plastic cup, rehearsing the words clinking around in his brain like the ice cubes clinking inside his cup.

Steady. Firm. Kind.

"Rick, Helen, glad you could come."

The bruise around Rick's eye had completely faded in the weeks since Logan had seen him. Helen managed a taut smile despite the strain tightening the summer air between them. "We like Friday nights in the park as much as anybody."

Logan rubbed his free hand over his jeans. "Uh, Charlie's right over there, but before you join the party, I'd like to say something. I'm not sure you're going to like it, but it needs to be said."

His father-in-law's face was a steely mask—unreadable.

"I love both of you. Charlie and I are lucky to have you in our lives. Your support in these past two years has been amazing."

Rick's arm dropped from around his wife. "But?"

"But I won't be leaving Charlie in your care. Not long-term. Not now or ever. And if you choose to move forward with any kind of legal custody challenge, I will fight it as hard as I can."

"Logan—" Helen began, but he lifted a hand.

"I know I'm not the perfect father. But I'm doing my best and, at least lately, praying, too. I was wrong to think for so long I was on my own and capable of keeping everything together by myself." He set his cup on a nearby table, ignoring the unbending glint in Rick's eyes. "I hope you always play a large role in her life. But asking me to leave her behind is wrong. You know Emma wouldn't have been okay with this, any of it."

"He's right." Helen's voice was barely above a whisper. "He's right, Rick. It'd break her heart."

Logan waited, willed himself to hold Rick's stare. *Steady. Firm. Kind.*

And then he saw it, the flicker of grief in his father-in-law's eyes. The barest of cracks. It was exactly what Dad had said. Rick was just trying to hold on to Emma any way he could.

Rick only nodded, then reached for his wife's hand. Relief as thick as the clouds bounding overhead tumbled through Logan as they moved on to greet Charlie. He caught Kate's gaze from across the grass. Gave a single nod.

Dad's voice sounded from behind him. "Quite the party you've pulled together."

He turned. "Well, Maple Valley does love a good party."

"Would it be way too sappy if I told you I was proud of you?"

"No sappier than Kate telling me she's going to write this into her next novel or screenplay." He paused. "Hey, Dad?"

His father glanced over. "Yeah?"

"Thanks."

"For wrangling the entire town into keeping this a secret?" He shook his head. "I mean, yeah, thanks for that. But also, thanks for what you had with Mom. A huge part of the reason Emma and I had a good marriage for as long as we did is because of what I learned from you."

And maybe, someday, probably—he might have another good marriage. It'd look different from the first time around, that was for sure. Emma had helped him focus. Grounded him. She'd given him just what he needed as a young adult ready to run into the world, but not sure where to start.

Amelia? She did the opposite of ground him. She opened up his world, filled it with possibilities and promises he hadn't even begun to unpack. But he couldn't wait to.

"That's all. Just wanted to say thanks. How's *that* for sappy?"

"Pretty darn good, I'd say." Dad's blink wasn't quick enough to hide his emotion.

Logan crossed his arms and looked around the square once more. The music, the people, the quirky decorations. His family and friends. Colton holding Charlie, and his guitar sitting on the picnic table. The honey-sweet hint of the expectation in the air.

"Do you think I'm crazy?"

Dad laughed. "Completely. And I love it." He turned to face Logan. "Where's the guest of honor, anyway?"

"She'll be here." The grin started on his face and reached for his heart. "Soon."

Pale violet light trickled in rivulets through gathering clouds and wispy willow branches that swayed in the breeze as if waving goodbye. The evening air tingled with something like anticipation, windy whispers promising rain. Maybe soon.

Raegan hoisted Amelia's suitcase into her trunk while Amelia stood with her hands in the pockets of her shorts, gaze hooked on the barn, a chorus of memories chirping through her. That first night here. The Klassens telling her they'd just known she was coming. Birthday dinners and movie nights and quiet evenings alone.

That sunset with Logan. The loft doors open.

Maybe not a house, but it was definitely a home.

Rae's sandals crunched over sand and gravel, and she slid her arm around Amelia. "You're not saying goodbye to the barn, are you? Because you promised this isn't goodbye yet. You don't leave 'til tomorrow."

"Not goodbye. Not yet, I promise."

Yet. Hope and fear and curiosity and a whole host of swirling emotions nested in the word. She may only be driving out to Chicago for a couple weeks. Long enough to meet the staff of the website and check out living spaces. Get a feel for the city and see if she could picture herself there.

Pray and decide if this was the *something new* she was meant for.

But something told her—and probably Raegan sensed it, too—soon she'd be packing more than a suitcase. She was pretty sure Lenny and Sunny had already started praying for whatever hungry soul might come along next, looking for a fresh start, a new landing place.

"Come on, let's go." Rae tugged on her arm.

"Can't I change out of these dingy overalls first?" She'd spent the afternoon helping Megan, the coffee shop owner and new mom, get moved into a new duplex—one with room for a nursery. Weird that Kate had only stopped by for a few minutes. Raegan, too. In fact, Rae hadn't even shown up until the end of the afternoon, and she'd insisted on coming back to Amelia's place with her.

"You look fine," she said now.

Amelia glanced down. "I look like Rebecca of Sunnybrook Farm." She even had the twin braids to complete the look. But the people of Maple Valley had seen her looking worse—like last summer when she'd been a muddy mess sandbagging before the flood. Or after the tornado when she'd worked alongside everyone else to clean up the park.

The drive into town was quiet, memories replacing conversation. Man, she was going to miss this town.

"I need to find some way to thank Kate for letting me stay in her townhouse while I'm in Chicago. Lucky for me she hasn't sold it yet. I—" She broke off as she turned onto Main Avenue and the town square came into view. The beat of music pumping through speakers floated in, and parked cars crowded both sides of the street. "What's going on?"

"I don't know." Raegan's voice lilted.

"It's not Fourth of July. Summer Fest isn't until August." And why in the world was there a glitter ball hanging from the band shell?

She found an open parking spot along the curb and pulled over, confusion crackling through her as she got out of the car. Clouds hunched overhead. All those people in the square better have umbrellas.

"Amelia!"

She froze at the sound of a voice—*his* voice. Logan.

Logan?

She turned, and there he was, at edge of the park, standing there like he'd been waiting for her.

"Well?" Raegan whispered from behind her. "What are you waiting for?"

"You totally knew, and you didn't say a word."

He was walking toward her now.

"He's my big brother, Amelia. If there's one thing Walkers don't do, it's squeal on each other's secrets. Go talk to him."

She took a breath and forced her feet to move. Swiped at a strand of hair that'd pulled loose from one of her braids. Oh man, the braids. The overalls. Why hadn't she forced Raegan to wait while she changed?

And of course Logan looked like . . . Logan. All the more attractive for the wind-tousled hair and shadowed jaw. No tie tonight—only dark jeans, an untucked white button-down, and a dark jacket.

She stopped in front of him. "W-what are you doing here? Shouldn't you be in LA? Or . . . somewhere? Do you know what's going on in the park?" A drop of rain landed on her cheek, and she stopped, taking a breath and grasping for the composure she must've packed away with her suitcase in the trunk.

And Logan just stood there. Smiling.

Another raindrop, this one tapping against her arm. Distant music floated in on a tumbling breeze. "If you don't say something soon, Logan Walker—"

He held up his hands and stepped closer. "Just wanted to see if you could make it to twenty questions."

"You're rude."

"And you're . . ." He broke off, as if catching his breath for the last word. "Beautiful."

"I'm sweaty from helping Megan move all day. I'm wearing overalls that are leftover from the first time they were fashionable. I'm . . ." *Out of words.* Because the way he was looking at her right now? It stole her breath and filled her lungs at the same time. It puddled inside her, warmer than any summer sun and sweeter than any cool rain.

"What's going on in the park, Logan?"

"Looks to me like a going-away party." He looked over his shoulder to where umbrellas were beginning to pop open.

And realization, it rambled in slow. A going-away party. And she was the person going away. "But I'm not even sure I'm moving. Not yet. This is just a . . . a short trip. An interview."

"Then call it a good-luck party instead."

Ribbons of emotion tangled inside her. "You did this?" Her question was a whisper.

He nodded, hands in his pockets and the first hint of nerves scampering over his face. "The thing is . . ." He cleared his throat and tried again. "The thing is, Charlie and I . . . we're coming with you."

"What?" The word leapt from her lips.

"We're coming with you."

Raindrops turned into rainfall, hushed patters tapping against grass and branches, bouncing off her car. Logan reached around to pull off his jacket. He closed the gap between them and held the jacket with both arms over their heads like an umbrella.

She tipped her head. "Stop joking, Logan."

"I'm not joking. You should've seen Charlie this morning with her little red suitcase. Adorable. I was thinking we'd take my car. I left it here when I flew back to LA last time, since I wasn't sure where Charlie and I were going to end up. It's got a lot less miles than yours—"

"Logan. Stop. Slow down. I'm processing here. What are you saying?"

"I'm saying . . ." His jacket flapped in the wind above them as he met her eyes. "I'm coming with you. Because I love you."

"I . . . you . . . *what*?"

"I love you, and Charlie loves you, and we'd like to come with you to Chicago. If you'll have us."

He loved her. "But the campaign and D.C. and your office—"

"There'll be other campaigns. And we closed the office."

He loved her. "You don't have a job or a plan?"

"This *is* the plan."

"Y-you love me?"

The answer was in his eyes, rich and warm and melting. And that did it. She launched herself at him, arms flinging around him and face burying against his shoulder. "I love you, too. I *love* you."

He lowered the jacket that'd shielded her from the rain, wrapping her in his arms. Raindrops slicked over her hair and down her cheeks, mixing with salty tears and the sound of cheers from the park.

"So we can come with you, then?" His voice brushed over her ear. "Because it doesn't matter whether you end up staying in Chicago or decide to come back here or go off to Paris to see for yourself where Lindbergh landed. We want to come with you."

She could linger here forever. At the park, in the rain, on the edge of so many dreams-come-true at once. She nodded into his neck, not even capable of talking right now.

"Good, 'cause in true Boy Scout fashion, I've already filled the gas tank and checked the oil and filled bags of snacks for Charlie. I made her a travel kit with coloring books and—"

"Logan." She lifted her arms to loop them around his neck and kissed him.

"—and I've already got the GPS programmed. Though it's basically a straight shot, and I always bring an atlas just in case—"

Another kiss.

"Okay, okay." He laughed the words against her lips. His arms tightened, and he took over the kiss.

Until the patter of footsteps interrupted. "Lia!"

Charlie. Logan swooped his daughter into his arms before Amelia could blink. Made room in the embrace for three.

See, I am doing a new thing.

A new season. A new family. A new hope. Amelia buried herself against Logan, Charlie's arm around her neck.

Filled with a joy like never before.

The End . . . except not quite.

Epilogue

~~~~~~

Dear Charlie,

If one day soon you're my daughter, I'll tell you all about how I had a crush on your dad before I even met him. Technically, it was a crush on his writing. He's brilliant with words, Charlie. Someday when you learn to read, you'll know what I mean.

~~~~~~

By the way, sorry about the rain at the party last night."

Amelia closed the notebook in her lap. The road was too bumpy to write, anyway. And the scenery too tempting.

Logan held a travel mug in one hand, the other on his steering wheel. The pinkish orange of dawn traced his profile and lit his eyes, and when he turned to her and smiled, she saw her future.

"You don't have to apologize for the weather, Logan. Not

even you, in all your glorious preparedness, can control that." Amelia stuck a handful of Cheerios in her mouth.

In her car seat in back, Charlie slept. Maple Valley had faded into the horizon an hour ago.

"Those snacks were supposed to be for Charlie."

She took another bite. "I don't know how something so tasteless actually counts as a snack. Almost as bad as carrots."

"And I don't understand how you can throw out a phrase like *glorious preparedness* when in one fell swoop, I walked away from a presidential campaign, quit my job, and started driving cross-country with you. Or at least cross-Midwest."

"Touché." She tipped her sunglasses from her eyes to her forehead. "As for last night, I like rain almost as much as snow. And it was fun seeing a rainbow of umbrellas." The whole night had been perfect, even if she had looked hilarious—hair, overalls, all of her drenched. But probably even more laughable, the way she hadn't been able to let go of Logan all night. As if he'd poof and disappear back to LA if she released his hand.

"I still can't believe you sold the newspaper to Jenessa Belville, though." She sealed up the baggie of Cheerios and reached for the princess backpack she'd found in the backseat. The one with everything they could possibly need for the day-long drive. "I thought she was a paralegal or something."

"She watched you in action. She thought it looked fun. And she's lived with her parents for nearly ten years, not paying a dime in rent—which means she's kinda well off, actually. No, she couldn't pay me what Cranford could, and she may need to take the paper online until she can afford to buy a new press, but the *Maple Valley News* still lives."

Amelia pilfered through the backpack, looking for a better snack. She paused when she recognized the cover of one of the books inside. She slid it out. "Logan?" She held it up. The

Amelia Earhart picture book. The one he'd inter-library loaned. "The due date was weeks ago."

"I know. I'm going to have the worst overdue fines ever." His smile stretched. "Worth it."

She couldn't help it—she abandoned the backpack to the floor and leaned over to kiss his cheek. "Well, anyway, it's a good thing someone's manning the helm at the paper because I've got a great headline."

"Oh yeah?"

"Yeah, I'm pretty sure Kendall Wilkins's body is going to end up being exhumed."

Logan spit out a drink of coffee, and it splashed against the steering wheel. "What?"

"You prematurely sent that story of ours to Belle. I might've solved the deposit-box mystery."

Logan's sunglasses slipped down his nose, and she could practically hear the cogs turning in his brain. "You did? And you're just now telling me?"

Oh man, he's adorable . . .

And he loved her. And he was following her to Chicago.

It was almost too much.

"Talk, Amelia."

"I'm pretty sure Charles Lindbergh's helmet was buried with Kendall."

She shifted in her seat and reached over to wipe off the wheel with her sleeve, catching a whiff of Logan's aftershave or soap or something—intoxicating, whatever it was. Enough to in one moment dissolve all thought of graves and missing helmets and dead men . . .

She flipped up the console between them, turning the middle spot into a seat, and scooted as close to him as she could, lacing her arm through his. She kissed his cheek again.

"I'm trying to drive here, woman."

"I know, and you're doing a fine job."

"But . . . how . . . what made you realize . . . ?" His voice was incredulous. "You're telling me Charles Lindbergh's helmet— the one he wore across the Atlantic—might be in a man's grave back in Maple Valley?"

She buried her face against his neck.

"Shouldn't we, like, do something about that? Tell someone?"

"Eventually, yeah. But for now . . ." She sighed, warmed by sunlight and surprise and Logan's kiss to her forehead. "Just keep driving."

A Note From the Author

So you know that Amelia Earhart children's book that Amelia Bentley talks about? Somewhere that book actually exists. I checked it out from the Kendall Young Library in Webster City, Iowa, over and over as a kid. But I've never been able to find it since. I can't even remember what it's called—I just know it had a salmon-pink cover.

My childhood fascination with Amelia Earhart, coupled with multiple trips to Little Falls, Minnesota, where Charles Lindbergh spent the bulk of his growing-up years, led to the light historical angle in this book. I sifted through plenty of sites and articles as I dreamt up the Lindbergh helmet storyline, but the one I came back to most was the Pulitzer Prize–winning biography *Lindbergh* by A. Scott Berg.

However, I definitely took some historical liberties. It's true that Lindbergh's helmet was never recovered after his historic flight across the Atlantic. And it's also true that after he landed, his helmet temporarily ended up on the head of an American named Harry Wheeler, whom the crowd mistook for Lindbergh. Many sources, including Berg's biography, say that the American was a journalist. Others say he was a Brown University student in Europe on holiday. At least one, a *Pittsburgh Press* article from June 6, 1927, says Harry Wheeler was a fur buyer from New York who'd gone to Europe to purchase rabbit skins for a hat manufacturer.

For the purpose of my story, I decided Harry was a Brown University student. I gave him a friend from Iowa and made up a backstory for him. I also let myself daydream about what might've happened to that helmet of Lindbergh's. I like to think it's out there somewhere . . . an incredible piece of history just waiting to be discovered.

Acknowledgments

*W*ell, anyone who has heard me talk about this book has probably also heard me talk (read: gush and swoon) about Logan Walker. I think I found the fictional love of my life!

But believe it or not, Logan wasn't the best part of writing this story. The best part was rediscovering the joy of writing and storytelling after a somewhat difficult creative season. I believe that was a gift straight from God . . . and I'm so grateful to him.

I'm also thankful to:

Mom and Dad—Thanks for letting me hide away in your sunroom and write. Thanks for all the meals and prayers and cups of coffee. And most of all, thank you for being you.

My siblings—Once again, thanks for inspiring all the best parts of the Walker family members.

Grandma and Grandpa—I can't tell you enough how much your encouragement and prayers mean to me. Thank you!

Raela Schoenherr, my editor—Thanks for putting up with my plot schizophrenia and helping me do the Walkers justice.

Amanda Luedeke, my agent—You're as fun as you are savvy. Thanks for everything.

Charlene Patterson, my line editor—I'm so grateful for your keen eye and careful reading and editing of this story.

Everyone at Bethany House—I'm hugely honored to be a part of your publishing family.

Beth Vogt and Rachel Hauck—Thanks for that much-needed conference call last spring and for helping me sort through the tangles to find the heart of this story. And Susan May Warren, as always, thank you for the teaching and mentoring that's shaped me as a storyteller.

Lindsay Harrel, Alena Tauriainen, and Gabrielle Meyer—My partners in crime . . . er, writing. Thank you for your constant encouragement and prayers and support and friendship and everything! And Gabe, thanks for all those tours of the Lindbergh house and museum in Little Falls.

Rachel McMillan and Hillary Manton Lodge—Can you say *moral support*? Thanks for being just one (or a bazillion) Facebook messages away.

Readers—I don't even have words. Except, yes I do. You bless me like you wouldn't believe. Huge thanks to those of you who have read, reviewed, and spread the word about my stories. If I could, I'd host a huge party and invite all of you, and we'd eat pizza and ice cream and talk and laugh the night away. Instead, please accept my very sincere, very heartfelt thanks. (And if you're ever in Iowa, just let me know and we'll have that party, after all.)

MELISSA TAGG is a former reporter and a total Iowa girl. In addition to her homeless ministry day job, she is the marketing/events coordinator for My Book Therapy, a craft-and-coaching community for writers. When she's not writing, she can be found hanging out with the coolest family ever, watching old movies, and daydreaming about her next book. She's passionate about humor, grace, and happy endings. Melissa blogs regularly and loves connecting with readers at www.melissatagg.com.

Also From Melissa Tagg

To learn more about Melissa and her books, visit melissatagg.com.

Kate writes romance movie scripts for a living, but after her last failed relationship, she's stopped believing "true love" is real. Could a new friendship with former NFL player Colton Greene restore her faith?

From the Start

Blake Hunziker has finally returned home to Whisper Shore, and he's planning to stay. Local inn owner Autumn Kingsley, on the other hand, can't wait to escape. When the two of them strike a deal to help each other out, they may get more than they bargained for.

Here to Stay

Miranda Woodruff, star of the homebuilding TV show, *From the Ground Up*, has built a perfect—but fake—life for herself onscreen. Will it all come crashing down when she falls in love for real?

Made to Last

◆ BETHANYHOUSE

Stay up-to-date on your favorite books and authors with our free e-newsletters. Sign up today at bethanyhouse.com.

Find us on Facebook. facebook.com/bethanyhousepublishers

an open book

Free exclusive resources for your book group! bethanyhouse.com/anopenbook